The Extraordinarily Ordinary Life of

Cassandra Jones

Springdale Bulldogs Year 1: Age 15

Springdale Bulldogs Year 1: Age 15

The Extraordinarily Ordinary Life of Cassandra Jones

Tamara Hart Heiner

paperback edition
copyright 2020 Tamara Hart Heiner
cover art by Tamara Hart Heiner

Also by Tamara Hart Heiner:
Perilous (WiDo Publishing 2010)
Altercation (WiDo Publishing 2012)
Deliverer (Tamark Books 2014)
Priceless (WiDo Publishing 2016)
Vendetta (Tamark Books 2018)

Goddess of Fate:
Inevitable (Tamark Books 2013)
Entranced (Tamark Books 2017)
Coercion (Tamark Books 2019)
Destined (Tamark Books 2019)

Kellam High:
Lay Me Down (Tamark Books 2016)
Reaching Kylee (Tamark Books 2016)

The Extraordinarily Ordinary Life of Cassandra Jones:
Walker Wildcats Year 1: Age 10 (Tamark Books 2015)
Walker Wildcats Year 2: Age 11 (Tamark Books 2016)
Southwest Cougars Year 1: Age 12 (Tamark Books 2017)
Southwest Cougars Year 2: Age 13 (Tamark Books 2018)
Southwest Cougars Year 3: Age 14 (Tamark Books 2019)

Tornado Warning (Dancing Lemur Press 2014)

Eureka in Love Series
Shades of Raven (Tamark Books 2020)
After the Fall (Tamark Books 2018)

Table of Contents

EPISODE 1: BECOMING CASSANDRA

CHAPTER ONE

No More Mustache

Why would the phone be ringing so early on the first day of summer break?

The ear-piercing siren jarred Cassandra from her dreams and jerked her into an upright position. Where was that dratted phone? She reached her hand around the pillow until she found it.

Sunlight streamed through the window behind her bed, indicating that it wasn't as early as she'd first thought. But her sister Emily still slumbered, mouth slightly open as she slept on the twin bed beside Cassie's.

Andrea's name flashed across the screen. Andrea! Cassie flipped the phone open to talk to her best friend, forgiving her for waking her. "Andrea? What's up?"

"I need to come over," Andrea said, her sobs filling the space between the phone and Cassie's ear. "My mom and I got in a huge fight. Can I spend the night?"

"Hang on." Cassie rolled off the bed and padded out of the bedroom she shared with Emily. She stepped into the kitchen, where she found her mom already doing dishes. A quick glance at the clock on the stove showed it was after ten in the morning.

"Mom," she said, "Andrea's on the phone. She fought with her mom and wants to know if she can come over and spend the night."

Mrs. Jones turned off the sink and sighed. "All right. That's fine."

"Thanks." Cassie flashed her a grin and went back to her room. "Sure,

Andrea. You can come over."

"Okay," Andrea said, her voice still choked. "Thank you so much. I'll be right there."

Cassie closed the phone and glanced around at the mess on her bedroom floor. Good thing her mom hadn't come in, or she certainly would have said no to Andrea spending the night! Cassie gathered the dirty clothes into her arms and dropped them into the hamper, then organized her books onto the shelf and put her shoes away.

Two hours later, Andrea still hadn't arrived. The room was clean, Cassie was dressed, and now she stared vacantly at the television with her brother and sisters, wondering when she'd see her friend. When she tried calling Andrea, no one answered.

Typical.

"Is Andrea still coming?" Mrs. Jones asked at two in the afternoon.

"I don't know," Cassie replied, too frustrated to elucidate.

Six hours after she had called, Andrea's mom pulled the car into the driveway. Andrea flounced out, her hair coiffed and curled, a light floral dress bouncing around her thighs.

"Hello!" she crowed as she came in and dropped her bags on Cassie's bed, all radiant smiles.

"How are you?" Cassie asked, searching her face. She didn't see any signs of trauma.

"Have fun," Mrs. Wall said, giving Andrea a hug. "See you later. Love you."

"Love you too," Andrea said, beaming.

As soon as Mrs. Wall left, Cassie said, "So? Are you and your mom okay?"

"Oh, yes," Andrea said breezily, pulling her toiletry bag onto the bed. "She took me shopping. Do you like my new dress?"

Andrea twirled for Cassie, and Cassie eyed the gorgeous material.

"Yes," Cassie said. "Did you guys even fight?"

"Yeah, but then we went shopping, and everything's all better." Andrea opened a small white box. "I brought this for you."

Cassie's annoyance at Andrea's melodramatic behavior faded as took the box from Andrea. "What is it?"

"It's a hair removal product. It melts the hair right off your face. We can try it on your mustache!"

Cassie frowned. Thanks to her ethnic heritage, she had darker hair on her upper lip. She didn't love it, but she wasn't thrilled at the idea of melting it. "That sounds scary."

"It's perfectly safe! I'll do it for you." Andrea grabbed Cassie's shoulder and steered her into the bathroom. "Let's see. It says to leave it on for two minutes." Andrea squeezed the tube until the white cream landed on her finger, and then she smeared it all over Cassie's upper lip. "Yours is pretty dark, though. We should probably do three minutes."

The cream felt cool at first, and then it warmed up, getting hot on Cassie's skin. "Ouch."

"Does it hurt?"

"It's getting a bit uncomfortable."

"That means it's working."

Cassie wanted to wipe it off now, but she knew it hadn't been on long enough. "So you've tried this?"

"I don't have any dark hairs to remove. I got this for you."

They waited in silence while Cassie fidgeted. "How much longer?"

"Another thirty seconds."

It really burned now. Cassie stared at her reflection, the dark almond-shaped eyes with blue contacts, the olive skin, the straight hair, and the creamy mustache. "Now?"

"Yes."

Cassie grabbed a washrag and began removing the offending substance. "Oh, it stings!" she said, wincing each time the rag touched her face.

"Rinse it with warm water."

Cassie did so, and Andrea turned her to face her.

"There! The hair's all gone!"

Cassie swiveled away and looked at her reflection. Sure enough, the small hairs on her lip were gone. But the skin was bright red and raw-looking. She touched it with the tip of a finger and drew in a hiss. "Is it supposed to be like this?"

"Oh, sure. It will be normal in a few minutes. That's just a reaction from the cream."

Andrea said this as if she knew from experience, but Andrea had just said she hadn't tried it.

"Girls?" Mrs. Jones poked her head into the bedroom. "Want to go out for Mexican food?"

"Yes!" Andrea said, tugging Cassie into the room.

Mrs. Jones' eyes landed on Cassie's mouth. "Is your lip okay, Cassie?"

"Yes," Cassie said, her face warming. "We did this hair removal cream. It still hurts."

"It worked, at least."

A little too well. The burning had not subsided by the time they reached the Mexican restaurant, and Cassie couldn't even eat the chips and salsa because her mouth hurt to move. If the salt or tomatoes touched her lip, it burned worse.

"I think we burned my lip," she told Andrea.

"Sorry," Andrea said, and she collapsed in a fit of giggles. "I hope it doesn't look bad later."

Cassie glared at her. "Thanks a lot, Andrea."

The next morning was worse. Instead of looking red and exposed, the skin on the upper lip had crusted over and was a darker brown.

"Crapola," Cassie murmured, grabbing her makeup bag and dabbing concealer over the scab. "Ow, ow, ow, ow!" The wound immediately began to burn. Cassie's hands trembled as she wet a washrag with warm water and hurriedly removed the make up. Then she scowled at her reflection and the brown scab, now dabbled with bits of peach-colored concealer.

"Great way to start summer vacation," she grumbled.

Cassie did her best to conceal her scab the next morning at church. It had hardened a bit and didn't hurt when she put on makeup this time, but she felt conspicuous in Sunday School. The color didn't match her skin tone, and it didn't glide smoothly over the bumpy scab.

Still, no one seemed to notice, or at least say anything. Cassie sat with Riley, her other best friend, and talked about their summer plans when class ended.

"I'm leaving for Camp Splendor this afternoon," Riley said.

A pang filled Cassie's heart as she remembered the previous summer, the fun she'd had there, and Ben. "I wish I could be there."

"Maybe you can come later."

Cassie nodded. "I hope so. I have a family reunion in Iowa. But maybe after that."

Tyler, Jason, and Beckham walked by and waved at them. Cassie waved back, glad that she no longer had a crush on Tyler. It made it a lot easier to be friendly with him.

"And then we have church camp together," Riley said.

Cassie frowned. "And the youth retreat." Suddenly she worried she wouldn't see her other friends all summer. Would Maureen, Cara, Andrea, Amity, and Janice forget her if she didn't hang out with them? Would they have a whole collection of inside jokes without Cassie? She already struggled to fit in with them.

"So we will get to spend most of the summer together!" Riley said.

"Yes." But what about the other girls? In August they would start high school. Cassie wanted her ring of popular friends around her. She needed them so she wouldn't feel alone or out of place at the big building with all the other kids.

"I guess I better go." Riley stood up, stooping to give Cassie a hug.

"See you soon."

"If you see Ben—" Cassie began, and Riley waited.

Cassie shook her head. "Nothing."

Riley gave her a small smile. "I will."

꩜ ⚘ ꩜

Mrs. Jones had all the kids packing for the family reunion on Monday, and Cassie's thoughts were on Riley at Camp Splendor. Was she there with all their old friends? It was different this year, because Riley hadn't gone as a camper but as a kitchen helper, like Ben had been the year before.

Cassie hadn't thought of Ben in months, but she thought of him now. The summer before had been magical, the way the two of them came together, and she wished something like that would happen again.

Her family had just sat down to dinner when Cassie's phone rang. Her dad gave her a stern look. "No phones at the table."

"Let me just see who it is." Cassie peered over at it on the counter. "It's Riley! Can I talk to her? Please? She's at camp and this might be her only time to call!"

"Go ahead," Mrs. Jones said, and Cassie leapt from the table.

She hauled the phone back into her room and closed the door. "Riley! How's it going?"

"Great, it's great." Riley giggled. "It's a lot of work, but I'm having fun. I've seen lots of our friends from last year. And—" she let the word linger. "Guess who else?"

Cassie already knew. How could she not? "Ben."

CHAPTER TWO

Memorable Dishes

"Yes," Riley said into the phone. "Ben's here. He hung out with us last night while we cleaned dishes."

Cassie gripped the phone tighter, hardly breathing. "And? Did he say anything?"

"So I was complaining about Connor Lane, how he's so arrogant and mean at school, and Ben said, 'guys are jerks.' I looked right at him and said, 'yes, they are.' And he kind of laughed and said, 'yeah, I know what you're thinking about! I know it!'"

Cassie laughed along with Riley, but she wanted more. "Then what?"

"Then we went back to cleaning and didn't talk about anything else."

"I wasn't brought up again?" Cassie let out a sigh of disappointment.

"No."

"And you didn't ask anything else?"

"No."

Why not? Cassie wanted to ask, but she knew she couldn't put that on Riley. It wasn't her job to fish out juicy details for Cassie.

Besides, she and Ben were over. Ancient history.

But it was fun to remember.

Andrea called the next day wanting Cassie to spend the night.

"Can I?" Cassie asked Mrs. Jones.

"Are you packed for reunion?"

"Yes."

"You have a youth meeting tonight. You can go after that."

Cassie didn't feel like going to church. She just wanted to go to Andrea's. But she agreed.

"We're going to teach you girls how to do hair and makeup tonight," Sister Mecham said in the youth room inside the church building that

6

evening, smiling at the girls in front of her. "We've brought in a professional hair dresser and makeup artist to show you tricks."

What fun! Cassie's spirits lifted. Now she wished Andrea were here. Andrea loved makeup, but Cassie thought she often wore too much. Cassie touched the skin on her upper lip, evidence of Andrea's obsession with appearances. She was glad the scab had peeled off and her mouth didn't look discolored anymore.

Cassie got in line for the hairdresser first. She watched him pin up the other girls' hair so that soft tendrils fell out and framed their faces. Others he put in a fancy bun. Cassie didn't want a bun. She fingered her stick straight hair and hoped he'd find a way to pin her hair up, too.

Then it was her turn.

"Your hair is very straight," he said, gathering it in his hands. "And it's thick but super fine. So you'll have to use lots of pins to keep it in place or it will slide right out." He twirled it on one side. "It will be a lot easier to put it in a bun. Let's do a French bun."

Cassie sighed inwardly. She wanted something trendier, but she didn't complain.

"What do you think?" he asked when he finished, showing her a mirror.

The hair pulled away from Cassie's face but did nothing to mature her features or make her look elegant. She may as well have it in an odd-shaped ponytail. "It looks great," she lied.

"Perfect. Now go get your makeup done."

The woman had Cassie sit in a chair. She examined her face, pushing her finger into Cassie's skin and smoothing it. "Your skin is perfect. The kind of skin tone every model wants. Your eyelashes are long and dark and definitely your best feature, followed by your eyes. But they're a tad bit too close together. So you want to put eyeliner on them and tail it out at the end to lengthen your eyes." She ran the eyeliner over Cassie's eyelids and showed her the effect in the mirror. "See?"

"Yes," Cassie said, pleased with the result. Now she looked older than thirteen. Never mind that she was fifteen; people often confused her age for someone younger.

"And you definitely want to use mascara and a little lipstick. You don't need much, but you don't want to leave your face naked."

Cassie kept quiet while the artist made up the rest of her face.

"You are so pretty!" the woman said, stepping back and examining her. "You could be a model! Everyone come look at her!"

Cassie felt a blush creeping up her face, but as the other girls gathered around and exclaimed over her, she couldn't help feeling pleased.

Mrs. Jones dropped Cassie off at Andrea's house, French bun and all.

"Your makeup looks good," Andrea said as Cassie dumped her overnight bag on the bed. Andrea's hair was curled, her blue eyes framed by thick mascara, and she wore a blue tank top with shorts.

"Thanks." Cassie felt frumpy in her white blouse and jean shorts. She sat next to Andrea at the vanity and pulled out the French bun. "We did makeovers at church."

"Lucky! Come on. We're going to the store with my mom."

"The store?"

"She needs groceries. I bet we can find some hot guys."

Hot guys sounded nice. Andrea was always on the lookout for those, and Cassie didn't mind the eye candy.

Cassie and Andrea loitered in the parking lot while Mrs. Wall went inside to get her groceries. A truck with two teenage boys pulled up beside them.

"Hi," the boy driving said. He only looked a year older than them. "You guys from around here?"

"Yes," Andrea said, tossing her hair and smiling.

The boys smiled back. They weren't very cute, Cassie thought, but in the end, what did that matter? At least they had nice smiles.

"We're just here for a swim meet," the driver said. "Maybe we could meet up with you guys sometime tomorrow?"

"Absolutely," Andrea said, tilting her head and batting her lashes.

"What is there to do for fun around here?" the passenger asked.

"Lots of stuff," Andrea said. "Swimming, movies, food. The normal."

The boy looked at Cassie. "Does your friend talk?"

Cassie's face warmed, and Andrea said, "Sometimes. She's shy."

Cassie elbowed her, embarrassed, but what else could she say? It was true. Boys made her get all tongue-tied.

"Well, we better go," the driver said. "Can we call you sometime?"

"Of course," Andrea said, and she gave him her number. Then she looped her arm through Cassie's and started to pull her away.

"Wait," he called. "We didn't get your friend's number."

"Oh," Andrea said, and even Cassie heard the note of surprise in Andrea's voice. "Cassie?"

Cassie cleared her throat and gave them her number also.

"Thank you, Cassie," the passenger said, and he gave her a shy grin that made something lurch in her stomach.

Maybe he was cuter than she'd first thought.

"See you girls later," the driver said, and they pulled away.

"We didn't even get their names," Cassie said. Something about the interaction left her giddy, almost glowing, inside.

"That's okay. They won't call."

"They won't?"

"Nope. It's just fun to get numbers." She pulled Cassie inside the grocery store. "Let's get donuts."

<hr/>

Andrea got Cassie home by noon the next day since Cassie was leaving for her family reunion in the morning. Cassie unloaded the dishes, swept the floor, and emptied the trash. Then she sat down on the porch to play with the kittens.

Her phone rang, and she tilted her head, studying the unknown number before answering it. "Hello?"

"Hi, is this Cassie?" a male voice asked.

She leaned back on the porch. "Yes." Who knew her but she didn't know him?

"This is Trevor. We met yesterday at Harps."

"Oh!" That same tremor of pleasure rippled through Cassie, and she sat up straighter. Andrea had said they wouldn't call! "Hi!"

"Hi. I'm the one who was sitting in the truck. Not driving." He cleared his throat. "So are you busy?"

"No. We're going out of town tomorrow, but today I'm just sitting around."

"Great! Want to hang out?"

Hang out.

Just a boy and a girl, hanging out. Going to the movies. Getting fries. Driving through town.

She couldn't. She didn't know him. And she wasn't old enough.

He was still talking. "We could meet at Harps. You can drive, right?"

He thought she was sixteen. Cassie bit on her lower lip, then said, "Yeah, but my mom has my car right now. She's running errands before we leave on our trip."

"I can pick you up, then."

Crapola, why was he being so congenial? "I don't live in the city. You don't want to come all the way out of town."

"I don't mind."

Cassie sighed. "I'm sorry, Trevor. I can't today. Maybe when I get back." Yeah, right. And then she'd have to admit to him that she had lied.

"Well, tell me about yourself. What do you like to do?"

Read. And write. She sounded so boring. "I like to sing."

"Really? Sing something for me."

"Oh, no way." Cassie laughed.

"Why not?"

"Over the phone? I'm too embarrassed."

"Come on. Someone as pretty as you has to sing good."

The flattery won her over. She hummed for a second and then sang a few lines from the latest song Ms. Malcolm had her working on.

"I knew it. You sing pretty."

"Thanks," Cassie said.

"You're sure I can't come get you? We could just go to the mall for a few hours."

"I can't today."

"Okay. Call me when you get back in town, then. Maybe I can come to Springdale."

"I will," Cassie said, though she doubted it.

They hung up, and Cassie grinned at the phone. Then she called Andrea.

"Andrea! Guess who just called me!"

⁂

For once, the family wasn't driving to another state. The Joneses were out the door early so they could catch their flight to Iowa.

"I've never been on a plane," Cassie's littlest sister Annette said, her eyes wide as she eyed the big jets on the runway.

"Yes, you have," Cassie said. "You just don't remember. We all flew to Grandma's house a few years ago." While her mom's mom lived in Fayetteville, Cassie's dad's parents lived in Arizona. They'd gone out to visit when Cassie was eleven—right before she got bit by a snake and spent a week in the hospital.

"Oh," Annette said. "Is it scary?"

"Nah." Cassie looped an arm over Annette's shoulders. Annette was nine now, six years Cassie's junior but hardly a small child. "They're lots of fun."

That was what Cassie told herself as the plane bumped and dipped through a patch of clouds for an hour. Around her, she heard people vomiting into the little paper bags, and Annette squeezed her hand.

"It's just like a ride at Disney World," Cassie said, squeezing back. "Easy peasy."

"Is it supposed to be this way?"

"This is normal," Mr. Jones said, not even looking up from his book.

Annette looked to Cassie for confirmation, who gave her a tight-lipped grin. "Yep. Perfectly normal."

And it must have been, because they landed without incident.

As soon as the Joneses got checked into the hotel, the kids changed into their swimsuits and ran to the pool.

"Now we can watch everyone arrive!" Emily said, keeping her eyes on the check-in desk.

"Do you think we'll recognize anyone?" Cassie asked. "It's been years since we had a reunion."

Emily shrugged, not looking away from the lobby.

Cassie tried to remember her cousins. She knew a set on her mom's side fairly well, since they saw them at Thanksgiving nearly every year. But her dad's side, she didn't see them often. She remembered Emma, who was a year older than her, and Clementine, a year younger. And Jordan, her male cousin who was about her age. She and Jordan had grown up together in Texas before the family moved to Arkansas. Cassie hadn't talked to him since then, and she wasn't sure they would still be friends.

"Look!" Emily cried, jumping up. "It's Bridget! Uncle Mike is here!"

That meant Jordan was here also. Cassie straightened up in her deck chair, watching the group of tow-headed children rushing toward the pool.

"Hi, guys!" Bridget cried, bursting into the solarium. Her hair was cut short to her chin, her blue eyes sparkling. She was about Scott's age, maybe eleven or twelve.

"Are you coming swimming?" Annette asked.

Jordan came in behind her, and Cassie felt her jaw drop. He had added about a foot to his height since the last time she saw him, and he'd bulked up, no longer looking like a scrawny kid but like a strong young man.

"We don't have our swimsuits on," he said. "We'll have to swim later." He spotted Cassie, and his eyes widened. "Cassie?"

"Hi," she said, giving a timid wave.

"We'll get our swimsuits on and come back," Bridget said, and she hurried from the pool room.

"Yeah, we'll see you guys later," Jordan said, following her out.

The other cousins slowly arrived. A few quickly changed into swimming suits, but before long the parents came and called all the kids out.

"We're going to dinner," Mr. Jones said, hussling everyone out the door. "You can talk with your cousins there. Let's go change."

Cassie quickly changed into something more appropriate for dinner, shorts and a tank top. Then she continued down to the hotel restaurant.

Her dad and his brothers all hugged each other, and the cousins were sitting in clusters around tables, having small, friendly conversations. Cassie spotted her cousin Emma and tried to catch her eye, but Emma didn't look her way. So Cassie sank into a chair at a different table by herself.

"Hey." Jordan sat down across from her. "How are you, Cassie?"

"I'm great." She smiled, pleased he wanted to sit with her. "You've gotten taller."

"I hope so. It's been like five years."

She nodded. "Even I've gotten taller."

"Yeah, but I don't think you're gonna catch me."

She laughed. "How's life in Texas?"

"Hot and humid. Arkansas?"

"About the same. It's nice. You guys should come visit. It's not that far."

"You're right. I wonder why we haven't ever come? I'll tell my dad."

The waiter came, and Cassie looked over her menu while her siblings placed their orders. When he got to her, she said, "I'll take the veggie burger and sweet potato fries, please."

"Veggie burger?" Jordan squinted at her. "You know there's no meat in that."

"I don't eat meat." She grinned. "I'm a vegetarian."

"Whoa. We totally can't mix, because I'm a vampire."

Cassie laughed. And she didn't stop laughing throughout the meal. When their burgers arrived, Jordan showed her the blood still oozing from his meat, and he flinched when Cassie waved the garlic-laden veggie burger at him. He flicked a tatertot at her, except it went right past her and hit Uncle Chad in the head, and when he turned around, Jordan ducked under the table. Cassie snorted as she took a sip of her water, and the liquid splashed out on their plates and the table.

"Nose water," Jordan said, using his napkin to mop at the table. "That's a new one. Is it good on burgers? Because I'm pretty sure mine's covered in it."

Cassie couldn't even answer, she was laughing so hard.

She had the feeling she and Jordan were going to be great friends this week.

CHAPTER THREE

Nose Water

The next morning, the family members gathered in the lobby to head to a park for a concert.

"How boring," Emily murmured next to her.

"I know," Cassie whispered back. "I don't even want to go."

Jordan jumped to Cassie's side, bumping her arm with his. He crossed his arms over his chest and put on a stern face as he listened to Uncle Chad explain the details of the concert in the park.

Cassie bit her lip, reassessing her analysis of the day. It might not be boring after all. "Did you sleep well?"

"I had a terrible cough," Jordan said, tapping his throat for emphasis.

"A cough? Are you sick?"

"Garlic." He thumped his fist against his neck and grunted. "It affects my fangs. Makes me sick."

She pressed her lips together to keep from giggling.

Uncle Chad finished talking. "All right, let's move out to the cars!"

"But it's all right," Jordan added as they turned to leave the lobby with the rest of the family. "Nose water helps clear it up. I think it could have been worse."

Now Cassie couldn't keep the laughter inside.

They rode in the Jones's car together with her family, and Cassie and Jordan teased each other the whole way. It almost felt like—*flirting*. But it couldn't be, because he was her cousin, right? So it was just teasing. Really fun, harmless teasing.

The park had an amphitheater set up near the baseball diamond, and a small band warmed up on the stage. The children looked for a playground, but there wasn't one. Just a fountain. The little kids dipped their fingers in it until the adults shooed them away.

"This is so boring," Scott said.

"Totally agree," Bridget said, and a handful of younger cousins murmured their agreement.

"I have an idea," Cassie said. "Come here." She motioned to Bridget.

Bridget stepped over uncertainly, and Cassie took her hands. "Ready?"

"For what?" Bridget asked, and then Cassie lifted her into the air and spun her.

Bridget squealed and laughed, and the other kids clamored around, wanting their turn. Jordan joined her, taking smaller children by the hands and spinning them.

Cassie panted after setting down her fourth child. "That's tiring. Who's going to spin me?"

"My turn!" Annette said, running to Cassie.

Cassie grabbed her little sister's hands and twirled her around.

"I'm pretty sure I can do it," Jordan said.

"Do what?" Cassie asked, glancing at him as she set Annette down.

"Spin you."

"No you can't. I weigh like—"

"What? Sixty pounds? Come on." Jordan took her hands.

He might have gotten her feet off the ground. Cassie wasn't sure. What she was sure of was that the next moment Jordan dropped her hands, and she fell flat on her stomach in the grass beside Jordan as he also collapsed in a heap. He struggled for breath, and Cassie gasped as she laughed, clutching her side.

"I'm so sorry," Jordan said. "I couldn't hold on."

"I thought I pulled your arms off!"

"Nope." He grinned and lifted his arms out. "Still there."

By the evening, Cassie felt like she'd found a new best friend. And he was her cousin. It couldn't get any better than that.

The next day had nothing planned until dinner. So Cassie changed into her swimsuit after lunch and headed for the pool.

She spotted Jordan in the hot tub with Emma and her brother Liam, and her smile dimmed. She wasn't sure Emma liked her. Cassie dipped into the big pool and splashed around a bit, then settled into a lawn chair with her book. Her cousins laughed and joked with each other, and Cassie felt left out. Why didn't they include her?

Why don't I just join them? Being shy wasn't doing her any favors. Gathering her courage, Cassie wrapped the towel around her and walked over to the hot tub.

"Hi, Cassie!" Liam said, and Emma scooted over to make room for her.

"Hey, nice of you to join us!" Jordan said.

"I didn't know I was invited," Cassie said.

"Of course you are," Emma scoffed. "You're our cousin."

"Not that anyone would know that from looking at us," Liam snorted.

It was true. All of them took from her dad's side with blond hair and blue eyes, while Cassie's family had enough of her mother's ethnic heritage to have darker skin and darker hair.

"I wish I looked like you," Emma said. "So exotic."

"Thanks," Cassie said, not sure what else to say to that.

Jordan pressed the On button on the hot tub. Big white bubbles spilled out, bubbling up over their shoulders. "Bubble fight!" He grabbed a handful and threw them at Cassie.

She shrieked and threw some back, then splashed wildly in Liam's direction when he also tried to attack her. Emma joined in, and Cassie couldn't even see who was splashing who as she squinted her eyes against the onslaught of water.

The jets turned off and the four of them sat there laughing, soaking wet.

"That was the most fun I've had all week," Emma said.

"It's always fun around me," Jordan said.

It was, Cassie thought. But she hoped Emma and Liam wouldn't hang around. She liked having Jordan to herself.

The families drove back to the park for a barbecue dinner and a game of soccer. This time Cassie rode with Jordan's family. She skipped the hamburgers and hot dogs, piling up on potato salad and grapes with chips instead.

"Do you know how healthy hot dogs are for you?" Jordan asked, sitting across from her under the pavilion.

"They're terrible for you!" Cassie said.

"No. You've got it all wrong. You're buying into the conspiracy theory." He waved the bunned hot dog at her. "There is enough protein in here to keep a starving child alive for four days."

"Did you, like, just make that up?"

"Yes," he said, not cracking a grin. "But it's a statistic that sounds good and is likely to play on the sympathies of the common people. So, like politicians, I don't care if it's factual or not."

She cracked up. Somehow she could never be serious around Jordan.

"Soccer time!" Mr. Jones called, gathering the families together. "Who wants to play?"

"I'm in!" Jordan said, jumping up. "Cassie?"

She stood slowly. "I like soccer. But I'm not very good at it."

"I've never played." He shrugged and grabbed her hand. "Let's do this."

Cassie ended up on a team with Liam, Jordan, Emma, and Clementine. They played against Scott, Bridget, Uncle Mike, Uncle Chad, Emily, and Mr. Jones.

"Uh, Houston, we have a problem," Jordan said into his hands. "We're outnumbered."

"You're also younger and fitter," Uncle Chad shouted. "You can do this."

"We got this," Liam said, nodding.

"Yeah, there's no problem here." Jordan dropped his hands.

The game began. Cassie forced herself to run even when she got tired, and she only winced a little when the myriad of elbows and knees collided with her body. She didn't have shin guards and knew her legs would be black and blue the next day.

"I'm out," Clementine said, stopping and clutching her side. "Good luck, guys."

"Me too," Emma said, gasping for breath.

"What?" Jordan said, his jaw dropping. "You can't abandon the team!"

"Let them," Liam said. "We're winning anyway."

"Cassie?" Emma said. "You coming?"

Cassie sure wanted to. But when she saw the way Jordan looked at her, with such expectancy, she knew she couldn't. "No, I'm good."

Jordan crowed and Liam gave her a high-five.

They finished the game on a win and sat in the grass, panting and rubbing their sore legs.

"Good game," Jordan said, holding his hand out to both of them for palm slaps. "We rock."

"I'm sore," Liam groaned.

"Me too," Cassie said. She hadn't played soccer in years. She needed a drink.

There was a water fountain in the pavilion. Cassie stood up just as Jordan did. They glanced at each other but didn't say anything as they started walking side by side toward the pavilion.

He must be getting a drink too. Cassie moved a little faster. His strides matched hers. Cassie bit her lip, and then she broke into a run.

Jordan didn't miss a beat. He broke into a run beside her, and she quickened her speed, racing him to the fountain.

She inched in front of him, her side aching from the sprint. Almost there. The fountain was in sight.

She didn't know there was a step up into the pavilion until she missed it. Her foot twisted beneath her and she lurched forward, flying over the lip of the concrete. Her hands lanced outward, searching for support, and she grabbed Jordan's shoulder as he ran past her. It twisted under her hand and Cassie let go, grabbing instead a pole next to the table. She swung around it and landed on her rear, tears leaking from her eyes as she grasped her ankle and laughed hysterically, trying desperately not to cry.

Jordan came over, holding his shoulder. "Congratulations. You just broke the long jump record." He took her hand and helped her to her feet, putting an arm around her waist as she hobbled. "Still want that drink of water?"

"Yes." She cried and laughed at the same time, slapping his hands away. "That was so your fault."

"You did that all on your own. I'm lucky I got to keep my shoulder."

She shook her head and sucked up the cool water, happiness bubbling in her chest like the liquid from the fountain.

The families gathered in the lobby after dinner when they returned to the hotel.

"It's been a fun reunion," Uncle Chad said. "We hope you've all been able to spend quality time together. This is our last night, so we invite you to stay down here and play games as long as you'd like."

Cassie couldn't believe it. It was already almost over. She hadn't expected to enjoy it so much, and it hurt her heart to think of not being around Jordan. Why couldn't her cousins live closer?

He set up a table with a card game on it and pushed a chair out for her. Emily and Clementine and Scott joined them.

"I'm dealing," Jordan said, setting up the game.

Everyone accepted their cards, but they had only made it through one round before Mr. Jones came over to their table.

"My crew, we have to go to bed. Our flight is super early in the morning."

Cassie's heart sank. "One more game, Daddy." This couldn't be the end.

"Nope. Time to go."

Cassie looked at Emily and Scott, and they all stood. Was this goodbye? She turned to Jordan, who had also stood. "Bye," she said lamely, then reached up and hugged him. "It was fun to get to know you again."

"You too," he said, giving her a tight squeeze.

The elevator ride was silent. Just as they reached the room, Mr. Jones said, "Cassie, if you want to stay downstairs and play with your cousins, I guess that's okay."

"Really?" Cassie said.

Her younger siblings immediately began to complain, but Cassie hobbled back to the elevator before he could change his mind. Her dad could handle them.

But when Cassie got back downstairs, everyone else was clearing out, also. Jordan stood next to Bridget and his mother waiting for the elevator.

"My dad said I could play another game," Cassie said, disappointment evident in her voice when she saw them. "Are you going to bed?"

Jordan looked at his mom, who shook her head.

"Go on. You can have ten more minutes."

"Yes." Jordan fist-bumped her, and they returned to the lobby.

"Yahtzee," Jordan said, setting up the unfamiliar game. "You know it?"

"No," Cassie admitted.

"Well, it's time you learned."

The game had a bit of a learning curve, and Cassie lost terribly on the first round until she got the gist of it. But by the third round, she knew how to play, and she rolled the dice with enthusiasm, then cheered as she added up her points.

Ten minutes turned into twenty, and then thirty, and finally Aunt Kayla called Jordan's phone. He listened without a word, then made a face and said, "Okay." Putting the phone away, he said, "I have to go to bed."

Cassie looked at their points, but it wasn't the thought of not finishing the game that left her disappointed. "Yeah. I probably should too."

"What time is your flight tomorrow?"

"At six in the morning. We leave the hotel around four."

"Whoa. That's super early. Are you sure vegetarians are supposed to get up that early?"

She giggled. "What about vampires?"

"Way too early."

They took the elevator together, though Jordan got off first. He turned and gave Cassie one last hug.

"It's official," he said. "You're my favorite cousin."

His words warmed her. "And you're mine."

He stepped out and waved, and then the doors closed behind on him.

CHAPTER FOUR
Return of Splendor

Four o'clock in the morning came too early for Cassie. Mr. Jones woke the family, and the light turned on in the hotel room as her siblings stuffed objects into their bags and checked under the bed for socks. She buried her head under the blankets as long as she could before her dad shouted, "Cassie! We're not missing our flight because of you!"

Groaning, she stumbled to her feet. She'd slept in her clothes the night before, so basically all she had to do was haul her suitcases to the car.

The door was open as the family made multiple trips to and fro. Cassie spotted Annette going up the stairs when Cassandra exited the elevator to put her first suitcase in the car, then she turned around and went up the stairs to get her second.

As she pulled her second suitcase from the elevator, she noticed Scott standing at the stairs talking to someone. "What are you doing, Scott?"

Scott turned around. "Cassie, it's Jordan!"

"What?" Cassie tugged the suitcase forward. It couldn't be. Not at four o'clock in the morning.

Sure enough, Jordan's lanky body was stretched over the stairs as he sat there watching them.

"Jordan!" A lump of emotion formed in Cassie's throat. "What are you doing here?"

Jordan shrugged. "I've been up since four watching you guys pack up your stuff."

Cassie hauled her last bag to the car and then returned, climbing the steps to sit by him. "Do you always get up this early?"

He bumped her shoulder with his. "Only on special occasions."

"You're crazy."

"Yeah, maybe."

She returned his shoulder bump. "You're my favorite cousin too."

They stayed that way until the car was loaded and Mr. Jones called Cassie away. Her siblings climbed up to say bye to Jordan, but Cassie already had. She went to the car without glancing back, knowing it would be a long few years before she saw him again.

⟳~✳~⟲

Riley called almost as soon as Cassie walked in the door at home.

"My mom talked to Zelda," she said, "and it's okay if you come and work in the kitchen with me."

"Really?" Cassie had so much to tell Riley. She wanted very much to go up to Camp Splendor and spend time with her. She would tell her all about Iowa and Jordan.

And she might even see Ben.

"I guess it's all right," Mrs. Jones said when Cassie asked, though she looked drugged from exhaustion. "Do all your laundry and repack, and I'll take you tomorrow."

"How long can I stay?"

"Let's start with one week."

One week. That would be enough time to see all her friends.

It only took a few hours to do her laundry and repack, so the next morning Mrs. Jones took Cassie to Camp Splendor.

Riley greeted her as she came out of the car. "You can put your stuff in my cabin!"

"We have cabins?" Cassie followed.

"Yes! No tents. We're not campers, we're staff!"

Staff. Cassie liked the sound of that. She still had the staff dog tags Ben had given her last year.

Was he here? She looked around but didn't see him.

Mrs. Jones said goodbye, and Cassie set about unpacking her things.

"Knock knock."

Cassie looked up as Zelda stepped into the cabin.

"I told Riley you could come. But I just want to lay down some ground rules," Zelda said, looking directly at Cassie. "You don't eat with the campers. You don't do special activities with them. You don't visit their units. And there will be absolutely no flirting or fraternizing with members of the opposite sex."

Cassie nodded, working hard to keep her jaw from dropping. She slid a glance toward Riley as soon as Zelda left. No eating with the campers? No activities with them? "What's going on? It's like a prison camp!"

"At least we're allowed to talk to the campers." Riley shrugged. "I got the same speech. Minus the last line about flirting."

Cassie smirked. "Ha." Then she sobered. "Have you seen Ben lately?"

"He comes by every few days. I told him you were coming to Camp Splendor."

Cassie's stomach twisted at that. Would he come by to see her or would he avoid her?

She stayed near the doorway at dinner time, watching the campers come in and looking for familiar faces. She spotted Tiffany, her friend from two years earlier, and waved. Tiffany ran over, and they hugged tightly. She also saw Brittany, the girl who had kissed up the counselor two summers earlier and stolen Cassie's Keeper of the Ashes award. She swallowed past any lingering feelings of jealousy or misgivings, giving her a hug also.

Satisfied she'd seen everyone there was to see, Cassie returned to the kitchen. She spotted the big freezer and gave a laugh. "Ben locked the two of us in there once," she said.

"Why did he do that?" Riley asked.

"So we could make out without his sister seeing us." Cassie grinned, remembering. She hadn't liked all the kissing, but she wouldn't mind just one kiss now. It had been too long.

Cassie set out the food plates for the campers to take to their tables, accepting them from the cook. Then the vegetables came out of the scullery, and she paused in mid-motion.

Okra.

She stared at the green star-shaped slices, a sharp pang in her chest. Maybe being here wasn't such a good idea. It brought back memories. So many memories.

She hurriedly put the plates out for the campers to grab and then excused herself to the bathroom. She'd come back out when the food plates were gone.

A tap came on the bathroom door. "Cassie? You in there?"

Crapola, she'd been noticed. Cassie flushed the toilet and came out, all smiles. "Did I miss something?"

Riley eyed her suspiciously. "You were gone awhile."

Cassie shrugged, trying to look innocent. "I didn't want to serve the okra."

Riley didn't know about the private joke between her and Ben. She wouldn't know how Cassie had just admitted to missing him.

"Well, come on," Riley said. "Zelda said we can sit with the campers during singing time."

"Oh, great." Cassie followed Riley into the dining hall and sat by her friend Tiffany.

"So," Tiffany said, lowering her voice, "I guess we've both gone out with Ben now."

Cassie winced. Not Ben again. She'd tried to forget that Ben went out with her friend the year before he went out with her. "I hope you're not mad."

Tiffany shrugged. "I kind of was, when I first heard. But we'd broken up. It was a long time ago."

"Same," Cassie said. "It was a year ago for me."

"Would you go out with him again?" Tiffany asked, settling back to study Cassie.

"I would," Cassie admitted. "But he's different now. I'm different. It wouldn't work." At least, that's what she told herself.

"He's had like three girlfriends since you."

That hurt. "I guess we all move on."

The girls sang the familiar songs, but Cassie's heart wasn't in it. Suddenly she just wanted to go home. Some things were better left in the past.

She was quiet as she and Riley washed dishes in the kitchen once the campers left.

"Are you okay?" Riley asked. "I thought you'd be happier here."

Cassie took a moment to answer. She didn't want to admit her feelings to anyone; they made her feel weak. "I guess I'm thinking a lot about last year."

"About Ben, you mean."

"Yeah."

"He did say something," Riley said. "That he's afraid to see you because he thinks you might cry."

"He said that?" Indignation burned up in Cassie's throat, shoving her achy-heart down to her toes. "What does he think, that I'm still not over him?" Suddenly she wanted to see Ben just to laugh in his face and show him how much she didn't care.

"I know. I told him in his dreams."

"Yeah! That's right!" Cassie said, all fired up.

"So you won't cry if we see him?" Riley sounded relieved.

"No way! I'm like, so done with him!" She grabbed a towel and wiped the sweat from her brow. "This is hard work."

"No kidding." Riley grinned. "Why do you think I wanted you here?"

"Ha!" Cassie snapped the towel at her, and Riley leapt out of the way.

"You need a camp name," Riley said, picking up another soap-covered dish. "Since you're staff."

"What's yours?"

"Twiggy."

"What should mine be?"

"I don't know. Violet because you like the color purple?"

Cassie tossed her head back. "Olive. I'll be Olive." Because she had olive skin and it sounded cute.

"Olive it is, then," Riley said. "Get to work, Olive, before Ben sees you being lazy."

Cassie whipped around, eyes wide. "Is he here?"

Riley rolled her eyes. "Yeah, you're so over him."

She laughed at Cassie, who scowled.

"Just you wait," she grumbled. "I'll show you."

She'd show them both. She hoped she'd get the chance.

CHAPTER FIVE

Lost in a Memory

Zelda put Riley and Cassie in charge of the camp out for the younger girls.

"This is one of your assignments as junior staff members. You figure out what the campers are going to do," she said. "Plan the evening and build the bonfire. They have to pass off an outdoor camp out, and this is your major project while you're both here."

After the dinner dishes, Cassie and Riley gathered in the empty mess hall.

"What should we do?" Riley asked, sitting down at a table with a paper and pencil.

Cassie sat across from her. "Music, of course. We have to sing songs."

"And s'mores, then. Everyone loves s'mores and a campfire with songs."

"Then I guess we better have a campfire!"

"Ha, yeah." Riley wrote that down too.

"Maybe we can do a one-match A-frame," Cassie said, her mind flashing on a memory.

Riley squinted at her. "A what?"

"Remember what they taught us in Girls Club all those years ago? The best fire is the one you can light with one match. We have to try it!" No one had succeeded at the camp out they'd had three years earlier, even though Trisha had yelled at them all and insisted she could do it.

"Yeah." Riley grinned.

"Where should we do this awesome camp out?" Cassie asked.

"We could do it here in the mess hall."

Cassie shook her head. "It has to be outside for a big bonfire!"

"I know! We could do it at the amphitheater. Where they have the last night ceremonies."

Cassie pictured the round outdoor theater, with benches ringing the concrete slab. "Great idea! We'll have the girls bring their sleeping bags and pillows, and we'll sleep under the stars."

"And hope it doesn't rain."

She and Riley spent the afternoon gathering the wood and setting it up in the amphitheater. Cassie layered the kindling on top of the tinder, and Riley loaded up the wood into an A-frame.

"We'll light it after dinner," Cassie said, standing next to Riley and staring at the fire with hope and expectation.

"With one match."

All they could think about during dinner was the upcoming camp out.

"Should we have any snacks besides s'mores?" Riley asked as they washed the dishes.

"I don't think so. The girls just ate dinner."

Ma came into the kitchen and examined their work. "Don't you girls have a campfire to prepare?"

"Yes," Riley said. She and Cassie grinned at each other and hurried back to the amphitheater.

The wind blew their hair as they crouched beside their A-frame pile of logs. Cassie looked at Riley, and Riley pulled out the matchbox.

This was it. Their chance to make the perfect fire.

"One match," Riley whispered.

"One match," Cassie breathed.

Riley lit the match. Cassie leaned forward and watched as Riley held it to the tinder. A piece caught, then another. Then the kindling on top smoked and burst into flame. And then finally, the fire beneath the large branches engulfed one of the larger pieces of wood, catching it with the flame.

"We did it!" Cassie cheered.

Riley whooped, and they hugged, pleased with themselves and their one-match fire.

The campers arrived as it began to get dark. Cassie led them in songs, but they wanted scary ghost stories, so Riley took over. Cassie cozied up in her sleeping bag and let her drowsy eyes close.

And then several sleeping bags crowded around her.

"Can we sleep next to you, Olive?" a voice said, and several others picked up the chorus.

"We're scared," another girl said. "We want to be close to you."

"Twiggy!" Cassie groaned, barely remembering to call Riley by her camp name. "You scared all the girls!"

"Sorry," Riley said. "Good thing they've got you to keep them safe!"

The girls moved their sleeping bags closer to Cassie. They whispered and giggled and talked for hours. It was well after midnight before they finally, finally drifted off to sleep.

Only then could Cassie also close her eyes and rest.

❧

The campers woke before seven the next morning, as soon as the sun lit the horizon. They went up to the mess hall, where their well-rested counselors led them to their unit. Grumpy and exhausted, Cassie cleaned up the fire debris and gathered up the trash left behind from the s'mores. Barely had she and Riley finished dumping the trash before it started raining.

"Good thing we did the camp out last night," Riley said.

"Good thing," Cassie said, though her head pounded and all she really wanted was to find a bed and sleep.

She and Riley stayed in the dining hall all day, helping with meals and cleaning and the trading post.

"I can't believe you go home tomorrow," Riley said in the afternoon.

"Has it already been a week?" Cassie had lost track of the days. To be honest, she didn't really mind. This wasn't the fun reunion she'd envisioned. A part of her had been wanting to relive the magic of the previous summer, but those events had been a one-time thing. "I guess so."

So much for seeing Ben. That ache would have to stay in her heart.

Because of the rain, there was no closing flag ceremony, and the campers left quickly after singing time. Cassie washed up and then went to use the bathroom, but Riley was in it.

"Riley!" she crowed. "I need to go!"

"Go to the one in the other building!"

Cassie would have to go out in the rain, and she didn't want to. "I'll just use the men's." There were no men here, anyway.

She was almost done in her stall when Riley banged on the door.

"Cassie!" she hissed loudly. "Hurry and come out! Ben's here!"

Cassie's stomach lurched. Ben was here? Cassie washed her hands and dried them, then smoothed her hair down in the mirror. Deep breaths. She stepped out, trying to appear calm.

Ben stood at the sink helping Riley with the dishes, and she was chatting a million miles a minute. Then Ben looked up, looking at her with the same startling blue eyes, the same face, the same crinkle around his lips.

"Hi," he said, breaking into a smile.

"Hi," Cassie said, raising her eyebrows as if surprised to see him. "You haven't changed much."

"You either," he said.

"You look good," she said, and then her face warmed.

Riley turned from the sink, dripping water everywhere. "Water fight!" She splashed water at both of them.

Cassie shrieked and Ben laughed. She ran for the ice maker and grabbed a handful of ice.

"She means business!" Ben said.

Cassie threw the ice on the floor as he ran toward her with a glass full of water, and Ben slipped. He clutched the wall for support and threw the water at her.

Riley joined Cassie at the ice, and soon they were slipping and sliding all over the floor. Cassie fell, twisting her sore ankle but laughing too hard to care. Riley helped her up, then straightened just as Ben dashed over with a glass in his hand.

What happened next happened so quickly that Cassie couldn't quite be sure how it occurred when she played it back in her head. All she knew was one moment Ben was running toward them, and the next, Riley had knocked her face into the glass and split her forehead open.

The glass shattered when it collided with Riley's head. The gash spewed blood down her shirt and onto the floor.

"Riley!" Cassie cried.

"Here, put this on her," Ben said, his expression instantly sobering. He grabbed a rag from a drawer and placed it in Cassie's hands, then pressed her hands against Riley's face. "Stay here. I'll get my dad."

He ran out of the kitchen, avoiding the mess of ice and water and broken glass. Riley began to cry, and Cassie swallowed a hard lump in her throat. "Riley, I'm so sorry. It's gonna be okay." She sure hoped it would be.

Ben's dad, Mr. Fix-It, returned shortly after in the jeep, with Ben beside him. Ben hopped out, and his dad taped the rag to Riley's forehead before putting her in the jeep.

"I'm taking her to the hospital," he told Cassie. "I called Zelda and told her what happened. She'll be here in a minute."

"I want to come," Cassie said, trying to climb in.

"No," he said firmly. "You and Ben stay here and clean up this mess. You'll be in enough trouble with Ma and Zelda as it is."

Cassie nodded, tears running down her face.

"I'm sorry," Ben said when she turned around. "It was my fault."

All she'd wanted was a moment alone with him. A moment to see how she felt, what he felt. But now that she had this moment, she just prayed Riley would be okay. She nodded and pushed past him to clean up the blood and shattered glass shards.

They worked together in silence until Zelda arrived.

"That's what you get for horsing around," she scolded both of them. "I'd send you home if you weren't leaving tomorrow anyway, Cassie. Riley had to get four stitches."

"Four stitches!" Cassie's stomach knotted. Her eyes welled up with tears again.

Ben looked at her. He reached over the dustbin and gave her hand a quick squeeze before facing Zelda. "She didn't do anything wrong. They were washing dishes and I came in goofing off. There's no one to blame but me."

"Go home, Ben," Zelda said. "Go to your cabin, Cassie. Riley will be back soon."

Ben bobbed his head and left the kitchen without a backward glance.

∼⁕∼

Cassie cried when Riley returned that evening with stitches above her eyebrow, but Riley was fine.

"I'll have a scar," she said. "But it won't be noticeable because my hair will mostly cover it. And it makes a great story."

"I feel so bad," Cassie said.

"You got to talk to Ben at least, right?"

"Not really," Cassie mumbled. "Zelda came along and sent him home."

"At least you saw him."

Yes, she'd seen him. But as Cassie tumbled into bed, she wished she'd done more than that.

She helped set up for breakfast in the morning, taking Riley's spot even though Mrs. Jones would arrive any moment. Ma threw sausages on the griddle, and Cassie ignored the ache of disappointment in her chest.

"Hey, you're doing my job."

Cassie turned away from the plates she'd stacked as Ben stepped into the kitchen. "I didn't think they'd let you back in here!"

He had on a baseball cap again, like he always had when they'd dated. "I have to cover for Riley until she's able to be in here. So a few days, at least."

"I'm about to leave. My mom's on her way." Cassie tried a smile, but it felt fragile. "It was good to see you."

"You too." His eyes crinkled in a smile. "I like your eyes."

"My eyes?" And then Cassie remembered her colored contacts, the ones that turned her brown eyes blue, and she laughed. And laughed harder. "The funniest thing—no, maybe it's not funny."

28

"What?" Ben tilted his head.

"I got these before we broke up," she said, her voice dropping. "And all I could think about was how I couldn't wait to show you."

"Huh. That is funny." But he didn't laugh. "I'm sorry about all that."

She shrugged. "We were just kids."

"We're still kids. And I'm still sorry."

Her heart pounded a little harder at the way he looked at her, and suddenly she remembered how his kisses made her feel. Would he kiss her now?

He looked like he might. But then he said, "I have a girlfriend."

"Oh." Her hopes plummeted. "That's awesome. Good for you."

"I mean." He held her gaze. "If I didn't, I would kiss you. Because I want to. But it wouldn't be fair. Not to her, not to you."

Her heart soared upward again. So he did still like her. She gave him a small smile. "That's all right."

Mrs. Jones arrived, and Cassie left, but she didn't feel bad anymore. She'd gotten what she needed out of Camp Splendor.

CHAPTER SIX

Matchmaker Fail

Cassie didn't see Riley for another week. She hoped things were going well at Camp Splendor.

Oddly enough, when Cassie got home, she didn't feel like talking to her other group of friends. She almost didn't call any of them, but she finally called Amity and Janice, just to say hi before she left again for the church youth retreat.

"It's so good to hear from you!" Amity said. "We miss you so much!"

She said it over and over again, enough that Cassie started to believe it. She hadn't seen them in so long, it almost felt like they weren't a part of her life anymore.

The youth retreat was in Dallas, and Cassie rode with her neighbor Beckham and his sisters to the campus. As soon as they arrived, she looked for Riley.

"Riley!" Cassie called, spotting her and waving.

"Hey!" Riley said. She came over and pushed the hair back from her face. "No stitches."

The stitches were gone, but the painful red mark remained. "Ouch."

"It doesn't hurt. And the doctor said it will fade to a small white line. So it's all okay."

"How was Ben?" Cassie couldn't help asking. "Did he seem okay after I left?"

"Yeah, he came by a few more times. But he didn't say anything about you. Sorry."

"That's okay," Cassie said, and she meant it. She had Ben's last words, and she'd treasure them.

They separated to go to their host homes to eat dinner and change for the dance. Cassie and Riley met Jessica, their third roommate for the duration of the three-day retreat.

"Want some salt and vinegar chips?" Jessica asked, holding the bag out to Cassie.

"I don't know," Cassie said, eyeing them uncertainly. "I've never had that kind."

"So try them."

Cassie took one, then lifted her eyebrow in surprise. "These are actually good."

"I know, right?" Jessica grinned. "They're my favorite."

Cassie grabbed several more handfuls and decided they were her favorite also.

Dinner was chicken nuggets and French fries, which was somewhat problematic for Cassie, since she was a vegetarian. She ignored the nuggets and nibbled at the fries. Good thing Jessica had chips for them to eat.

"What are you wearing to the dance?" Jessica asked.

Cassie showed her the long black dress she'd brought.

"Oo, nice. I think the dances are everyone's favorite part."

"They're mine," Riley said, pulling her own dress out. "I'm so excited we get two dances."

"I wish we had three," Cassie sighed. "There are so many boys here!" Boys had come from as far away as Texas and Tennessee for the extended retreat.

They had another class after dinner, which meant the dance didn't start until nine o'clock. Cassie waved to friends from other congregational units but stayed sitting next to Riley. As soon as the class ended, the girls jumped up with the rest of the youth and worked their way through the hallways to the big auditorium where the dance would be held.

"Noah's here," Riley said, taking Cassie's hand and squeezing it. "I saw him walk in."

"Who's Noah?" Cassie asked.

"Oh, that's right, I never told you. He's friends with one of Zack's brothers. From Fayetteville."

"Ah. And you like him? When did you meet him?"

"At the church dance while you were at your family reunion." Riley sighed. "He's so cute."

The music started, but no one moved yet.

"Which one is he?" Cassie asked.

Riley pointed, and Cassie spotted him. He looked younger than them, only a bit taller than Cassie, with short blond hair and a blue polo shirt. She took a step his direction.

"What are you going to do?" Riley asked, panicking.

"Ask him to dance," Cassie said, sliding her hand out of Riley's.

Riley let her go, and Cassie stepped up to him with a big smile.

"Want to dance?" she asked.

"Sure," he said, his cheeks turning bright pink. He took her hand in his and placed a hand on her waist, and then they moved onto the dance floor with the other couples.

"You're Noah, right?"

"Yeah. Do I know you?"

"Don't think so. I'm Cassie."

"Cassie Jones? From Springdale?"

Cassie gave him a startled look. "Yes. How do you know me?"

His face flushed even brighter, in spite of the dimmed lights. "Um, uh —"

And then Cassie knew. "Are you friends with Zack?"

"Yes. He might have mentioned you a few times."

"Zack, he's awesome." Yet another boy Cassie would gladly date. She'd have to look for him later.

"He speaks highly of you."

Cassie smiled, pleased by that. "I need you to do something for me."

"Does this have to do with Zack?"

"No, not at all. I have a friend who has a crush on you, and I need you to ask her to dance."

"Oh!" He looked around. "Who? Sure!"

This kid was so much easier than Tyler had been. When Riley had a crush on him, he'd acted rude and stuck up about it. "She's got short blond hair and is wearing a black dress with flowers on it. Behind me. Her name is Riley."

Noah's eyes focused somewhere over her shoulder. "Okay. I see her."

"Ask her to dance on the next song?"

"Yeah, I will."

The song ended, and they separated. Noah gave her a smile.

"Thanks for the dance, Cassie."

Cassie returned to Riley, who was biting her fingers anxiously.

"What did he say?"

"Nothing," Cassie said, not wanting to reveal the plot she'd laid. "He's really nice. I'm sure he'll ask you to dance."

"Where'd he go?" Riley murmured as another song came on.

"I don't know," Cassie said, not even turning to look.

Riley moaned. "He's dancing with another girl! Why, why, why doesn't he like me?"

What? Cassie turned to look and saw Noah dancing—with a girl who had short blond hair and a black floral dress.

Cassie fought back laughter. "I'm sure he'll get to you, Riley." She turned around as a boy asked her to dance, but the whole time her eyes scanned the dance floor for Zack. He always asked her to dance, and she hadn't talked to him in a long time.

She spotted him as the song ended and excused herself to move his direction. But he turned away as she neared, almost as if avoiding her.

Cassie frowned. Had he seen her coming? Or was it coincidental? Maybe she'd get the chance to dance with him tomorrow.

She danced a few more songs, and the dance was nearly over before she remembered Noah and Riley. She broke away from her partner and rushed to Noah's side.

"Noah!" she cried.

He gave her a perplexed look from where he stood, another girl in his arms.

He couldn't do anything at the moment. He was dancing. Cassie would just have to wait.

As soon as the song ended, she stepped forward and tapped Noah on the shoulder. He turned to her, a confused smile on his face. "Did I dance with the wrong girl?"

Cassie burst out laughing and nodded. "How did you know?"

"Because she didn't even know my name . . . And that seemed odd. And then I asked her name, and it wasn't Riley."

The lights turned on, and Cassie realized the dance was over. "Well, you'll just have to dance with her tomorrow, she's like about to cry."

Noah's eyes widened, and he cupped a hand to his mouth. "Tell her not to cry!"

Cassie glanced behind her and saw Riley watching. "Tell her yourself. There she is."

He shook his head very slowly. "I won't mess up tomorrow. I'll dance with her."

"She'll be waiting." Cassie gave him one last smile and slipped away.

❦

Cassie, Riley, and Jessica stayed up late talking about the guys they'd met and the people they'd danced with. Finally, giggly and exhausted, they fell asleep without even turning off the light.

Still hungry from not eating dinner the night before, Cassie stuffed herself at breakfast. The cheese danishes were her favorite.

The host family drove them back to the conference center, and Cassie and Riley sat together. The speakers in each session were inspirational and funny, making Cassie laugh and want to live a better life all at the same time.

But mostly she kept thinking about the dance. She really hoped she'd get the chance to dance with Zack this time. And thank goodness Josh, her ex-boyfriend from Tahlequah, wasn't here. She hadn't had to hide at all.

There were so many cute boys. Cassie could only hope some of them would ask her to dance.

This time the host family was more prepared at dinner time, and they served noodles with cheese sandwiches.

"Thank you," Cassie said, glad to eat dinner with everyone else.

"Of course," the wife said, her face pink. "I'm so sorry we didn't know. We would have made sure there was something for you to eat."

"Don't worry about it," Cassie said, trying to put them at ease. "My youth leaders always forget." Or maybe they just thought she was making it up. They seemed annoyed every time she reminded them she was a vegetarian.

Cassie's dress for the second dance was blue with pink flowers on it. Cassie liked the way it accentuated her slender body. She posed with her roommates for pictures, and then they were off to the dance.

She spotted Noah right away, and he waved at her. Cassie waved back, pleased he remembered her. Cassie hurried to his side.

"Short blond hair, green dress," she said, nodding her head toward Riley.

"Got it," Noah said. "I won't mess it up this time."

The dance started, but before Cassie could move away, someone tapped her shoulder.

She turned, her pleasant smile already in place, and saw Zack. "Zack!" she cried, throwing her arms around him and giving him a hug.

"Hi, Cassie," he said, laughing.

She pulled back, slightly embarrassed. She and Zack had never hugged or anything before. "I didn't think you were going to ask me to dance."

"Well, you didn't seem to have any empty dances yesterday," he said, and his face turned pink also.

"I've always got a dance for you," she said, giving him a knowing look. She wished she could talk to other guys the way she did Zack. He made her feel confident.

He took her hand in his and pulled her to the dance floor. "I'll remember that."

"I saw your brother somewhere," Cassie said. "He was dancing with some older girls."

Zack made a face. "People always think he's older than me. And he pretends he is."

"Oh, I hate that." Cassie rolled her eyes. "I get it all the time. I'm shorter than Emily and thinner, so people think she's the big sister."

"Like height's everything."

"Right?" Cassie giggled.

"But you seem older than you are. You're only fifteen, right?"

"Yes." Cassie sighed. "People always think I'm twelve."

He gave her a weird look. "You do not look twelve."

She squeezed his arm. "You're sweet!"

"And you act like you're seventeen or eighteen. The first time I met you, I thought you were that old."

"Let's dance again. You always say such nice things."

The song ended a minute later, and Zack said, "Thanks, Cassie."

"Seriously, Zack," Cassie said. "I'd love to dance again."

He smiled and nodded and slipped away, and somehow Cassie knew he wouldn't ask her. She sighed. It always seemed like he liked her. So why didn't he act on it?

Cassie turned her attention back to Noah. She stepped his direction, and he looked up. He widened his eyes and inclined his head, giving her a look that clearly said, "I'm going to ask her, just leave me alone." Then he flashed a big smile.

Cassie realized he was already moving toward Riley. She watched him ask her to dance and clapped her hands in delight. Right after they started dancing, he met her eyes and raised an eyebrow.

"Thanks," Cassie mouthed. He smiled again.

As soon as they finished dancing and Noah had stepped away, Cassie hurried to Riley's side. They squealed and jumped around for a moment while Riley caught her breath.

"How was it?" Cassie asked.

"Oh, he's so cute. His smile is so dreamy. We didn't really talk much, but he's so nice!"

"I'm so happy for you," Cassie said, beaming.

A guy stepped over and asked Riley to dance, and Cassie went to find Noah. He was at the punch table and put his cup down when he saw her.

"Dance?" he said.

"Sure." Cassie took his hand and slid it into place. "Thank you so much for doing that. It meant the world to her."

"I'm glad I made her happy."

He meant it, she could tell. "I wish there were more guys like you."

"Like me?"

"Yeah." She nodded. "You didn't dance with Riley because you had to or even because you wanted to. You did it to make her happy. Just to be kind."

"Well." Noah shrugged. "That's the way I was raised. To be kind. Especially to girls." He gave her a little twirl and then pulled her back into place.

If only all guys were, Cassie thought.

CHAPTER SEVEN

A New Person

Cassie had no recovery time from the youth retreat before she was off to church camp. She gathered with Michelle and Sue, two girls her age from church, on the shores of Beaver Lake for their long canoe trip.

"Some things to remember," Brother White said, his bald head shiny in the tree-dappled sunlight, "if your canoe tips over, you'll lose everything in it. So tie your shoes to the strap in the middle and hope your sleeping bag doesn't end up in the middle of the lake!"

"Great," Michelle said, rolling her eyes. "This sounds like so much fun."

Brother White ignored her. "You three are the only fifteen-year-olds who haven't done the advanced hike yet. We've got two canoes and four people. Who's pairing up?"

"I'm with Michelle," Sue said immediately.

Of course. Cassie fidgeted, feeling out of place.

"Okay." Brother White picked up her sleeping bag. "I'm with Cassie. I'll carry her stuff."

Ha! Cassie smiled smugly and followed after him.

They put on life jackets, tied their shoes down, and pushed their canoe out into the water. At first, the two of them couldn't seem to make the oars work properly, going in circles.

"I got it," Brother White said. "You turn the paddle this way at the same time I turn mine this way."

"Sure," Cassie said, giving it a try.

It worked, and the canoe slowly began to move forward, slicing through the water.

"Help!" Michelle called. She and Sue kept bumping into the shoreline.

"We're going nowhere!"

"Let's paddle toward them," Brother White said.

Cassie followed his instructions, and soon they were next to the other canoe.

"You have to do it like this," Brother White said, demonstrating. "Work together."

The girls slowly moved away from the shore, and then their canoe nearly tipped. Sue yelped, and Michelle gripped the edges.

"You're okay," Brother White encouraged. "Keep coming this way."

Slowly they continued, making their way across the cove to the campsite. Cassie loosened up as they paddled beside each other, and soon she and Michelle and Sue were laughing and telling stories together.

They reached the other side without incident and sat around the campfire, cooking their foil dinners.

"I love you guys, you're so funny," Sue said. "Let's share a tent together even after the other campers arrive and camp starts for everyone else."

"That sounds like fun!" Michelle said.

Cassie beamed, thrilled she'd finally become friends with these girls who she had known for years but never bonded with.

They put their tent up and giggled all night. The rocks were uncomfortable, but after canoing and hiking to get to the campsite, Cassie managed to fall asleep anyway.

The next morning the other campers arrived at the clearing, popping up their tents next to Michelle's. Lily, a younger girl from church, showed up with Riley in the midmorning.

"Hi!" Cassie said, stepping over and hugging Riley. "We had such a great time on the canoe trip!"

"Wish I could have gone," Riley said.

"You'll be fifteen next year." Cassie nodded at Riley's tent as she put it up. "Who are you sharing with?"

"Lily."

"Nice. I'm with Michelle and Sue."

"Cassie!"

Cassie and Riley both turned as Lily came out of Michelle's tent with Cassie's sleeping bag in her arms.

"I'm taking your spot," she said, chucking it at her. "You can be with Riley."

Cassie's jaw dropped. "You can't just kick me out!"

"Michelle said it was fine."

Cassie stomped over to the tent and looked at Michelle and Sue, who studied their nails or stared at the ground. "Really?" Cassie said. "You're letting Lily take my spot?"

Neither looked at her, but Sue finally ventured, "Riley's your best friend. We thought you'd want to be with her."

"Fine," Cassie said, turning and storming back to Riley's tent. She blinked back angry tears at the rejection. Just when she'd thought they were friends!

"Sorry," Riley said.

"I'm not." Cassie threw her things inside Riley's tent. "I'd rather be with you anyway." She mostly meant it.

"There's a new girl here. I guess Tyler likes her."

"Really?"

"You know her. We ate lunch with her in seventh grade."

That piqued Cassie's interest. "Who?"

"Farrah?" Riley sounded unsure.

Farrah! No way. It couldn't be the same girl Cassie had been friends with a few years ago. "Is she here yet?"

"Yes. Over there. Putting her tent up."

Cassie had to see now. She hurried away from Riley and stepped over to the blond girl helping with the tent. "Farrah?" she said cautiously.

The girl turned around, and Cassie caught her breath. "Farrah! It really is you!"

"Cassie!" Farrah put down the tent pole and threw her arms around Cassie. "Riley told me you'd be here! I couldn't wait to see you!"

"You've moved back. And you—" Cassie didn't want to be insulting by saying now Farrah went to church, but she never had before.

"Yes, we just moved back, so we'll go to high school with you. And I always said I wanted to go to church with you, so here we are!"

"You look great." Cassie looked her friend up and down. She'd filled out a bit, gotten taller, but still had a pretty smile and friendly features. The same scar as before cut across her chin, but it didn't mar her face.

"I'm so excited we'll get to spend time together again! Since you quit texting me years ago, I've completely lost track of what you're doing."

"I'm sorry." Cassie's face warmed. "Not so good at that."

"That's okay." Farrah hooked her arm through Cassie's. They stopped at the tent and collected Riley, and with one of them on each arm, Cassie made her way down the dirt road toward the dining hall.

Who cared about Sue or Michelle? Cassie didn't need anyone else in the world.

⟳≈⟲

Riley was right: Tyler definitely liked Farrah.

Cassie spent a lot of time with Ana Julia and Brother Moda, singing songs every evening. Riley usually joined her, but Farrah stayed by the pool, talking to the lifeguards.

One of whom was Tyler.

"Did you see Tyler's feet?" Riley said Thursday morning as they headed to breakfast with several other girls. "He burned them so bad, they have huge blisters on them."

"I didn't see," Cassie said.

"Pay attention when we're swimming."

"He should put socks on them," Sue said. "It looks terrible."

Cassie checked them out the next time they were at the pool, and she winced when she saw his blistered feet. It looked like red balloons clung to the surface of the skin. Cassie swam to the edge of the pool. "Tyler!" she called.

He looked down from his lifeguard stand at her. "What?"

She gestured at his feet. "You should put socks on," she said, echoing Sue's idea.

The look he gave her was as if she's suggested he put straws in his nose. "Why should I?"

"Your feet," Cassie said. "So they don't burn worse."

"I'm not stupid!" he snapped. "I've been putting cold water on them!"

Cassie pushed away from the side of the pool, stung by his response. "Okay, then."

The other girls crowded around her.

"What's wrong with him?" Sue said.

"Is he mad at you?" Jessica asked.

Cassie just shrugged like it didn't matter. So she and Tyler weren't friends anymore. No big deal.

Riley found Cassie resting in the tent a little later. "Farrah's looking for you. She heard what Tyler did and wanted to talk to you."

Cassie rolled her eyes. "It's so not worth discussing. He's her boyfriend anyway."

"But he's your friend."

"Was." Cassie rolled over. "I'm just going to rest for a bit."

Riley came back for Cassie at dinner time, and Cassie knew she would have to leave the tent. She had a headache and suspected her eyes might be red, but hopefully no one would think she'd been crying. Just tired. She ate her corn and green beans and bread, then threw away the rest of the food. Why were there never any vegetarian options?

The evening devotional followed, and Cassie forgot about Tyler's rebuttal as campers got up and spoke of their love for each other, how much they'd learned at camp, and how it made them want to become a better person. Her heart warmed as she remembered the real reason she was here: to draw closer to God and her friends, to learn about herself. What did Tyler matter? He didn't even belong here.

A woman Cassie recognized as Zack's mother approached Cassie after. She put her arms around her and gave her a hug.

"You never call anymore," she said. "Ever since I teased your grandma."

Cassie's face warmed. "I was worried I wasn't supposed to."

Mrs. Amos laughed. "I was just picking on her. Call anytime!"

"I will," Cassie said, though she knew she wouldn't. Just like she'd known Zack wouldn't ask her to dance again. The connection they'd had to each other was fading.

⚬ ⚬ ⚬

"I have to go back to Camp Splendor," Riley said as she and Cassie packed up the tent after their week of church camp. "But I need you to do something for me."

"Of course," Cassie said.

"Call Noah for me."

"Call Noah?" She remembered the cute, friendly blond Riley had crushed on at the youth retreat.

"Sure. I'll give you his number."

"Okay," Cassie said slowly. "I'll call him."

"Tonight?"

"Tonight."

She said goodbye to Riley and Farrah and went home with her sister Emily. She showered for half an hour, washing away the sweat and grime and relishing the hot water. Then she sat down at her desk and stared at the number Riley had given her.

Call Noah.

She punched his number into her phone, shoving her wet hair over one shoulder.

"Hello?" a male voice answered.

"Is this Noah?" Cassie asked.

"Yes," he said. "Who is this?"

"This is Cassie. Cassie Jones."

"Hi, Cassie," he said, his voice pleasant and friendly.

Why was he so easy to talk to? "Have you had a good week? I just got back from Camp Cherokee."

"Oh, I know that place," he said. "It gets hot. Super hot."

"It was so hot." Cassie laughed, settling into her chair and putting her toes on the desk. "One of the lifeguards burned his feet."

"Ouch. Not so good."

"Not at all. They were kind of grumpy, actually."

"I heard about that."

"Wow, news travels fast! How did you hear that?"

"Some of the girls complained to my mom. She told my dad. I don't think the boys will get to be lifeguards again."

"Serves them right." Cassie took a deep breath and plunged on to the reason she was calling: what Riley really wanted to know. "So. About my friend Riley."

"Yeah. The second one I danced with."

The laughter was evident in his voice, and she smiled. "Do you like her?"

He paused, then said, "Well, I don't really know her. So I'm not sure if I do or don't. She didn't talk when we danced."

"That's a problem," Cassie agreed.

"I kind of like someone else."

"You do?" Cassie arched an eyebrow, eager for the information. "Who?"

"Well, I can't tell you."

"Why not?" Cassie dropped her feet and bounced in her chair, giggling. "You can tell me."

"You're not an unbiased party. Your friend wants me to like her."

"Oh, come on. I won't tell her."

"No." He laughed. "I'm not telling you."

Cassie grinned. "Fine. Be that way. Can I still talk to you, even if you have a crush on another girl?"

"Yes."

They talked for another half an hour, and he made Cassie laugh, and she felt warm inside when she hung up.

"You picked a good one, Riley," she murmured to herself, and then she called Riley to tell her the conversation.

♦

Maureen called that night.

"Hi!" Cassie said, startled to hear from her. "How are you?"

"How are you, stranger?" Maureen replied. "I haven't seen you all summer."

"I haven't really been here," Cassie said. "I've been off."

"You sound perky. Been having fun?"

"So much fun." Cassie sighed, remembering her adventures so far this year. She missed her cousin Jordan, though she felt certain they would be friends again when she saw him in two years. She'd run into Ben and cleared the air between them. And she'd gotten to know some cute boys at the youth retreat. "I feel really good. Better than I have in a long time."

And suddenly, it hit Cassie. One of the reasons she felt so good was because she wasn't hanging out with her old friends anymore.

Was this possible? She remembered how they'd bring her down, make her feel inferior and rejected. Right now she felt so confident. So pretty. So likable and sure of herself.

She didn't want to lose this feeling.

Maureen was still talking, and Cassie tried to pay attention.

"You missed my birthday party," Maureen said. "But maybe you can come over this weekend."

"Yeah, maybe," Cassie said.

But she didn't want to.

"When are you going school shopping? We can go together."

School shopping. That made her pause as she remembered with a rush of nerves that she was about to start high school.

Who did she want to be this year? Someone different than last year. Someone confident and beautiful and smart.

Not someone's shadow or puppy.

"I'm changing my name," she said suddenly, decisively.

"Oh?" Maureen said. "To what?"

"Cassandra," Cassie said. "I'm going by Cassandra now."

CHAPTER EIGHT

Rites of Passage

A phone was ringing in Cassandra's dream. She stood in a large ballroom surrounded by girls in fancy dresses and boys with tails on their suit jackets. She turned her head, trying to find the phone in the crowd of dancers, but it kept ringing, just out of reach everywhere she went.

Her eyes opened as she woke up. The phone was actually ringing. She wasn't dreaming.

And with a spurt of adrenaline, she remembered. It was orientation day.

Crapola!

Cassandra bolted to her desk and grabbed the phone. "Riley!"

"Hey, we're almost to your house. Just another ten minutes," she said.

"I'll be ready." Cassandra hung up and ran a hand through her long, tangled hair. Crapola crapola! She was so not ready!

This was the first time all summer that she'd see most of her friends from junior high. She'd meet lots of new kids from the other junior highs, also. Today was a day for first impressions. Not sleeping in!

Ten minutes later, she was dressed, with her teeth brushed and her hair combed. Riley gave her a big smile as Cassandra got into the seat behind her, though the smile looked a tad nervous.

"Are you ready for this?"

"I think so." Cassandra grabbed her seatbelt and pulled it over her shoulder. Her stomach tightened. Her old friends would be there. Cara, Janice, Maureen, Amity, and Andrea.

She hadn't seen them all summer. She hadn't even missed them. What would happen between them now?

Mrs. Isabel dropped the girls off, and Cassandra stared up at the large dome resembling the White House that stood as sentry to the hallways and classrooms within it. Riley pushed the door open, and Cassandra followed her inside.

A long line of incoming sophomores had formed inside the high school, wrapping through the corridor and leading to the office. Cassandra stepped up to Riley and kept pace with her as they walked past the kids in line, heading to the back. Cassandra kept her eyes forward and her chin up, fighting to hold onto the confidence she'd built all summer.

Then she saw them, all together: Andrea, Cara, Maureen, and Amity.

Together. They hadn't even called her and invited her, and yet here they were, clearly together.

Did they have a slumber party the night before? Ride over together?

Her heart lurched and her step nearly faltered, but it didn't.

Amity spotted her then. "Hi," she said.

"Hi," Cassandra replied, and she kept going.

She didn't stop. She didn't look back. She didn't need them.

The line slowly moved forward as kids shuffled into the office and got their schedules. Soon Riley and Cassandra both had one in hand. Cassandra's eyes scanned over the sheet.

"Crapola!" she said, her heart sinking. "They gave me Spanish I again! I took that last year!"

Riley took her arm and pulled her over to the next line, the one where they waited to get their photos taken for the mandatory school IDs. "Can't you just get it changed?"

"Yes." Cassandra looked at the rest of her schedule. "It just means the rest of this is worthless. It could all change."

"Hey, Cassie," Maureen said, coming over with Andrea. They held their schedules in their hands. "What classes do you have?"

"Hi, guys," Cassandra said. They wanted to see her schedule. They wanted to be in a class with her. Pleasure spurted in her chest in spite of herself. "I have to get my schedule changed, so I don't know. Are you doing choir?"

Maureen shook her head. "I'm done with that."

"Oh. I guess I won't see you in there, then."

Cara joined them, dragging Amity with her. "You didn't stop to talk to us," Cara said, reproach in her voice.

"Sorry," Cassandra said. "I was focused on making sure I got to the right place." Riley fidgeted beside her, and Cassandra couldn't help noticing how none of them even acknowledged her.

The line crept forward, ever so slowly as the camera took pictures and churned out plastic IDs for the student lanyards.

"Where's Janice?" Cassandra asked.

Maureen shrugged. "We haven't seen her all summer. Like you. She has new choir friends now and just hangs out with them."

So it wasn't just Cassandra drifting away. She wanted to see Janice. She missed her, even though she still felt a spasm of jealousy that Janice made Unity when Cassandra didn't.

"We're having a sleepover at my house tonight," Andrea said. "Want to come?"

"Can't," Cassandra said without missing a beat. "I'm going to the mall with Riley and then staying at her house."

Amity and Maureen turned to look at Riley, their eyes scanning her from head to toe. Taking in the short haircut, the colorful, satiny blouse.

"With Riley?" Amity said.

"Yep," Cassandra said, practically daring them to say something snotty about that.

They didn't. She could tell from the way they looked at her that they also knew something had changed over the summer.

"Well, it was good to see you," Cara said, turning around. "Hopefully we'll see you again before school starts."

"Bye," Maureen said.

"Bye," Cassandra said, and she only relaxed once they had walked away.

That was that. Maybe none of them would ever talk to her again. The thought made Cassandra sad, and she realized she still cared for them. But she was different now. She could handle it.

❧

"Are you sure you're ready for this?"

Cassandra didn't answer for a heartbeat as her mother pulled the van to a stop in front of the Department of Motor Vehicles. School orientation had been the day before, and this was the next step: getting a driver's license. Cassandra nodded.

"I'm ready. I want to be driving the moment I turn sixteen. That means I need to start studying for my permit now."

"I'm not sure I'm ready for this," Mrs. Jones muttered, and Cassandra smiled. She followed her mom into the small building and waited with her in line.

"What can I do for you, Ma'am?" the guy with a Smokey the Bear hat behind the counter asked.

"My daughter needs a manual. So she can start studying for the test."

"Here you go." He handed a thick booklet back to Cassandra. "Just memorize that, and you won't have any problems passing the driving test."

Memorize it! Cassandra tried to stay calm as she stared at the book. She could do this. It was time to learn to drive.

She went with her mom to the grocery store and then to the post office, but she sat in the car each time with the windows down, reading through the driver's manual. She'd have to make flashcards, or she'd never pass the test.

Her phone rang, and she opened it without looking, her eyes still on the book. "Hello?"

"Cassie? It's Cara."

That got her attention. Cassandra sat up straighter. "Cara! Hey!"

"Hey. Listen, we're going to the Grape Festival tonight and then having a slumber party, just like we do every year. Do you want to come?"

Cassandra heard the hesitation in Cara's voice. Like she thought Cassandra might not want to. Like maybe they weren't important to her. But they were. She still loved them. She just didn't know if she wanted to be friends with them anymore.

"Yes," she said. "I want to. I'll be there."

"Great! Meet us at the Grape Festival at ten tonight."

She told Mrs. Jones as her mom drove them home, waiting for the third-degree lecture about boys and remembering who she was. But for once, her mom just said, "Okay. Have fun. I know you haven't seen them all summer, so enjoy yourself."

And it might be the last time. Cassandra didn't say that, but she felt it in her core.

She chose her clothes very carefully. She picked a tank top that showed off her tanned shoulders and shorts that emphasized her slender legs. She wanted to look like them. She wanted to see if she could fit in.

Cara's mom waited for Cassandra at the white church by the festival, then she took her over to the other girls. They squealed when they saw her, throwing their arms around her.

"You came!" Amity said. "We weren't sure you would!"

"Cara, you cut your hair!" Cassandra said. She reached out and fingered the short blond locks, the fringe of bangs. "I love it."

"Me too." Cara grinned. "It makes me look older."

"I guess I should cut mine," Cassandra joked, and the other girls laughed. It was a running joke that Cassandra only looked twelve while the others looked fifteen or even sixteen. Cassandra listened for the edge in their voices that meant they were laughing at her, not with her, but she didn't hear it.

They moved through the crowd, and Cassandra took the time to really examine them. Cara, Amity, and Andrea had grown up. They were filling out, with bigger breasts and wider hips. Their faces looked more mature, their hair less like a little girl's and more like a woman's. Cassandra felt a pang of jealousy. They were beautiful, and next to them she felt plain.

Especially when every boy they passed stopped to stare at them and ignored her as if she wasn't there.

They didn't even ride anything, just walked around like they were too good for the fair, laughing and pointing at cute boys. Andrea started talking about how many boys Amity had kissed over the summer, and Amity couldn't stop giggling. How much had Cassandra missed? No wonder she didn't know them anymore.

"Let's go home," Cara said. "Mom already ordered pizza."

"Right, and we can talk about that awesome party last week at Connor's house," Amity said.

"Or the one coming up at Phillip's," Maureen said, and they hooked arms, squealing in anticipation.

They included Cassandra, but she felt on the outside anyway. Party at Connor's? And who the heck was Phillip?

Cara put on country music at her house and they gathered in her bedroom, telling stories and eating.

"Where's Janice?" Cassandra asked Cara, helping her pull another blanket from the closet.

"I don't know. She doesn't talk to us anymore." Cara gave her a meaningful look. "It's like she thinks she's too good for us."

Cassandra understood that look. "I don't think that, Cara."

"But?"

"But." Cassandra hesitated. "I always want to be close to you guys. I always want to be able to talk about anything and everything. But I don't feel like I can. I always thought we'd be friends forever. But I'm gone for a few weeks, and it's like no one remembers me. Everything continues without me."

"It wouldn't take long for you to be apart of everything again. You just have to spend more time with us."

Yet Cassandra remembered how often last year her friends made her cry, made her feel like she wasn't good enough. "It's more than that," she said.

"I know," Cara said. She handed her the blanket. "But a lot of it is up to you."

Yes, it was.

CHAPTER NINE

The Rat Race

C assandra's alarm went off at six in the morning, and she shot out of bed like a rocket.

The first day of high school. Nerves jumbled up in her stomach, and she thought she'd be sick. Crapola! She wasn't ready for this.

She attacked her long dark hair with a curling iron, trying to give it volume and wave. Then she pulled out her makeup and outlined her eyes. She puckered her lips and examined her reflection. How would others see her? Did she still look twelve, or could she at least pass for fifteen?

"Time to go, Cassandra!" Mrs. Jones called. "I have to drop the younger kids off first!"

"Right," Cassandra muttered, swiping gloss over her lips.

Panic broiled in Cassandra's stomach as they neared the high school. She felt like she had just climbed the ladder to the high-dive and was looking down at the frightening blue pool. She couldn't do it! She couldn't jump!

But she had no choice. Mrs. Jones pulled up in front of the school and smiled at her.

"Good luck, Cassie."

Cassandra inhaled slowly and then let it out. "I've got this," she murmured to herself. Then she pushed the car door open and stepped out.

Springdale High School was a sprawling campus, with a dome that looked like the capital between two wings of classrooms. The first class she had was Spanish II. She'd had to get her schedule changed to accommodate the class and hadn't walked around the school yet to map out her classes. Luckily Spanish was just inside the massive school atrium. Cassandra slipped inside well before the tardy bell rang and sat there, shaking in her shoes, feeling like she would throw up.

"*Bienvenidos, estudiantes!*" the teacher said, smiling down at all of them.

Behind her, a girl giggled. "*Muchas gracias*," she said in a mocking accent, just quietly enough that the teacher didn't hear.

"I'm your Spanish II teacher, Ms. Elliot. I know we'll have a great time this year exploring a new culture!"

"*Mas que claro*," the girl whispered.

Cassandra turned around and smiled at her. "I'm Cassandra."

"Mia," the girl said. Her straight red hair flowed down her back, and freckles dotted her skin. "Spanish can be *muy aburrecido*."

"I think your Spanish is better than mine," Cassandra said. She wilted in relief to have made a friend already. "What junior high did you go to?"

"Central. You?"

"Southwest."

They hushed when Ms. Elliot looked at them, but Mia waved when class ended.

"See you tomorrow," she said.

"See you," Cassandra echoed.

She had P.E. second hour and had to race across the courtyard outside to get to the old gym, one of the originals left from the early days. The bell rang just as she ran in, but she wasn't last, and the teacher didn't reprimand her.

"Cassie!" Farrah called, waving when she saw her come in.

Cassandra moved over to her friend. "Oh, my goodness. This campus is huge."

"Isn't it? I can't believe we're in high school now!"

Cassandra wasn't sure she wanted to believe it.

"Welcome, girls!" the teacher, a short Hispanic woman with short hair, said. "I'm Ms. Lynn. Tomorrow you bring clothes to change into. We will change out every day!"

Cassandra groaned. Just great. She already knew she'd hate this class.

"And my goal this year is to get each one of you moving. You need to lose fat and gain muscle!" Ms. Lynn flexed a skinny arm. "Even you skinny people!"

Farrah giggled. "She's talking to you."

"Right," Cassandra muttered. She was skinny, but she had no muscle.

After P.E. she had math, and then she hurried to the science wing for her biology class.

Cassandra recognized Ashlee, a friend from Camp Splendor, in her fourth hour class. Ashlee spotted Cassandra at the same time, and she brightened.

"Hi, Cassie!" she said. "I forgot I'd see you here!"

"Same," Cassandra said, exhaling.

"At least we have a class together," Ashlee said, motioning Cassandra to sit with her.

"At least I wasn't late to this one," Cassandra muttered, pulling her backpack out and placing it on the table in front of them.

Ashlee laughed. "I've had a hard time finding my classes, too."

Emmett and Andrew, two friends from Cassandra's last school, stepped into the room, chatting together. Cassandra waved them over.

"Guys!"

"Hey, Cassie," Emmett said, giving her a fond smile.

"Sit at our table," Cassandra said, gesturing to the empty seats next to Ashlee.

The two boys sat down just as the teacher came in. They fell silent while he droned on in a monotone voice about the important and intricate details to biology and life on earth, then the bell dismissed for lunch. Ashlee stood, shouldering her backpack.

"Better luck tomorrow," she said.

"Soon this will feel like home," Cassandra said. She hoped, anyway.

Cassandra stopped at her locker and dumped her books off, then wandered into the cafeteria. She faltered a few steps in and examined the round tables. Where was she supposed to go now?

"Cassie." Cara touched her arm, tugging her forward. "Sit with us?"

She had nowhere else to go, so Cassandra nodded. She followed Cara to a round table with her old group of friends. She sank down into a chair, and they moved over without questioning. She was still one of them. For now.

"Want to come over after school?" Maureen asked. "I'm having a celebration. Surviving the first day of high school."

"We have to survive it first, moron," Amity said.

"I'm planning to, even if you're not," Maureen answered.

"What do you have next?" Amity leaned over to peer at Cassandra's schedule.

"Choir."

"Oh, me too! We can walk together!"

"Do you know where it is?"

"Yes."

Cassandra exhaled in relief. She wouldn't be late for that one either, then.

"And we've got history together," Maureen said. "This is great. We'll still get to hang out."

Cassandra smiled, but she felt like someone slowly pulling off a band-aid.

"My birthday party's this weekend," Amity said as they walked the circular hallways toward the choir room. "Want to come?"

"Of course," Cassandra said.

"Great. Melanie will be there too."

Cassandra had almost forgotten about Amity's cheerleader friend, the one no one liked. She hadn't come to Cara's party at the Grape Festival, and Cassandra had hoped no one hung out with her anymore. "How come she wasn't at lunch?"

"She has B lunch."

"Ah."

They entered the choir room, and Cassandra waved when she saw Riley. She broke away from Amity to sit on the riser with her.

"I'm an alto," Riley said.

"I know. But I'll sit here until I have to leave."

The music director, Mr. Cullen, came in and cleared his throat. "Your previous choir teachers put you into parts for me. So let me just call your name and tell you where to go. We have first sopranos, second sopranos, tenors, basses, first altos, second altos, in that order on the risers."

Cassandra gave Riley a mournful look, knowing they were about to part ways. She got up when her name was called and went back to the first soprano section, close to Amity, who had already found Melanie and sat close to her. She spotted her friend Miles and gave him a headbob, glad they were finally in choir together.

The boy beside Miles stared at Cassandra as if he knew her, but when his name was called—"Ethan Matthews"—Cassandra knew she'd never seen him before. He was kind of cute.

"Betsy Walker—"

Betsy. Betsy Walker? That was a name Cassandra hadn't heard in a very long time. Betsy had been a good friend in fifth and sixth grade, but then her parents got in trouble with the law and Betsy moved away to live with her aunt. Cassandra hadn't seen her since. She straightened up, scanning the choir room. She almost couldn't breathe with anticipation.

There she was. It had been three years since Cassandra saw Betsy, but her face was the same. The last time Cassandra had seen her, Betsy had been like a waif, thin and pale and almost invisible. This time she looked all right, cheeks flushed, smiling and laughing with the kid beside her, and completely well-adjusted.

Cassandra couldn't wait to talk to her, but Mr. Cullen wasn't through. He made them go through a warm up and site-read a song before the bell rang, dismissing them for sixth hour.

"Betsy!" Cassandra ran over and spun her friend around.

Betsy just frowned at her for a moment, and then her face wreathed into a smile. "Cassie? Is that you?"

"Yes!" Cassandra laughed and hugged her tight. "I never thought I'd see you again!" She pulled away and studied her. "Where are you? Who are you living with?"

"I still live with my aunt," Betsy said, and there was no anger or animosity in her voice. "She's like a mom to me. We moved back to Springdale last year. I finished up junior high at Central, and now I'm here."

"I'm so happy!" Cassandra squeezed her arm, unable to even explain her joy. Betsy was here. Betsy was all right. She gave her another hug and then jerked away. "I better go. I keep getting lost and don't want to be tardy again!"

She was tardy to her next two classes, but the teachers were lenient about it.

What she couldn't believe was that four of her seven teachers had given her homework on the first day of school.

Her head pounded by the time school finally ended. She'd survived it. Besides Maureen, her friends Leigh Ann and Nicole were also in history with her. Nicole was in her English class, also. And Mia, the girl she'd met in Spanish that morning, was in choir.

She hurried outside after seventh hour and paused in front of the school. She looked for a bus loop or a parking lot with the long yellow vehicles, but she didn't see any. Where were the buses? She dashed back through the atrium to the courtyard, but there was no parking on that side. She hurried into the office, pushing past a mob of kids asking for help with schedules and lockers.

"Excuse me," she said, finally getting the registrar's attention. "Where are the buses?"

"In the gravel lot," the woman said without looking up.

Cassandra's frustration rose. "And where is that?"

The woman finally lifted her eyes. "Across the street from the stadium. You can't miss them."

She most certainly could miss them. Cassandra ran back outside, eyes darting to the stadium and then to the parking lot across the street.

There they were. All the little buses, pulling out onto the street one by one. Even if she sprinted, Cassandra wouldn't make it in time.

She groaned and put her face in her hands. First day of school, and she'd missed the bus.

Mrs. Jones only sighed a little when she picked Cassandra up from the high school. "Try not to miss the bus tomorrow."

"I won't." Cassandra's face burned. "I didn't know where to go." She pulled out her driver's license manual and began to study. "Besides, it won't be an issue in a few months."

"Six more months," Mrs. Jones muttered, and Cassandra smiled. They were both counting it down.

Mrs. Jones peppered her with questions about how school was, but Cassandra fended them off, not wishing to rehash her day of tardies and awkwardness.

Cassandra caught the bus to school the next morning and felt more calm as she entered the atrium and walked to her locker. First hour. Spanish. She knew where to go.

Spanish went by smoothly, and Cassandra changed into shorts and a T-shirt in P.E., just as commanded. And then Ms. Lynn got on the phone and left the girls sitting on the bleachers, doing nothing.

Farrah stretched across from Cassandra and watched her read the driver's permit manual.

"I made flashcards," she said. "That helped me remember it all."

Cassandra looked up at her. "Did you take your test already?"

Farrah nodded. "Yes. And I passed on the first try."

Cassandra's eyes went wide. She didn't know anyone who had done that. "Guess I'll make flashcards, then!" She closed her book and peered at her friend, remembering her summer romance. "How are you and Tyler?"

Farrah shrugged, giving a sheepish smile. "Fine, I guess. We don't have lunch or any classes together. But he always smiles and says hi when he sees me in the halls."

"Well, that's something," Cassandra said, though she really didn't know. She hadn't had a boyfriend since Ben, the summer before ninth grade. "I wish we had lunch together." She would probably sit with Cara and her old friends again, but that felt like putting on shoes that didn't fit right.

"You'll make new friends soon enough."

The second day was much better. Cassandra only got lost going to math class and managed to get to all her classes without any tardies.

"You're coming to my birthday on Friday, right, Cassie?" Amity said at lunch.

Cassandra nodded. "Yes." She hesitated a moment, not sure she wanted to invite her, but then she decided to. "There's a dance at church on Saturday. If you guys want to come." It was tradition, after all. For two years, she and her friends had gone to the dances in Rogers together.

"Yes!" Amity squealed, and Andrea and Maureen quickly agreed.

"Well, awesome," Cassandra said.

She tried to make herself feel excited, but for some reason, a knot of dread formed in her stomach.

Her old world and her new world were about to collide.

EPISODE 2: ON THE EDGE

CHAPTER TEN

Perfection

On Friday after school, before Amity's birthday party, Mrs. Jones took Cassandra to the DMV to take the written part of the driving test. If she passed, she'd get her permit and be able to legally learn how to drive. She studied her flashcards the whole way there, praying she wouldn't forget anything.

She had to wait for an available testing station first.

A boy was in the waiting room with her. He smiled at her, revealing white teeth contrasting with his dark skin tone. His eyes and handsome face intrigued Cassandra, and she wondered if he went to her school. He said something to her in Spanish, but Cassandra's limited one year of the language failed her.

"I'm sorry," she said, smiling awkwardly. "I don't speak Spanish." She knew enough to say those words in Spanish, but she was willing to bet he also understood the English.

He shook his head, then pointed at her and mimed holding a steering wheel.

She nodded. "Yes. I'm getting my learner's permit. Are you?" She pointed at him, and he nodded also.

He pointed at her again, and then he said something in Spanish. She just stared blankly. He sighed, and then he said again, very slowly. "*Tu . . . es . . . muy . . . bonita.*"

Cassandra translated in her head. *Tu es . . .* you are . . . *muy . . .* very . . *. bonita . . .* Oh! Pretty! She did know these words!

"Thank you," she said, face hot. "*Gracias.* You too." She blushed harder, both at her attempt at Spanish and her telling him he was cute.

He just smiled and said something else, to which she had no understanding.

"Cassandra Jones?" the man at the reception called.

She stood up, keeping her eyes down as she walked past the boy. It would have been nice to communicate better.

The deputy led her over to a computer to take the test. "Remember, you can only miss five," he warned. "If you miss more than that, you have to take it over."

Cassandra nodded, her heart beating too hard in her chest. She wanted this over with!

The questions popped up on the screen one by one, and at least they were multiple choice. She felt confident on most of them, but there were enough she had to guess on that trepidation rolled like a rock in her stomach. She might have missed too many!

When she finished she went back to the reception counter and waited for them to give her score to her.

"Cassandra," a large woman in a tan button-up shirt called. She stepped up to the counter, and Cassandra raised her hand.

"Here."

The woman handed her a slip of paper. "You missed five, which means you passed. One more wrong and you wouldn't have, but you did. Good job."

"I passed?" Cassandra gasped. She took the paper that gave her permission to begin learning how to drive. "I did it!" She squealed and ran outside, eager to tell her mom.

⟲⟶✹⟵⟳

Mrs. Jones took Cassandra over to Amity's house after the testing for Amity's birthday party.

"You ready?" she asked as she parked in front of the house.

"Yes," Cassandra said, still excited about having her driver's permit. She hesitated before opening the car door, the coldness of reality splashing over her. "These aren't really my friends anymore." She didn't fit in. Next week she planned to start eating lunch with Ashlee and Betsy and a few other choir friends.

"Then enjoy your weekend with them. It might be the last."

"Yeah." Cassandra pushed the door open and walked up the steps to Amity's house.

"Cassie!" Amity gave her a big hug and hauled her into the kitchen where everyone else was gathered.

"Guess what?" Cassandra said, and she reached into her purse to pull out her signed permit paper.

But then she stopped mid-motion. One face had drawn her attention.

Tyler Reeves.

That gave her a jolt of surprise. Tyler was from church, and he was supposed to be dating Farrah. What was he doing here?

58

"Hi, Cassie," he said.

"Hi," she said, then looked away from him. He'd been rude to her all summer, and now he wanted to be friendly? She didn't think so.

"We're about to get in the pool," Amity said. "You have your suit on?"

"Not yet." Cassandra unzipped the bag she had slung over her shoulder. "I've got it, though."

"Get changed and meet us out there."

Everyone had gone to the pool when Cassandra came out except Melanie, Amity's cheerleader friend, and Tyler. They sat at the kitchen table talking softly, with Melanie giggling every few words.

"You guys going swimming?" Cassandra asked, pulling her cover up closer around her as she came into the kitchen. It bothered her to see Tyler talking to Melanie, for some reason.

"Yes." Melanie stood, pushing her blond hair behind her shoulders and sashaying down the steps that led to the pool. She wore nothing except a tiny bikini over her voluptuous body.

Cassandra lingered. "What are you doing here?"

"Amity invited me." Tyler shrugged and stood up.

"Why? You guys aren't even friends."

"I guess Melanie likes me. So I came to get to know her better."

What did it matter if Melanie liked him? "What do you think now that you know her?"

"She's really cute and super nice. I'm going to ask her out. She'll be at the dance tomorrow, too."

"The church dance?" How dare Amity invite Melanie! "What about Farrah?" Cassandra asked, her blood boiling. Farrah talked about him every day. How much she liked him, how sweet he was, how they'd become such good friends over the past few months.

"Things change," Tyler said, but he wouldn't quite meet her eyes.

Cassandra turned around and stormed for the pool, so mad she saw spots. She wasn't going to tell Farrah, but if Melanie came to the dance, Farrah would learn soon enough.

"And I was like, oh my gosh, no way," Maureen was saying when Cassandra sat on the edge of the pool, letting her feet cool off. "And then Michael said, 'only white girls move it that way,' and I said, 'you are so sick! I'm outta here!' and I left."

Everyone roared with riotous laughter, but the knot in Cassandra's stomach didn't dissipate. She didn't know Michael, and she didn't like the sound of the conversation. This was what she had missed all summer, and she was glad.

Amity turned on the music, and it blared across the pool.

"Oh, I know this song!" Melanie said. She climbed out of the pool, water streaming down her body, her breasts barely covered in her skimpy bikini. She moved to the concrete and began dancing to the song. "Come on, Amity, dance with me!"

"I don't know the song," Amity said, but she obliged. She also wore a bikini. Cassandra glanced around and realized she was the only one who didn't.

The song ended and the girls returned to the pool, laughing and gossiping. But nobody talked to Cassandra. She sat on the edge, literally and figuratively.

The pizza and cake and presents went by in a blur. Cassandra wished she hadn't come. When everyone went back outside, she put her clothes on and sat down at the kitchen table.

Andrea came in to get something and spotted her. "Cassie? Why aren't you swimming?"

Cassandra shrugged. "I don't feel like it."

Andrea pulled out a chair and sat next to her. "Because of Melanie?"

Cassandra could go with that. "Because of her and Tyler. Tyler's been dating a friend of mine all summer."

"That's Tyler for you," Andrea said, and she sounded quite pleased about it. She had also dated Tyler in junior high.

"How was your first week of school?" Cassandra asked.

Andrea shrugged. "Not so bad. There's a lot of work. My teachers are giving homework already, but I'm like, meh. I'll do it if I feel like it."

"I know. I made a mistake taking advanced biology and advanced English. Those classes are already killing me."

"That's all on you," Andrea said, and they both laughed.

For a moment, the hardness in Cassandra's chest eased. She'd been friends with Andrea for so long. Wasn't there a way for that friendship to continue?

Someone knocked on the front door, and Cassandra followed Andrea to answer it.

"Hello?" Andrea said, pulling open the door.

"Hi," a male voice said. "I'm here to pick up Tyler."

It was Jason, his brother. Cassandra pushed the door open and smiled at him. "Hi, Jason."

"Oh, hey, Cassie," he said, returning her smile.

Unlike Tyler, Jason was always kind. He was president of the early morning Bible study class this year, and he'd asked Cassandra to be his assistant. She was honored he even knew who she was.

"They're swimming out back," she said, turning and leading him through the house.

Someone had turned out the porch light, and Cassandra flipped it on as she stepped outside, Jason and Andrea right bend her. "Tyler," she called, "Jason's h—"

That was as far as she got before the girls in the pool began screaming and ducking into the water, arms flailing and covering themselves.

Andrea grabbed her arm and shoved her and Jason back into the house.

"They're skinny-dipping!" she gasped, her face going red while her eyes danced wickedly.

Cassandra felt her own face burn with embarrassment. Thank goodness she wasn't with them!

Tyler's face had gone quite pale. "And where is Jason?"

Cassandra reached for the wall to support herself. "I'm sure he's not out there," she said as calmly as she could.

"I'll find him," Andrea said, and she darted back outside.

Cassandra couldn't meet Jason's eyes. He must think horrible thoughts about her now. He'd probably ask her not to be his assistant after today.

The side door leading to the road opened, and Tyler came in, his own face bright red.

"I didn't know," he said hurriedly to his brother. "They told me to wait in the yard for a bit. So I did. I wasn't there, I promise."

Jason nodded. He hadn't relaxed, though his features looked a little less stern. "I believe you. Let's go." He cast her a quick look. "Cassie."

That was it, and then they left. Cassandra sank into a chair, weak-kneed.

Andrea sat beside her. "That was so close," she said, and then she started giggling. "I can't believe we took Jason out there!"

Cassandra put her face in her hands and groaned. "Oh, that was awful." And then she couldn't help it. Her shoulders shook as she laughed too. "Did you see his face?"

"Priceless."

And they both laughed, Cassandra weak with relief at the crisis averted and what had almost happened.

⁂

Mrs. Jones picked Cassandra up the next day, and she said goodbye to her friends for a few hours while she went home and changed for the dance.

"How was it at Amity's house?" Mrs. Jones asked as they made the drive to Rogers.

"I didn't like it," Cassandra said, not bothering to explain the skinny-dipping incident. "I don't fit in with them. I never did. I'm tired of trying."

"I'm sorry, sweetie," Mrs. Jones said.

"Don't be. I'm not." She had Riley and Farrah, and she just knew there were more people she would meet and become friends with.

Cassandra arrived early enough to help set up the decorations in the gym. Noah, Riley's crush, arrived soon after, and Cassandra waved him over.

"Don't worry," he said as he joined her. "I won't forget to ask her to dance."

She smiled. "I knew you wouldn't."

He stayed beside her as they unrolled streamers and put out cups by the punch bowl. People began to trickle in, and Cassandra knew when Amity and her friends arrived: they came in like a herd of elephants, trumpeting to announce their presence. They waved at Cassandra, who waved back, then stayed next to Noah and the other kids from Fayetteville.

Farrah came in just as the dance was getting going. She looked beautiful in a light pink shirt and black skinny jeans.

"I'm so excited," she said. "This is my first dance."

Cassandra's chest tightened and she glanced toward Melanie, wearing a nearly see-through shirt with no sleeves. Cassandra almost expected an adult to go up to her and tell her to change.

"Do you think Tyler will dance with me?" Farrah asked.

"He's weird about dancing sometimes," Cassandra said, trying to defuse the situation. "But lots of guys will ask you."

Zack came over, smiling and extending a hand toward Cassandra. "Want to dance?"

"Love to."

They made small talk about school, what she thought about high school.

"I got my driver's permit," Cassandra said.

"Good for you! That's not easy."

"I'll be sixteen in March," she added, giving him a meaningful look. "You'll take me on a date, won't you?"

He laughed. "Of course."

She smiled, relieved she'd have at least one date after her birthday.

Andrea came over to Cassandra as soon as their dance finished. "Who was that? He's hot!"

"Really, Andrea? You don't know?" Cassandra turned her direction. "That was Zack! I had such a crush on him last year!"

"But you don't this year?"

Cassandra shook her head. "He's just a good friend."

"Great." Andrea pushed past her, shoes clomping as she headed

Zack's direction.

"Good luck, Zack," Cassandra muttered.

"Who is that girl, Cassie?" Farrah moved to Cassandra's side, her eyes fixated on the dance floor.

Cassandra followed her gaze and squinted, pretending she didn't know what she was looking for. There was Tyler, holding Melanie a little too closely, gliding across the floor.

"That's Melanie. She went to Southwest last year."

"How does Tyler know her?"

Cassandra shrugged. "I really don't know." She turned to Farrah. "Everyone dances with everyone at these dances. It's lots of fun!"

Farrah narrowed her blueish eyes. "But he's danced with her twice and hasn't glanced at me at all. Hasn't even said hi." Her voice nearly broke on these words, and Cassandra felt the pain she held back.

She squeezed Farrah's arm. "I'm sorry. Guys are fickle like that."

The song ended, and Tyler suddenly crossed the room in their direction. Farrah clutched her hands and waited, but Tyler said, "Dance, Cassie?"

She would have said no, for Farrah's sake, but Farrah turned and ran out of the gym. Cassandra took his hand. "Yes."

As soon as they were on the dance floor, she let him have it. "What's wrong with you? What are you doing? How can you be so cold and uncaring toward someone you used to like?"

He looked uncomfortable, and she knew he regretted asking her to dance. "I haven't liked her in a month. We weren't dating, so it's not like I owe her an explanation."

"You couldn't tell her? She's thought this whole time the two of you had something going on!"

"Well, that's not really my fault, is it? I never said there was."

She wanted to smack him for his idiocy. "You traded Farrah for Melanie? Really, Tyler? You want the kind of girl who wears tiny bikinis and skinny dips with a boy in the yard?"

"She didn't do anything wrong," he said, avoiding her eyes as his cheeks went pink.

"It didn't feel right to me!"

"But you're Cassie." He shot her a quick glance and lifted a shoulder. "You're perfect."

He didn't say it like it was a compliment. He said it like she was untouchable, unattainable. Too good for everyone.

She let go of his hand, not sure why his words stung so bad. Why did perfect sound like such a bad thing? She turned around and walked out, looking for Farrah.

CHAPTER ELEVEN

Driver's Ed

Farrah spent the rest of the evening in the bathroom sobbing. Cassandra tried to enjoy the dance, but she couldn't. She kept checking on Farrah and anxiously looking at the time on her phone, just wanting the dance to end.

Tyler did not seek Farrah out. He did not ask Cassandra where she was or try to talk to her. In fact, he avoided Cassandra for the rest of the night while he danced with Melanie for nearly every song.

Even church was awkward on Sunday, with Farrah sitting as far from Tyler as possible during Sunday School and Tyler making a conscientious effort to talk to everyone except her.

Cassandra had hoped that by Monday Farrah would be feeling better, but she moped through P.E., her form wilted as they did crunches and toe touches.

"I never thought he'd hurt me that way," she said, her eyes red, though she didn't cry. "He was always so kind and respectful."

"Guys are while they like you," Cassandra said, a lump of empathy in her throat. "Once they're over you, you're nothing. They don't care about your feelings anymore."

Ms. Lynn cleared her throat, and the girls stopped talking.

"We're going to concentrate on building muscle mass this year in P.E.," Ms. Lynn announced. "So that means I need to take measurements of everyone here so we have a starting place. We'll just go in alphabetical order."

"I don't understand that," Farrah whispered while they waited for their names to be called. "He'll always be something to me."

"That's the difference between guys and girls," Cassandra said. "We never forget."

"Cassandra Jones," Ms. Lynn called out.

"Oh, yippy," Cassandra muttered, climbing down the bleachers and following Ms. Lynn into the little office.

"You don't weigh very much," Ms. Lynn said after putting Cassandra on a scale. She used a tiny pair of forceps to pinch Cassandra's arm, waist, hip, and back. "But you have a lot of body fat."

"I do?"

"Yep." Ms. Lynn showed her the percentage on a graph. "This means you don't like to exercise even though you aren't very big. You're what we call skinny fat."

Cassandra didn't like that. "What do I have to do?"

"We'll be teaching you exercises to build muscle mass. Do more cardio. Also avoid dieting. It makes you skinny but eats away at your muscles so you aren't in good shape. Eat lots of protein."

Cassandra didn't like to run or break a sweat. And it was hard to get protein as a vegetarian. Apparently there were a few things for her to work on. "Okay," she mumbled, then shuffled out of the room so the next person could have their turn.

School was a lot better now that she knew where her classes were. She had someone to talk to in every class. She'd made friends with Mia in Spanish class, had Farrah in P.E., Ashlee in biology, and Mason sat behind her in English and always talked to her. Nicole was in there also. It was probably her favorite class.

Amity didn't walk with her to choir now that they didn't eat lunch together. She didn't sit with her, either, but close to Melanie. Cassandra sat next to Miles and John, another boy she'd made friends with. Amity wasn't far away and she frequently said hi, but Cassandra kept to herself, sometimes talking to Harper, a talkative, friendly soprano who sat on her other side, but usually laughing at Miles' and John's conversations.

Leigh Ann, Nicole, and Maureen were in her history class, so she felt like she had someone to talk to everywhere she went.

Cassandra usually sat with Cara on the bus, but today Cara was sitting with a boy, so Cassandra sat with Leigh Ann.

"History is so boring," Leigh Ann said. "Our teacher speaks in such a monotone. He puts me to sleep."

Cassandra nodded in agreement. "He needs to do something to make learning about dates more interesting."

"That's Cassie," Cara said, attracting Cassandra's attention.

She turned her head to see Cara pointing at her as she talked to the guy beside her.

"She's so sweet," Cara went on. "She's so happy and hyper. She's the sweetest person I've ever met."

"What?" Cassandra laughed. "No, Cara is. She never has anything mean to say about anyone."

Cara smiled at her, and Cassandra wished she could keep their friendship going strong. But they didn't have any classes together, and now they didn't even have friends in common.

The only thing they had was the bus.

⊙⌒◦⚙◦⌒⊙

"Today's cardio is running!" Ms. Lynn said in P.E. the next day. "All the way around the parking lot three times!"

"No," Cassandra groaned, her side aching at the mere thought.

"We can do this," Farrah said.

"No," Cassandra moaned, but then they were out the door, running. And Cassandra was dying.

Her shins hurt after a minute, her neck after two, and after three minutes, the hitch in her side forced her to slow to a walk.

"Run!" Ms. Lynn shouted when she and Farrah passed.

Grumbling, Cassandra forced herself to pick up the pace. One more lap.

She hated this.

Farrah left her in the end and waited at the door. Cassandra wasn't the last one in, but very close to it.

"I think it's safe to say running is not your strong point," Farrah said.

"I knew that already!" Cassandra snapped, wiping sweat from her brow and gasping for breath.

At lunch Cassandra sat with Miles and Betsy and a few people from choir she didn't know. Even though she was new to this group of friends, they welcomed her warmly and made her feel connected.

She glanced over once to where Tyler sat with Maureen and Amity and Melanie. There was no empty chair for her. And that was okay.

Amity found Cassandra after lunch and walked with her down the hall. "You never even talk to us anymore."

"Sure I do," Cassandra said. "I talk to Cara on the bus and Maureen in history and you in choir."

"You don't even sit by me."

Cassandra was fairly sure it was the other way around. "I just sit down."

"Well, sit by me today."

Cassandra obliged, setting her chair by Amity instead of by Harper and Miles.

Amity then spent the whole time talking to Melanie and Olivia without saying another word to Cassandra. Cassandra rolled her eyes. Next time, she'd sit where she wanted.

"How is high school treating you?" Ms. Malcolm asked at her music lesson.

"Pretty good, actually," Cassandra said. "I thought it would be super hard, but I just had to get into a routine. Now I'm able to get my homework done before class, so that helps."

"Well, that's good." Ms. Malcolm struck a chord on the piano. "As long as you remember to practice your music. Are you in choir?"

"Of course. Speaking of which." Cassandra pulled out the sheet music from her bag. "Mr. Cullen gave us the music for All-Region." Her heart constricted when she considered how badly she wanted to make this. Every year she tried, and every year she failed. "I was hoping we could go over it."

"This is your year, Cassie." Ms. Malcolm set the sheets up on the piano. "Let's make sure you have it down."

⊙━◈━⊙

Saturday morning Mr. Jones came into Cassandra's room and woke her up.

"Hurry and get dressed," he said. "I'm going to take you driving today."

That got her up. Her first time behind the wheel!

She dressed and brushed her teeth and pulled her hair back, then ran outside to meet her father.

Mr. Jones had already pulled his sports car into the circle drive, so at least she wouldn't have to learn how to back up first thing. He stood next to the passenger side, and that's when it sank in that Cassandra would be in the driver's side.

Her heart skipped a beat, both parts excitement and anxiety rushing through her veins. She dropped into the driver's seat beside her father, placing her hands on the wheel and taking a deep, steadying breath.

"You're too far from the wheel," Mr. Jones said. "You need to scoot up."

"Okay." It took a moment to find the lever, but she moved her chair up.

"Now put one foot on the clutch and one on the brake. It won't start if you don't have both of those down."

"Clutch?"

"The one in the middle. The brake is on the left."

"Okay." She found the appropriate paddles and put her feet on them.

"Make sure you're in Neutral. Now turn the key."

67

"I can do this." Taking another deep breath, she turned the car on. The engine roared to life, and the car hummed beneath her.

"Great. Sit here for a moment, feel what it's like to be in a vehicle. Now, move your gear shift to first gear. See the number one? Yes, that one."

Cassandra did as she was told, holding the egg-shaped handle in her palm.

"Release the clutch and slowly push on the gas. That's on the right."

She lifted her foot from the clutch and put her foot on the gas pedal. The car roared and jerked forward, slamming her against the seatbelt.

"Slowly!" Mr. Jones shouted. "I said slowly!"

Panicking, Cassandra yanked her foot from the gas pedal. The car gurgled and then died.

She gasped, heart pounding, and gulped in rapid breaths of air.

"Try again," Mr. Jones said, sounding defeated already. "You'll have to turn it on. Put your feet on the clutch and the brake."

Brake. That was the one on the left . . . and the clutch. Clutch. Middle. She did so, shaking slightly. This was harder than she'd expected. She turned the key, but nothing happened.

"Put it in Neutral," Mr. Jones growled.

"Oh. Yeah." This time when she turned the key, the car purred to life.

"Put it into First. Now slowly lift your foot from the clutch and push on the gas."

Slowly. Slowly. Feeling like she was under water, Cassandra moved her foot off the clutch. She barely pressed on the gas. Nothing happened, and then the car died again.

Mr. Jones sighed. "You didn't give it enough gas. You have to move faster than that, Cassie. You release the clutch at the same time you push on the gas."

At the same time! It would have been nice to know that. She nodded, swallowing against a painful lump in her throat.

"Try again. Remember all your steps."

Neutral. Foot on clutch and foot on brake. Car on. First gear. Slowly release clutch and push down on gas—*at the same time.*

The car crept forward.

"Bravo. Push down on the clutch again and let's move to Second gear."

She didn't even respond, just did as she was told.

"Push on the gas. A little more. Let's get out of the driveway."

Everything about this was harder than she expected, even turning the steering wheel. She moved the car off the gravel driveway at a snail's pace, lurching forward when it turned onto the asphalt. She fought nausea as she pushed the car up the hill.

"Slow down on the curve. Slow down, Cassie!"

The urgency in his voice made her panic, and she slammed on the brake. The car halted, sighed, and died.

"You killed it," he said flatly. "Turn it on and let's try again."

She just wanted to go home. Forget this driving thing. Cassandra pushed on the clutch and the brake and turned the key.

Nothing.

"Neutral," Mr. Jones growled.

Of course. Neutral. Why were there so many steps to this?

She tried again, and this time she did the steps in the right order. She went down the hill and back up, gripping the steering wheel in a death hold, knuckles white.

"Use this driveway to turn around. I want to see you slow down better on that curve."

The car stalled when Cassandra tried to turn around in the driveway. And then Mr. Jones wouldn't stop yelling at her, and no matter what she did, she couldn't find the right combination of releasing the clutch and pushing on the gas.

Mr. Jones unlatched his seat belt. "Get out. I'll drive us home."

Cassandra scooted over to the passenger side, trembling and sick to her stomach, and she didn't even care. She'd had enough driving for one day.

CHAPTER TWELVE

School Identity

Monday was Clash Day at the high school. Cassandra remembered how important Spirit Week had been in junior high when she and her friends made sure to dress up and show their support. She wanted to set the right tone for her high school career. Cassandra dressed in mismatched socks with shorts and a tie-dyed shirt. She put one side of her hair in ribbons but left the other down. She got ready quietly, not wanting to wake Emily. Emily didn't have to go to the early morning Bible class yet, and she got angry if Cassandra was noisy.

Her throat hurt when she swallowed. Cassandra opened her mouth and peered into the bathroom mirror. Were those white spots on the back of her throat? Hard to tell. She took a sip of water and hurried out of the bathroom.

"Why are you dressed so odd?" Mr. Jones asked when she came into the living room.

"It's Spirit Week," Cassandra said. "Today's Clash Day."

He gave her a funny look but didn't say anything else.

Mr. Jones made Cassandra drive the car to the carpool spot before her church class. He yelled at her when she stalled at the stop sign, and her heart beat too hard all the way down the road. But they made it, and finally she parked the car, taking deep breaths while they waited for Riley to arrive so they could ride together.

"You've got to make your transitions smoother," Mr. Jones said. "You're jerking the car all the way down the road."

"But I got us here," Cassandra said, feeling wounded. "I'm doing better, aren't I?"

"If not killing us is considered an improvement."

Cassandra certainly thought so. Driving was going to give her a heart attack.

"What are you wearing?" Riley asked when Cassandra climbed into the car with her.

"It's Clash Day." Cassandra looked her over. "You're not clashing."

"No one actually dresses up for those things. That's so elementary." Riley rolled her eyes.

"Really? We did last year." Now Cassandra felt horribly stupid.

"That was last year." Riley laughed. "No one will ask you to Homecoming dressed like that."

Cassandra's heart squeezed. She wanted a date so badly. Had she just ruined her chances?

Cassandra's eyes scanned the students as she stepped into the hallway after their early morning class. Sure enough, she was one of the only people dressed up. Her friends laughed and other kids stared at her when she walked by.

Crapola. This wouldn't do. She would rather wear her P.E. clothes than these.

Which wasn't a bad idea. She changed for P.E. in second hour and then stayed in her T-shirt and shorts.

She wouldn't dress up again.

⟡

The white bumps in the back of her throat didn't go away, and each day felt a little harder to swallow. To top it off, Cassandra's head began to hurt, and each morning was a harder to get out of bed.

Mrs. Jones came into Cassandra's room Wednesday before music lessons and church.

"Tonight I'm taking you driving. I think your dad needs a break."

"He needs a break?" Cassandra grumbled. "I need a break."

Mrs. Jones smiled. "Let's see how you do in the van."

"I have to drive the van?"

"That's my car."

Cassandra got behind the wheel of the giant vehicle, feeling tiny and insignificant. How could she control this beast going down the road?

Mrs. Jones handed her the keys, and Cassandra searched the floor. "Where's the clutch?"

"This is an automatic. There's no clutch. The brake is on the left. Push down on it while you turn the car on, then put the transmission in reverse and lift your foot."

That sounded rather simple. Suspicious, Cassandra turned the car on and lifted her foot. Nothing happened. The car didn't sputter and die, but it didn't move, either.

"Keep your foot on the brake and put it in reverse."

Oh, right. She'd forgotten that part. Cassandra pressed on the brake pedal and moved the transmission to reverse.

"Now check your mirrors and all around you. Turn around and look over your shoulder. Slowly ease your foot off the brake. That's right."

Still looking behind her, Cassandra lifted her foot. The car rolled backward. She let the car ease its way out of the driveway.

"Put your foot on the brake when you're ready to stop."

Cassandra slammed her foot on the brake, panicking, and the car halted. "Oh. I thought maybe—"

"You're fine. Just move the transmission into Drive."

That was it? No yelling at her for jerking the car? "Okay."

"Now take your foot off the brake and press on the gas. Just a little. We're going slow down this road."

The car eased forward, and Cassandra almost cried with relief. "This is so easy!"

Mrs. Jones smiled. "Is this better than driving your dad's car?"

"Can you teach me from now on?" Cassandra begged. "I don't want to ride with Daddy in that car again!" Even steering was easier. She didn't have to grip the wheel as hard, and the car responded to her lightest touch.

Mrs. Jones laughed. "I'll help when I can. But be patient with your dad. This is a first for him."

"It's a first for me too, and he's not patient with me."

Mrs. Jones gave her an understanding look but didn't say anything.

"You sound a little congested, Cassie," Ms. Malcolm said during her music lesson. "Are you feeling okay?"

"My throat hurts a bit," Cassandra admitted. "I'm all right, though."

"Hmm. Take it easy and gurgle salt water."

How would that help? Cassandra nodded anyway, though her head throbbed when she did.

Riley called later that night.

"Can you pick me up at my house for Bible study tomorrow?" she asked. "My dad is sick and can't take me to the drop off spot."

"Of course," Cassandra said. "I'll let my dad know."

"You're driving," Mr. Jones said when Cassandra told him.

"Me? All the way there?"

"Yes. You should feel more comfortable now."

She'd been driving for almost a week, and he yelled at her the whole time. Why should she feel more comfortable? But she knew better than to argue.

Mr. Jones woke her super early so she would have plenty of time to drive to Riley's house. Anxiety filled her veins, twisting her stomach the moment she sat behind the wheel. And as soon as she backed out of the driveway, the yelling started.

"Did you look behind you? Careful with the clutch! Too much gas! Are you in second gear yet? Stay in your lane! Slow down on the curves! Turn right. Now. Now!"

And so on. It was enough to give her a panic attack. But Cassandra managed to focus on the car, and she only stalled once at the stop light. When they stopped in front of Riley's apartment, she ran up to it and knocked on the door.

"I drove all the way here!" It hurt to talk, and she clutched her throat, suddenly wanting that salt water Ms. Malcolm had recommended.

"Good job," Riley said, sounding sleepy. "Are you driving us to church?"

"No." Cassandra shook her head. "My dad won't let me drive with you in the car."

"Maybe after you get your license."

"Yeah, maybe." But she wasn't sure if even then. Mr. Jones had no confidence in her driving ability.

⁂

By Friday, Cassandra knew she was sick. But it was only the second week of school, and if she missed now, her teachers would think she was a slacker. So she forced herself to get up and attend Bible study before stumbling through each class.

She woke up Saturday hardly able to move. There was no reason to get up, so she lay in bed as long as she could, then winced when she stood up. Her ear hurt something terrible. She coughed, a deep, rattling sound.

"Mom!" she called. Her voice startled her. It sounded like a man's voice, low in her chest. "Mom!" she called again.

The bedroom door opened, and Mrs. Jones came in. "Cassie? What's wrong?"

The words percolated strangely into Cassie's ears, like she was hearing them from underwater or through a squeaky microphone.

"I don't feel well," Cassandra said. "I think I'm sick."

"You sound terrible." Mrs. Jones came over and pressed a cool hand to her forehead. "You're hot. Just lay down and rest. Don't worry about doing anything today."

Cassandra didn't argue. She had no desire to even think.

She slept all day Saturday and most of the day Sunday, even missing church. She lay in bed, body convulsing every time she coughed.

"I don't want you to go to school tomorrow, either," Mrs. Jones said when she checked on her that night.

How behind would she be in her classes if she missed a day? But it was a moot point. Cassandra had no strength to go. She merely nodded, not even trying to use her vocal chords.

❦

"Guess what!" Emily said, coming into the bedroom and dumping her backpack on the carpet Monday after school.

"What?" Cassandra mumbled. It still hurt to swallow, and she'd spent the day coughing, but she hoped to be back in school the next day.

"I saw your car!"

"My car?"

"The one you get when you start driving!"

Cassandra sat up, excitement stirring in her chest and dispelling some of her grogginess. "I get a car?"

"Yes! What car did you think you'd be driving?"

"What's it look like?" She wanted to go see it now. She couldn't wait to tell Riley!

"It's small and black."

"Is it nice?"

Emily shrugged. "I don't know. It's a car."

It was a car! She'd have her own car!

"How are we feeling?" Mrs. Jones asked, coming into the room.

"Better," Cassandra said. "I need to go to school tomorrow."

"Are you sure?" Her mom patted her face. "You still feel warm."

Cassandra shook her off. "I'm fine."

"Okay. But if you don't feel well in the morning, just let me know."

She'd feel well. Even if she had to fake it.

The next morning, though, she wasn't so sure. Her body did not want to respond when her alarm went off, and she dragged herself out of bed too late to meet Riley. She dressed quickly, and Mrs. Jones let her drive the van to the chapel.

"Is my new car an automatic?" Cassandra asked, praying it was.

"New car? What makes you think you're getting a car?" Mrs. Jones shot her a smile.

"Emily."

"Ah. Well, then, yes, it is."

Cassandra breathed a sigh of relief. "Thank goodness. I like driving this car so much more."

"Would you like to see it?"

"Can I?" Cassandra looked at her mom hopefully.

"We'll go by on our way to school after Bible class."

That only made the class that much harder to sit through. She

74

squirmed in her seat, trying to focus on the scripture study while imagining what sort of small black car it could be.

She saw soon enough. Mrs. Jones pulled the van into a used car lot and pointed it out.

"That black one right there."

Cassandra looked at a four-door Honda, at least ten years old. The paint was chipped in some spots, and the pin striping was peeling.

"That?" she said, her heart sinking. Hardly the snazzy sports car she'd been imagining.

"At least you get a car, Cassie," Mrs. Jones said, chastisement in her voice.

"Yes." Cassandra tried a smile.

"My parents are getting me a car," she told Farrah as they ran beside each other in P.E. This running thing never got easier.

"Wow! Is it nice?"

"No. It's ugly." Cassandra tried to laugh like that was funny. "Doesn't matter, right?"

"No one cares. Have you been asked to Homecoming?"

Homecoming again. The dance was only a month away. Technically Cassandra couldn't date yet, but she was sure she could find a way around that. "No. Have you?"

Farrah nodded. "Yes, but I'm not sure I'll go. I don't really like him."

Cassandra felt a pang of jealousy. "Who goes to Homecoming?"

"Most everyone. The cheerleaders all have dates already. The rest of us wait for the leftovers."

Cassandra had heard this sentiment before, that cheerleaders were hot commodities, and she was slowly starting to witness it for herself. "Maybe I should be a cheerleader."

"Yeah, right." Farrah laughed. "You, a cheerleader? You're not the type."

Cassandra elbowed her. "Why not?"

"Can you even dance or do cheers?"

"No, but I could learn."

"And why? So someone will ask you to Homecoming?"

Cassandra didn't answer. Was that a bad reason?

"You're not like them, Cassie," Farrah said, getting serious. "You wouldn't like it. Trust me. I used to be like them."

Cassandra considered that. She remembered how out of place she'd felt with her old group of friends, even when they accepted her. "Yeah, maybe."

But there had to be something she could do to make herself desirable.

CHAPTER THIRTEEN

New Hampshire

Mr. Jones let Cassandra drive all the way to church the next morning because Riley woke up late and said she wouldn't make it. Cassandra only messed up once when turning a corner, and then she didn't quite make it into a parking spot and had to redo it.

"You're ten minutes late. Turn off the headlights and go in."

Turn off the headlights. Where was that button? "Where are the headlights?"

"On the spindle on the steering wheel."

She grabbed the spindle and turned it. The windshield wipers came on. She pulled the spindle toward her, and soap sprayed on the glass.

"The spindle on the other side!"

Why didn't he ever tell her how to do something the first time? She found the right knob and turned off the lights, then threw the keys at him and went inside before he could say another word.

It took a full ten minutes of studying the New Testament before Cassandra finally felt calm enough to face her dad again.

"Ready to drive to school?" he said, eyeing her as she got in.

Cassandra smiled sweetly. "Ready." She turned the car on and revved the gas.

"Cassandra!" Mr. Jones bellowed.

"What?" She gave him her best innocent look. "I was just getting the engine warmed up."

He glared at her like he knew what she was up to. "Just drive."

"Gladly," she breathed, and then she peeled out of the parking lot. If he was going to yell at her, she was going to give him a reason.

She was still giggling when she got to school.

"We don't have to dress out today!" Farrah crowed when Cassandra walked into the gym for P.E. "Someone sprayed all the lockers with water, and our clothes are soaked!"

"Ha!" Cassandra said, delighted. "So no running?"

"No running!"

She and Farrah sat on the bleachers and talked through the rest of class, and Cassandra was in high spirits through third hour. When she reached fourth hour, Ashlee motioned for her to sit down quickly.

"New boy," she whispered, nodding her head at the front of the class.

Cassandra swiveled to look. The boy was thin and a few inches taller than her, with dark hair and light skin. He spoke with Mr. Reems, his hands fidgeting nervously with the edges of the desk. Then Mr. Reems motioned for him to sit down, and he moved to the row behind Cassandra, keeping his eyes down.

He looked anxious and out of place, and Cassandra felt bad for him. She turned around when he sat. "Hi. I'm Cassandra."

He lifted his head, meeting her eyes and giving her a smile. Something about the warmth of his gaze made her heart skip a beat. "Hello, Cassandra." He lengthened the sound of her name, the vowels coming out like "ah" instead of "aa." Cah-ssahn-drah. "I'm Grayson."

She loved the way he talked. "Where are you from?"

"New Hampshire." It sounded like "Noo Hamp-shuh" the way he said it. "Just moved in a few days ago."

She gave him a big smile. "Welcome to Arkansas, Grayson. You'll like it here."

"Yeah?" He looked a little less nervous. "I hope so. Big change for me."

She wanted to move her seat back and talk to him, or at least just listen to him talk, but class was about to start, and Ashlee might not appreciate being abandoned. "We'll catch up later."

He nodded and gave her another smile, and something fluttered in her stomach. She clutched her hands together and faced front, trying not to think about his light brown eyes.

"Hi," Mason said when Cassandra stepped into English class. He'd been talking to Nicole when she came in, but now he faced forward to talk to her.

"Hi," Cassandra breathed, dropping her bags and collapsing into the chair behind her desk.

Nicole gave her some kind of look she couldn't quite decipher.

Ms. Ragland began the lecture, but Cassandra's mind flashed back to Grayson. What grade was he in? What other classes did he have?

Mason leaned forward and handed her a note, and Cassandra quickly scanned it.

Have a date to Homecoming yet?

Not yet, she replied, sending it back. At this rate, she'd be the only girl in school with no date.

Nicole walked with Cassandra from English class to history.

"Mason likes you," she said.

"He does?" Cassandra stopped and looked at her. "How do you know?" She pictured the boy with dark brown hair and freckles who had been friendly with her since school started. He was one of the people who made English class bearable.

"He told me."

"Oh, that's so sweet."

But Cassandra couldn't bring herself to feel anything in response. Because there was another fair-eyed, dark-haired boy who had her interest.

She couldn't wait for biology the next day.

❧

Cassandra greeted Grayson as soon as he came into class the next day.

"Hi," he said in response, settling behind her with a smile.

"How was your first day yesterday?" she asked, turning her chair slightly to face him.

"Awkward. Which I guess is to be expected. I don't know anyone."

"You know me." She gave him what she hoped was a winning smile.

His eyes crinkled in response. "Yeah."

Even that single syllable sounded foreign and sophisticated when he said it.

Mr. Reems got class started and Cassandra turned around, but she spent the rest of class thinking up things to say to Grayson.

It turned out not to be necessary, because he kept the conversation going all the way to the cafeteria, telling her about New Hampshire and the weather and his dad, who had moved him to Arkansas.

At the cafeteria they parted ways, but Cassandra replayed their conversation the rest of the day. Every time she considered the way he said her name, her heart melted.

She spent sixth hour writing him a note instead of listening to class.

Hey Grayson,

I hope you don't mind me writing you. I know it can be hard to move in somewhere where everyone knows everyone except you. I did that a few years ago. I hated it here at first, but I love it now.

So what's different between New Hampshire and Arkansas? I've never been there. I've always wanted to go.

Anyway. I hope things are going well for you.

Cassandra hesitated on the closing line. What should she say? "Love" was too presumptuous. "Sincerely" was too formal. "Always" sounded too much like a love letter. She finally settled on, "Later, Cassandra."

She thought she'd have to wait until fourth hour the next day to give it to him, but Grayson surprised her by tapping her shoulder as she walked to Spanish the next morning.

"Hey," he said with a wave.

"Oh, hey! Wait!" She paused to dig through her bag, looking for the note. "I have something for you."

"For me?" Surprise registered on his face.

"Yeah." She pulled out the note, warmth creeping up her face. "It's nothing."

"Thanks." He tapped it in the palm of his hand and nodded, then disappeared into the classroom across from hers.

He found her again as soon as she stepped out of Spanish class. "Here," he said, handing her a folded slip of paper.

Cassandra's eyes shot to his, and this time she was the surprised one. He'd written her back!

"See you in biology," he said when she took it, and then he climbed up the stairs out of the A-wing.

Cassandra could not wait to get to P.E. to read his response. Breathless, hands trembling in anticipation, she paused by her locker and opened the note.

Hi, Cassandra,

Sure, I don't mind you writing me. You can write me any time. It's nice to have friends to talk to already. It's not the first time I've had to move, but I think it gets harder every time. The big difference is how quiet it is here. Like, what is there to do for fun? Go hiking? Ha ha. Just kidding, it's not so bad here.

I've had a few weeks to get used to it. I just started school this week but we moved here in August. I thought I was going to Fayetteville High, but then we ended up moving to Springdale.

I'm in English class and we're doing vocabulary. So don't mind me if I practice on you. Sorry if I'm not particularly loquacious. I'm still trying to figure out what people are saying.

Write again.

Grayson

Cassandra giggled all the way to third hour, and then she could hardly wait to see Grayson.

They exchanged notes every day that week, and he walked her to lunch the rest of the week also.

Cassandra knew who she wanted to go to homecoming with.

When Monday rolled around, Cassandra devised different ways to bring up the topic. Each time, though, she chickened out. It took three days, but by Thursday, Cassandra was determined to ask him herself.

"So you're a sophomore, but you're in the Biology II class," Grayson said as they walked toward the cafeteria just as they had for the past week and a half.

"Yes. And you're a junior."

"Yeah, but juniors are supposed to be in Bio II. It's not like I'm smart."

"I just like to be challenged, I guess."

"Come on, just admit it. You're smart."

She smiled at that. "So why did your dad move to Arkansas?"

"He got married," Grayson said, and his tone frosted over. "To this woman who lives here. So we both had to move. Now I have a new sister and every thing's weird."

She lingered on his every word. She could listen to his lyrical accent all day. "But it's not all bad, right? You've made friends?"

"A few." He nudged her arm with his. "You."

Her body tingled where he'd touched her. "You'll make more." She held her breath before the next question. He'd just moved here and hardly knew anyone. Surely, surely, that meant he didn't have a date to homecoming. "What are you doing for Homecoming?"

He stopped walking and looked at her. His brown eyes had flecks of green in them, and he furrowed his brow. "Why?"

Because she didn't have a date and wanted to go with him. Because she melted just listening to his voice and wanted to hear him say her name over and over again.

But she lost her nerve just short of asking him to go with her and said instead, "I just wondered if you're going with anyone."

"I am," he said, and the breath rushed out of her, disappointment clubbing her in the chest. "This girl in my class, Charlotte, asked me to take her. She's new, too. I thought every one must have a date by now, so I said yes."

"Oh," was all Cassandra could say, deflated.

"You don't have a date?" he said.

She shook her head. "No. I don't think I'm going to go." And now she feared she would cry.

"Come on." Grayson bumped her arm again. "It'll be fun. I'll dance with you."

She wanted nothing more than to dance with Grayson. "What about your girlfriend?"

He gave a low growl in the back of his throat. "She's not my girlfriend. I'm doing her a favor. She won't care if we dance."

"Maybe I'll go, then," she said, wanting to hold him to that.

"All right." Grayson leaned over and hugged her. "See you tomorrow." He waved, then walked away to eat with several juniors at their table.

Cassandra studied them, wondering jealously which one must be Charlotte. And how she had beaten Cassandra to the punch.

Mason passed Cassandra another note in English class.

Will you go to Homecoming with me?

She read it several times, thinking it over. She had no reason to say no. No one else was asking. Grayson was going with someone else. So she pulled out her pen and wrote a response.

Yes.

She passed it back, strangely depressed by the series of events.

☙◈❧

Grayson caught up to Cassandra in the hallway before class started on Friday.

"I have a friend who's not taking anyone to Homecoming," he said. "If you want, we could all double date."

Watching Grayson be another girl's date did not sound like a fun time to Cassandra. "That's really nice of you. I actually got asked yesterday."

He nodded. "I'm not surprised. I wish I'd known you didn't have a date."

"Me too," she said, and then her face warmed. "I mean, it would have been fun to go together."

"Some other time." He squeezed her shoulder and then went to his seat behind her.

She replayed the conversation over in her head again and again, not hearing a word Mr. Reems said. What did he mean by some other time? Did he intend to ask her to the next dance? Or were they meaningless words? And then the shoulder squeeze. What was that?

"Cassandra, wait," Grayson said when class ended, catching up with her in the hall.

She stood just outside the classroom door, waiting for him. "I wasn't going to leave you. We walk to lunch together." And this was by far her favorite part of the day.

"Yeah." He gave a half-smile. "Going to the game tonight?"

"Wouldn't miss it."

They walked in silence toward the cafeteria, then Grayson said, "Want to sit with us?"

She looked at his group of friends, all of them a year older than her. "Which one is Charlotte?"

"The one with red hair. She moved here from Kentucky."

Cassandra nodded. Charlotte had short red hair and dark eyes lined in black. "She's pretty." Figured.

"She's all right."

Cassandra shook her head. "I'll sit with my friends. But thanks for the invite."

They parted, with Cassandra sitting next to Betsy and Miles. But her eyes stayed on Grayson, and her heart ached.

Riley rode the bus to Cassandra's house with her so they could get ready for the football game that evening.

"I'm so jealous you have a date to Homecoming," Riley said.

"It's not even important," Cassandra said. "This whole time, all I've wanted was a date, but now that I have one, I don't even want to go with him. I want to be with Grayson."

Of course Riley knew all about Grayson. "You've only known him for eight days."

"Ten," Cassandra corrected.

"Whatever. How can you like him so much?"

Cassandra pictured Grayson's face, his smile, and felt something ignite in her chest. "I don't know."

"When do I get to meet him?"

"Maybe at the game tonight. He'll be there."

Cassandra took more time than usual, using the curling iron on her thick dark hair and pinning up the sides. She outlined her eyes like Charlotte had and smeared on dark lipstick.

"You look way too good for a game," Riley said.

Cassandra shrugged. Grayson would be there. Her heart pounded at the thought.

Mrs. Jones drove them to the high school, dropping them off in the parking lot in front of the stadium. They joined the throng of students, hugging people they saw and clasping the hands of friends as they passed. Cassandra swiveled her head from side to side but didn't see Grayson. Disappointed, she sat with her classmates on the bleachers.

The game started with a bang, and soon she was involved with cheering and screaming. Each touchdown sent a thrill through her, and she felt immense pride in her school.

"Cassandra!" someone called, and she turned to see Grayson making his way up the bleachers toward her.

"Grayson!" She stood up, pushing past Riley to get to the aisle. Riley followed.

"Hey!" She reached out to take his hand, but he pulled her into a hug.

"You look nice," he said, his hand lingering on her back.

She smiled, giddy at the praise. "Oh, this is my friend, Riley."

"Hi, Riley." He shook her hand and turned his attention back to Cassandra. "I have to go sit with my friends. I'll find you after the game, okay?"

"Of course."

She and Riley went back to their seat, then she gripped Riley's hands and squeezed. "Riley! I think he might like me too!"

"I think he definitely does." Riley looked over her shoulder. "He's still watching us. If he didn't have a date to Homecoming, he would definitely have gone with you."

"I know!" Cassandra groaned and buried her face in her hands. "Bad timing on my part!"

"He's really cute, too. And I know what you mean about the way he talks."

"It's adorable." She could hear it now, the way he said her name. Her heart skipped a beat just at the memory.

Their high school team won, and Cassandra hugged all her classmates before they ran onto the turf to congratulate the players. She looked behind her for Grayson but didn't see him.

"I'm going to find Grayson," she told Riley.

"Okay. See you later."

Cassandra made her way down the bleachers and toward the concession stand, all the while looking for him. Then she saw him walking toward the parking lot.

"Grayson!"

He turned and waited for her. "Hey, Cassandra." He nudged her foot with his when she reached him.

"Good game, right?" She matched his pace, walking with him toward the gates.

"It was fun."

"Are you leaving?"

He shrugged. "It's over."

Where was Charlotte? She must not have come. This was Cassandra's moment, her chance to have him to herself.

And do what?

Yet her pulse pounded in her neck with anticipation. As if this moment mattered.

They reached the gates, and both of them stopped.

"Come with me to my car?" he asked.

Cassandra wanted to. Very badly. But if she left, they wouldn't let her back in, and she didn't want to be stuck out in the parking lot waiting for her mom. "I'm not ready to go yet."

"Okay. I'll see you Monday."

"What's your phone number?" she blurted.

He grinned. "Why, you want it?"

"Yes." She pulled her phone out.

"Nice phone," he teased.

"Gets the job done."

He fed her his number, watching as she put it in into her old-school flip phone.

"Thanks," she said, putting her phone away.

"Are you going to call me?"

"Yeah, maybe."

"See you later." He nudged her foot again and then walked away.

That was it. Cassandra watched him go with an air of disappointment, feeling somehow she'd held something magical in her hands and let it go.

CHAPTER FOURTEEN

Disgruntled

Everything went wrong Monday morning. Cassandra stalled the car three times on the way to Bible study, and then she forgot her Spanish flashcards for first hour. She quickly used Mia's to make new ones, but she was frantic and nervous the whole time.

Then P.E. ran late because Ms. Lynn wasn't watching the clock. She still had the girls doing calisthenics when Mariah called out, "Ms. Lynn! We have to get to our next class!"

"Is it time already?" Ms. Lynn looked at the clock. "Oh! You're late! Hurry, hurry!"

Hurry, hurry. Like that would help. Cassandra changed quickly from her P.E. clothes to her street clothes, then she ran out the door for her math class. She was out of breath and late, and it left her slightly out of sorts even in biology. Grayson didn't say hi to her or comment on her appearance, and she almost hurried out the door to go to lunch without him, feeling unable to bear any more rejection. At the last minute, she waited for him, and she was glad she did when he fell into step beside her.

"You haven't called me yet," Grayson said as he walked with her to lunch.

You haven't even asked for my number, Cassandra thought. But she didn't say that. It kind of hurt that he hadn't, though. If he liked her, wouldn't he ask? "I will if I need something."

"Only if you need something?"

She shrugged.

"You okay?" he asked, looking at her closer.

"Fine. Just one of those days."

"I'll find you after lunch."

She nodded and went and sat with her friends, feeling sad and lonely.

"Cassandra." Grayson caught up with her as she headed toward the choir room. He chattered about his pencil the whole way there, what color it was, how it sharpened, the way it felt in his hand, which Cassandra found rather amusing.

She stopped in front of the choir room and looked at him. "Your pencil is so fascinating. What if you had a pen?"

"It would be a whole new element to talk about. We could go on for hours."

She gave a crooked smile.

"What's wrong?" he asked, frowning.

She knew he liked her. But she also knew he would be spending all his time with Charlotte at Homecoming, and that wouldn't be good for Cassandra. So she just shook her head. "I'll see you later."

She stepped into the classroom, and then heard, "Cassandra."

She went back into the hallway, where Grayson looked at her with concern.

"What's wrong? Are you all right?"

She made her smile more real this time. Guys liked happy girls, not sad ones. "I'll be fine. It's just been one of those days." *Cheer up, Cassandra!* she told herself. *No one likes a storm cloud!*

"Be happy." He poked her arm with his pencil.

"That's *the* pencil."

He looked at her oddly, and Cassandra said, "You just touched me with the special pencil."

Now he grinned, his eyes crinkling. "Yep. I guess you know what that means."

She did, and this time her smile was genuine. "See you later, Grayson."

"I know everyone is super concerned with Homecoming on Friday," Mr. Cullen said as the singers filed in. "But don't forget All-Region is the day after! Be prepared to sing your hearts out Saturday morning! Which means take care of your bodies on Friday!" He gave them all warning looks.

All-Region. Cassandra groaned. She'd hardly practiced at all. Between learning to drive and Grayson and school, it wasn't even on her mind. This was the first year she hadn't given it much thought.

Maybe she could change that this week.

Cassandra plopped down next to Cara on the bus.

"Who's that guy you're always talking to?" Cara asked. "He's so cute."

"Probably Grayson." Cassandra smiled to herself as she remembered their daily conversations.

"Is he your boyfriend?"

"I wish." She sighed.

"You'll have one soon. Everyone knows you. Everyone likes you."

"I'm nobody." Cassandra rolled her eyes.

"So not true. I wish I was as outgoing as you. You're friends with everyone."

"You want to be like me?" Cassandra looked at her incredulously.

"I've always wanted to be just like you."

Cara laughed. "You're crazy. No one wants to be me."

"We all do!" Cassandra exclaimed. "You just don't know how wonderful you are!"

"You're just saying that," Cara said, but she looked pleased all the same. "Are you going to Homecoming?"

"Yes," Cassandra said, relieved she could answer that way.

"With Grayson?"

"No. A different guy."

"See?" Cara giggled. "You've already got so many guys."

Cassandra had to laugh. It did look that way. "It's not like that."

"Well, I'll see you there. It will be so much fun."

"Yeah." Maybe. If she were going with Grayson, anyway. At least he'd promised her a dance.

⁓◌⁓

"Good job, Cassandra," Mr. Jones said when she parked the car in front of the church building Wednesday morning. "You didn't make any mistakes this time, and you got to class on time."

Cassandra grinned widely. Maybe she'd be able to do this driving thing after all.

All anyone could talk about at school was Homecoming. Cassandra had mixed feelings, both dread and excitement. She had a date. It would be fun.

Grayson would be there with someone else. That just hurt so much. How would she be able to handle seeing him dancing with another girl?

Grayson found her before her first hour class.

"Hey," he said, coming up to the door. "My classroom is across from yours."

"Yes, I know." She peered down the hall. "English, right?"

"Yeah. What's this?"

"Spanish."

"It's a lot easier to stick to one language." He smirked at her.

She smiled back. "I don't do easy."

"That's right. Bio II girl. How are you doing today? Better?"

"I'm fine." She shrugged. "I was just having an off-day. You know how it goes, right?"

"Sure. We all have those. Hey, what's your number?"

She blinked in surprise. "You want it?"

"Seems like you're not going to call me, so . . ."

Heart pumping with absolute delight, she fed him the numbers, watching as he put them into his phone.

"Now are you going to call me?"

"Maybe." He smirked at her, then put his phone in his pocket. "Oh, and I've got something for you." He pulled a folded paper from his back pocket and handed it to her, then went to his classroom without saying another word.

Cassandra's heart leaped. He'd written her a note. All on his own. She hurried to her seat and unfolded it as Ms. Elliot started class.

Hey Cassandra,

Just wanted to say cheer up! Yesterday you seemed disgruntled. Sorry. Still practicing my vocabulary on you. But it makes me feel smart.

What are you wearing to Homecoming? I didn't realize the dress is such a big deal. What are you doing before the dance? Maybe we can meet up at the game.

Smile! It looks good on you.

Grayson

She read the note over and over again, and she couldn't help the smile that plastered itself to her face.

Mason was waiting in the hallway before sixth hour.

"Cassandra," he said, stopping her before she went into the classroom.

"What is it?" She scanned his face, saw the frustration in his eyes.

"I've got some bad news."

No. She couldn't do bad news. She blinked at him and waited for the revelation.

"I'm grounded. I don't think my parents will let me go to Homecoming."

"Seriously?" How could he get himself grounded now? Homecoming was in two days! What would she do if he couldn't go? "I've already got my dress." Never mind that it was a dress she'd worn to a recital last year. "I've made plans."

"I know, and I've even bought the tickets. I'm going to talk to my parents tonight. I'll let you know by tomorrow. I'm so sorry."

There wasn't anything she could do about it, and she wasn't even sure there was anything he could do about it. "Fine. Just let me know."

She stomped into her English class and heaved a sigh. Just her luck.

❦

"I don't even know if I'll have a date Friday," Cassandra said to Riley, opening her locker Thursday morning. Mason hadn't called her, and she had no idea what was going on.

"Hey, there's Grayson," Riley said, bobbing her head.

Cassandra turned and saw him, dressed down in a T-shirt and jeans. He spotted her and moved her direction.

"Morning, Cassandra," he said, touching her arm.

"Good morning, Grayson." She leaned into his touch, wanting so much more.

He nodded at Riley. "Cassandra's friend."

"Riley," she said.

"Riley," he echoed. Then he looked at Cassandra. "What are you wearing to Homecoming?"

"What, want to coordinate colors?" she teased, and then she blushed, thinking she'd been too bold.

But he only laughed. "Yeah. I want to match you. No, so I can find you."

She gave him a knowing look. "I'll be the shortest girl out there."

He put a hand on her head, his fingers massaging her scalp. "You are pretty short."

The side door to the A-wing opened, and a red-headed girl with thick eyeliner came in. She wiped her feet on the mat, and then her face lit up when she saw them.

"Grayson!" she said.

He took a step sideways, effectively separating himself from Cassandra. "Hi, Charlotte," he said, and they went down the hall together. He didn't even glance back.

"There goes my heart," Cassandra whispered.

"Cassie!" Andrea ran to Cassandra's side and grabbed her arm. "Is that the guy you're going to Homecoming with?"

"No," Cassandra laughed. "We're just friends." Her chest tightened at the truth in the lie.

"I'm going to talk to him. Everyone says he talks funny." Andrea rushed off.

"That was fun," Riley said.

Cassandra took her books and closed her locker. "Oh, Riley. I'm going to die."

Riley gave her a sympathetic look.

They started down the hallway, and then Grayson was back, walking beside them.

"Do you know that Andrea girl?" he asked.

"Yes." Cassandra rolled her eyes. "Did she come over and talk to you?"

He smirked. "She's weird. She said I didn't sound any different, then I said something else, and she goes, yes you do."

"Sounds like something she would say."

He moved in front of them down the hall. Not that Cassandra minded the view. He glanced over his shoulder, then came back when he saw they'd lagged behind.

"Slow down, Grayson," Cassandra said.

"Move your legs, short stuff."

Cassandra halted by her Spanish class. "This is me."

"And I'm here." He gave her shoulder a squeeze. "See you later."

"Riley," Cassandra whimpered as he walked away.

"I know. Who knows? Maybe after Homecoming."

"Maybe."

Mia's eyes followed Cassandra when she stepped into Spanish. "Why are you glowing?"

"Grayson." Cassandra dropped her books on the desk and let her head fall on top of them. "I'm in love with Grayson."

"Was he just with you?"

"Yes. Yet he's not with me. He's with someone else."

Mia shrugged and pushed her straight hair behind her shoulders. "It's just a date."

Cassandra had told Mia all about Grayson and Homecoming. "It's just a date," she confirmed. "But I think Charlotte wants it to be more."

"But does he?"

Cassandra sighed. If only she knew.

"You seem happier today," Grayson said when they walked toward lunch after biology.

Because I'm talking to you. "It's been a good day."

"You excited for Homecoming?"

"As long you give me that dance."

"Promise." He tugged on her purse strap.

Cassandra turned around to wave before he walked away, and for a moment, her hand slipped into his. He gave it a squeeze and winked at her, then he pulled away.

Cassandra shook herself, breathless. She'd fallen bad.

Mason waited outside the English classroom again, and Cassandra knew when she saw his face it was bad news.

"I'm so sorry," he said miserably. "My parents won't let me go. I told them you've got your dress and I've got the tickets, and they still won't."

She sighed. "It's okay. There's nothing you can do about it."

"Here." He reached into his pocket and pulled out the tickets. "Take these. Maybe you can find someone else to take you."

The day before Homecoming? She doubted it. But it was a nice gesture, so she stuck the tickets in her pocket.

"Say you'll go," he begged. "I feel so bad. I'll feel even worse if you don't go."

Grayson would be there. With her promised dance. "I'll go."

CHAPTER FIFTEEN

Heartbreaker

"**I** cannot believe your date canceled on you," Riley said for like the hundredth time as she and Cassandra walked to first hour before class started on Friday.

"I know. It's like the worst thing ever." Well, not quite.

"What are you going to do? Are you still going?"

Cassandra shrugged. "Farrah said I can just hang out with her and her date. Betsy and Miles will be there." They were going together, which Cassandra thought was super cute. "I just hate feeling like a fifth wheel. Hey, I know." She grabbed Riley's hand. "I've got two tickets. Why don't you come?"

"Without a date? No way."

That was how Cassandra felt. "I hear you."

"You should tell Grayson. Maybe he'll take you."

She shook her head. "He's too nice. He wouldn't do that to Charlotte."

"Speaking of the devil," Riley said, and she inclined her head down the hall.

"Cassandra." Grayson approached them, tapping a piece of paper in his hand.

She couldn't bear to see him, not right now. Not when he was who she wanted to be with. "I've got to go." She turned and went into her classroom, leaving him in the hall with Riley.

She didn't talk to him in biology, and she escaped ahead of him after class. She doddled in the cafeteria after lunch and sat talking to Mia at a table in the cafeteria when the door opened and he stepped inside.

"Cassandra." He motioned her toward him.

She and Mia both turned, and there was no pretending she hadn't seen him. Besides, something in Cassandra's chest fluttered at the sight of him, and she longed to be next to him.

"Who's that?" Mia asked.

"Grayson."

"Grayson? As in, the Grayson?"

Cassandra didn't bother responding. "I'll be right back." She stepped over to him.

He frowned at her as she approached. "Are you mad at me?"

"No, of course not. Why would I be?" But there was a sting in her heart when she thought of him. She felt a tiny bit of resentment, even if it wasn't his fault she no longer had a date to Homecoming.

"You didn't wait for me after class."

She shook her head and rolled her eyes. "It's not you that's the issue."

"Yeah, it's obviously you." He grinned. "You going to choir?"

He knew her schedule, and that lifted her spirits somewhat. "It's about that time, isn't it?" She started down the hall, and he fell into step beside her.

"You're upset about something."

"Ugh." She looked heavenward. "Am I that easy to read?"

"You wear your heart on your sleeve."

Did she? Did he know what she felt? She looked at him and saw the way he peered at her. She suspected he did.

They stopped outside the choir room, and he touched her cheek with his knuckle. "What's wrong?"

Why did she want to cry now? "There really is something wrong this time." And then she did start to cry.

Grayson pulled her into a hug, holding her close for a moment. Then he let her go. "Cheer up, Cassandra." He looked concerned, but also wary, like somehow he knew this had to do with him.

She wiped at the tears. She couldn't go into choir crying. "I'll be okay."

"Tell me what's wrong."

She could tell him part of it, anyway, even if not everything. "My date for tonight canceled."

"Are you serious?" His eyes flashed, and his jaw tightened. "How can he cancel the day of Homecoming?"

"He got grounded. So he can't go."

"But you're still coming." Grayson's eyes peered into hers.

"I don't know. He gave me the tickets, but I don't want to go alone."

"Come. I'll be there."

"With Charlotte." She didn't mean to say it, and she didn't mean it to come out so bitter, but it did. There it was.

He fell silent. Then he said, "I better go. The bell's gonna ring, and I'll be tardy. But I'll see you tonight."

"I'll be at the game," she said.

"Me too." Grayson bobbed his head, then turned and continued down the science hall, away from the choir room.

All Cassandra could do was watch him walk away.

Cassandra rode with Betsy and Miles to the game, then she found Farrah on the bleachers and sat with her. Cassandra had put her hair in a messy side braid, and her dress was in Miles' car, waiting for the quick change after the game and before the dance. But she still wasn't sure she was going.

The Homecoming parade was beautiful, and she cheered up a bit when the high school team scored their first touchdown. She booed when the other team tackled their quarterback and stomped her feet and screamed when her team ran the ball down the field. She knew almost nothing about football, but the excitement in the air was palpable.

"See? Aren't you glad you came?" Farrah leaned over and hugged her.

"This part's fun," Cassandra agreed.

She excused herself to the concession stand to get a water bottle at halftime. She was standing in line checking her phone for messages when someone touched her shoulder. She turned around to see Grayson.

"Hi," she said, a goofy smile spreading across her face in spite of herself.

"You look nice," he said, fingering a strand of hair on her braid. "Does this mean you're coming to the dance?"

"I brought my dress," she admitted. "But I haven't decided yet."

"I can't dance with you if you don't come inside," he said, and there was a lot of promise in those words.

That did it. She wanted that dance. "I'll be there."

He made a fist and tapped her chin. "Are you happy now?"

Her fingers came up and touched his hand before falling away. "I have the worst timing in the world."

He put his hand on her shoulder and squeezed it, then turned and left her there in line.

Springdale High won the Homecoming game, and spirits were high as the students flooded the fields, singing and cheering. The euphoria lifted Cassandra's heart, and she couldn't stop smiling as they walked out to Miles' car.

"So you're coming?" Betsy said, looping her arm through Cassandra's.

"I'm coming."

Miles unlocked the car, and they drove back to his house to finish getting ready. Cassandra pulled the backpack from the car and stuck close to Betsy.

"I'm getting that dance with Grayson," she said.

"Of course you are," Betsy said. "Show him what he's missing."

Miles went to talk to his dad while Ms. Hansen let the girls take over the master bathroom. Betsy slipped on a pale green dress and helped Cassandra pin her bra in the right places so it wouldn't show with the plunged backline of her dress.

"This dress is so sexy," Betsy said.

"As long as Grayson gets to see me in it," Cassandra muttered.

"Do you think he'll ask you out after Homecoming?"

"I sure hope so."

The game had ended late, so the dance got started late. Cassandra was anxious to get there, but she had to be patient while Betsy and Miles snapped pictures of each other and together. They finally arrived at the school and walked in together, handing their tickets to the teacher in front of the gym.

That was where they separated. Betsy and Miles walked off hand in hand, clinging to each other like every other couple in the room. Cassandra tried not to be a wallflower, but everyone was there with a date, and she was by herself. And where was Grayson? She watched every couple that came in and didn't see him.

She walked to the snack bar and grabbed a cup of punch.

When she turned around, she saw Grayson just coming inside, guiding Charlotte onto the dance floor. He wore a fancy light blue suit, and she wore a long, stunning silver dress. He held her hand, and Cassandra's stomach twisted at the sight. His eyes scanned the gym-turned-dance-hall, and they landed on Cassandra. He said something to Charlotte, then released her hand and walked over to Cassandra.

"You came," he said, but he didn't touch her, and she knew why.

She nodded, not trusting herself to speak.

"Save me a dance," he said, and then he was gone again, back to Charlotte's side.

Cassandra sighed. She had nothing to do now but watch him and wait. She moved from side to side, humming a bit and smiling at people, pretending like she had a reason to be here. She checked on Grayson every few minutes to make sure she knew where he was.

And then she caught her breath, because the next time she looked at him, he and Charlotte were locked in a mouth-to-mouth embrace.

It felt like someone had kicked her in the stomach. She couldn't breathe. Her throat hurt. Her ears pounded.

He didn't like Charlotte that way. Hadn't he said he didn't like her that way? How could he kiss her?

One thing was for sure. He obviously felt nothing for Cassandra, or he wouldn't leave her standing there while he made out with another girl.

Charlotte took his hand and led him toward the exit. Cassandra's stomach lurched. No. He couldn't leave like this. The only reason she was here was for him! Even if he didn't like her, he'd promised her a dance. Cassandra jerked forward, not caring how stupid she looked as she darted in front of him before he could leave the gym.

"Where are you going?" she asked, smiling, knowing her eyes glistened with unshed tears.

"I have to take Charlotte home," he said, glancing back at her.

Cassandra refused to look at his date. "But you just got here!"

"I know. My car broke down, so we got here late, and Charlotte has a curfew. So I have to go."

Cassandra was going to cry, right here, right now. She felt her face go flat, every emotion hiding as she tried to control herself.

"I'll see you Monday," Grayson whispered. "I'm sorry."

Then he was gone. And Cassandra ran from the gym, throwing herself into a bathroom and dissolving into tears. Why had she let herself believe this night might have a different outcome?

❧❦❧

Cassandra woke up Saturday morning wanting to throw up. A heavy weight sat in her stomach, pulling her down. How had she misread Grayson? How could she have thought he liked her?

"Are you ready?" Mrs. Jones asked, coming into the bedroom. "Don't you have All-Region tryouts?" She looked at her daughter and frowned, then sat down on the edge of the bed. "What's wrong? Did you not have a nice time at Homecoming?"

"No." The tears came again, and Cassandra finally spoke the words she hadn't been able to tell to anyone, not even Riley. "Grayson doesn't like me. He was there with another girl."

"Well, honey, you already knew he had a date."

"As a friend!" The tears wouldn't stop now. "But he was kissing her! And he didn't dance with me!"

Mrs. Jones reached over and pulled Cassandra into a hug, and all Cassandra could do was sob.

Pulling back, Mrs. Jones said, "Are you going to try out?"

"Yes." Cassandra wiped her eyes. "I'll get ready."

She didn't say a word in the car. She tried to think of the music in her head, but all she could do was visualize again the image of Grayson pressing his mouth against Charlotte's. The tears sprang from her eyes, darting down her cheeks. She shoved them away with the palms of her hands.

The choir had gathered in the cafeteria of Rogers High School, where the auditions were, and Cassandra sat down with her peers, but she didn't talk and joke with them. Instead she pulled out her biology notebook and studied.

Mia noticed and said, "Are you okay?"

"I'm fine," Cassandra answered, and offered no more. She wished Riley were here, but Riley wasn't trying out.

The different sections practiced their music, and Cassandra tried to rehearse with the other sopranos, but her heart wasn't in it. No, her heart was broken.

Miles sat down next to her. "You okay, Cassie?" he asked, his voice gentle.

She hadn't told him and Betsy what happened. But when Cassandra came out of the bathroom red-faced and begging to go home, it wasn't hard to guess.

"I'm sorry I ruined last night for you," she said softly.

Miles gave her a side hug. "You couldn't. We were worried about you, though."

"I'm fine," she repeated.

He didn't ask her any more questions, but he stayed by her side until it was his tryout.

It wasn't her turn until after lunch. Cassandra tried to act engaged, to feel like she cared. But nothing felt important. What was music? What was All-Region? Her voice shook when she sang, and there wasn't enough energy in her voice to reach the high notes. She didn't need to see a judge's sheet to know she'd blown her tryout.

Mia and Betsy and Miles and John were all laughing around a table when Cassandra came out.

"How did it go?" Betsy asked, motioning her over.

"Terrible," Cassandra said. "But I don't even care."

"Cheer up, Cassandra Jones," John said.

The group told stories and jokes for the next few hours while they waited for their parents to come get them, and Cassandra felt a tiny bit better by the end of the afternoon.

She still didn't know how she would face school on Monday.

Cassandra stayed in the bathroom as long as she could before class started Monday morning. She filled Riley in on everything that happened over the weekend while Riley put on her makeup, making all the right noises of sympathy and hugging Cassandra when she cried again.

She didn't want to see Grayson. Riley left for class before Cassandra, who stayed in the bathroom until the last minute. Right before the tardy bell rang, she flew out and ran to class.

He was standing outside her classroom, looking the opposite way down the hall. What was he doing there? How could she slip past him?

Someone called his name, and he moved a few feet in the other direction. That was when Cassandra hurtled past, bolting into her class. She sensed him turning, but by then she was in her classroom, safely at her desk in front of Mia.

"You were almost tardy," Mia murmured.

"Grayson was in the hallway," Cassandra said, not looking up as she pulled out her flashcards.

"Yeah? Did you talk to him?"

"No," Cassandra said shortly. Even though they'd spent Saturday doing All-Region tryouts together, Cassandra had not explained what went down with Grayson. "And I don't want to."

"I take it Homecoming didn't go well?"

"You could say that."

"Sorry."

Cassandra just bobbed her head.

She didn't escape him after class, though. He called out to her as she made a beeline for the exit to get to P.E.

"Cassandra."

She froze, the way he said her name melting to the inside of her brain.

"Don't say hi," he said, giving her a wounded look as he stepped beside her.

"I have to get to class," she said, and she tried to flee.

He reached out as if he was going to touch her arm, but she jerked it away. And then she fled.

Mr. Reems told them to pull out their notebooks in biology, and that's when Cassandra realized hers wasn't in her backpack.

She searched frantically through her things, checking inside other notebooks, searching her memory for when she had it last.

At All-Region tryouts. She'd taken it with her to study.

She must have left it there.

"Oh no," she moaned.

"What's wrong?" Ashlee asked.

"I've lost my notebook. With everything. All my notes, my assignments." Her breathing came faster, and she felt close to panic.

"It's okay," Ashlee said, rubbing her shoulder. "I'll make copies of my stuff, and you can use it to study for the midterm."

"Okay. Okay." Cassandra forced herself to breathe deeper. "Thank you."

She didn't glance behind her to see if Grayson was listening. He didn't try to talk to her in biology, and he didn't call out to her when she left for lunch without him. She breathed a little easier, relieved to have successfully evaded him, even if it hurt not to be near him.

Cassandra picked at her food at lunch, listening to Betsy and Miles chatter on about nothing. Betsy elbowed her.

"Grayson keeps looking over here."

Cassandra turned her face to see Grayson and Charlotte sitting at a table nearby. Sure enough, he was looking at her. Charlotte said something to him, and Cassandra faced Betsy, becoming deeply involved in their conversation.

"What's he doing now?"

"Charlotte's playing with his hands. Now she put his arm around her."

Cassandra swallowed, glad she wasn't watching. "Now what?"

"They stood up. Now they're dancing together."

Cassandra closed her eyes. "Is he trying to hurt me?"

"I think he likes you both. But what's he going to do? He's not going to let go of the bird in his hand to catch the other."

Cassandra stood up. "I'm just going to choir."

⟲⟳⚜⟲⟳

Riley called Cassandra later that evening.

"I heard something," she said.

"What?" Cassandra coiled up in the chair in the living room, ready for whatever news Riley had.

"There's a girl in my French class who is friends with Charlotte. And she said Charlotte was upset that you talked to Grayson at Homecoming. She said she could tell there was something between you, and she didn't like the way you flaunted yourself at him."

"Flaunted myself!" Cassandra exclaimed. "I'm so sure! I just stopped him!"

"Cassie, are you listening to me? She could tell there was something between you!"

Cassandra paused, taking a moment to let that info soak in. "Was there something between us?"

"There still is. Cassie, you need to talk to him."

And say what? She couldn't even imagine what she'd say now. "Okay. Maybe tomorrow."

Instead of hiding in the bathroom before class, Cassandra stayed at her locker with Riley, waiting to see if Grayson would come over.

"I never liked him, you know," Riley said. "Matt was the best guy you've had a crush on. I wish it had worked out with you guys last year."

"Matt was a jerk," Cassandra said without looking up from her book. "He wasn't even a real friend. Just pretended to be and then went out with Amity."

"Yeah, well, Grayson has kind of done the same thing."

"Grayson is—"

"Grayson is what?"

She and Riley both spun around to see Grayson standing there. Cassandra closed her book and straightened up, and Riley said, "See you later, Cassie."

Grayson waited until she was gone, then he said, "Do your friends call you Cassie?"

"No. Yes. I guess. Don't call me that."

"Because we're not friends?"

"Because I like the way you say Cassandra."

He smiled, though it didn't reach his eyes. "Why are you avoiding me?"

I'm mad at you. I'm so, so, so mad at you. She didn't say that, though. "I heard your girlfriend got mad about me talking to you. I didn't want to cause trouble for you." She intentionally used the word girlfriend, waiting to see what he would say.

Grayson shrugged. "She's cool that way. I can talk to you."

He didn't deny it. Cassandra's heart sank to her toes. Charlotte was his girlfriend.

"I thought . . ." She swallowed hard, trying to keep control of her emotions. "I thought you were only friends."

"Something changed," he said, very quietly.

The tears stung her eyes. She'd had such high hopes. "I better go to class."

"Timing, Cassandra," he said before she walked away. "It's all about timing."

"And mine's off." She hurried down the hall before he could see her cry.

CHAPTER SIXTEEN

A New Wind Blows

Midterms meant two things: cramming like crazy for three days of tests, and getting to leave campus in between those tests.

Cassandra only had two tests on Monday, Spanish and biology, and then she was done for the day. She made plans with Riley and Farrah to meet up for lunch.

Grayson found her in the hall before the door to the Spanish classroom had opened. "Good luck today, Cassandra," he said, taking her hand.

"You too." She tried to extricate her fingers, but he tightened his grip and tugged on them. Then he winked at her and let go.

She wished he wouldn't be so kind. Wouldn't touch her. It made her wish for things she couldn't have.

"Who was that?" Olivia, a girl in her class, said when Cassandra stepped through the door.

"That's Grayson," Mia said, answering for her.

"He's so fine!" Olivia said. "How do you know him, Cassandra?"

"He's my friend," she said. Her words were true, but they tore at her heart. It wasn't enough for her.

Grayson walked past her desk three times in biology: once to get his test from Mr. Reems' table, once when he went to turn it in, and finally on his way back to his desk. Each time he passed her desk, he patted her head.

He finished way before Cassandra. She concentrated on the definitions and physical components of biology, trying not to think about the boy who sat behind her. Her brain stuttered. She hadn't found Ashlee's study notes nearly as concise as her own, and now the answers didn't come to her mind the way she wished they would. She penciled in responses, fearing the worst.

"You have about five minutes," Mr. Reems said. "Finish up and turn your test in."

Crapola! Now she couldn't think at all. Cassandra hurried on the remaining answers.

She was just handing her test in when the bell rang and the class bolted, scurrying away to lunch. Grayson was one of the first out of the classroom. Cassandra watched him go, her heart sinking to her toes. She could only assume he was meeting with Charlotte.

Mr. Reems cleared his throat. "Ms. Jones? Were you going to turn that in?"

"Hm? Oh." She looked at the exam still in her fingers. "Yes." She placed it on the desk and walked somberly out of the room.

Only to find Grayson in the hall, waiting for her.

"I figured I had to be stealthy so you wouldn't escape from me," he said. "You wouldn't run off if you thought I was already gone."

She smiled in spite of herself. He'd left before her as a ruse? "Escape from you?"

"Yeah. Or run away from me. Because I know you're mad at me."

She looked away as the smile dropped from her face. "Are you getting lunch with Charlotte?"

"I think so."

"Because she's your girlfriend."

He took her arm and stopped her. "Cassandra."

She closed her eyes, loving how the sound of her name molded to his lips.

"I'm sorry I didn't get to dance with you. I really wanted to."

"Some other time," she said, not believing it for a second.

He lifted a shoulder and glanced down the hallway, not meeting her eyes. "I have to—I have to find her."

What about us? Cassandra screamed in her mind. *What about our happy ever after?* But she just smiled and nodded, and he left her.

And then he turned around and ran back. "Cassandra. I really am sorry." He took her hand and ran his fingers over her knuckle. "Things could have gone very differently."

She held her breath, waiting for him to say more, but he didn't. "It's not too late," she whispered, begging him to agree with her.

He squeezed her hand. "It's not the right time."

She swallowed and spoke the words she hardly dared to think. "So I'm supposed to—wait?"

"No. I would never ask that of you."

But if there was even the possibility, the chance that he might want her some day, that was what she was going to do. She'd wait forever if she had to.

He let go and lowered his head, and this time he didn't come back after he hurried down the hall.

She found Riley and Farrah outside waiting, and the three of them walked to Arby's, then McDonald's before finally settling on Taco Bell. Cassandra told them all about Grayson and why she'd been late.

"He said if it weren't for Charlotte, he would be with me," Cassandra said, picking at her bean burrito.

"He said that?" Farrah said, exchanging a look with Riley.

"Well, not in all those words," Cassandra admitted. "But basically. And he said when they break up—someday—maybe we can be together."

Silence descended upon them, and Farrah rolled her eyes. "You won't last that long. Some other guy will steal you first."

"Yeah," Riley said. "If he wants you, he should break up with Charlotte and be with you."

Cassandra faked a smile as her friends defended her, but in her heart she knew she wouldn't fall for anyone else. Not ever.

⁂

Wednesday was the last day of midterms, and Cassandra and Riley decided to celebrate by going to a Chinese restaurant.

There was no exam in choir, but Mr. Cullen made all the students come in and sign the roll book to prove they hadn't skipped class. After that, they were free to go.

Cassandra and Riley spotted John leaving the choir room at the same time as them, heading for his car in the parking lot behind the building. They looked at each other, then ran over to him.

"Where you going, John?" Cassandra said, leaning against his car door.

"All done with testing?" Riley leaned on his hood.

He looked back and forth between the two of them and laughed. "What do you want?"

"Let's go to lunch." Cassandra grinned. "Chinese. Come on."

"You paying for me?"

"No, but you're paying for me." Riley flashed him a smile.

John grinned. "With an invite like that, how can I say no?"

Riley and Cassandra cheered and climbed into the backseat.

"Where am I headed?" John asked as they drove.

"Just take seventy-one to Vincent's #2. It's a good restaurant."

"Got it."

A truck full of high schoolers stopped at the red light next to them. It revved its engine, and Cassandra and Riley peered out the window. The boys inside waved, and the girls laughed and waved back.

"They're gorgeous," Riley said.

"Really nice," Cassandra agreed.

"Hey," John protested. "I'm right here!"

They giggled and patted John's shoulder while he drove to the restaurant.

Cassandra felt lighter than she had in days. She hadn't seen Grayson since Monday, and maybe that was for the best. When he wasn't around her, he didn't dwell in her thoughts as often. John and Riley cracked her up all through lunch, and then the waitress gave them their fortune cookies. Cassandra read hers. *Only finding love will heal your broken heart.*

"This one's true," Cassandra said, showing her friends.

"Do you have a broken heart, Cassandra?" John asked.

"Shattered," she said.

"In pieces," Riley added.

"So sorry," John said, deep brown eyes studying her with concern.

She shrugged. "I guess that's life."

They paid for their meal (Riley even paid for her own) and climbed back into John's car. But when he turned the engine, nothing happened.

"That's weird." He tried again.

It was getting hot in the car. Even though it was October, the days were hot enough that Cassandra wore shorts and Riley a T-shirt. She opened the car door, trying to let cooler air in.

"We kind of have to get back to school," Riley said. "We still have seventh hour tests to take."

John looked at his phone. "I can call my mom for help."

Cassandra also checked the time. "We need to be back in twenty minutes." Her heart sped up with worry as she did some quick calculations. Even if John's mom was at home and he lived five minutes away, it would take time to get in the car and drive over. If all that happened like clockwork, they would still be cutting it close to get back to school in time.

"What should we do?" Riley said.

Cassandra got out of the car and closed the door. The other two did as well, staring at her.

"I guess we better run," she said, suddenly grateful to Ms. Lynn for making them run in P.E.

"What about my car?" John cried.

"Come back and get it later!" Cassandra said. Then she took off down the street.

The three of them ran all the way back to school. They ran through the side doors with only two minutes to spare, all of them gasping, holding their sides, and laughing.

"I think that was the most fun lunch I've ever had," John said. "But I'm not taking you girls anywhere ever again."

Riley and Cassandra busted up again.

♦

The weather changed almost overnight as the last week of October arrived. Rain pelted Farrah and Cassandra as they raced across the courtyard after P.E. Cassandra stood inside the doors to the A-wing a moment, dripping wet, trying to catch her breath. Farrah pulled a jacket out of her backpack and put it on.

"Where's your jacket, Cassie?"

"I left it in my locker," she said.

"Well, that was smart!"

"What was smart?"

There was no mistaking that accent, and both girls turned to see Grayson coming the other way down the hall.

"Cassie left her jacket in her locker."

"Super smart." He stopped next to them in the hallway.

"The rain was hurting my ears." Cassandra poked at her head, trying to keep her wits together. It was hard with the way Grayson stood there, smiling at her. They'd barely exchanged more than hellos and goodbyes in the week since midterms. "Like needles going through them."

Grayson smirked, a little twist of his lip. "I think they were sticking your brain."

"What brain?" Farrah chortled, and Cassandra couldn't stop laughing either.

"You'll freeze, all wet like that," he said, and he pulled her into a hug, wrapping his arms around her. "Here." He took his sweater off and handed it to her. "Wear this."

Cassandra stared at it, then at him, disbelieving. "No. I'm not taking your clothes."

"I'm offering. Take it, Cassandra."

Cassandra took it, and Farrah made a noise in the back of her throat. Both of them looked at her, but she turned her face away.

"Thanks," Cassandra murmured, tucking into the sweater and inhaling his scent. Grayson. It smelled like Grayson.

"See you later, Cassie," Farrah said, and then she took off down the hall.

Cassandra's class was just a few doors away, but she didn't move. Neither did Grayson.

"How's Charlotte?" she asked, playing with sleeve of his sweater.

"She's good. We're good for each other. We're both new, we get it. We get along well."

"I've been new before too," she murmured. "I get it." Even if that was six years ago.

"I know you do." He patted her head, then gave her another hug. "I'll see you next hour."

Cassandra walked into math class feeling both elated and numb. Grayson did care for her. He liked her. And she felt like she was something special to him. But at the same time, she couldn't be what she wanted to be to him. And she felt rotten, hanging on the sidelines and pining for another girl's boyfriend.

How fair was life?

She pulled out a sheet of paper and began scribbling, writing down words as they came to her. A poem. She hadn't written one in ages, but her heart was crying out right now, crying for her to put the bleeding emotions down as poetry.

My Light in the Dark

There are days when the sun doesn't shine.
When the clouds encircle me.
Then my only solace comes from without.
A smile through the gloom.

That smile warms my soul.
It's the light in my tunnel.
My hope in the dark.
And it belongs to you.

A calmness in spirit. maybe.

Or a sincerity in tone.
But I hope you know how much
I value our friendship.

She would never give this poem to Grayson. But she hoped he would always be there for her, even if she never had him as more than a friend. She clung to their fragile connection, terrified of losing him.

Mr. Reems handed out their midterm test scores in fourth hour. Cassandra looked at hers and exhaled in relief. She'd gotten an A, just barely. She pulled out her phone and did some quick calculations. That meant she'd have an A in the class for the first half of the term. Mr. Reems had told her she had a 93% going in, and this test would put her at a solid 91%.

"Cassandra," Grayson whispered.

Ashlee looked at Cassandra. "Ohhh," she said, her eyes going soft and wide.

Cassandra cocked an eyebrow and then swiveled her chair to face Grayson. "What?"

"How did you do?"

She showed him her test, proud of the grade.

"Good job." His lip quirked, and he lifted his paper, exposing a 96%.

Her mouth dropped. "How did you get a better score than me?"

"I memorized the text." His eyes danced merrily.

"Oh, hey." Cassandra pulled his sweater off and handed it back to him. She felt the eyes of all her classmates on them as she did. "Thanks for that."

He took it, sliding it on over his shirt. She watched, feeling a strange intimacy, knowing the sweater had just been on her body and was now on his.

"Anytime," he said.

Charlotte waited for him in the hall after class, barely letting the class end before she poked her head in. As soon as he stepped out, she took his hand and led him down the hall.

"Good thing I took his sweater off," Cassandra grumbled. Charlotte would have noticed that for sure.

"Talk about possessive," Ashlee said, watching them go. She looked at Cassandra. "I'd never heard him say your name before. No wonder you like it."

"I love him," Cassandra whispered. She'd never said that about any boy before, but she had no doubt. She'd never felt this way before, either.

"He let you wear his sweater?"

She nodded, afraid to speak. Afraid she'd cry.

The need to sob followed her through lunch and choir. She stopped at her locker before going to English and sank to the ground, letting her face fall into her hands.

"Cassie."

She looked up to see John and Miles walking over. Both of them stopped and started patting her on the head, as if spontaneously.

"Why are you on the ground?" Miles asked.

"What are you doing?" Cassandra laughed and covered her head, trying to shield herself from them. "I'm not a puppy dog!"

They laughed too, but they didn't stop patting her. She leaned forward.

"Okay, okay. We'll stop," Miles said.

She sat up, but the patting resumed.

"Guys!"

She lifted her head, but it wasn't Miles or John this time. It was Grayson. And then all the boys laughed at her, and Cassandra's heart lifted. She laughed too, and then stood up and practically skipped to class.

CHAPTER SEVENTEEN

Playing Games

The office had report cards ready for students to pick up after sixth hour, and Cassandra stopped and grabbed hers on her way to history class. She paused at her locker, reading over the grades.

"This isn't right," she murmured, her eyes landing on the biology score.

B. Mr. Reems had given her a B. But she knew she should have an A.

Someone patted her on the head, and she turned around, not surprised to see Grayson.

"My grade's not right," she blurted.

"What's wrong with it?" He stepped behind her and read over her report card. "Looks like good grades to me."

"Biology." She jabbed her finger at it. "I should have an A. I know I should."

He took a step back. "Let's talk to Mr. Reems about it."

Let's. "Really? You would go with me?"

"Grayson." Charlotte sidled up to them and slid an arm around Grayson's waist, her gaze dark as her eyes cast over Cassandra before she pulled him away.

Argh! Cassandra wanted to punch her in the face. She took a deep breath, reminding herself that she was the interloper. Grayson was Charlotte's boyfriend.

She would have to talk to Mr. Reems about her grade after class tomorrow.

She saw Grayson with Charlotte before school the next day, and Charlotte was at his classroom door after first hour. If she saw

Cassandra, she gave no indication, just took Grayson's hand and went down the hall, clearly claiming her property. Cassandra fumed silently but kept the peace.

She got anxious going into fourth hour, knowing she'd have to talk to Mr. Reems. But too many people were in the classroom, and she lost her nerve, instead standing behind her table and staring at his desk, wondering what she would say.

Grayson came in and stopped behind her, then began patting her head. "Everyone pat Cassandra on the head. It makes her feel like a puppy dog."

A smile creased her lips in spite of her nerves. "Grayson, go away."

His eyes crinkled as he grinned and handed her a small slip of paper. She sat down and then opened the note.

Stay in here after class.

She glanced toward him, but he was deep in conversation with Katie, the girl next to him.

"We have a special guest today," Mr. Reems said. "Wait till you see this."

Special guest? Cassandra raised an eyebrow. That sounded intriguing.

The classroom door opened, and a man came in with a large snake wrapped around his neck.

"Crapola!" Cassandra said, and she ducked her head under the desk, reminding herself to breathe.

"Cassandra?" Emmett asked.

"You all right there, bud?" Aiden, a dude who always wore a leather jacket, asked.

"That was fast!" Andrew said.

"Hey, Cassandra, I think they dropped it on the floor!" Aiden said.

"Don't joke that way," Ashlee said. Cassandra remembered how she'd told the snake story to everyone at Camp Splendor a few summers ago. Ashlee knew what was going on.

"Are you afraid of snakes or something, Cassandra?" Grayson asked.

"She has a snake thing," Ashlee said. "She was bit by a poisonous snake a few years ago and spent a week in the hospital. It was awful."

Murmurs of sympathy filled the classroom, but Cassandra kept her head down until Mr. Reems finished showing off the snake and the special guest left. Only then did Cassandra come out from under the desk, her body quivering.

"There's tears in your eyes," Emmett said, looking closely at her.

"I'm okay," she breathed. "I'm okay." She felt like she was reassuring herself.

Ashlee patted her shoulder. "You did great."

Yeah. She hadn't hyperventilated and required a paper bag like last time.

Class finally ended, but Cassandra stayed put. Grayson put his things away, then moved around the tables to sit by her after Ashlee, Emmett, and Andrew left. Cassandra turned to face him.

"I can't stay right now," he said softly, looking directly into her eyes. "Charlotte will be in the hall waiting for me. But meet me here after school. We'll talk to Mr. Reems together."

She couldn't believe he was willing to help her on this. "Why?"

"So we can get your grade fixed."

"But why are you helping me?"

He picked up his bag and grinned at her. "Don't you know, Cassandra Jones?" He walked away, taking her heart with him. Again.

She passed Grayson after sixth hour. He winked at her, and then barked, loud enough to be heard across the heads of the other students.

"Shut up!" Cassandra said, but she was laughing.

"What's going on with you guys?" Mia asked from the desk behind her in history.

Cassandra turned around and doodled on Mia's notebook. She was aware of Maureen on her left and Leigh Ann on her right. Nicole was also behind Mia, but Cassandra didn't care if Nicole overheard.

"Why do you ask?"

"He's always by your locker. I see you together a lot. But everyone knows he's dating another girl."

Maureen leaned closer, and Cassandra knew she had to be careful what she said. "He and I became close before he and Charlotte started dating. So we're still good friends. She doesn't like it, but that's all we are. He's pretty devoted to her." The words stabbed her in the heart. But they were true. Mostly.

The girls seemed satisfied with that response, and they backed away. And Cassandra went back to her notebook so she could write more heartbroken poetry. She'd see Grayson soon.

Cassandra was having second thoughts by the time school was over. Maybe it would be better to just let the grade slide. She needed to catch the bus, anyway. She shoved her books into her locker and prepared herself for the run to the bus stop.

Farrah stepped over to her locker and handed her a folded piece of paper. "I have this for you." She gave Cassandra a knowing look.

Cassandra put her bag down and opened it, also knowing what it would be.

Don't chicken out. See you at Reems.

That did it. She would go. "I'll miss the bus." It would be worth it.

Farrah followed her down the hall toward the science rooms. "Is he cheating on Charlotte with you?" she whispered.

"No," Cassandra whispered back. "He's loyal to her."

"You shouldn't have taken his sweater."

Maybe she shouldn't have. But she would not defend her decision. And she would do it again if given the opportunity.

Grayson was waiting outside the door when they arrived, and he stepped toward her and hugged her. "Hi," he said.

He took her hand and pulled her toward the classroom, and Cassandra felt Farrah's eyes burning into her back, felt the accusation. Was this cheating? Letting him hug her, holding his hand? He would've been hers. He should've been hers.

He let go when they stepped inside, and she wished he hadn't.

Mr. Reems looked up at them. "Mr. Arend, Ms. Jones. What can I do for you?"

Grayson looked at her, but she didn't say anything, so he stepped forward. "Cassandra noticed a discrepancy in her grades, and she feels a bit disgruntled by it. She wanted to talk to you about it."

Discrepancy. Disgruntled. Grayson and his big vocabulary.

Mr. Reems peered over his glasses at her. "Ms. Jones. Care to speak up?"

She cleared her throat. "I'm not sure why I have a B. By my calculations, I should have an A."

"Let's see what's going on here." Mr. Reems opened his grade book and scanned it. "There's an assignment you never turned in. So that gave you a B in the end."

"No." Cassandra shook her head, trying to stay level-headed. "I haven't missed any assignments. I've turned them all in, on time."

"Do you have the assignment?"

Her heart sank, and she exhaled. "I lost my notebook. I lost everything."

He raised an eyebrow. "How did you study for the midterm?"

"Ashlee made me copies of her material."

"Well, I don't know how we can prove you turned it in, then."

"Come on, Mr. Reems," Grayson said. "It's Cassandra."

"You told me I had a 93% going into the exam," Cassandra said. "So I should have a 91% now."

"Well, let's pretend you turned in that assignment." Mr. Reems pulled out a calculator and plugged in the numbers. "That would put you at a 93% going into the midterm." He plugged in a few more. "And that would give you a 91% after." He put the calculator down. "I'm going to give you the benefit of a doubt because you've done so well in the past. But keep better track of your things."

"I will," Cassandra said, her heart soaring.

Grayson squeezed her shoulder, and the two of them left the classroom.

"Good job."

"Thank you," she said. "I feel so much better about that. Thanks for coming with me." She pulled out her phone. "Now to tell my mom I need a ride home."

"You need a ride?"

She nodded. "I usually ride the bus, and it's long gone."

"I can give you a ride."

She looked at him, at his somber light brown eyes, at that face she wanted so badly to touch. And she knew what would happen if they were alone in a car. "I—I better not," she said, and her voice shook.

He heard the quiver in her voice, and his brow furrowed. "Are you afraid of something?"

"Myself. I'm afraid of myself." Oh, she wanted to kiss him so bad. "And then afraid of what your girlfriend might do to me."

He laughed and then gave her another hug, bending to reach her and holding her extra long. "See you tomorrow, then."

⁂

"We have a short P.E. class today," Ms. Lynn said. "Because there's an assembly. We'll be listening to the governor speak to us."

"The governor," Mariah, another girl in class, said. "Anyone even know who that is?"

Cassandra laughed until Farrah grabbed her arm and pulled her away.

"They were talking about you in first hour."

"Who?" Someone was talking about her?

"Charlotte's best friend. She said she's really upset at you."

"Her best friend is upset at me?"

Farrah whacked her forehead. "Charlotte is! Someone saw Grayson with you in the hall after school. Told Charlotte you guys were kissing." Farrah searched Cassandra's face as if waiting for a confession.

"He hugged me. No kissing involved."

"Well, I guess he told her he couldn't give her a ride home because he had detention. And then he was with you. So it didn't look good."

Cassandra felt her face go cold. And then hope flared in her chest. "Did they break up?"

"Not that I know of. But he's in trouble with her. And so are you."

Maybe that meant they'd break up. Oh, if only!

"So after we do our morning run, follow me to the assembly hall. We'll figure out how to work this."

Cassandra rolled her eyes. She didn't want to figure anything out. Let Charlotte think the worst of her. "Do we have to do this governor assembly? We could just skip."

Farrah smiled, a devious glint in her eyes. "Why, Cassandra Jones."

"What?"

Farrah didn't say anything more. They ran their laps and then followed Ms. Lynn and the rest of the class across the street to the auditorium. As they filed into a row of seats with the Springdale High student body, Farrah grabbed Cassandra's arm and jerked her backward.

"What are you doing?" Cassandra hissed, stumbling over legs and armrests.

Farrah pulled her past the other students and down a hallway. Then they went out a side door, and suddenly they were in the courtyard.

"Come on." Farrah ran over to the old gym, and Cassandra followed.

"What are we doing in here?" she asked, her voice echoing in the empty chamber as they crossed the room. "Did you forget something?"

Farrah pushed open the back door, revealing the parking lot they ran laps on. Only now there were buses and band students from other schools crowding the area.

"We're skipping!" Farrah said, laughing and throwing her arms out wide.

"Farrah!" Cassandra nearly panicked. "We'll get in trouble!"

"Relax. We're not even leaving school property. Everyone's at the assembly. There's no way we'll be caught."

Cassandra glanced around at what looked like junior high band students and felt her shoulders relax. Farrah was right.

They walked around, enjoying the sunshine and leaning on the fence, watching the band students practice marching. Cassandra saw a few of her sister Emily's friends and waved at them.

Farrah checked her phone. "The assembly is probably almost over now. We should head back for fourth hour."

"Right." Cassandra took a step just as a kid shouted, "Watch out!"

She turned her face in time to take a hackey-sack to the eye. She cried out and crumbled to the ground, grabbing her face.

"Cassie?" Farrah hurried to her side. "Are you okay?"

"Sorry!" the kid shouted.

Farrah waved him away. "Cassie?" she said anxiously. "Should I take you to the nurse?"

Her voice was tight, and Cassandra knew why. If they went to the nurse, they would be caught. Everyone would know they'd skipped the assembly.

"I'm okay." Cassandra forced herself to her feet and blinked a few times, both eyes watering. "Let's go to class."

Farrah guided her to her locker because everything was blurry in one eye. "I'm really worried. If it's still like this after school, we have to tell someone."

"It'll be fine." Cassandra pulled out her books and gave a grim smile.

"Let me walk you to class, at least."

Cassandra relented, though she could see. Out of one eye, anyway.

Ashlee noticed right away and stood up. "Cassie! You okay?"

"I'm fine." She blinked, and water spilled over. "I got hit in the face."

"What happened?" Emmett leaned over. "Looks painful."

She shook her head. "It's nothing. Really." Where was Grayson? She glanced back and saw him watching them, but he didn't say anything.

Which was odd.

She wiped at her watering eyes and stole another glance at him. He had shadows under his eyes, and he looked a little pale.

She lingered after class, hoping to talk to him, but he packed up and left quickly, not giving her a chance. Now she knew something was wrong.

She watched him and Charlotte at lunch, leaning close enough for their shoulders to touch. They definitely had not broken up.

The lunch bell rang, and he kissed her before she went down the hall for the other wing. Cassandra kept her head down, pretending not to notice. Grayson passed her table without a word, tossing something in the trash before continuing out.

Cassandra counted to five, then she jumped up and ran after him. "Grayson?"

He turned around, a look of resignation on his face, like he'd known she was coming. She neared him and stopped several feet from him. He didn't look approachable.

"What's wrong?"

"Nothing." His voice came out aloof, distant, and it froze her heart.

She blinked again, her eyes still stinging. Stinging worse. "Something's wrong."

"No. It's nothing. Nothing's wrong." He started to turn away.

"Grayson?" she said. It was almost a whisper, but her heart was pattering painfully in her chest, and it was all she could get out.

He shook his head. He didn't look at her, didn't look back, just shook his head and kept going.

Cassandra turned and hurried the other direction, almost running to get to choir on time. She ached inside, tears welling in her eyes.

Grayson couldn't break up with Cassandra because they weren't going out. But it kind of felt like he just had.

EPISODE 3: DREAM CRUSHER

CHAPTER EIGHTEEN

Caught

Cassandra didn't sleep well. Different worries and thoughts plagued her mind, mostly centering around Grayson. She felt muddled and confused inside, desperate and lonely. She couldn't lose him.

She woke up late, and her mind felt groggy as she threw her clothes on. Riley had slept in also and called to say they shouldn't wait for her, so Mrs. Jones let Cassandra drive the van to Bible study. But Cassandra drove too slow, and they were late.

She regretted it as soon as she stepped inside and saw who their substitute teacher was: Brother Garrett, Noah's father.

Riley had developed a crush on Noah over the summer, and Cassandra had developed a friendship with him while she acted as the voice between them. She glanced around for Noah but didn't see him. Riley hadn't come either. She would be disappointed! Cassandra collapsed into a chair in the front row and tried to appear as if she hadn't just arrived.

"You are a fine-looking bunch of kids," Brother Garrett said, smiling at all of them. "I'd say you're the finest looking people I've seen this morning, other than my wife and son Noah."

Cassandra smiled at the reference.

"I want to talk to you about outside influences that can affect your life, that can affect how you see yourself."

Why did it seem he looked right at her when he spoke? Why had she sat on the front row?

"You have to remember who you are. You have to remember the light you have. You can share that light, but only if you keep it burning bright. Don't let anyone take it from you or dim it. Don't let anyone have that kind of power over you. Nobody should be that powerful."

Brother Garrett kept on talking, but those words seared into Cassandra's soul. *Nobody should be that powerful.* No matter what she felt for Grayson, he shouldn't be able to take away her light.

"Surround yourself with people who add to you light. Who make it grow. Who make you better. If someone is not doing that for you, you have to be their light. Do not let them diminish yours."

Her heart pounded in acknowledgment. She could be a light for Grayson, but she could not let him diminish hers.

She didn't see Grayson before first hour. She suspected he stayed in his classroom, but that was all right. Cassandra sat down in front of Mia in Spanish and pulled out her notecards to review for the quiz.

The bell rang, and an office runner came by with a note. Ms. Elliot read it, then said, "Cassandra Jones? You're wanted at the principal's office."

A murmured "Oo" carried through the room, but Cassandra's blood froze in her veins.

"Did you do something?" Mia murmured.

Cassandra couldn't even answer. She *had* done something. But surely not . . . surely she couldn't be in trouble for that. She clutched her fingers together as she walked toward the office, her heart pumping harder with each step.

There were four chairs outside the principal's office, and one of them was occupied. By Farrah.

Cassandra's heart skipped a beat. They had been caught.

Farrah shot her a wide-eyed look when she sat down. "What do we do?"

"I can't believe this," Cassandra breathed.

"We're going to lose our senior privileges. Get suspended."

Cassandra took several deep breaths. She closed her eyes and uttered a silent prayer, one of total regret for skipping and begging to help them get out of this mess. She opened her eyes and blinked rapidly. "We were just at the football fields! It was just one hour!" So not worth this kind of trauma.

"What do we say?" Farrah clutched her fingers together, her hands trembling.

"Let me handle this," Cassandra whispered.

The door opened, and Mr. Harris, the school principal, stood there. "Ladies." He beckoned them inside.

They stepped inside and sat down again, very quietly, backs straight, as he folded himself into his chair. He looked at them somberly.

"Do either of you know what this is about?"

They looked at each other and shook their heads very slowly. Better to see what he knew.

He looked down at a paper and back at them. "Ms. Lynn marked you truant during yesterday's assembly. She said neither one of you was in the row when she counted heads."

"Oh!" Farrah said, but Cassandra already saw a way out of this one. She wasn't supposed to lie, and she prayed God would forgive her this one time. Because the words forming on her tongue were a lie.

"We didn't know we had to sit with our classes," she said. "Ms. Lynn never told us that."

Mr. Harris leaned forward in his chair and frowned at her. "Where were you?"

"I had to use the bathroom," Cassandra said, remembering the chain of events. "So Farrah and I left the row. I'm sure Ms. Lynn saw us. When we came back in, it was all dark, and there was an empty seat in the back, so I sat there. Farrah found one a few rows ahead of me."

"We just didn't know," Farrah said, trembling. "We didn't know we needed to stay with our classes."

Mr. Harris shuffled his papers and studied them, then looked at the girls again. "Neither of you has any bad marks on your record, and you're both good students. So I'm going to give you the benefit of a doubt. But if anything like this happens again, you will be written up for truancy."

Cassandra nodded, trying not to wilt with relief. She had never even been in detention! She couldn't be punished for truancy!

"Go on, then. Off to class."

They both fled. Farrah looked close to tears, and Cassandra gave her a quick hug before hurrying back to Spanish class. She slipped into class and sank into her seat in front of Mia, wanting to disappear.

"What happened?" Mia demanded to know as soon as class let out. "You looked like you'd seen a ghost."

"Ms. Lynn reported me truant from the assembly yesterday," Cassandra said. She felt a flash of anger toward her teacher and wished she didn't have to go to P.E. right now.

Mia's eyes went wide. "What did you do?"

"I told Mr. Harris I'd been in a different row and she didn't see me."

"I would vouch for you. I know you're the kind of person who would never skip."

Her words gave Cassandra a pang of guilt, but she brushed it aside.

She'd never intended to skip. Another prayer went up, this one of gratitude that she'd escaped unscathed. And it included a promise that she would not ever allow herself to be in that situation again.

Ms. Lynn didn't say anything to Farrah or Cassandra about the incident, and neither girl brought it up. Cassandra hoped that meant it was behind them.

She did not see Grayson until fourth hour. He was already at his desk, and he didn't look at her when she walked in, even though she kept her eyes on him. She sat down next to Ashlee, her hands trembling as she pulled out her binder. What was going on?

He slipped out quickly again, not giving her a chance to talk to him. And she wasn't going to chase him to fifth hour. She'd seen how that went last time.

She wanted to wait at his locker, but Charlotte was everywhere. So instead she wrote him a note.

Grayson,

I just wanted to see how you are. I'm sorry if I did something wrong. I can tell you're upset. I'm concerned. I miss your smile.

She almost erased that last line and decided against it. He knew how she felt. How should she end it? Not love. Too honest. Yours? Too assuming. Sincerely? Too formal.

She finally just put her name. *Cassandra.*

She knew which way he went before sixth hour, and she intentionally walked the opposite direction in the hallway so she'd pass him. She saw the moment he noticed her because he gave a slight pause in his step. Charlotte wasn't with him, for once. Cassandra took advantage of the hesitation to move next to him, grab his hand, and slide the note into it. Then she kept going down the stairs, blushing at her own brazenness, grabbing his hand that way.

Of course, with her classroom being upstairs, she had to go back up. But she made sure Grayson had already gone to class.

She saw him after sixth hour as she moved the few doors down to her seventh period class. Grayson stood talking with another junior outside her classroom door. Was he intentionally waiting for her? She slowed when she approached, just in case.

He turned slightly as she neared, not breaking conversation with his friend, and held his hand out as if giving her five. She saw the note there, tucked under his thumb, and she returned the five, sliding the note out as her hand pulled away.

She sank into her seat, shaking. She wasn't sure she wanted to know what he said.

"You okay?" Leigh Ann asked, and Nicole and Mia both looked at her. "You look pale."

"Are you still upset about this morning?" Mia asked.

Cassandra shook her head. Keeping her hands under her desk, she opened the note from Grayson.

> *Cassandra,*
> *I can't talk to you anymore. I'm sorry. For everything.*
> *Grayson*

That was it. But the three lines explained everything, and inexplicably, Cassandra burst into tears.

CHAPTER NINETEEN

Sticky Webs

Cassandra hated biology.

Of all her classes, it was the one she most despised going to. It was the class where she would sit in front of Grayson and listen to him ignore her.

The first few days after getting his note, Cassandra did her best to avoid him as well. If she saw him, she went the other way. If he looked at her, she became engrossed in studying her nails or talking to the person next to her. If she saw Charlotte, she laughed and flirted with the boys around her.

She hated Charlotte.

She was quite certain Charlotte was the reason he wouldn't talk to her anymore. The reason why Cassandra had gone from being one of his closest friends to being someone he couldn't look at.

But then her anger passed, replaced by a cold, drizzling ache. A desperate desire to see him smile at her again. To feel him hug her.

Her skin prickled as she walked past his classroom before first hour, knowing how near he was. She saw him coming down the hall, but instead of fleeing into her classroom, she stopped at the water fountain and bent her head to get a drink.

He stopped at the fountain beside hers and also got a drink. "Hi," he said before continuing down the hallway.

Hi. The word burned a flaming path of hope in her heart.

She stood up, and he was looking back at her, standing outside his classroom door. Were they talking again? Was he allowed? She went to her classroom, saying, "Good morning" as she passed him. He gave a smile and disappeared inside.

"What's with the look on your face?" Mia asked when she sat down in

Spanish.

"He's talking to me again," Cassandra breathed.

"Grayson?"

"Yes."

Mia gave her a disappointed look. "He's using you. Find a guy that's not dating someone."

"He wouldn't use me. He really cares about me."

"Then why is he with another girl?"

Because he cares about her more.

The thought occurred to her. But no, it couldn't be true. "Because he's too kind. And because he's loyal. Admirable traits."

"Admirable traits, unless he's with a girl he doesn't want to be with. Then it's dishonest and cowardly."

Neither of those attributes fit on Grayson, and Cassandra scowled at her. "That's not how it is."

Mia shrugged and didn't say anything more.

Cassandra stayed standing when she got into biology, organizing her notebook and pencils while waiting for Grayson to walk in. He would do something. She knew he would.

He did. He poked her side with his pencil as he passed her. When she looked at him, he said, "That's *the* pencil."

She smiled, warm and fuzzy inside that he remembered their joke.

He didn't rush out the door this time, either. She dropped her pen near his table and stooped to pick it up, then said softly when she stood, "Are we talking again?"

He didn't respond for a moment, his eyes on his notebook. "I really care about Charlotte," he finally said. "And she sees you as a threat." His eyes darted toward her before returning to his notebook. "I have to prove to her that you're not."

"I'm not." Cassandra shook her head. "I would never do anything—"

"I know."

"So . . . we can be friends? We can talk to each other?" She hardly dared breathe.

He shouldered his bag. "Maybe."

"Why maybe?"

"I'll see you later." He left the room, quickly, and she stayed behind, knowing Charlotte would be in the hall and it would look bad if they left together.

⁂

"I don't think it's fair," Riley said. "The way he strings you along."

Cassandra stretched out on her bed after school, the phone to her ear. "I'm happy to be his friend. I'm happy for any interaction with him."

"Yeah, but he cares for Charlotte? What about you?"

"Well, yeah." She rolled onto her stomach. "He obviously cares for me too."

"Then he should just say, 'Charlotte, she's my friend and I'm gonna talk to her.'"

Cassandra hadn't told Riley about him offering to take her home. About the way he'd touched her face and hugged her. She swallowed, feeling a tightness in her abdomen. "I think he knows that maybe things were going too far."

"What are you not telling me, Cassandra Jones?"

"Well." She sat up. "Maybe I'm reading too much into it."

"Into what?"

"We almost kissed."

"You did?"

"No." She shook her head. "Not exactly. But almost."

"Just spit it out."

"He was helping me with something in biology. And he touched my face. He held my hand. Then he offered to give me a ride home. I was afraid he would kiss me, and I'd let him, and then we'd really be cheating. So I said no. And he hugged me. But he hugged me really tight, really close. That's what Charlotte's friend saw when she told her we'd been making out."

"Oh. So maybe he thinks Charlotte's right in making him stay away from you?"

"I don't know." Cassandra sighed. "I'm trying to figure it out."

"Well, the good news is, I like someone new!"

"You do?" Cassandra grinned, happy to have someone else to focus on. "What happened to Noah?"

"Oh, Noah's sweet and all, but he's still in junior high. And he lives in Fayetteville. I never see him. No, it's time for me to like an older guy."

"Yeah? Who?"

"He's a senior. And he's in my French class, and he's so hot."

Cassandra leaned back on her pillow and let her friend ramble while her thoughts drifted back to Grayson and their almost-kiss. Would he ever break up with Charlotte? Her soul longed to kiss him. She wasn't sure she'd be happy until she did.

⁕

Grayson didn't talk to Cassandra for two days, and it drove her crazy. But she followed his lead, not saying anything, not doing anything.

Friday night was a football game, and Riley's mom picked up Farrah and Cassandra. They stood at the fences along the field instead of sitting at the bleachers, cheering and clapping to stave off the chill in the air.

Farrah poked her. "There's Grayson. You gonna say hi?"

Cassandra turned enough to see him and felt the way her heart skipped a beat. "We're only kind of talking. Maybe." She giggled at the ridiculousness of it.

He was walking past them, and he saw them looking. He gave a brief smile. "Hi, guys." His hand came out, squeezed Cassandra's arm, and then he was past them.

"I'm sure he'd be with you if not for his girlfriend," Farrah said.

"Yeah, well." Cassandra shrugged. He did have one.

There wasn't anything else to say about that.

Charlotte showed up midway through the first quarter, and the two of them sat together in the bleachers. He put his arm around her and she leaned on him, and Cassandra's heart roared with jealousy.

"Stop staring at them," Farrah said. "It'll only make you feel worse."

"I can't watch." Cassandra pushed away from the fences and went to find a different seat, one with a better view of the field instead of the student body.

She found Cara and her boyfriend sitting together, and she dropped down beside them.

"Hi, Miss Cassie!" Cara said, turning to give her a hug.

"Where are the other girls?' Cassandra asked. She had history with Maureen and choir with Amity, but she hardly talked to them.

"Around. Hitting on guys."

"Of course." She smiled. She shouldn't have expected anything different.

"Where's your boyfriend?"

"Boyfriend?" Cassandra gave her a blank stare. "I don't have one."

"Oh. I thought you were dating Hampshire."

Hampshire. Was that what they called Grayson? Cassandra felt a little glow inside that people thought they were together. "I'm not. We're just friends. But his girlfriend doesn't like me, so." She shrugged. "We don't get to talk much."

"Who's his girlfriend?"

"This girl named Charlotte. She's sitting with him now."

"Show me."

Cassandra leaned out and looked over the railing, then settled back. "Look over the side. You'll see him sitting with a tall red-head. That's her. Like third row back."

Cara and her boyfriend both leaned over to look. "I think she's leaving. She just grabbed her purse and walked away. Now he stood up . . . he's stretching . . . I think he's looking for someone." She gave Cassandra a sly expression. "Is he looking for you?"

Cassandra shook her head. "He won't talk to me in public. Someone saw us together and told Charlotte."

"What?" Cara's mouth fell open. "Jerks."

"Yeah." Cassandra laughed. But if there was a chance she could talk to Grayson now . . . Cassandra stood also. "Good to see you. I'm going to wander."

"Good luck, hon," Cara said.

Cassandra went down the steps and paused by the concession stand, remembering when she'd run into Grayson here before Homecoming. Back when she still thought she had a chance to be with him. Now she was begging for a chance to be his friend.

As if summoned by her thoughts, Grayson was suddenly there in front of her. "Have you seen Kevin?"

She didn't even know who that was. "No."

"Can you help me look for him?"

"Sure . . ."

He leaned close to her as more cheering went on in the bleachers. "If anyone asks, we're looking for Kevin."

Ah. She got it now. She walked beside him, careful not to touch him, to keep it platonic. Every few steps Grayson stopped and asked people if they'd seen Kevin. Then they reached the bathrooms. He bent near her ear and said, loudly to be heard over the noise, "Go through the bathroom to the hallway inside." Then he walked away, going into the boys' bathroom.

Okay. Cassandra stepped into the bathroom. She walked past the stalls and sinks to the door on the opposite side, the one that led into the building. She pulled on it, but it was locked. Well. So much for that plan.

There was an audible click on the other side of the door. Curious, Cassandra pulled again. This time it opened.

She stepped through and found Grayson on the other side of the hallway, waiting for her.

"How did you do that?"

"I saw someone else go through the door from the men's bathroom earlier. So I knew it was unlocked in." He went and sat down on a bench by the entrance doors, motioning her to sit beside him. No students were nearby, and the doors were kept locked during the game.

"I guess Charlotte still doesn't like me?" Cassandra lowered herself beside him.

He didn't answer her question. "It's not easy, is it, to be friends when you can't talk to each other."

"No," she agreed. "I feel like we're drifting apart."

He yawned, stretching his arms wide, then wrapped them around her and pulled her into his chest. "We can pretend, for a moment, that you talked to me first. That I went to Homecoming with you."

Oh, yes. She closed her eyes, very willing to discuss this fantasy with him.

He released her, and she sat up to look at him.

"Where would we be now?"

"We'd be dating. I liked you before Charlotte asked me to Homecoming."

Her heart tightened at the confirmation. "You liked me before her."

He nodded. "But it's not that simple now. Because I like you both."

She sighed, looking away from him. "And while you and I drift apart, the two of you get closer."

His hand touched her back. "It's not fair, is it?"

She shook her head, tears springing to her eyes. Her throat throbbed with unshed tears, and the words were there on the tip of her tongue. *I love you.* But she couldn't say them.

She cleared her throat, swallowing back the words and the tears. "So is this how we get to talk to each other? Sneaking around locked buildings?"

His arms went around her again, smoothing her hair and holding her close. "Maybe, Cassandra Jones. Maybe this is all we'll ever get."

That was the saddest thought ever.

The Bulldogs won the football game while Cassandra lay in Grayson' arms, hidden from the world, secluded from prying eyes. When she finally left the bathroom, her classmates greeted her cheerfully, announcing how the school team was going to conference. Cassandra smiled, pretending to be glad, when her heart was equal parts soaring and breaking at once.

CHAPTER TWENTY

The Great Pretender

Cassandra went over to Farrah's house after church on Sunday, and they baked cookies while talking about life.

"My dad and I fight a lot," Farrah said. "He wants me to be this perfect little girl, and I just can't."

Cassandra nodded. "I get it." She didn't fight with her dad that much, but she'd learned there were subjects she couldn't discuss with him. Mainly, boys.

Farrah finished mixing the batter, and Cassandra got the cookie sheets so they could spoon the cookies onto them.

"Are there any boys you like?" Farrah asked.

Cassandra had to smile. It was a silly question, and all her friends knew it. "No. None." Except for one boy, who ruled her heart and she could not have.

"How's Grayson?"

Cassandra trembled at the question. She paused over the cookie sheet, spoon poised to deposit another mound, and she wanted to tell Farrah everything. But she also felt like the moment they'd shared in that hallway was secret; it was theirs.

"What is it, Cass?"

She turned to Farrah, and the tears pricked her eyes. "He's not going to break up with her, Farrah. Every day that he's with her, he likes her more. I'm losing him."

Farrah opened her arms and Cassandra fell into them, sobbing.

"How do I get over him? How do I get over a boy I never even had?"

Farrah plopped the cookies into the oven and sat Cassandra down at the table. "Maybe you should stop talking to him."

"We already hardly talk at all!"

"Then maybe you should stop hoping you will."

Cassandra considered that statement. She spent every moment at school looking around corners for Grayson, barely breathing through biology because she might miss something he said. Her entire being revolved around him, tingled with anticipation that he might be near. "How? How do I do such a thing?"

Farrah traced a magazine on the table with her finger, thinking. Then she said, "Pretend like he's nothing to you."

"Like he's nothing to me." Cassandra looked away.

"No, I'm serious. Act. Be an actress and laugh with other people when he's near, distract yourself, throw yourself at another guy just for the heck of it. Pretend."

Cassandra pressed her hand to her chest and massaged it. "How can this hurt so much? How? It's real. It's physical. I'm in so much pain."

"That's love," Farrah said softly, and Cassandra wished it wasn't so.

"How long until it goes away?"

"I don't know, Cassie."

On Monday, Cassandra put "Operation: Forget Grayson" into practice.

Or "Operation: Pretend to be Strong."

Or was it "Operation: Laugh When You Want to Cry"? She didn't even know.

At any rate, she smiled and talked with Riley at her locker before school and kept her eyes focused on her friend. She didn't look from side to side with her breath half-held, waiting to see Grayson's face. They walked to her classroom when they felt like it, and she said bye to Riley and went inside, not even checking to see if Grayson was in the hall.

She sat down at her desk and smiled at Mia, keeping up a constant storm of conversation.

She had to, or the ache inside might burst into a flood of tears.

She didn't bring it up in P.E. with Farrah, but talked about everything in the world except boys.

She ignored the rush of adrenaline when she walked into fourth hour. Instead of sitting by Ashlee, she sat by Emmett and Andrew and drew flowers and hearts all over their papers during class, then took their pencils away and giggled when they tried to get them back. Then she stole Andrew's wallet and ran out of the classroom the moment the bell rang, leaving him to run after her. He caught her at the lunch table as she slid in beside Miles, and both of them were laughing too hard to breathe.

It was working. She felt giddy and more in control than she had in months.

In choir she sang as if nothing could be more important than hitting the right notes and blending with the other sopranos. And in English, she turned around and flirted with Mason, really speaking to him for the first time since Homecoming. His face flushed with pleasure, and he followed her down the hall to her seventh hour class, where they stood in the hallway chatting until he had to run to seventh hour.

The mask was wearing on her. Her face hurt from smiling. She stepped into history class and kept up the chatty, giggly charade with Maureen and Leigh Ann.

Go home. Cry. Sleep. Repeat.

She did not talk about Grayson. She would not.

"You've been really happy lately," Mia said on the third day. "Are things better with Grayson?"

His name was like a dagger to her heart, and she felt her smile slip. She forced it back into place, but she felt like she would break. "I'm over him. I'm in a really good spot right now. I've realized he's not for me." The lies caught in her throat, and she leaned away to cough.

"That's good," Mia said. "I'm happy for you." She didn't look like she quite believed the story, but she didn't press it.

Cassandra hadn't even looked Grayson's direction all week. When she walked into fourth hour, she sensed him at the table behind her, felt his eyes pulling her toward him. She took a deep breath and forced herself to plop down between Emmett and Andrew without looking at him. Then she forced herself to laugh and giggle and flirt like she had each day.

Thursday morning Grayson stood at the water fountain next to her classroom. There was no evading him. Cassandra clutched Riley's arm, holding her close as she started up a nonsensical conversation about her brother and their dog. She tried really, really hard not to look at Grayson as they walked past.

But she could not resist his gaze. Their eyes met, and in that brief moment, she knew he knew what she was doing. And he looked wounded, hurt, and his expression nearly undid her resolution.

Then she straightened her spine and turned away. She said bye to Riley and went into class, still smiling. She let anger replace her longing. He had no right to be hurt. Every day he held Charlotte in front of Cassandra, even kissed her in front of Cassandra. She would not let him diminish her light.

By the end of the day Thursday, Cassandra felt like she'd been doing mental gymnastics for days. She fell into bed after school and buried her head in her pillow. She couldn't think anymore. She just had to sleep.

Friday morning, she woke up with a pounding headache and feeling as if she hadn't rested at all. She couldn't seem to pull up a smile, not even a fake one. Her body felt like one large festering wound, from the inside out.

She couldn't do it anymore. She couldn't keep pretending. Not today, anyway.

Riley noticed her silence as soon as she climbed into the car on the way to Bible study. Mrs. Jones was driving, but Cassandra sat in the middle row.

"You okay?" Riley asked, looking her over.

"Fine. Just tired."

Cassandra didn't say anything else. Not in the car, and not in class.

Riley pulled her into the bathroom when they got to school. "You seem really down. What's wrong?"

Such a stupid question. Nothing was wrong. Nothing had changed. Everything was wrong. "Let's just stay in here until it's time for class."

"I have to go to my locker."

"Will you go to mine too?" Cassandra couldn't stand there and pretend not to see Grayson. A week ago he'd held her tenderly in the hallway during the game. Her heart throbbed with longing. One week since she'd spoken to him at all.

Riley went without saying anything, collecting Cassandra's books and bringing them back to her in the bathroom.

Cassandra put her jacket on the bathroom floor and sank onto it. She closed her eyes and rested her head against the brick wall behind her.

Riley sat beside her. "This is about Grayson, isn't it."

There was no question in her words. And Cassandra started to cry. "I miss him."

Riley took her hand and held it all the way until the warning bell rang. Girls came in and out of the bathroom, shooting weird looks at them but saying nothing.

Cassandra stood and gathered up the books Riley had brought her.

"I'll come spend the night tonight," Riley said.

"Okay." Cassandra nodded. "That will be great."

They left the bathroom, and Cassandra saw Grayson at his classroom door, talking to someone, but his eyes followed her. She held her books close and went into her classroom without looking back.

She kept quiet in all her classes. Compared to how chatty she'd been all week, it was an extreme difference, and those around her noticed. She didn't tell them this was the real her. This was how she felt. She just said she was tired and ready for the weekend.

A sense of dread filled her when she approached the biology classroom. She slipped into her seat beside Ashlee and opened her notebook, then rested her chin on her hand and stared at the clock on the wall. Over. She just had to get this over with.

She followed along as Mr. Reems went through their homework from the night before, but she didn't have to correct her answers. Hers were right. Instead she kept her gaze on the second hand on the clock as it wound around and around and around.

"Ms. Jones," Mr. Reems said, snatching her out of her reverie, "since you're looking at the clock and obviously want to leave, will you read the next answer, please?"

Cassandra straightened up, her face flaming with embarrassment. Last thing she wanted was to draw attention to herself. She looked down at her paper and winced.

The answer to number nineteen was three paragraphs long.

She took a deep breath and then started reading. Her voice faltered halfway through as her classmates turned to stare at her, but she couldn't stop now. Andrew muttered, "All right, already!" just loud enough for her to hear.

She read the last word and lifted her gaze.

"That," Mr. Reems said, his eyes locked on her, "was an A-plus-plus answer." He went on to praise the thoroughness and thought put into her response and how that answer alone would raise any test score by several points.

Cassandra couldn't even enjoy the nice things he said about her. She lowered her head, letting her hair fall around her face. Would this class never end?

The bell finally rang, and Cassandra shot up like a bullet. But Emmett was blocking her way with his chair, and Andrew was stuffing his backpack with books. While she stood there waiting, Grayson walked to the end of his row and stopped.

Crapola. She would not get past him.

She met his eyes as she moved down the row and then dropped her gaze. He grabbed the sleeve of her sweater and pulled her to the opposite wall.

"Hey, good answer," he said, and she had to laugh.

"Oh, gosh. I was so embarrassed."

He smiled, his eyes studying her face, so many unspoken words between them. "Is this how it goes, then?"

A lump jumped into her throat, the lump that had plagued her all morning. She looked down at his fingers on her sleeve. "I guess."

He let go of her and slid slightly to the right as the last few classmates shuffled out. "I want to talk again."

She lifted a shoulder. "Sure. Whenever." Like they'd ever get the chance.

He gave her another searching, probing gaze, and then he melted into the crowd and left the room.

She thought it would make her feel worse, talking to him. But it didn't. For the first time in a week, she could breathe easier. Her chest felt lighter. She closed her eyes and wished she could hold onto this feeling. If only she could have Grayson.

⊙ ᗡᴥᗡ ⊙

Cassandra picked Riley up that evening, and she was in a goofy mood.

"You're a hundred percent happier than this morning," Riley observed.

"I didn't make any mistakes driving over here," Cassandra said.

"You're doing great," Mrs. Jones said. "Though you did have to turn around once."

"That was your fault," Cassandra said. "You got us lost!"

"You got lost coming to my house?" Riley exclaimed.

"I wasn't paying attention," Mrs. Jones said, sounding sheepish.

Both girls laughed. Mrs. Jones let Cassandra drive all the way back to the house, and she could just imagine the day when she drove without a parent. Riley could sit up front, and they would play and goof off the whole time.

Riley let herself into Cassandra's room and immediately started bouncing on the bed. "So why are you so happy? I know this isn't a driving thing."

"It's nothing."

"Cassandra . . ."

"No, really." She put on some lipstick and then faced Riley, giving her a big grin. "It's nothing."

Riley arched an eyebrow. "So if by nothing, you mean Grayson . . ."

"Yes." She giggled. "That's nothing."

"So Grayson is nothing."

"Yes." Cassandra was laughing now. "He's nothing."

"You are so weird. So what happened with nothing?"

"Nothing." She shrugged. "Maybe a few words. Maybe a touch. Nothing." Cassandra came and sat cross-legged on the bed in front of Riley. "I'm going to survive this. Sometimes it hurts so bad I want to die. But then it eases, and I can breathe, and then I'm happy again, and I can do this."

"What if he never breaks up with Charlotte?"

Cassandra shook her head. She was beyond hoping for that now. "I can do this."

"Well." Riley grabbed her face and smashed her cheeks together. "I think that deserves a kiss."

Cassandra shrieked and jumped back, then grabbed her pillow and attacked Riley any time she came close. Finally the girls collapsed on the separate twin beds. Cassandra's side hurt and she couldn't breathe, she had laughed so hard. She smiled up at the ceiling, letting the lightness she felt right now envelope her.

CHAPTER TWENTY-ONE

Fortifications

This time, Cassandra didn't feel like she was faking it when she walked into school smiling on Monday.

She saw Miles in the hallway before school, his hands all red.

"What happened to you?" She stopped him by his locker and took a hand, examining the minuscule cuts and chapped skin.

"Oh, it's nothing." He pulled his hand away and picked at the skin. "I was playing a game outside. This is normal."

"Doesn't seem like such a great game."

"It's lots of fun. Hey, you're always here early. Come join us sometime."

"No thanks. But thanks." She waited for him to get his books, then hooked her arm through his and dragged him to her locker.

Miles laughed at her. "Why are you so happy?"

"I'm moving on." She retrieved her books and smiled at him. "And I feel good about it."

"Hi, guys!" Betsy joined them, smiling brightly.

"Hey, Betz." Miles slung an arm over her shoulder. "Cassie's finally getting over what's-his-face."

"Grayson." Betsy arched an eyebrow.

"The guy with the accent," Miles said.

Cassandra waved an arm breezily. "It's done, it's over. We don't have to talk about him anymore." She pulled out her Spanish book and then paused, searching her memory. "Oh, crapola! I didn't do my Spanish vocab! See you guys!"

They both laughed at her as she raced down the hall and slid into class. No one was there yet, so she pulled out her book and got to work, not even glancing up as her classmates came in.

"Forget to do your assignment?" Mia asked.

"Yes." Cassandra wrote down the last one and slammed her book. "Done." She turned around in her chair to chat with Mia.

"Grayson is in the hall."

Cassandra honestly hadn't even thought of him, she'd been so anxious about her vocab. "I got into class quickly."

"Did you want to go talk to him?"

She shook her head. "I'll see him later." But she wouldn't talk to him then, either.

She left choir with John and Aiden, and they escorted her to English, both of them making her laugh, teasing her about her handwriting. She was so engrossed in their conversation that she didn't see Grayson until he had nearly walked past her. He waved as he walked by, and she waved back without thinking. Then she swiveled her head around and looked over her shoulder.

At the exact same time he did.

She spun back around, heart pounding again. These little things. They kept her from moving on.

Mason was at his desk and she threw herself at him, leaning over his paper and doodling and touching his arm.

It was easy to make boys feel something for her. If only she could make herself feel something for them.

Maureen called Cassandra that night while she was doing her history homework.

"Hi," Cassandra said, surprised to hear from her. "I'm working on history. Did you get it done?"

"No. Cara's over here. Did you want to come over?"

Cassandra arched an eyebrow. That wasn't something she'd been pining for, no. "I've got to get this assignment done. What are you guys doing?"

"Just hanging out. More fun than history, I'm sure."

"Yeah, probably." Cassandra laughed.

"Cara wants to know what's going on with that guy you like."

Cassandra made a face. She didn't mind discussing this with Cara, but she didn't want to with Maureen. "Oh, nothing. That was months ago. We've both moved on."

"So he's still with his girlfriend?"

"Yeah." Cassandra twiddled her pen between her fingers. "They're like, perfect for each other. Probably gonna get married."

"Who do you like now?"

No one. I'm still stuck on him like glue. "I can't decide. It's a toss-up between Mason and Josh and John and Miles."

Maureen gave a hearty laugh. "Sounds like fun."

"So much."

"Well, next time we have a party I want you to come, okay? We miss you."

Cassandra smiled, wistfully. That was a time from her past, and she looked back on it with nostalgia, but she didn't want it again. "Sure. Just let me know."

Cassandra drove her and Riley to Bible study with Mrs. Jones in the passenger seat. Her mother pressed her lips together a few times when she thought Cassandra did something wrong, but she didn't say anything.

Cassandra parked behind a car, making sure she stayed in her parking lines. She kept a foot between her bumper and the other car. She looked at her mom.

"How was that?"

Mrs. Jones nodded. "I think you did well. I'll take you to the DMV after school so you can do the test. If you drive like that, I'm sure you'll pass."

Cassandra squealed and hugged her mom, then leaned back and hugged Riley. She got out of the car and skipped into the church, totally excited.

Farrah was the first of them to have gotten her license. She had turned sixteen a few days earlier, and knowing her friend could drive only made Cassandra that much more anxious. Farrah was only allowed to have one other person in her car when she drove. So she and Cassandra drove to Braum's after Bible study class to celebrate.

"To driving!" Cassandra said, raising her hot chocolate.

"To sweet sixteen!" Farrah said.

They touched the Styrofoams cups together and lifted the hot chocolate to their lips. Cassandra tilted hers back, and Farrah let out a shriek.

"What?" Cassandra cried, lowering her cup.

"My lid came off!" she gawked, looking down at herself. Hot chocolate trailed from the bottom of her shirt all the way down her pants.

"Oh no!" Cassandra said. She grabbed napkins and immediately tried to help Farrah clean up, though the paper just shredded on the fabric instead of drying.

"It's okay." Farrah blinked hard and pushed Cassandra's hands away. "Let's go to school. I'll change into my P.E. clothes."

Cassandra bit her lower lip and nodded.

She waited in the gym while Farrah changed, then couldn't help laughing at the sweat pants and over-sized shirt she'd put on.

"Don't I look sexy?" Farrah said, striking a pose.

"So sexy." Cassandra hooked her arm through hers. "If anyone can pull off that look, it's you."

Nothing could dampen Cassandra's euphoria. She saw Grayson before first hour and gave him a big smile before disappearing into her classroom. As soon as Mia came in, she said, "I'm taking my driving test after school."

"That's great!" Mia said. "Then will you be driving to school?"

Cassandra shook her head. "I won't be able to drive by myself until I turn sixteen in March. But I'll be ready!"

She hummed as she walked to P.E. The happiness was genuine, not some show she put on for other people.

She hoped it would last through fourth hour.

She saw Grayson as soon as she walked in. He met her eyes, and she smiled at him, feeling the way her heart soared just from looking at him. He smiled back.

Maybe, maybe, they could really just be friends.

She didn't try to bolt from the classroom, and neither did Grayson.

"You look happy, Cassandra," he said, stepping into her row while she put her books away.

"I am." She met his eyes and smiled at him. "I'm taking my driving test today. I'm excited."

"Good luck." His thumb touched the back of her fingers.

He started to leave, and she blurted, from nowhere, "Remember when we used to walk to lunch together?"

He turned back around. "I remember."

"I do miss that."

He gave a half smile. "Me too." He hesitated, as if about to say something else, then shook his head and left the classroom.

Oh, dang it, there was that ache again. At least they were talking.

Miles and Betsy walked with Cassandra to choir after lunch. Betsy went to sit down, and Miles grabbed Cassandra's arm before she did also.

"Wait, Cassandra."

She stopped and lifted an eyebrow. "What's up, Miles?"

"You know that girl who sits close to you, with the long blond hair?"

Cassandra could guess who he meant. She was friendly, talkative, and very pretty. "Harper?"

"Yeah." He smiled at the name.

Huh. Interesting reaction. "What about her, Miles?"

"She seems nice. Is she?"

"Yes. She is." Cassandra waited for more, but Miles didn't add to the conversation. "I'm gonna go sing now."

"Yeah. Let's do that."

Cassandra sat down near Harper and watched her, suspecting Miles had a crush on her. Wasn't there any guy who had a crush on Cassandra? Someone who liked her more than any other girl?

There was Mason in English class, and he attempted to flirt with her just as he did every day. But she wasn't attracted to him.

Okay, so she wanted a guy to like her who she might also like.

Someone like . . .

Someone like Grayson.

He was standing in the hall outside her seventh hour class, his back to her. Cassandra slowed as she approached. He turned as if sensing her, and they made eye contact. Heat rushed over her body at his gaze, at the magnetic pull of his body to hers.

"Hi," she said.

"Hi. How are you?"

She glanced around. The hallway wasn't empty, but there weren't a lot of other people in there. "I have to go to class."

"Where will you be after school?"

"Well—" she hesitated. "My mom's picking me up so we can do my driving test."

"So the back lot?"

She nodded.

"Okay. Good luck, if I don't see you."

She watched him go, knowing he had every intention of seeing her before then. Trepidation burned in her chest, and she eased herself into her desk. What was he going to say?

"Uh-oh," Mia said, taking one look at her face. "Something going on with Grayson?"

"No," Cassandra said, probably a little too quickly. She wiped any emotion from her face. "Nope. I'm just excited because I'm taking my driving test after school."

"You are?" Nicole gasped. "That's so awesome!"

"You'll turn sixteen before the rest of us," Maureen said. "At least we'll know who to bum rides from."

"Anytime," Cassandra said breezily.

Her classmates' attention distracted her until school was over, and she took her time getting her books out of her locker, liking how she didn't have to rush to catch the bus.

"What's your hurry?" she teased Miles a few lockers down as he shoved books out of his backpack into the metal cabinet.

"Rub it in," Miles said, slamming his locker. "I have to run and catch the bus."

"I'll drive you home after I get my license," Cassandra offered.

"I think I'd rather take the bus."

"Thanks!" she exclaimed.

"Just kidding!" He waved and dashed out the door.

"Do you have a crush on Miles again?" Riley asked, walking over to join her.

"No, but I think he has a crush on Harper. You not riding the bus today?"

"My mom's coming."

Cassandra dug through her wallet and pulled out a wad of cash. "I want a bag of chips. Come with me to the vending machine?"

"Sure."

They went down the hall toward the old gym, and Cassandra's mind fluttered toward the back parking lot, where she had told Grayson she would be waiting for her mom. What if he went and she wasn't there?

"Hi, Cassie, how are you, sweetie?"

Floral perfume invaded her nostrils seconds before Andrea, Cassandra's former best friend, threw her arms around Cassandra and hugged her.

"Oh, hey, Andrea," Cassandra said, stepping back. Riley looked annoyed.

"I never see you anymore. You look so cute!"

"I guess I better go," Riley said. "My mom is probably here."

"I'll call you later," Cassandra said. "Let you know how it goes."

"I think she hates me," Andrea said, watching her go.

"No, she doesn't." Cassandra dumped her money into the machine. "She actually likes you the most out of all you guys."

"Why?"

Cassandra shrugged and waited for her chips to drop. "I don't know. You're more real, I guess." Sometimes. When she wasn't lying.

"Well, that's sweet." Andrea walked with her down the hall toward the back lot. "Hey, it's Hampshire. Let's go say hi!" She waved toward the boy leaning against the back doors.

Grayson was there for Cassandra, not Andrea, but she couldn't say that. She let Andrea take the lead, watching as she flirted shamelessly with him, poking his face and touching his shirt, and he smiled and joked back.

Why couldn't Cassandra do that?

Then he looked at Cassandra over Andrea's head and said, "Hey. Can we talk outside?"

CHAPTER TWENTY-TWO

Legal Driver

It was a clear request for privacy, and Andrea didn't miss it. Her eyes volleyed between Grayson and Cassandra, and she stepped back.

"Bye, Cassie," she said. "I'll call you later."

Cassandra bet she would.

Grayson didn't even wait for Andrea to leave before he took Cassandra's hand and led her to a bench outside. "Is your mom here yet?"

"Not yet." She didn't recognize the other kids out, either.

"How are you?" He kept his hand on hers, the soft touch of his fingers clasping her own.

"I'm good."

"Are you really good?"

"I think so. Most of the time. How about you and Charlotte?"

"I don't want to talk about Charlotte with you."

"Why?" Did it make him feel guilty?

"Because it's not fair."

There were so many ways to interpret that, but she wanted to know his interpretation. "What do you mean?"

He didn't answer directly. "It bothers me when I see you with other guys."

Ah. That was why it wasn't fair. "Yes, well. That's what happens when you're single."

"Does it make you jealous? When you see me with her?"

She looked away, the heat rushing to her face.

"Cassandra?"

She slipped her hand from his. "You have no idea. It makes me—it makes me want to hurt something. Really bad." He'd opened up a can of worms, and she couldn't stop now. "But I have to accept the fact that you're with her, and you're going to be, and the only place for me in your life is as a friend. You and I will never be together."

"Hey." He touched her face, turned her to look at him again. "I never said never."

She trembled at the way he held her gaze. What was he trying to tell her? Did he still think there was a possibility for them?

Or did he just want to make sure he had her as a backup?

A van pulled up and honked, and Grayson dropped his hand.

"That's my mom." Cassandra stood and shouldered her backpack.

Grayson stood as well. "I don't want you to give up on us."

"But I can't hold on to nothing."

He grabbed her backpack strap before she could leave. "It's not nothing."

"What is it, then?"

He didn't have an answer, and she just smiled sadly before pulling away.

"Who was that?" Mrs. Jones asked as Cassandra got into the van.

"That," she said, pulling her seatbelt across her torso and buckling it, "was Grayson."

"That's the infamous Grayson?" Mrs. Jones peered out the window, but he'd already gone inside.

"Yes."

"What's going on with you guys?"

Cassandra sighed, hating this question, hating her non-answer. "Nothing. He has a girlfriend and it's not me." *And I can't get over him.*

"It didn't look like nothing."

"Funny," Cassandra mumbled, "his girlfriend doesn't think so either."

Mrs. Jones remained quiet, then she said tactfully, "Are you ready for your test?"

Cassandra nodded, grateful for the subject change.

Betsy was at the DMV, picking up her manual. "Hi, Cassie!" she said, waving when Cassandra walked in. "Are you getting your permit?"

"No, I'm taking the driving test." Her stomach twisted with nerves.

"Oh!" Betsy squealed. "Good luck! You'll do great!"

"I hope so." She wanted to puke.

Mrs. Jones sat down in the waiting room and winked. "I'll be here when you get back."

Cassandra had no words, so she just bobbed her head.

The deputy inside assigned her to an examiner, and then he led her outside to the parked cars.

"Which one is yours?"

"The blue van." Cassandra pointed.

"All right, let's do this."

Her heart hammered in her throat, and she whispered a prayer for help.

They both put their seat belts on, and the guy put a clipboard in front of him.

"Let's put it in reverse and back out of here, then go right onto the main street."

She knew how to do this. Cassandra looked over her shoulder and slowly backed up until she could turn around. Then she pulled up to the street and made a right.

"Now go straight until we get to the three-way stop."

She did, braking long before they reached the stop sign.

"You don't have to slow down that early. But make sure you stop before you get to the sign." He made a few notes on the clipboard, and her anxiety ratcheted up a notch.

"Turn right. Let's go back out to the main road. Stop before the stop sign."

She did. But she was too far back and couldn't see any of the cars coming from the left.

"You're going to turn right again."

"I can't see anyone coming," she said, wishing she wasn't so short.

"Inch forward little by little until you can."

She took her foot off the brake, relieved when the car moved up just a bit.

Now she could see. There were no cars coming. Cassandra hit the gas too hard, and they jerked as she made the right turn onto the main road.

"Don't push it so much. A little goes a long ways." He made another note, and her heart sank. She was going to fail!

"Pull over."

"What?"

"Pull over."

Crapola! He didn't even want her to drive anymore. Cassandra moved the car to the shoulder of the road, trying not to cry.

An ambulance roared past, sirens blaring.

"You always pull over for an emergency vehicle."

That was why he had her pull over! She nodded, shaking in her shoes. She hadn't heard the ambulance, but she didn't want him to think she hadn't been paying attention, so she kept quiet.

"Let's go back to the DMV."

The drive back was uneventful. She parked the car and got out. He wrote on his clipboard, got out, and handed a slip of paper to her.

"You passed. Take this inside and they'll give you want you need."

"I passed?" she gasped, hardly believing it.

"You'll do fine. Just don't forget those things I told you."

She laughed and nearly collapsed, giddy with relief. She'd passed! Cassandra turned around and ran inside to tell her mom.

⟋⟍⟍⟋⟍⟋

She was a legal driver.

Well, she still wasn't sixteen and couldn't drive by herself, but that was a mere technicality. Cassandra Jones had her license.

She showed off her signed form during Bible study before school, and then showed it off some more to everyone she found in the hallways.

"Remember I'm gone on a field trip today," Riley said before first hour started.

"I know," Cassandra said.

"That means I won't be here to save you from looking for Grayson."

"I'm done looking for him," Cassandra said breezily.

Yeah, right. If only she could get him out of her head.

She smiled wider, trying to make her bravado real.

"I'll see you when I get back, then!"

Cassandra panicked as Riley walked away. There was no one to distract her in the hallway, and what if Grayson came by? She turned and fled into her first hour class, preferring to just sit in Spanish class.

While she sat there, she hatched a plan.

"I need a new crush," Cassandra said to Farrah in second hour. "Right now. ASAP. Someone else I can dote on and look for in the hallways and pine for after school."

"You're on the rebound."

"Call it what you will. I'm done wanting someone I can't have."

"Is that so, *Cassandra*?" Farrah said her name the way Grayson did, lengthening the vowels.

Cassandra put her hand to her chest, sucking in a breath at the pain that lanced through her heart. "Don't call me that."

Farrah gave her a most sympathetic look. "Okay. Who can you like instead?"

Cassandra considered the guys she knew. "There's John in choir. And Emmett, Andrew, and Aiden in biology. And Mason in English, but I'm not interested in him."

"How about Emmett? You've been friends with him for a long time."

Which made developing a crush on him feel incredibly wrong. "It's got to be someone new."

"So Aiden. You just met him this year."

But she couldn't crush on someone in front of Grayson. Besides, the feelings would pale in comparison. "Maybe John. I sit by him in choir."

"Good choice."

"Okay." Cassandra forced a smile. "I like John. Did that sound good?"

"Not convincing at all," Farrah said, laughing. "You have to actually like him."

"I'll try. I've got to. I need to."

I like John, she told herself as she did stretches in P.E. *I like John*, she repeated as she did triangulations in geometry. *I like John*, she reminded herself as she walked into biology and her eyes tracked toward Grayson's table.

"Did you finish the homework?" Andrew asked her.

"Of course," she said.

"Can you help me?"

"Sure." She opened her book and settled next to him.

Someone walked into the class, and she spared them a glance before turning back to Andrew's paper. Only then did she realize it was Grayson. He'd cut his hair, and she hadn't recognized him right away.

"Hi to you too," he said, walking behind her to his desk.

She looked over her shoulder, a strand of hair falling in her face. "Hello, Grayson."

"How did your driving test go?"

A rush of pleasure flooded her body, and she beamed. "I passed!"

"Good job. I knew you would." He beamed back, looking proud of her.

She wanted to climb over the table and throw her arms around him. But she couldn't, so she just went back to helping Andrew.

I like John, she chanted. *I like John.*

In choir she moved her chair closer to John and chatted with him about her driving test.

"How did it go for you?" she asked. "You got your license last year."

He nodded. "My guy was so mean. He acted like he thought I was going to kill us both. I didn't think I'd pass, either, but I did."

She bobbed her head as he spoke, focusing on his eyes, willing herself to fall into them and feel something. Anything.

Nothing.

Just pretend.

They couldn't talk while they were singing, but she walked beside him as they left the classroom and nudged his arm with hers.

"See you tomorrow, John."

"See you, Cassandra."

They waved and parted ways, and she searched desperately for some deeper feelings. Still nothing. Talking to him bored her. She sighed. Maybe she'd have to try a different guy.

"Cassie!"

She turned to see Miles walking her direction, with Harper behind him. So the two of them were talking now. "Hi, guys."

They fell into step with her. Harper chatted the whole way about something that had happened at lunch as they climbed the stairs to the A-wing.

"Move over, short-stuff," a voice said behind her.

She turned, already smiling, knowing it would be Grayson. He poked her side with his pen and then continued down the hall.

That one touch, that small interaction. Like a small reminder that he hadn't forgotten her.

"Hey!" she said, and he shot her a grin over his shoulder.

Miles gave her a knowing look, but Harper hadn't even noticed. She was still laughing about the lunch incident.

"See you guys," Cassandra said, stepping into class.

She made a list of potential crushes in seventh hour while Mr. Grant droned on about theology. None of the guys on the list made her heart skip a beat. Was there potential with any of them?

Nicole tapped her desk. "Cassie. Look out the window."

Cassandra lifted her face to the window in the door and saw Riley standing in the hallway. She made signs through the glass and funny faces, and Cassandra giggled. She glanced at Mr. Grant, but he had his back to her and hadn't noticed.

Cassandra mouthed, "I like someone else now."

Riley mouthed something back that looked like, "I like snails now."

Cassandra raised an eyebrow. "No more Grayson."

Riley bent over and reappeared with a phone in her hand. "No more great songs?" She rattled the phone.

Cassandra giggled and lowered her head.

"Ms. Jones?" Mr. Grant moved over to her desk. "Is there someone in the hall that needs to join our classroom?"

Her eyes darted toward the window, but Riley was gone. "No. Sorry. I was just distracted."

The rest of the class laughed at her expense, and Cassandra's face warmed, but she couldn't stop smiling.

And she would stick with liking John. He was her best bet.

"Our Christmas concert is coming up," Mr. Cullen said in choir the next day. "It will be right after we get back from Thanksgiving break. So today we're going to rehearse on the risers and see how it goes. I'll tell you where to stand."

Cassandra waited to be put on the front row, where they always stuck her because she was short. But instead, Mr. Cullen said, "Cassandra Jones, back row."

Really? She got the top riser? She raised an eyebrow and climbed to the top, not about to complain.

She was next to John again, and she smiled at him. Amity was in front of her, and Ethan in front of Amity.

"I'm not used to being on the back row," Cassandra said, a little unnerved by the height.

Ethan turned around, peering around Amity at her. "Would you rather come stand by me?"

Cassandra cocked her head. He hadn't so much as looked at her since the beginning of the school year. And now he was talking to her? "I think I can do it from here."

"You're a little wobbly," John said, grabbing her shoulders. "We don't want you to fall."

"Well, I won't if you don't grab me!" she exclaimed, clutching Amity's shoulder for balance.

"Let's sing!" Mr. Cullen said, and he ran them through a warm up before they began practicing the actual piece.

Amity turned around. "Sing louder, Cassie. I need your voice."

"I'm trying," Cassandra said.

"Can you hear me?" Amity leaned her head back and sang near Cassandra's chin.

Cassandra giggled.

Ethan turned around, focusing his brownish-green eyes on her, and said, "Shh!"

Cassandra mimed zipping her lips shut, and then Mr. Cullen shouted, "Sing, Cassandra!"

She did, trying to put on her serious face.

Mr. Cullen stopped the choir. "We're singing too low at measure thirty-four. Does anyone have any questions about their part?"

Cassandra raised her hand. Mr. Cullen's eyes swept the choir, but he didn't notice her.

"Right, then, I expect it to be perfect this time."

Cassandra bounced on her heels as he turned back to the piano.

"Mr. Cullen!" she called, jumping up and down. Suddenly she lost her balance, and with a squeal, she tumbled off the back of the risers.

John rushed to help her up as the whole class laughed.

"I don't think Cassandra can be on the back row," Ethan said.

"Cassandra, what is it?" Mr. Cullen said, sounding annoyed.

She got back into place with John's help. "I can't remember."

That just led to more laughter, and Mr. Cullen glared. "Move to the edge of the row so you don't fall again."

He turned to the other side of the choir and started coaching the altos.

"I'm too short to be up here," Cassandra complained to those around her, secretly enjoying the attention. "Not even Mr. Cullen can see me."

Ethan moved off the risers and went over to the chairs in the corner of the room. Cassandra watched him, along with everyone else, as he brought a chair over to the risers beside her. Then another, stacking it on top. Then another, and another, until he had stacked several chairs up to the height of the top row.

"There," he said.

"Um, thanks," Cassandra said, looking at the tilted tower of chairs.

The whole section looked at her with expectation, so Cassandra stepped onto it.

It made her maybe a millimeter taller.

John snorted and Amity laughed, and Cassandra couldn't help laughing also.

Ethan shrugged. "Worth a try."

Cassandra smiled at him. She could like him.

But he also had a girlfriend.

Her mom took her after school to a different department of the DMV so she could get her picture taken for her license.

The lady behind the desk looked the form over and then studied Cassandra. "You this same girl? Sure you're old enough for this?"

"I'm fifteen," Cassandra said, embarrassed. She hated it when people thought she was younger than she was.

"Look like you're twelve," the fat lady said, tottering away from the desk and telling Cassandra to sit in the chair in front of the white wall.

You look like a beached whale, Cassandra thought, but she kept her biting thoughts to herself.

"Oh, you do not, sweetie," the other lady with huge blond hair said. "You're adorable. Just smile for the camera."

Cassandra did.

They printed her license and showed it to her.

"That good, honey?"

"Yes." She pocketed it, pleased with how it turned out. "That's good."

Thanksgiving break brought a welcome reprieve from school and all things school related, such as Grayson.

A whole week without seeing him. Without wondering. Cassandra actually looked forward to it.

Mrs. Jones's sister and family arrived from Georgia on Wednesday. Cassandra hoped she and Carla would get along again. They'd really hit it off the previous year.

"Carla's not feeling well," Aunt Jadene said once the family had unloaded the car. "Can she rest for a bit?"

"You can use my bed, Carla," Cassandra said, taking Carla's bag and leading the way.

"Thanks so much, Cassie," Carla said.

Cassandra settled on Emily's bed and watched Carla climb under the covers. Carla was a year older, but that didn't seem to matter like it had when they were younger. "Was it an okay drive?"

"Fine. We're all just tired. I hope I don't have the flu. What's up in your life?"

Cassandra squeezed her hands together, considering her normal answer: nothing. Instead, she blurted, "I'm in love with this guy, and he likes me too, but he has a girlfriend and he won't break up with her to go out with me."

Carla slowly sat up, her eyes widening. "Tell me everything."

It took hours, but Cassandra did, from the beginning. And she cried sometimes remembering, the hope, the expectation, the thought that they would be together. And then she cried again as she saw that hope slip away, as she and Grayson drifted apart, even though neither of them wanted to.

"That's so sad," Carla said when she finished. "So sad."

Cassandra exhaled and smiled, glad to have that out. "And you?"

Carla shrugged. "No boyfriends. No heartbreaks. Life is boring."

"I would take boring over heartbreaks any day," Cassandra said fervently. "So many times I wish Grayson had never moved here."

"Would you wish him away?"

And never see him again? Could she handle that? "I don't know."

Carla stayed in bed during dinner but came out after, when Braden set up a card table and wanted to play games. Cassandra was not any better at it than she had been the year before, but she felt lighter and happier than she had in months as her cousins teased her and coached her through the game.

Carla stayed in the room with Emily and Cassandra, and that night they talked about guys and church and school.

Everything except Grayson, but that didn't matter. Cassandra had already gotten him out of her system.

CHAPTER TWENTY-THREE

A Little Bit Off

Carla's family stayed through the holiday, and right when Carla started to feel better, Cassandra started to feel sick. So she spent the last two days sleeping off a cold. She hated missing time with Carla and wished she or Jordan lived closer. She enjoyed her cousins when they were around, but the friendships always grew cold between months.

By the time Monday rolled around, Cassandra felt rejuvenated and relaxed after Thanksgiving break and ready to face her teachers, her classes, and most of all, Grayson.

She saw him before first hour on Monday and smiled at him. He gave a head bob and then ducked into his classroom. Cassandra went into her own and chatted with Mia about what a great break it had been.

She got to biology after Grayson and put her books down, then turned around to talk to him. "Hi."

He wrote very carefully in his notebook, the familiar writing stiff and stilted in its precision, and didn't even look up. "Hi."

"Did you have a good break?"

"Yeah."

Even that one word had an accent. Like he didn't know it had an "e" in it.

He didn't ask about hers, so she asked about his. "What did you do?"

"Flew to New Hampshire to be with my mother. Spent time with Charlotte."

"Was it a good trip?"

"It was fine."

He still hadn't looked at her, and a coldness settled in her heart as she finally got the hint. She turned around and faced forward, blinking against the sudden heat in her eyes.

Something was off.

Something had changed, and she didn't like it.

"What do you think it is?" Farrah asked before school the next morning as she gathered with Riley and Cassandra in the bathroom after Bible study.

"I don't know," Cassandra said.

"Maybe it has nothing to do with you." Farrah applied her eyeshadow with expert hands. "Maybe he's upset after seeing his mom."

"Maybe it's Charlotte," Riley added. "Maybe she put him in a bad mood."

"Maybe." Maybe it was all of those things. Or maybe he'd simply stopped caring for her.

They left the bathroom and wandered down A-wing, and then they went for a walk down C-wing. Farrah nudged Cassandra.

"Look, there's Grayson. He's talking to Kevin."

"Let's go back," Cassandra said. She'd rather no interaction than a negative one.

"I'm friends with Kevin. Let's say hi." She grabbed Cassandra's arm and pulled her forward, not accepting any other answer. Riley trailed them.

"Good morning, Kevin," Farrah said brightly. "Grayson."

Cassandra smiled at Kevin and then lowered her eyes.

Farrah kept up a steady conversation with Kevin, but Grayson didn't say a word.

But he did look at her. She lifted her eyes, just briefly, and he gave her a nod. A very deliberate nod. She frowned and turned away, glad Farrah had finished the conversation. What did his attempt at communication mean?

"He looked at you," Farrah said. "He nodded at you. I saw it."

"Me too. But I don't know what it means."

Farrah put an arm around her and squeezed. "Probably that nothing's changed. You're in the same limbo you were in before."

Cassandra laughed. Not like that had been a good place.

She got to biology before him and pulled out a book, pretending to be immersed so she wouldn't have to notice him come in.

But he was impossible not to notice. He came in, talking in a loud, boisterous voice and banging his books around. He laughed at something Katie said, knocked his chair into the table behind him, and then he swore at Mr. Reems when the teacher asked him a question.

Cassandra's face burned with embarrassment for him. "What's wrong with him?" she whispered to Ashlee.

"I don't know. He's usually so quiet."

If only he would talk to her. She could get him to tell her what was in his mind.

Cassandra remembered she was supposed to have a crush on John during fifth hour. She sat next to him and giggled at everything he said. He went through her purse and took her gum, and she hissed at him and hit his leg, which made him laugh.

She looked down when she saw her purse inching away from her across the floor, and there was Ethan, reaching in and stealing a piece of gum.

"Ethan!" she cried, but this time she really didn't mind. She snatched the purse away and glared at him.

I refuse to be interested in another guy with a girlfriend, she thought, keeping her purse in her arms and resisting his attempts to get it from her. But he made her laugh, which made her feel light and giddy inside, and why oh why couldn't she feel this way over John or Mason?

"I need volunteers for the Christmas Feast tomorrow night," Mr. Cullen said. "I always ask my sophomores to help out with this. Sign this clipboard as I pass it around if you can come."

"Are you going?" John asked.

"Yes." Cassandra signed her name. "I think it sounds like fun." Nicole had already told her she could borrow one of her Renaissance dresses for the occasion.

"I'll come, then," John said.

"Me too." Ethan took the clipboard and signed his name really big.

She smiled weakly and willed herself to have a crush on John.

☙❀❧

Riley and Cassandra rode to the Christmas Feast together.

"I wouldn't miss it for anything," Riley said. "Lucas will be there."

Lucas was the senior Riley had had a crush on since the beginning of the school year. He pretty much ignored her, and Cassandra wished she would like Noah again.

"But he's singing in the festival. We won't really see him. We're serving-wenches." Cassandra giggled.

"Yeah, when they yell, 'here, wench!', that's when we come running." They laughed.

Janice was there with the elite singers, and she and Cassandra hugged and talked for a minute. It was the most they'd spoken to each other in months. They didn't have any classes together, and Cassandra never got to hang out with her.

Amity was there, too, in a really snug dress that made her boobs pop out. John stuck next to Riley and Cassandra, talking with them in between courses.

Unity did the musical performances. The singing was beautiful, and Cassandra hid in the sidelines and sighed, wishing she was a part of the elect choir. She had tried out, but she hadn't made it.

"We're low on pudding," John said, coming to her. "Can you get more from the kitchen?"

"More pudding." Cassandra went down the steps in the little white chapel, dashing into the kitchen for more dessert.

Lucas was there, and she stopped when she realized they were the only people downstairs. Riley's crush looked at her, and she looked at him. Broad-shouldered and dark-haired, Cassandra didn't see any appeal to him. But Riley liked him, so . . .

"I need pudding," she said, watching him steal a spoonful.

"Oh, here. I'm not eating it all."

She took a few plates, keeping her eyes trained on him. Had he ever even noticed Riley? "I know someone who likes you."

That got his attention. "Who?" He put the spoon down and faced her.

"Not telling."

"Come here, wench!"

She just laughed and fled up the stairs with the pudding.

"We'll need more than this," John said when she handed him the plates.

"I'll get it."

Lucas was waiting this time when she came down.

"Who?" he said.

"Nope!" she crowed, and took a few more plates before running back up.

Lucas was onstage next, so he couldn't ask her again.

Cassandra was on a total high by the end of the night. John kept teasing her, asking if she'd been at the cider, and Ethan just shook his head at her.

She didn't tell Riley she'd talked to Lucas. "Wasn't this fun?" she said. "We get to do the whole thing again tomorrow!"

"You're just happy because guys flirted with you all night."

That did help. She poked Riley's arm. "They flirted with you too."

"Not like with you."

"You'll get another chance tomorrow!"

❧

The whole school day Cassandra looked forward to the festival again. She tried not to feel bad that Grayson didn't say hi to her, or look at her, or poke her. So it was over. It could be over. It needed to be over.

There was John, and she'd see him tonight.

She helped set up the table settings for the Festival, then went into the kitchen to make sure the first course was ready to go. She hadn't been down here before dinner the previous night, and she hadn't seen the fake wild pig with an apple in its mouth and everything, decked out on the table. She crouched in front of it, poking the whiskers on the rubbery nose.

"Tell me you're not kissing the boar."

She jumped back and turned to see Lucas there. "No. Not kissing the boar."

"I'm going to find out," he said, stepping into the kitchen area. "I'm a pretty good detective."

Crapola, it wouldn't take much. There weren't a lot of girls she talked to. Still, she flashed a confident smile. "Good luck!" Then she hurried away before he asked her anything else.

"You're back," Ethan said, spotting her as she grabbed mugs for the cider. "You're my favorite wench."

She paused and gave him a closer look. "Don't you have a girlfriend, Ethan?"

"Yeah, but she's not a wench."

I'd be your wench if you broke up with her, she thought. But she didn't say that. All the eligible guys had girls.

She went down to get the puddings before the last act.

"Hey!" Lucas called after her, and then ran down the steps.

Uh-oh. "Yes?" She turned to face him.

"I figured it out." He had a smug expression on his face. "I saw you talking to a girl in my French class, so I asked her if she knew you. She said yes. She's the one, isn't she?"

"Who?" Cassandra said, playing dumb.

"I think her name is Riley."

CHAPTER TWENTY-FOUR

Consequences

Cassandra raised her brows. "Good job, detective." Crapola. Why hadn't she lied?

Riley was furious with Cassandra when she told her. She barely spoke to her the rest of the night, even though Cassandra followed along and pleaded with her.

"Isn't it better he knows? Now if you like each other, you can work something out!"

"He doesn't like me!" she fumed.

"But he knows your name! Isn't that a good thing?"

"It doesn't make him like me!"

She was still mad when Mrs. Isabel dropped Cassandra off at home.

Saturday was the last day of the festival, and Cassandra knew she would miss all the attention she got from the boys.

"Hey, it's you again," Lucas said when she came downstairs to collect the dinner plates.

"My favorite wench," Ethan said.

"I think she might be mine too."

Cassandra smiled at both of them and turned to Lucas. "Are you going to talk to Riley?"

"Should I?"

"It might make her happy. And you got me in trouble. You have to make up for that."

"Sure. I can do that."

Cassandra had ridden with her mom instead of Riley. She watched for her friend to arrive, but when she did, Riley wouldn't look at Cassandra. Cassandra left her alone, hoping Lucas would follow through and make Riley be nice again.

Janice came to the kitchen area between acts and found Cassandra. "Are you guys having fun?" she asked.

"Oh, this is a blast," Cassandra said. "And I love listening to the music. You guys sing so well." She said it with a sincere smile, pushing down the constant jealousy. She spotted Lucas then, moving in Riley's direction, and caught her breath. "He's going to talk to her!"

Janice followed her gaze. "Who, Lucas?"

"Yes. Riley has such a crush on him."

Janice rolled her eyes. "Every girl does. But he's such a jerk."

Cassandra turned back to her. "Really?"

"Yeah, he's so full of himself. He's always mean to me because I'm just a sophomore. I can't wait till he graduates."

Cassandra furrowed her brow. He had seemed so nice.

"I'm sure he'll be nice to Riley," Janice added. "She doesn't have to hang around him much."

"What?" Lucas said, so loud Cassandra could hear him from where she was. "You put the spoon on the wrong side of the table? Who does that?"

Riley just laughed and laughed, and Cassandra relaxed. He'd made her evening, at least.

Riley came to her side as soon as he walked away, her eyes dreamy. "I'm not mad at you anymore. He's so wonderful." She sighed happily.

Cassandra poked her side. "Just trying to help you out."

⟆⟋⟊⟍⟋⟎

Grayson and Cassandra weren't talking to each other, and it was killing her.

No more "hi"s or pokes in the hallway. No more eye contact across the room. No secret meetings by benches or in parking lots.

It was like she had ceased to be anything to Grayson.

She caught his eye midway through the week when she headed to first hour, but he turned away, his eyes hooded, his gaze uninterested. Like he didn't even like her.

"You look like you're about to cry," Mia said when Cassandra sat down in front of her in Spanish class.

"No, I'm not." She blinked rapidly.

"Is this about Grayson again?"

"No." Cassandra shook her head. There was no more Grayson. She wouldn't say his name again. She opened to the back page of her notebook and scribbled a poem, her feelings bleeding from her pen to the paper.

I have only one thing to say to you:
I hate you.
Day after day.
I have to live with the pain
I've tried to hide it.
I've tried to cope.
But when your eyes are only half-lit
Every time you see me.
The fire burns within me.
The anger consumes me.
And I hate you.
Who do you think you are?
Walk into my life
And steal my heart.
Then you forget me.
I've served my purpose.
What is the reason for your being here?
Why must I face you day after day?
I am nothing.
My heart is a hole.
Love and hate
Are one emotion.
And how I hate you!

    It was an angry poem, full of exaggerated emotions, feelings she would never share with anyone. But how could Grayson go from telling her not to give up hope on them, to not speaking to her at all? It hurt so bad she could barely breathe.

She walked with John from lunch to choir, trying so hard to feel a connection to him. He touched her arm and played with her hair, and she knew he felt something for her.

She'd toyed with him, led him on, when her heart was an empty vacuum.

"Hi, Cassie," Amity said, stopping her as Cassandra and John neared the choir room. "Are you going to call me?"

Cassandra looked at her and blinked. "If you want me to."

John laughed.

"Yeah, call me tonight. It would be great to talk."

"Sure." Whatever. What did friendship even mean, anyway? Grayson was willing to throw theirs away without a second thought.

How could he forget her so easily?

She was in a bad spot.

⟡

Cassandra forgot to call Amity, and Amity didn't mention it again. Instead, Cassandra spent the next week finishing up homework assignments before Christmas break and working on the Christmas cards she had made for her friends. She penciled their names out in calligraphy and then colored it in with special pens and wrote an individual message to each person.

She almost didn't make one for Grayson.

She had carefully written his name out weeks ago and pondered what to say to him. Now she wasn't even sure she'd give him one.

She went to church with Farrah on Wednesday, and they ate cheesecake with the boys while decorating cookies for different families from church.

"You've got to cheer up," Farrah said.

"I don't know how."

"What's the matter with Cassandra?" Tyler asked.

"She's just sad." Farrah gave him a deliberate glare. "Sometimes guys are jerks."

Jason popped a cookie in his mouth and laughed. "Guys are always jerks."

"But you've got us," Riley said. "Who needs a guy?"

"Yeah." Beckham joined the conversation. "Who needs a guy?"

Cassandra laughed and shook her head. "You guys are the best."

She sat down that evening with the card in front of her and tried to think of something to say. Nothing mushy. Nothing romantic. Nothing that Charlotte could get mad about. So she wrote out, "You know you're a great guy. I wish you the best in all you do. May God bless you and keep you in his hand."

She left out the part about how she loved him and missed him and wished she could be with him. He didn't need to hear it.

Then she focused on the ten-page research project on nuclear energy due on Friday.

Cassandra took her pile of Christmas cards with her to hand out in school. They still had one more day before break, but some people would be gone already, and she didn't want to miss anyone. It was freeing to watch the cards disappear as she gave them to each recipient, but her anxiety was back, the trepidation suffocating her lungs as she approached the biology room.

Grayson wasn't in there. Taking a careful breath, she handed a card to Ashlee, one to Emmett, Andrew, and Aiden. She tucked Grayson's under her binder, not sure if he would come. Not sure if she should give it to him even if he did.

But then he did, walking in with Katie and talking about snow shoes. He glanced at her and looked away as they went to their chairs.

Crapola, that had not been encouraging.

She turned around to his table, forcing the smile to stay on her face, and put the card in front of him.

"What's this?" he asked, staring at it.

"A Christmas card. I gave one to all my friends."

"Thanks. Did you do this or use a stencil?"

"I did it. I do calligraphy." She was self-taught, using a kit her mom had given her for Christmas the year before.

"Cool."

She turned back around, knowing that was the end of the conversation.

The class fell silent as Mr. Reems handed out their final exam. Cassandra finished hers up and put her pencil away, ready to leave.

"Wait for me, Cassie," Ashlee said. "I have to talk to Mr. Reems about something."

"Okay." Cassandra waited by the wall, but Ashlee had to stand in line, because Andrew also wanted to talk to Mr. Reems. Grayson stood behind Ashlee, waiting his turn.

She studied her nails to avoid studying Grayson. But when she looked up, he was watching her.

She met his gaze, almost fearfully, and he winked at her. Then he smiled, a half sort of smile.

Her heart lurched, and she was glad Ashlee finished so they could leave the room.

"The card was beautiful! How did you learn calligraphy?" Ashlee exclaimed.

"I taught myself."

Charlotte was in the hallway, waiting for Grayson, but Cassandra didn't look at her. She continued next to Ashlee as if there were nothing else going on.

She handed out more cards at lunch, then evaded John when he wanted to walk her to choir. She couldn't pretend to like him today.

Mia saved her by asking Cassandra to go with her to the bathroom before fifth hour. They both fixed their hair and added more mascara to their eyelashes, then stepped into the hall to continue to choir.

"I think you're battling depression, Cassandra," Mia said. "It seems like you have a lot of highs and lows but nothing in between. Those are classic symptoms."

Cassandra gave her an amused look. She didn't need Mia to tell her that; she already knew she was struggling with it. "Thank you, Doctor Mia."

A hand dropped on her shoulder, giving it a squeeze. Heat radiated down her arm, a warmth that spread from her shoulder to the rest of her body. Cassandra turned, and her heart stopped when she saw Grayson behind her.

"Thanks for the card," he said. His eyes peered directly into hers, and again she felt like he was trying to communicate something to her.

"You're welcome," she said, grateful she didn't stutter. *What's happening, Grayson?* she wanted to say. *What happened to us?*

He squeezed her shoulder again, then let his hand slide away and continued down the hall.

Cassandra stared after him. "Did you see? He talked to me. Did you see it, Mia?"

Mia burst out laughing. "Yes. It really happened."

Cassandra wanted so much more. But that would have to satisfy her.

CHAPTER TWENTY-FIVE

Bleeding Pearls

Cassandra woke up early Friday morning to finish her research paper on nuclear energy. She only had three pages to go. She fired up the computer in the basement office and glanced at the clock. A little after three.

Her mind flashed back to Grayson, and the touch of his hand on her shoulder before choir. She hadn't seen him the rest of the day, but that had been enough. Just a reminder that she meant something to him. Or at least, that she had.

The computer flicked to life, and she opened the online drive where she kept her school documents. She searched for the one she'd started two days ago but didn't find it right away. Had she moved it? She did a quick search, slowly beginning to panic as it still didn't show up.

Maybe she'd renamed it. She looked for any documents created in the last two days.

Nothing.

How could it just disappear?

She searched for ten more minutes before accepting it was gone. The first seven pages were gone.

Cassandra cried. She cried and yelled at the computer while she pulled out her handwritten notes and began the arduous effort of typing it up again.

She managed to get it done around 5:40 a.m., with Mr. Jones yelling at her that they needed to leave. She was bleary eyed and exhausted when they left for the Bible study class, but at least her paper was done.

Farrah gave her an odd look when Cassandra came into the classroom after her dad dropped her off, but she didn't say anything. She continued to look at her strangely after class.

"Want to ride with me, Cassie?" Farrah asked, stepping up beside her and wrapping her scarf around her neck.

"I thought you were coming with me," Riley said.

Farrah took a deep breath and blurted out, "I need to talk to you about something."

Riley looked put out, but Cassandra nodded. "Okay."

"What is it?" Cassandra asked when they were in Farrah's car.

Farrah took a long time replying. "I'll tell you when we get to school."

That got Cassandra worried. She turned up the radio and sang along, trying not to be concerned by whatever it was Farrah had to say. But that little bird of anxiety began to bat around her chest like a ticking bomb, making her stomach churn.

They parked the car in the student lot, and Farrah sat in silence. Finally, she swiveled in her seat and faced Cassandra.

"I wasn't even sure I was going to tell you."

"What is it, Farrah?" Cassandra couldn't bear the suspense.

Farrah opened the glove compartment and pulled out a small white box. She held it in her hands, staring at it.

Cassandra looked at it also, not sure what it meant. "Farrah?"

Farrah didn't look up. "I opened it. I know what it is. And I don't think you should accept it."

Cassandra furrowed her brow, her heart rate increasing. "Accept what?"

"I didn't want to give it to you," she continued. "But it's not my place to unaccept. That's yours. But I think you should."

It finally dawned on Cassandra what Farrah was saying. She snatched the box from Farrah's hand. "It's from Grayson," she breathed.

"He asked me to give it to you."

Cassandra opened the lid, pulse thumping in her neck.

Two tiny pearl earrings stared back at her. She touched them, her fingers trembling, feeling an electric connection to him just from the touch.

"Cassandra, it's an apology. He said to tell you he's sorry."

"What did he say, exactly?" Cassandra whispered.

"He asked me to give these to you. That he's sorry for how things turned out. That's it."

Grayson and Cassandra would never be together. That was what this meant. They couldn't even be friends.

But it didn't mean he didn't still have feelings for her.

She closed the lid on the box and held it to her chest, bowing her head as the tears freed themselves and coursed down her cheeks.

"Be discreet, Cassandra. You can't tell anyone who gave them to you."

"I won't." She dried her eyes, treasuring his gift. She unzipped her backpack and put the box inside. "Tell him I got them. Tell him thank you. And I love them."

"Them or him?"

She loved him. There was no doubt. "You can't tell him I love him."

Farrah turned the car off and sighed. "I knew you wouldn't turn them down. Let's go in. Get through the last day of this semester."

⤜◦❀◦⤛

Just like at midterms, it was another relaxed school day with a long lunch break. Cassandra turned in her history paper and went to P.E. with Farrah.

"Did you see Grayson?" Cassandra asked as they did their calisthenics.

"I did."

"And?"

"He was talking to Charlotte. But he came over to me when he saw me and I told him I gave them to you. I told him what you said."

Cassandra smiled, even though her heart was full of bleeding holes. "It's over, then." There was almost something peaceful about it.

Ms. Lynn came out of the office with a box of trophies. "You girls have worked hard all semester to increase your muscle tone and lower your fat percentage! I took your measurements last week, and I've got trophies for those who accomplished the most!"

They fell silent, waiting for Ms. Lynn to make her announcements.

"For the most weight lost: Mariah Hampton!"

Cassandra clapped tepidly along with the rest of the class.

"For the most increase in muscle tone: Addy Lewis!"

Again, she clapped.

"For the most body fat lost: Cassandra Jones!"

"Go Cassie," Farrah said.

"Really?" Cassandra stepped down the bleachers and took the trophy. She read the plaque on the front. She'd lost three whole percentage points. Without trying.

"That's what exercise will do for you," Ms. Lynn said.

"Thanks." She rejoined Farrah and let her see the trophy. "Huh. Maybe I'll have to keep running."

"Yeah, right." Farrah laughed. "You hate running!"

"What are you doing for lunch?" Cassandra asked. "Can you take me and Riley somewhere?"

Farrah made a face. "I'm sorry, I can't. My mom needs me to come home."

166

"No worries." Cassandra shrugged. Finding someone else to take her was part of the adventure.

Cassandra found Riley after P.E., and they went to the parking lot. They scanned the lot for their friends. More people could drive now than a few weeks ago, but it still looked like most students had already left.

"There's Tyler," Cassandra said, pointing. "We can go with him and Jason."

"No way," Riley said. "It will be awful."

"There's like no one left." Cassandra grabbed her arm and hauled her over to Tyler and Jason. "Can we ride to lunch with you guys?"

"If you don't mind Tyler's horrible braking," Jason said.

"I am not a horrible braker," Tyler growled.

"We don't mind." Cassandra opened the back door to the van and pulled Riley inside.

It turned out, Tyler was a horrible braker. First they drove to the Reeves' house, where Tyler finished up an assignment due for his final after lunch. Every time he braked, the car jerked forward, yanking the girls against the seat belts.

"Slow down," Jason said.

"I'm doing just fine."

They arrived without incident, and Cassandra stopped in the living room to admire their cat with the furry toes.

"Look at your cat!" She glanced at Tyler. "Can I talk to it?"

Tyler rolled his eyes. "Cassie, you can talk to the wall, for all I care."

"Hurry up with your homework, I'm hungry!" Jason shouted from the kitchen.

Riley crouched next to Cassandra and the cat. "What did Farrah want to talk about?"

Cassandra hesitated.

"Is it private?"

She shook her head. "I want to tell you, but you can't react crazy."

Riley searched her face. "You seem okay with whatever it is."

She gave a weak smile. "I am. I really am."

"Then just tell me."

Cassandra pulled her backpack over and took the small box out of the pocket. She handed it to Riley and watched her open it and examine the earrings.

"Who gave these to you?" Riley asked.

"Grayson."

Riley gasped. "Grayson gave these to you? What does it mean?"

"It means its over." She swallowed past the lump in her throat and put the earrings away with a long sigh. "It means whatever was going on between us is done. That's what it means."

"I finished!" Tyler shouted. "We can go to Braum's now!"

Cassandra shouldered her backpack. "Let's go to lunch."

She had no idea Tyler and Jason could be so goofy.

The four of them sat down in a booth at the fast food joint to wait for their food, and then they stared at Cassandra's veggie burger when it arrived.

"Something's wrong with your meat," Tyler said.

"It's got green things in it," Jason said.

"I wouldn't touch that if I were you," Tyler said.

Cassandra laughed at them. "It's a veggie burger."

"Whatever," Tyler said. "Looks like it came out of the wrong end of the cow."

"Ew!" Riley said.

"Gross, guys!" Cassandra said. Ignoring their stares, she picked up the burger and took a huge bite.

"Does it taste like poop too?" Tyler asked.

Cassandra choked on her bite, coughed, and spit it all over Tyler and Jason.

"That was sick," Jason said, and Cassandra hid behind a napkin, her shoulders shaking as she laughed.

"We're gonna need more napkins," Tyler said, using his to wipe his face. Riley sat in the corner, laughing so hard no sound came out of her.

"More napkins for Cassie." Jason threw one at her, missed, and hit her cup of water. It tipped over, flooding the trays and table with ice and water.

"Effective," Tyler said, "if you were trying to clean the table."

"I think whenever Cassandra's done eating her poop burger, we can go," Jason said dryly. Or not so much.

She couldn't eat, she was laughing too hard.

Twenty minutes later, after they'd cleaned up her messes, they headed back for the school.

"Jason, look!" Tyler cried as he pulled into the turning bay. "A blue beamer!"

He pointed out the window, or tried to. Instead, he hit Jason's face hard enough for Jason's head to bang into the window.

Riley and Cassandra both gasped, and she waited to see if Jason would explode.

"Sorry, Jason," Tyler said, instantly contrite. "I suck."

For a moment Jason didn't say anything, and then he shrugged. "Cool beamer."

Cassandra relaxed. She couldn't wipe the grin from her face. The two brothers had been just what she needed to lighten her mood.

"Thanks for taking us," Cassandra said, giving them big smiles as they walked back into the school together. "I had so much fun. I really needed that today."

"Anytime, Cassie," Tyler said. "We're like family anyway."

She mock-saluted them and followed Riley into the A-wing.

"Oh, Cassie!" Cara came down the hallway. "I'm so glad I found you. I have a present for you."

"You do?" Cassandra looked at her in surprise as she rummaged through her purse.

"Yep." She handed Cassandra a pack of gum and planted a big kiss on her cheek. "Because you're always stuck with me."

Cassandra hugged her. "Love you, Cara."

"You too, Cassie."

"I don't have an exam for you guys," Mr. Cullen said when they came into the choir room. "So you can just hang out or leave, whatever."

Cassandra dropped her backpack and shrugged. "We have to wait for the buses to get here at three."

"So hang out," John said, waving from the chairs. He and Miles and a few other people were on the stands.

Riley stood in the entry, looking at the photos of those in the elite choir. Mr. Cullen joined her.

"Who are you studying?"

"Lucas," Cassandra said, joining them.

"Lucas. You like Lucas, Riley?"

Her face turned red. "He's nice."

Mr. Cullen let out a feminine sigh. "Oh, Lucas. I love your face when you're singing. The way your mouth moves. Lucas, I love you."

Riley got even redder, but all the kids laughed.

Cassandra pulled her P.E. trophy out of her backpack and set it on the risers. "I won the award for the most body fat lost in P.E."

John tilted his head. "So what is your body fat now?"

Cassandra shrugged. "I don't know, but it's less than it used to be."

Mr. Cullen frowned. "You haven't lost any weight, have you?"

"No. It's not like that. It's fat percentage, not pounds."

"Okay. Because there's not any weight on you to lose."

Cassandra waved off his concerns. "I'm good there." This year, anyway.

The kids made small talk and bantered back and forth for awhile. Cassandra snuck another peek at her pearl earrings before closing the box and putting them away.

"It's probably time to go to the buses," Riley said, glancing at the clock.

It was ten to three. Cassandra gathered up her things. "Yeah, probably."

"Have a great break!" Mr. Cullen said.

The weather had turned wet and nippy, and Cassandra cuddled up next to Riley as they hurried across campus to the bus lot. She ducked her head against the wind and shivered.

"Where are the buses?" Riley asked, drawing to a stop.

Cassandra looked up. The buses that usually crowded the gravel lot were gone.

CHAPTER TWENTY-SIX

Surprise Ride

"The buses left already?" Cassandra cried.

"Maybe they never even came today!" Riley said.

"How will we get home?" Cassandra whirled around and spotted Ciera, a friend from choir, just getting into her car.

"Ciera!"

She flagged her down, and Ciera drove over to them.

"Can you give us a ride to Walker?" Cassandra asked. "We've got to catch the bus at the elementary school." The high school buses drove to the elementary school first, then let students meet up with the younger kids and take the most appropriate bus home. If they hurried, Cassandra might not have to explain to her mother what had happened.

"Let's go, then," Ciera said, unlocking her car door.

They battled traffic toward the elementary school, and Cassandra crossed her mental fingers that they would get there before the buses left. Then Ciera got stuck behind a red light, and she groaned.

"This light is red forever. We might not make it."

Even as she spoke, several buses made the left turn from Walker onto Sunset Road.

"There's my bus," Riley said, pointing.

Cassandra spotted her own behind it, and her heart sank.

"What do you want me to do now?" Ciera asked, pulling up to the elementary school.

"Just leave us here," Cassandra said. "I'll call my mom." She had no choice now but to tell her what happened.

"Okay. See you after break!" Ciera waved and drove off.

Cassandra tried to open the school lobby, but the door was already locked. Shivering, she pulled her phone out of her pocket.

"Hello, Cassie?" Mrs. Jones said.

"Mom," Cassandra said, wrapping her jacket up around her ears. "We missed the bus. Can you come get me and Riley?"

"Cassandra!" Her mom did not sound happy. "I can't come get you right now. You need to go to someone's house and wait for me."

"Okay." Cassandra hung up and scanned through her contacts. Andrea lived close by, but she didn't want to go there. Leigh Ann lived around here, didn't she? Cassandra called her number.

"Hello?" Leigh Ann said.

"Leigh Ann, it's Cassandra. Riley and I are stuck at Walker until my mom can come get us. Can we walk over?"

"Sure, of course. My mom's not home. Come on over."

"Great! What's your address?"

Leigh Ann gave it to her, and Cassandra hung up. "Let's go to Leigh Ann's."

"How far is it?" Riley asked, huddling close to Cassandra as a nippy wind blew in.

"Not far. Just a few blocks."

But by the time they'd walked two, it felt like a mile.

"I can't stand this cold much longer," Cassandra growled.

"Maybe someone will pick us up."

A van pulled over to the curb just as Riley spoke, and the passenger door opened. Amity poked her head out.

"Cassie? Need a ride somewhere?"

Cassandra could have kissed her. "Yes! Take us to Leigh Ann's house."

Amity looked them over as they climbed in. "Why are you stuck out here?"

"We missed the bus," Cassandra said with a sigh.

"You never did call me. You said you would."

She'd completely forgotten. "I'm sorry."

"That's all right." Amity unbuckled from the front and climbed into the back next to them. She lowered her voice. "I keep hearing that you have a secret relationship with Hampshire. I just wanted to know if it's true."

Was this really a rumor? Cassandra exchanged a look with Riley. "Why are you asking?"

Amity looked meek and devilishly curious at the same time. "He has a girlfriend. It wouldn't be like you to do that."

Cassandra let out a short laugh. What did Amity know? She'd cheated on Josh when she'd started going out with Ben, but she'd never told that to any of them. "Apparently I have a thing for guys with girlfriends."

Riley busted up laughing, and Amity's mouth dropped open.

"So it's true?" she gasped.

"Show her what he gave you," Riley said.

Cassandra turned and glared at her. That was a secret. Word could not get out. Grayson would kill her if Charlotte found out somehow.

Amity's eyes were wide, and she was practically drooling. "What did he give you?"

"It's not that big a deal," Riley said, sensing her mistake.

Cassandra faced Amity again. "There's nothing between us. Nothing at all. We're not even friends."

Amity smirked. "But we've all seen you guys. In the halls, behind the school."

Apparently they hadn't been as discrete as Cassandra thought. "Well, you won't anymore," she said softly.

Amity knew enough about relationships to pick up on the tone in Cassandra's voice. Her gaze softened, and her mouth turned down. "I'm sorry."

Cassandra nodded and looked away so she wouldn't cry again. She played with her jacket sleeve.

"We're here," Mrs. Stafford said cheerfully. "Have been for a few minutes, but I thought I'd let you guys finish talking."

"Thank you." Cassandra opened the door. "Thanks for the ride."

Amity followed her and Riley to the door. Leigh Ann answered when Riley knocked, and Riley hurried inside.

"What did he give you, Cassie?"

Cassandra turned back to Amity. "Something special. Something private. Something I can't share with anyone because if his girlfriend finds out, it won't be special anymore. It will be something he regrets."

"Maybe they'll break up," Amity said, sounding hopeful.

"They won't. I know that. So does he."

Amity gave her a hug. "Merry Christmas, Cassie."

"You too, Amity."

Cassandra followed Riley into the house to wait for her mom to arrive.

EPISODE 4: HARD TRUTHS

CHAPTER TWENTY-SEVEN

All Is Calm

The days leading up to Christmas passed in a hurry. Farrah threw a Christmas party, and Cassandra went, along with Tyler, Jason, Beckham, and Riley.

Farrah and Riley cornered Cassandra in Farrah's bedroom before the movie started.

"You're wearing the earrings," Farrah said.

Cassandra caught sight of her reflection. "Yes. I won't wear them at school, but I'm wearing them now."

"Maybe he wants to see you in them," Riley said.

"I don't think he cares to see me at all," she replied.

Farrah squeezed her hand. "How are you doing?"

Cassandra shook her head. She didn't bother to tell them about the constant ache in her chest. "Well enough. He was never mine. I haven't lost anything except dreams and fantasies."

Farrah's look turned mischievous. "What kind of fantasies?"

"Farrah!" Cassandra laughed and hit her.

Then they went out and watched the movie with the boys in Farrah's living room.

Maureen called Cassandra halfway through it.

"Maureen, hi!" Cassandra said, moving to the kitchen to talk to her.

"Hi, Cassie. We just wondered if you were coming."

"Coming?" She furrowed her brow. "Coming to what?"

"Our annual Christmas party. Everyone's here but you."

A strange longing sprouted in Cassandra's chest. She remembered these Christmas parties with fondness. "I didn't even know."

"No one told you?"

"You know that, Maureen. I didn't draw anyone's name and no one drew mine."

There was a pause, then Maureen said, "That doesn't matter. You can still come."

Cassandra smiled, appreciating the sentiment. "I'm at another party right now. But merry Christmas. I love you guys."

"Merry Christmas to you, too, Cassie. You can come later tonight if you want."

"Thanks, Maureen." Cassandra hung up, her heart warmed by the invite. She wouldn't go. But that group of girls would always be a part of who she had been. And thus, they helped make her who she was now.

⁊ﾟ☆ﾟ⁊

"We're going caroling in an hour!" Mrs. Jones called through the house on Christmas Eve. "Dress warm, it's chilly out!"

Cassandra picked out a black sweater and black jeans. She put them on and admired her thin frame in the reflection of the mirror. She looked good, and she looked happy. She *felt* happy. Not having to worry about seeing Grayson around every corner, or seeing Grayson and Charlotte, or seeing Grayson and wondering if he would talk to her—it made a world of difference on her emotional well-being.

She hoped she could hold on to this when school started back up in January.

The family hopped into the car with the plates of goodies Mrs. Jones had made, singing songs and laughing and generally feeling excited about the holiday season. The Loflands weren't home, so they left the tray of goodies just inside the front door. The Mechams were delighted to see them and invited them in, feeding them cookies before sending them on their way. They visited the Reeves and the McKennas and several other families from church.

"I think we need some dinner, dear," Mrs. Jones said to Mr. Jones once everyone was buckled into the car again.

"All right." He turned down the main street with most of the restaurants in town, but the lights were turning off.

"I think they're closing," Cassandra said, observing the signs as they went dark.

"It's only eight-thirty!" Mrs. Jones said.

"Denny's will be open," Emily joked, reminding them of a popular Christmas movie.

"Shogun's light is on." Mr. Jones pulled the car into the Japanese restaurant, which had a full parking lot. "They don't celebrate Christmas."

Apparently everyone who didn't want to cook on Christmas Eve or eat at Denny's was at Shogun. It took the waitress a moment to find them a table, and they were seated with people they didn't know. But the chef was hilarious, entertaining them with jokes and food tricks while he tossed their shrimp through the air, and Cassandra laughed so hard she had to hold on to Emily's arm to keep from falling over. He winked at Cassandra as he put two extra pieces of chicken on her plate. By the time she finished eating, she had to unbutton the top of her jeans.

She got sleepy when they piled back into the car. Mrs. Jones turned on the radio, and Cassandra leaned her head against Emily's shoulder, closing her eyes as the soft lullaby of "Silent Night" filled the van.

Silent night, holy night.

All is calm, all is bright.

She smiled, letting the peaceful melody wash over her.

The van bumped over the gravel drive and pulled to a stop in front of the brick house.

"All right, guys," Mrs. Jones said, turning around to look at the kids. "Tonight you get two presents. But you have to wait until we've read the Christmas story."

"Two!" Annette squawked. "Usually we only get one!"

"Pajamas and . . ." Scott said.

"Shh!" Cassandra swatted at him. "We're not supposed to know we get pajamas!"

"No pajamas for you!" Mr. Jones said.

Giggling and in good spirits, the four children piled out of the car. Everyone quieted down in the house once the scriptures came out, and Cassandra sat close to her mom, content and happy as her father read the Christmas story from the book of Luke. Happy happy. The warm fuzzies enveloped her like a soft blanket, wiping away her fears and frustrations and heartaches of the past few months. She wanted to cry again, but this time with joy.

Mrs. Jones handed everyone two presents. "Go ahead. Open them."

Cassandra ripped open the small one first and smiled at the matching pajamas. Then she ripped open the big one. "A whole box of Jelly Bellies!" She opened the box of gourmet jelly beans. Over forty flavors of jelly beans sat in tiny little compartments inside the rectangular box. "I love these!" She reached over to hug her mom, but the box slipped from her lap, and all the jelly beans spilled on the carpet.

"Good luck putting those back in the right spot," Mr. Jones said.

Cassandra picked up the yellow ones. "I'm pretty sure these are popcorn . . ." She plopped one in her mouth. "Nope! That was lemon!"

She had no chance of guessing the correct flavors. So she shrugged and grabbed up a handful. "I guess I'll have to enjoy mixing the flavors!"

CHAPTER TWENTY-EIGHT

Gamer

The days after Christmas passed in a haze of sleeping and eating and reading. Feeling sluggish after nearly a week of no activity, Cassandra welcomed the opportunity to head to a church dance before the New Year.

But this one was in Tahlequah. Cassandra had never been to the chapel out there, and the city itself summoned up memories of her ex-boyfriend Josh. Ugh. She shifted through the clothes in her closet and called Riley for moral support.

"I'm not going," Riley said when Cassandra explained her plan.

"What do you mean, you're not going to the dance tonight?" Cassandra demanded. "I can't go without you!"

"I can't," Riley said, sighing. "I have to go to Tulsa with my mom."

Cassandra put down the shirt in her hands. "Well, then I'm not going, either!"

"Come on, Cassandra. You'll have a fun time."

"With who?" Cassandra demanded. "The dance is in Oklahoma. Farrah's not going and neither are you."

"But Tyler and Jason are. And Sue, and Michelle . . ."

"Those aren't my friends," Cassandra growled. "What do I do if Josh is there?"

"Rebound?" Riley suggested, and Cassandra would have hit her if she weren't on the phone.

Mrs. Jones came into the room. "We've got to go, Cassandra, or we'll miss the carpool!"

"I don't want to go," Cassandra said.

"See you later, Cassie," Riley said, hanging up.

"Honey." Mrs. Jones came over. "Is this about Grayson?"

"No." Cassandra shook her head. "This is about my friends not being there and me not wanting to make new ones."

"Just go, honey. If it's boring, it's just one night. But if you have an amazing time, you'll be so glad."

"Fine." Cassandra sighed and picked up her shirt again. "Let me change."

"Do it fast! We have to go!"

Cassandra changed quickly into a ruffly turquoise top to go with her tight jeans, then she and Emily piled into the van. Mrs. Jones wouldn't let Cassandra drive because her mom planned on speeding to get there on time. Even with the speeding, they were late, and the cars were loading up in the parking lot.

"We still have room in this one," one of the youth leaders called.

Cassandra followed Emily inside the car, and she groaned when she saw all the twelve-year-olds. Normally only fourteen years and up were allowed at dances, but since this was a smaller activity, the younger kids had been allowed to come. "Really?" she muttered under her breath. Just her luck that she got to ride with them.

"It's your fault we're late," Emily said, though she didn't seem to mind. These kids were closer to her age, and they called out to her, telling Emily to sit with them.

The drive to Tahlequah was more than an hour, and the whole way there, all Cassandra could think was she shouldn't be there. She felt more and more out of place, listening to the younger kids tell stories and act immature. It was too late to go home, but she wished she could.

She didn't recognize anyone when they walked into the gym, set up as a dance floor. Only a few congregations were there, so not a lot of people to choose from, either. Not that she felt like dancing. Cassandra sat down on the floor against the wall, ready to spend the rest of the evening watching everyone.

A boy sat down cross-legged beside her. "Hi."

She gave him a once-over and then went for a second look. His dark-blond hair was just long enough to spike, and he had sharp blue eyes, almost teal, behind wire-framed glasses, high cheekbones, and a strong jaw.

He was *hot.*

So why was he talking to her?

Oh, right. There weren't many other people to choose from. "Hi," she said.

He bumped her knee with his. "You look sad."

She shrugged. "I just don't want to be here."

"It's more than that. You look like you're getting over someone."

Now she laughed. "That's probably true for half the people in here."

"Yeah, probably. So are you?"

"I don't even know you. Why would I tell you anything?"

He faked a hurt look. "Of course you know me. I'm Elijah."

At first she just stared blankly at him, and then the memory fell. Elijah. Josh's friend. The one who Amity kissed last year when she was supposed to be head-over-heels in love with Matt.

"Ha, yeah, I remember," she said shortly, turning her head away.

"I see the memory hasn't made you fonder of me."

She rolled her eyes. "You kissed my friend after only knowing her a few hours."

"Hey, now. Give me a chance to defend myself here. I never liked her that seriously. She was really aggressive. But it's hard to say no when a girl wants to kiss you."

"Well, maybe you should try."

Elijah laughed. "I can see why Josh liked you so much."

She faced him again. "And why is that?"

He tapped her knee with his fist, and she pulled away. "You've got spirit. I don't think you're easily swayed."

Cassandra turned back to watching the dance.

"And you're way heartbroken. Bitter. Hurt. I can see it in your eyes."

Could he? Was all that visible? She thought she hid it so well. But now she felt her eyes burning and knew she was close to tears.

"Hey, we're not all bad."

"He wasn't bad." She didn't mean to speak the words, but they crept out anyway.

"What happened?"

"Bad timing." That was what it boiled down to.

"Bad timing. Gets us all sometimes. What went wrong?"

The words tumbled out without her permission, as if they thought his interest was a reason to make a run for it. "We met right after he promised to go on a date with another girl. We liked each other, but he wouldn't break his date with her, and after the date, she somehow thought she was his girlfriend. He thought it wouldn't last long and we'd have a chance, but instead, they got more serious. And he told me, right before Christmas, that it's not going to happen. We're not going to happen." She said it without emotion, yet she could feel the tears making tracks down her face. "I don't even know why I'm telling you this."

"It happens a lot. Girls I hardly know pour their hearts out to me."

He looked so sincere, so sympathetic, that she had to smile. "It's your eyes."

He stood up and extended a hand. "Dance?"

She took his hand and let him pull her up. "All right."

He whisked her out onto the dance floor. Tyler and Sue danced by, and Tyler said, "You have to dance with me, Cassie!" They drifted a part, but when they passed each other again, he said, "And Jason wants a dance also!"

Beckham danced by with Emily. "Cassie, you were supposed to ride in our car. We saved a seat for you."

Elijah pulled her close and whispered, "You've got them all liking you, don't you? You're nothing but a flirt." His tone was teasing, playful, and Cassandra laughed.

A little light turned on her heart. A little bit of healing.

She danced with James next, a long-time friend of hers from Oklahoma. And then Elijah was back, claiming her as his.

"I'll be at the next dance," he said. "And I'm only going to dance with you."

"Yeah, right." Cassandra rolled her eyes. "Amity will be there. I know exactly who you'll be dancing with."

"No," he protested. "You don't know at all. I don't care about her. It's you I remember. I was always interested in you."

She snorted. "We didn't even meet until last year when you hooked up with Amity."

"We didn't hook up," he said defensively. "And just because you don't remember me doesn't meant I don't remember you. The first time I saw you, you were in a flowery blue dress that fit you loosely and flowed when you walked, and I thought, short, pretty, and young."

Cassandra did own such a dress, of course, though she could not remember if and which dances she'd worn it to. "If you prefer me over Amity now, why didn't you then?"

"I did. But you were dating my best friend. Josh."

"Oh!" Cassandra gasped. His story had a little more credibility now. Was it possible he'd always liked her more? The thought was flattering.

They finished the dance and returned to the side, but Elijah kept his hand on her waist. Then he slid it around her shoulders, pulling her in close. His nearness awakened something in her, the promise that her heart could find someone else.

Tyler asked her to dance next, and a few other guys from Tahlequah after him, but Elijah took her away for almost every other song. Another girl asked him to dance on the last song, so he left with her. Cassandra didn't mind. She danced with Jason, who made her laugh the whole time.

The last song ended, and Jason released Cassandra. He'd barely stepped away when James and Elijah joined her, framing her on either side as a kid was called on to say a prayer of closing.

"Now you're part of the cool crowd," Elijah whispered.

As soon as the prayer ended, he turned to her and said, "I'm so sorry I didn't get to dance the last song with you."

"It's all right," Cassandra said. "That's not a big deal."

"I feel bad because I really wanted to." He took her hand and squeezed it. "I'm really glad we were both here tonight."

Cassandra smiled. She could hardly believe this was the same Elijah Amity had been so crazy about. And he liked her!

Brother Reeves came along, gathering up all the kids. "We're headed to Braum's! We've got to go!"

Cassandra hated to leave. She wanted to hold onto this moment of happiness, this moment of feeling wanted. She turned to say bye to Elijah, but he wasn't in sight.

Had he already left? She exhaled in disappointment, then followed Brother Reeves out to the car.

She couldn't help feeling sad at the fast-food joint as they piled into the booths with their ice cream. It had been fun, finding someone interested in her. The moment had ended much too soon.

A side door opened to the restaurant, letting in a whoosh of cold December air, and then suddenly Elijah was there, squishing into the booth beside Cassandra.

"Elijah!" she said, surprised.

"Cassie." He grinned. "Did you think I'd let you get away without saying goodbye?"

Everyone was looking at them, her peers from church and Brother Reeves. She offered her ice cream to Elijah. "Want some?"

"I'm good." He slid his hand under the table and squeezed her thigh.

She looked at him, a shiver running down her spine. She didn't dare glance around to see if anyone else had noticed. Then he put both hands on the table and tapped her arm, giving her a smile. She turned back to her ice cream, keeping her eyes on it as she spooned it into her mouth. Elijah didn't say anything either, and they both listened to the conversations around them. But she was ultra aware of his leg up against hers.

"Well, I do have to go," he said, getting up.

Cassandra stood too. "I'll see you later?"

"At the next dance." He gave her a tight hug before leaving.

"Did he get your number?" Brother Reeves asked.

Cassandra shook her head before sitting down. "I'll see him again."

And if Amity dared dance with him even once, Cassandra would kill them both.

⟡

Cassandra woke up Saturday morning with a restless, joyful energy in her heart instead of the heavy sadness she usually felt every day. It took her a moment to remember why.

Elijah!

She stretched her hands over her head and wiggled her toes, remembering his piercing blue eyes and warm hands. How was it possible he actually liked her? When was the next dance? A month from now?

She couldn't wait that long. She needed to talk to him, to reassure herself these feelings were real. Who might have his phone number? Josh would for sure, but Cassandra was not asking him for it.

She was still pondering how to get the number as she put away her clean laundry after lunch.

That was when Andrea called.

Was it possible Andrea had his number?

"Andrea!" she said, genuinely excited to talk to a friend. "How are you?"

"I'm great!" Andrea said, and in the background, Maureen's voice shouted, "We're great!," followed by a farting noise and several giggling voices.

Cassandra rolled her eyes. Typical. "Who all is over there?"

"Me!" Maureen shouted.

"And me!" came Amity's voice.

So much for asking Andrea for Elijah's phone number. "Am I on speaker phone?"

"Yes," Andrea said. "What are you doing today? Why don't you come over?"

Cassandra considered it for a heartbeat. She liked these girls, individually. When they were all together, though, something changed, and they weren't so nice. "I'd love to do something with you, but I can't today."

"When's the next dance?" Maureen asked. "We haven't been to one in a while."

Coincidence? "You haven't missed much." Cassandra picked up her laundry, unable to focus on two things at once. "They've mostly been boring. There was a fun one last night."

"There was a dance last night?" Amity said, coming closer to the phone. "You should've told us!"

"Sorry," Cassandra said, though she wasn't sorry at all. If they been there, Elijah might not have noticed her. And last night had been her little miracle, a special gift to help heal her heart. Not even Farrah or Riley had been around to distract him from Cassandra.

"Was Elijah there?" Amity asked, and Cassandra's heart skipped a beat.

"Why?" she asked, slightly guarded. "You haven't seen him in almost a year, have you? Do you still like him?"

"Well, he's only the hottest guy I've ever seen," Amity said, and the other girls chortled.

Cassandra did not find this funny in the least. "Yeah, he was there."

"Did he ask about me?"

Amity sounded so hopeful, but Cassandra knew it meant nothing. Amity was always in love with at least five guys at a time. Elijah hadn't actually asked about Amity, though Cassandra had brought her up. She decided not to mention the technicality. "Yeah, you were mentioned."

"What did he say?" she squealed.

That he never liked you and he thinks you're aggressive. Cassandra would never say those words. "He plans to be at the next dance." She didn't offer anything more than that.

"Let us know when it is, I will definitely be there," Amity said.

Cassandra had no doubt.

⊙〜·⚜·〜⊙

Amity called Cassandra again a few hours later, which surprised her.

"Hi, Cassie," she said.

"Amity," Cassandra greeted. She put away the book she had been reading and leaned against the pillow on her bed. It wasn't like her old friends to call twice in one day. "What's up?"

"Oh, I'm at home now, so I thought I'd call," Amity said breezily as if they still talked every day.

"Well, that was nice of you to think of me," Cassandra said sarcastically.

"We think about you all the time, Cassie," she said, oblivious to the sarcasm.

Cassandra rolled her eyes and waited to see what Amity would say next.

"Um." Amity cleared her throat. "Could I get Elijah's phone number?"

Not that. Anything but that. Cassandra's stomach tightened in displeasure. "I don't have it," she said, glad she could be perfectly honest.

"Oh. Can I get Josh's number, then?"

Cassandra considered lying about this one. If Amity had Elijah's phone number, she could spend the next few weeks weaseling her way back into his heart. She would have Cassandra at a disadvantage.

"Let me see if I can find it." Cassandra flipped through her phone, wishing she had not kept his number. But she kept everything. "Okay, here it is." She fed the numbers to Amity.

"Thanks, Cassie!"

"Amity," Cassandra said, stopping Amity before she hung up.

"Yeah?" Amity said.

Cassandra hesitated, then blurted, "If you get his number, can you give it to me also?"

A pause, and then Amity said, "Sure." Then, as if she couldn't resist, she asked, "Why?"

Cassandra's defenses flared. What did Amity think, that she was the only one who got to talk to guys? "Because he's my friend too. And I'd like to talk to him, if that's all right with you."

"All right," Amity said, and Cassandra instantly knew her response had been too heated.

She should have kept her mouth shut. Now Amity would suspect something was going on.

Amity never did call back.

CHAPTER TWENTY-NINE
Healing Hearts

Riley was back in town in time for the New Year's Eve dance, the one that would go until midnight and serve breakfast to usher in the new year.

This dance was held in Fayetteville at the smaller chapel instead of the one in Rogers, and after the excitement of the last dance, Cassandra considered not going. But the thought that Elijah might be there got her out the door.

She did not bother telling Amity or Andrea about it.

Since the dance went till midnight, it didn't start until nine o'clock. Cassandra and Emily got there late, around nine-thirty. Cassandra did a quick headcount of the people present. James, Andy, and his sister Brooklyn were there. Cassandra put her jacket in a chair and then went and tugged on James's arm.

"Hey, Cassie!" He gave her a hug and then pulled back. "Great to see you here!"

She smiled back. "Is Elijah here?"

James made a contrite face. "I kind of thought this was a secret dance, so I didn't tell him."

Cassandra sighed. Oh well. Some other time. "That's okay. Tell him I said hi."

"I will.

Cassandra looked around to see who else was there, noting several people from the Fayetteville congregation. Belatedly, she realized she could always ask James for Elijah's phone number. But to be honest, she probably would not call him, so she didn't really need it.

But if the Fayetteville kids were here, Zack should be here also. She saw his brother and sister, but not Zack. What a disappointment. There was nobody interesting around.

"Cassie!" Riley came into the gym and waved her arm.

"Thank goodness," Cassandra mumbled, then she ran over to hug her friend.

"Is he here?" Riley asked, peering around her.

"Elijah?" Cassandra shook her head. "No. He didn't come."

"Okay, guys!" Brother White, one of the youth leaders, stood up and clapped his hands, an enthusiastic smile on his face. "Before we start this dance, we're going to play a mixer!"

A groan rose from the kids, Cassandra included. She hated mixers, forced activities where they had to be social with each other when all they wanted to do was dance.

Brother White ignored their grumbles. "Grab a chair. We're going to make a big circle, but place your chair facing out, with the back toward the middle."

"Do we have to do this?" Riley grumbled.

"It sure looks like it," Cassandra said, no more excited than Riley. They both grabbed folding chairs and hauled them into the circle.

The door to the gym opened, and Farrah stepped in.

"Farrah!" Cassandra abandoned her chair and ran over to hug her friend. Riley came also, and the two of them smothered her in affection.

"To think I almost didn't come," Farrah said, smiling at both of them.

"This game is called fruit bowl!" Brother White said, calling their attention back to the circle. "The way it goes is, you pick a fruit for yourself, and that's what you are. You can be a banana, an apple, a grape, or anything else you can think of. When I call out your fruit, you jump up and switch spots with other people."

Lame. Lame lame lame.

"If I call out 'fruit bowl!', everybody has to get up and find a new chair.

"But here's the rub. I will remove one chair every time there's a fruit bowl, and one person will be left without a seat!"

"Are we in second grade again?" Farrah giggled.

Cassandra wrapped an arm around her waist and laughed, resting her head on Farrah's shoulder. She was so happy to see her friends.

"Everyone in your seats!"

Cassandra didn't feel like running around, so she picked her favorite fruit, which she doubted would ever get called: mango.

"Ready? Grapes!"

Several people jumped up and ran, tumbling over each other as they searched out vacant seats.

"Apple!"

She giggled a little, watching people fight over a chair and then run across the circle to get a different one.

"Banana!"

The guy next to her bolted from his seat and ran, jostling her chair as he did.

"Fruit bowl!"

That was everyone! The seat next to her vacated as her neighbor ran into the melee, and Cassandra scooted over one. Then she grinned smugly at her own cleverness. Kids were laughing, fighting over the last chair, and she was pleased because she might not have to move much after all.

"Oranges! Kiwi! Mangoes!"

Cassandra gasped. Crapola! She had not expected Brother White to call her fruit! She had to actually get up and run this time, darting out in front of everyone because there were no empty seats beside her to jump into.

"Fruit bowl!"

As soon as the person next to her shot out of the chair, Cassandra hopped into the seat. She sat and waited for everyone else to get settled.

Suddenly, Tyler Reeves plopped down on top of her.

"Tyler!" she cried, pushing at his shoulders.

"Who's out?" Brother White asked. "I pulled a chair but I don't see anyone standing!"

Tyler wiggled his hips, shoving his body onto the chair beside Cassandra. "It's Cassie! She doesn't have a seat!"

"No, it's Tyler! He stole my chair!"

But by this point, Tyler had managed to shove Cassandra from her chair, and she crashed beside it, still trying to claim ownership.

"You're out, Cassandra!" Brother White said.

She stood up and walked away, fuming, even though everyone else was laughing. Stupid Tyler.

The game ended only a few rounds later. Jason came over and asked Cassandra to dance, and she accepted.

"I'm still totally annoyed at your brother," she said. "I should not have gotten out."

"Well, you kind of didn't have a chair," Jason said, arching an eyebrow.

"Because Tyler shoved me out!"

Jason laughed. "That's funny."

It kind of was. Cassandra managed to get over her annoyance with Tyler, and Jason made her laugh through the rest of the song.

They had just finished their dance when someone touched her arm and said, "Dance, Cassie?"

She turned around to see Zack. A smile spread across her face. "Hey! I didn't think you were coming!"

He put a hand on her waist and took her other hand, then led her out to the dance floor. "I got here late. What did I miss?"

"Fruit bowl." Cassandra giggled.

Both of Zack's eyebrows shot up. "Fruit bowl?"

Cassandra couldn't stop laughing, and she nodded her head. "Be grateful."

They switched partners at the end of the song, and Cassandra forgot she hadn't wanted to come. She danced with several more guys when an unfamiliar song came on. Something about the lyrics caught her attention, and she stopped listening to her partner's conversation. The male singer talked about being fair to the one he was with because she'd been good to him and she deserved it, so he had to let go of the girl he really wanted, never telling her that he loved her.

"Excuse me," Cassandra murmured, releasing her partner and exiting the gym. She went to the bathroom and stopped by the sink, head bowed, taking careful breaths.

Why could she not let a single day go by without being reminded of Grayson?

The door opened behind her, and Farrah came in. "I knew that song would do you in."

"No. No. I'm okay." Cassandra straightened, blinking rapidly.

Farrah came closer and laid her hand on Cassandra's back. "It's okay to cry."

That was all the permission she needed. The sobs erupted out of her, and she buried her face in her hands. The what-if's and what-might-have-been's stabbed at her heart. And above all of it, the chorus of "never, never, never" rang in her ears.

Finally the tears dried up, and she felt more in control. "Thank you. I can handle it now." She took Farrah's hand and squeezed it. She didn't know what heartache Farrah had been through before this year, but she always knew exactly the right thing to say.

She was in between partners when the last song started, and she saw Zack walking by.

"Are you dancing?" she asked him.

"Sure I'll dance. With you."

She cocked her head, a little confused by the response. And he gave a little laugh, as if he suspected there'd been a miscommunication but wasn't sure what.

She smiled and held out her hand. "Let's dance, then."

She might not still have a crazy crush on Zack, but his open, friendly personality and obvious devotion to God always made her feel happier. She leaned her head on his shoulder, as close as she dared get to him, and let some of her heartbreak melt away.

◌⟋ᨒ⟍◌

The first day of a new semester.

Cassandra was terrified. She didn't know what to expect. She had spent the past two weeks compartmentalizing her feelings for Grayson, trying to put him in a box so she didn't hurt every time she thought about him.

She had mostly succeeded. Was seeing him today going to undo all of that?

She had worn the pearl earrings he'd given her during the entire break. They represented to her the only piece of his heart she was allowed to have. She removed them from her earlobes now and put them back in their box. She couldn't wear them to school.

Early morning Bible study class hadn't started back up yet, so for the first time in months, Cassandra had to hurry out the door with her siblings to catch the bus. The frigid temperatures shocked her. She hadn't grabbed a hat or gloves, and she jammed her hands into her jacket pockets, praying the bus would arrive soon.

It did, though it wasn't much warmer inside.

Just a few more months, she told herself. *A few more months and you'll be driving, and then you'll never have to ride the bus again.*

She didn't see Riley or Farrah before class, so she went straight to her locker, greeting Miles and John and a few other people. John poked her side and teased her, trying to flirt, and she smiled back. Why couldn't she just have a crush on him?

Her heart skipped a beat when she walked toward Spanish. She was both parts anxious to see Grayson and dreading seeing him.

And there he was, laughing and talking with Kevin outside his classroom door. Cassandra did not avoid eye contact, but she didn't stare either. She started to go into her classroom just as he looked over and saw her. He gave a fleeting smile, and she bobbed her head in acknowledgment before going inside.

She sat down at her desk and took a careful breath. That had gone all right. She was okay.

She didn't have P.E. anymore. Instead, she had health class second hour. She would miss seeing Farrah, but she bumped into Riley on the way to class.

"I saw Grayson," Riley said.

191

"Me too, and I'm okay, it's okay. We said our goodbyes. I can move on."

"Good. I was really tired of hearing about it."

Riley said it like she was joking, and Cassandra forced a smile. But the comment didn't sit well with her.

She spotted Harper in her health class, and they said hi as Cassandra sat down in a desk in the next row over. Harper talked to another girl the whole time, and Cassandra took out a notebook and paid attention to the teacher. This class would be super easy.

It was the only change in her schedule, since Spanish and choir were both year-round electives. She slowed as she walked toward biology after math class, wishing she could somehow get out of this. The less she saw of Grayson, the easier it would be to forget him.

He wasn't there, and she sat down next to Ashlee and Emmett, hoping he wouldn't come at all.

But he did. He moved into the row behind her and said, "Cassandra."

She closed her eyes as a wave of nostalgia and longing washed over her. Why did he have to say her name like that? No one else spoke with his accent. She turned her head slightly and greeted him. "Grayson." Then she faced forward.

"Cassandra." He said her name again.

She turned around, lifting one eyebrow, not revealing any emotion.

"Do you have any lotion?" He lifted his hands, which were white and riddled with red cracks.

"I do." She dug through her purse and pulled out a small bottle. "What happened to you?"

"Exposure. Christmas in New Hampshire is brutal."

They were talking. A decent, normal conversation. And it felt nice, comfortable. "So you went home for Christmas? Did you see your mom?"

"Yeah, of course. I spent Christmas with her."

"That's great. I'm glad you got to be with her."

She turned back around as Mr. Reems came in and dumped his textbook on the desk.

"Cassandra."

Again. His voice, saying her name. He wouldn't talk to her if he had any idea what that did to her. She looked back at him, and he held out the bottle of lotion. "Thanks. Maybe my hands won't bleed anymore."

She accepted it without a word and put it away, not wanting to dwell on the desires within her, the need to take his hand and rub the lotion into those cracks to see if she could rub away the hurts.

She closed her eyes. Crapola! She thought she had conquered these feelings. How could they come back so strongly? "It's nothing, it's nothing," she whispered to herself. Focus. Focus on school. Forget him. But how could she when he sat behind her for an entire hour?

❦

Mr. Jones let Cassandra drive the stick shift all the way to Bible study the next week. Even with Riley in the car.

Cassandra didn't stall the car. Maybe she was getting the hang of this clutch thing.

When she crossed the railroad track in Johnson, a familiar car turned left in front of her. She recognized the van as Jason and Tyler's. The van pulled into the lane beside her, and Tyler looked out the driver's side window at her. Then he grinned and sped up.

Cassandra grinned, too. She sped up also, the engine revving as she pulled ahead. Then she switched lanes and got in front of him. Tyler gunned his engine behind her, but both of them had to stop at a red light. As soon as it turned green, Cassandra hit the gas, and try as he might, Tyler couldn't get in front. Mr. Jones was yelling at her, telling her to slow down, but Riley was laughing, and Cassandra couldn't stop smiling.

Mr. Jones dropped both of them off, and the two girls were still giggling when they walked in.

Tyler and Jason approached from the other door. Tyler spotted them and mock-saluted.

"Nice driving, Cassie. I'll take you on anytime."

Cassandra and Riley collapsed into laughter, and the incident left her grinning all the way into first hour.

Grayson didn't say anything to her in biology, but she refused to dwell on it. Refused to let it bother her. She was not going to spend the rest of this year with each day revolving around whether or not he spoke to her.

John caught up to her on her way to choir. She heaved an inward sigh, knowing she wouldn't be able to avoid him forever. Besides, she was supposed to have a crush on him. So she smiled playfully and giggled when he tried to take her books away.

"How's your second semester going?" he asked.

"So far it's boring. It's the same thing every day. I know what to expect. I can predict what's going to happen in every class. I'm actually looking forward to getting homework so there's something new."

John shook his head. "You're crazy."

"You wouldn't be the first person to tell me that."

They took their places in the choir room. Amity said hello, though

Cassandra knew she just wanted to maintain ties so she would know about any upcoming dances.

Cassandra didn't ask if Amity had gotten Elijah's phone number. It would look too obvious.

Harper leaned across two chairs. "Cassandra, did you write down the health assignment?"

"Yes." Cassandra opened her book and pulled out her notebook. "It's here."

"Thanks." Harper smiled broadly, her blue eyes sparkling. Then she said, stretching her head around Cassandra, "Hi, Miles."

He looked up from his sheet music. "Hey, Harper," he said, his face brightening.

They spent the rest of class talking to each other over Cassandra. She wondered sardonically if she should offer to switch places, but she didn't.

CHAPTER THIRTY

Kidneys and Stoning

Cold.

Wouldn't winter ever end?

The dark clouds outside and the frigid temperatures echoed the feelings in Cassandra's heart. She sighed as she pulled a sweater on over her shirt. It felt like one step forward, two steps back as she tried to get over Grayson.

All her hopes were pinned on Elijah, the cute boy who had flirted with her in December. She hadn't seen him since, but he'd made her heart feel something besides sadness. The next dance was in a week. She'd see him soon. She hoped to feel that same lightness again.

Mr. Jones was sitting at the kitchen table waiting for Cassandra when she walked into the kitchen. She stopped at the table to tie her shoes and pull on her jacket, then she looked closer at her dad.

"Are you okay?"

His face was pale, and sweat beaded along his brow.

"I think I might be coming down with something. Let's just get you to class so I can come home."

"All right." It wasn't like her dad to be sick, though. He should probably stay in bed, but she knew he was making a sacrifice to get her to her early morning Bible study.

He let her drive the car to the pick-up spot, where they waited for Cassandra's best friend, Riley. Then all of a sudden, Mr. Jones threw open the passenger door and vomited on the road.

"Daddy?" Cassandra asked, alarmed. She opened the glove compartment and searched for anything to help. She came up with a package of wet wipes.

Mr. Jones fell back into his chair, breathing hard. "Cassandra. I need you to drive me to the hospital."

Hot flashes of panic shot up and down her spine, and her eyes pricked with heat. "What's wrong?"

"I don't know, but I really feel terrible. Call Riley and tell her you're not going to class. If you don't know how to get to the hospital, I'll direct you."

"Okay," Cassandra said, trying to stay calm. She fought back tears as she dialed Riley's number. Her hands shook, and she took several deep breaths, waiting for Riley to pick up.

"We're almost there, Cassie," Riley said as soon as she answered. "Sorry we're a little late."

"Riley, I can't take you." Cassandra swallowed hard, not wanting to give away how worried she was. "Something's wrong with my dad. I have to take him to the hospital. We're on our way there now." Her voice caught as she tried not to cry.

"Do you need help? Should we meet you there?" Riley asked, her tone immediately reflecting her concern.

"No, I don't think so. Could you call my mom and tell her? I'm just gonna drive."

"Yes. Call if you need anything."

"Thanks, Riley."

Cassandra hung up. Mr. Jones directed her to the hospital, moaning and groaning every time the car made a turn. She gripped the steering wheel with sweaty palms, trying to obey the speed limit but wanting to plow through every light. Her heart pounded in her throat, and she blinked rapidly to keep the tears at bay. Was her dad having a heart attack?

"It's okay to drive fast right now," he wheezed out.

Cassandra lifted her eyebrows and drove as fast as she dared.

She pulled into the emergency drop off and jerked the car into park, then ran into the hospital. "I need help with my dad!" she shouted as she burst through the doors. "He got really sick in the car."

Hospital personnel immediately rushed to attention, grabbing a wheelchair and following Cassandra out to the car. They loaded Mr. Jones into the wheelchair, and one of the men said to her, "You can park the car in the lower lot over there."

He pointed to a parking lot across the street. Cassandra looked at it, then turned back to him.

"I'm not supposed to drive without an adult," she said. "I don't have my license yet."

"It's just a few meters away. You can do it."

She could do it. She took a careful breath and nodded. He left with her dad and she did as she was told, driving very carefully across the street to the other lot and parking away from any cars. Her breathing came in panicked gasps, and her hands shook. She jumped out of the car and slammed the door behind her, shouldering her purse just as her phone rang.

It was her mom. "Mom!" Cassandra gasped out, answering the phone. Then she immediately burst into tears.

"Cassie, honey, what happened? Riley's dad just called me and said you guys were going to the hospital!"

"I don't know," she sobbed. "Daddy got sick on the drive and asked me to bring him to the hospital. I just dropped him off and parked the car."

"I'm on my way there. Just wait for me. I'll be there in a moment."

"Okay," Cassandra said, trying to take a steadying breath. "I'll see you soon." She hung up the phone and clutched it tightly. Her mom would be here in a moment. Everything would be all right.

Cassandra stepped into the emergency room and went to the front desk. Her heart pattered in her neck, and she clutched her hands to control their shaking.

"Excuse me," she said, swallowing hard to keep from crying. "My dad arrived here a few minutes ago. Can you tell me where to find him?"

"What's his name, hon?" a mustached-man in a green scrub asked.

"Jim Jones."

The man checked a computer screen. "Wait right here for a second, and I'll let you know what's going on."

That wasn't the answer she wanted. Cassandra nodded and clenched her jaw, blinking rapidly. She curled up in a chair and looked out the window, waiting for her mom.

Snowing. Soft white flakes fell from the sky, dotting the green grass, melting on contact with the black asphalt. She watched them, mesmerized, losing herself in the crystalline display.

The automatic doors opened with a whoosh that brought in a sharp burst of frigid air, and then Mrs. Jones stepped through.

"Cassie?"

"Mom!" Cassandra jumped from the chair and ran to her mom, already crying, longing for comfort, for someone to tell her it would be okay.

"Shh." Mrs. Jones rubbed her back. "You did a good job getting your dad here. Come on." She took Cassandra's hand and led her to the counter. Cassandra let her take the lead, falling back into her own worries while Mrs. Jones talked to the man. Then her mom turned to her, patting her hair and smiling.

"It's all right, honey. He has a kidney stone. He's going to be fine."

A kidney stone. Cassandra wilted in relief. That wasn't life threatening. "He seemed so sick . . ."

"It was causing him a lot of pain, and it's not over yet. They can't remove it, so your dad will just have to wait for it to pass."

"But he's okay?"

"He'll be fine, honey."

Cassandra closed her eyes and exhaled, her shoulders relaxing. Then she opened her eyes and looked at her mom. "Do I have to go to school now?"

"It doesn't start for another hour. Just sit tight with me, and then I'll take you."

Cassandra sat down beside her mother and held her hand, for once not minding the parental touch. She watched the snow outside get thicker until she couldn't see the parking lot. It clung to the bushes and tree branches, a deceiving mask of calm.

Mrs. Jones' phone dinged, and she checked it, then smiled. "School's been canceled, Cassie. Looks like you get to go home after this."

"I won't say no to that."

⌒ஓ⚙ஓ⌒

School was out the next day also. Mr. Jones ran around the house like a woman in labor, huffing and puffing and panting. Cassandra watched him in amusement from where she sat on the couch reading and catching up on homework. He was on pain medication, but that was all the doctors could do for him. Now he had to pass the tiny pebble out of his system all on his own.

He finally got it out that evening and went to bed exhausted.

"You guys want to see the stone?" Mrs. Jones asked her family at dinner time, rather giggly.

"No thanks," Cassandra said, disgusted.

"It's his baby," Emily said.

"Ew." Cassandra refused to think about it more.

"Yes," Mrs. Jones said. "All that effort, and all he got was a little rock baby."

They told jokes at Mr. Jones' expense the rest of the evening, but he was asleep and had no idea.

The snow turned to gray slush and lined the streets, giving the city a dirty, dismal appearance instead of the clean, nostalgic one of the day before.

By Wednesday school was back in session. Cassandra dried her shoes on the the rug coming into the building, then went to her locker and removed her books. She stood up to leave when an arm went around her and started tickling her stomach.

Cassandra shrieked in surprise, dropping her backpack and banging against the lockers. Her heart hammered in her chest, and she whirled around around to see John, laughing at her. "Don't touch me!" she cried, shoving him hard. Embarrassment and indignation burned her cheeks.

People in the hall had turned to stare, and she spotted one familiar face—a red-headed girl with dark eyeliner.

Charlotte. And she had just witnessed Cassandra's freak out.

John laughed and went to put an arm around her shoulders, but Cassandra ducked away.

"You can't just grab me that way," she said.

"Sorry," he said, but he didn't look sorry. "I was just happy to see you."

"Then say hi!" Cassandra picked her backpack up, not caring if she'd been rude. She hurried to Spanish class, wishing the whole incident hadn't happened.

She steeled herself before going into biology, taking a deep breath and preparing to feel nothing. Before she could go in, though, a foot nudged hers, and she turned in the doorway to see Grayson, giving her that familiar half-smile.

"I won't touch you," he said, a hint of teasing in his tone. "I hear you're jumpy."

She laughed, but she heard the quiver in it and hoped he didn't. *Not with you*, she wanted to say. "With some people, I guess."

It was close enough to what she really wanted to say, and his smile softened. He knew it too. He touched her foot again, and then slipped past her into the classroom.

She blinked several times and then went into the room behind him, her throat aching. She concentrated on Mr. Reems' lesson, then bolted from the room as fast as she could. She ignored John in choir, hoping he got the message that she was annoyed with him.

Maybe he would quit talking to her altogether.

"We're going to try our hand at writing poetry today," Ms. Ragland said in English class. "This can be any kind of poem. Structured, rhyming, free style. I want you to pull your emotions and feelings into words and put them on paper."

Cassandra gripped her pen and stared at her notebook paper. Poetry didn't work that way for her. She couldn't just make it come. But when she felt something in her heart, she had to get it out.

"This is required by the end of class," Ms. Ragland added. "So get started."

No poetic lines or fancy imagery tickled Cassandra's mind. Briefly she recalled that in junior high she'd written an entire book and even had a publisher interested in it. Somehow, with all the school assignments and Grayson in her life, writing silly books about fictional characters didn't feel important.

But poetry did.

She wrote down a few lines about love and friendship and then crossed them out. She tried again, taking a different route, describing the beauty of the snow and then the harshness of the slush. Still felt empty.

For half an hour she tried, but nothing heartfelt came to her. Finally she wrote down a rhyming poem using the dirtied snow as an analogy for relationships.

But even that didn't feel right.

"All right, let's go ahead and pass your poems up."

Cassandra wrote her name across the top of the paper, unsatisfied with the results.

Then suddenly one came to her, almost fully formed in her head. Cassandra crumpled up the first paper and leaned forward, composing as fast as she could on a new sheet of paper.

Memories

The despair that has hung
Over my head all day
Was simply and clearly dispelled
By one word from you.
Not even a word.
Rather a nudge.
As you let me know you were there.
And you knew I was next to you.
Some might think it's absurd.
Others that I'm obsessed.
Maybe I am. but it's because

Of what used to be.
The sweet memories of happier times.
When you were my best friend.
And I fell in love.
Now it's all over.
And it often depresses me.
Thank you for that touch.
To let me know
That you remember too.

She sat up and passed her paper to the front, euphoria igniting her veins and clearing her head. Poetry helped her compartmentalize her feelings, to put her experiences in a box where she could look at them and deal with them with a more level head. She didn't feel sad anymore from talking to Grayson. Instead, she was grateful for his small gesture that let her know he still remembered her.

CHAPTER THIRTY-ONE

Sold Out

Saturday night of the dance finally arrived.

This was the one Cassandra had been anxiously waiting for since December. Elijah would be there.

So would Amity and Andrea.

Cassandra's heart two-stepped a nervous beat, and she needed to tell someone what was about to go down. So she called Andrea.

"Hey, Cassie!" Andrea said. "Did you want to ride with us to the dance?"

"No," Cassandra said, feeling queasy. "I have to tell you something. But can you promise not to tell Amity?" Even as she spoke, she knew what she was asking. It was highly possible Andrea would not be able to keep this to herself.

"Yes," Andrea said, her tone decidedly more intrigued. "What is it?"

"So." Cassandra took a deep breath and blurted it out. "At the last dance, Elijah and I kind of got together."

There was a pause, followed by, "You did?" There was no mistaking the shock in Andrea's voice.

"Yes." Cassandra swallowed hard. "So tonight at the dance, Amity might think it's a little weird. That he's spending all his time with me."

Andrea didn't say anything for a moment, and then she said, "Okay. What do you want me to do?"

Would she really be that supportive? Cassandra felt a wave of gratitude. "Don't tell her. Let her figure it out on her own. But don't be mad at me. And tell me anything you find out."

"All right. We'll see you tonight." Andrea sounded rather excited, and Cassandra could just imagine herself preparing for the show-down.

Cassandra made her mom drop her off at the dance fifteen minutes early. She wanted to be there, just in case Elijah also came early. And she wanted to make sure she beat Andrea and Amity. Her nerves battered against her throat and twisted her stomach in knots, and she worried she'd throw up.

People began trickling in, but Cassandra only looked for one person. Farrah arrived and waved, and James from Tahlequah walked in.

James was here already. Didn't they—?

A hand touched her elbow, and Cassandra swiveled around.

"Elijah," she breathed, the panic floating out of her.

"Looking for me?" He put his arms around her, hugging her to him.

Cassandra laughed, giddy with relief. She took a step back and examined him. He'd shown up in a tuxedo, of all things, and he looked gorgeous. "I'm so glad you're here."

The DJ started the music, and Elijah held out his hand. "May I?"

She placed her hand in his. "Absolutely."

He led her onto the dance floor and they swayed to the music, but now Cassandra was watching the door for someone else: Amity. What would Elijah do when she showed up?

The song ended, and Elijah led her over to the food table. Cassandra rarely ate at these functions, but she accepted a cup of punch from him.

She nearly spilled it when Andrea and Amity walked into the gym.

Andrea scanned the room and spotted Cassandra. She headed her way.

"Hi, Cassie," she said.

"Hi," Cassandra said. She put the cup down and motioned to Elijah, suddenly too timid to touch him. "This is Elijah."

"Cool!" Andrea said, giving him a wide smile.

Amity joined them then. She stood with her body tilted so her hip stuck out, the tight shirt squeezing her boobs together and emphasizing her cleavage. "Hi, Elijah," she said, twirling a strand of hair with her finger, a vapid smile on her face.

The jealousy ripped through Cassandra like a knife. A physical, hot sensation of slicing right through her chest.

"I got my hair cut," Amity said. "Don't ya like it?"

"I do," Elijah said. "It looks really nice."

The next song had started, and Cassandra grabbed his hand. "Come on, let's dance."

Elijah let her pull him onto the floor, though she sensed a reluctance in his movement. His hands didn't tighten around her, but held her loosely. And his eyes didn't focus on her the way they had before, but instead seemed to be distracted by something else. Or someone.

That was when Cassandra's chest started to hurt. She took short breaths, trying hard to keep the smile on her face and not reveal her inner turmoil.

He did not notice. They finished dancing without saying hardly a word, and he gave her hand a squeeze, finally meeting her eyes long enough for a smile.

"Thanks for the dance, Cassie." He walked away without a second glance.

Cassandra blinked and swiveled, following Elijah with her eyes.

Farrah stepped over to her. "Who's the cutie?"

"Elijah," Cassandra said. Elijah had reached Amity now. He took her hand and pulled her onto the dance floor.

"Are you guys together? Because if you're not, I might move in on that."

"Yes, we're together!" Cassandra snapped. She moved to the wall and pretended like she didn't care.

Beckham asked her to dance, and Cassandra accepted. See? Everyone danced. It didn't mean anything, that Elijah was dancing with Amity.

He didn't even let go of her hand on the next song, but kept dancing with her.

Cassandra headed back to the wall and watched as Elijah and Amity danced a third song together. Andrea came over and stood beside her.

"How's it going?" Andrea asked.

"He's dancing with Amity again. He promised me he wouldn't do that." Cassandra could not take her eyes off them.

"But if he says he likes you, there's nothing to worry about, right?"

Cassandra gave a short laugh, an unhappy sound from the back of her throat. "I don't trust him. And I don't trust her."

"If it makes you feel any better, Amity was jealous watching the two of you dance."

Cassandra turned toward her. "What did she say?" It did make her feel better, that she could make Amity jealous.

"She was just watching you guys, and she said, 'Cassie wouldn't do that to me.' And I said, 'Do what?' And she said, 'Cassie wouldn't take Elijah from me. I think they're going out. Do you think they're going out?' And I said, 'No, I don't think so.'"

Cassandra felt a tiny bit better at Andrea's words. But judging from the way Elijah held Amity in his arms, her victory would be short-lived.

She had been foolish to think someone like Elijah could help heal her heart. He was nothing but a player.

She danced with Tyler, and then some kid from Rogers she didn't know, and then she turned around and realized Elijah was taking her hands, pulling her onto the dance floor.

"Sorry," he said. "I just wanted to make sure other people got the chance to dance with me. Didn't want to deprive anyone."

He winked at her, but once again there was this suggestion that she was who he preferred. Cassandra melted into his words like sugar under hot water.

"That's okay," she said, very diplomatically. "I don't expect you to spend all your time with me." Although she would sure like it if he did.

They danced two more songs together, and Cassandra chided herself for being so insecure.

Amity stepped over when they finished dancing, her smile more timid this time. "Elijah, want to dance?" Then Amity glanced at Cassandra. "If that's okay with you."

It wasn't. But Cassandra didn't have to say anything, because Elijah said, "I'm sorry, I promised Farrah I would dance with her. But we'll dance again, I promise."

He gave Amity a smile, and Cassandra tried to see if there was anything deeper to it than the one he gave everyone else.

"Okay." Amity nodded. "I'll catch you another time." She gave Cassandra a fleeting smile and then walked away.

Cassandra watched Elijah and Farrah dancing, feeling like Farrah got closer than she needed to. The song ended, and Cassandra waited for Elijah to return to her. Amity stepped over and touched his arm. They spoke together for a moment, then turned around and walked out of the gym.

It took all of Cassandra's willpower not to follow them. Where were they going, and what were they doing? She knew her old friend too well not to be suspicious.

James came over and asked her to dance, and Cassandra tried to distract herself on the dance floor with him.

"Did you see Elijah come back in?"

He gave her a sympathetic look. "No."

They finished the song, and there was still no sign of those two. Cassandra bypassed all the other dancers and went to Andrea's side.

"Where are Amity and Elijah, and what are they doing?"

Andrea shook her head. "I don't know. She said she wanted to talk to him."

Something snapped inside. She felt as if she'd been stretched to a breaking point and then let go. Heat washed over her face. "Yeah, right," she snarled. Then she turned and stormed out of the gym, heading for the bathroom.

She stepped inside and gripped the edge of the counter, smashing her fingers against the yellowing Formica countertop. Then she screamed and hit the paper towel dispenser as hard as she could, not even caring when her palm throbbed. What a stupid, stupid idiot she was.

The door opened and heels clicked across the tile, and then Andrea stood there. She stepped over and wrapped her arms around Cassandra, but Cassandra pulled away.

"Cassie? Are you okay?"

"No!" Cassandra shouted. She dug her fingers into her scalp and pulled at her hair. "I am so sick of her taking every guy I like!" She picked up the bottle of soap on the counter and threw it across the bathroom, where the plastic bottle bounced harmlessly off the wall.

Andrea stared at her, wide-eyed. "I don't think I've ever seen you angry."

"Well, it happens!" Cassandra said. "I am sick of being walked on. I am sick of being treated like a dispensable commodity. I am sick of being second best!" She balled her fists, wanting so badly to punch something. Or someone.

The door opened again, and Farrah came in. "They're back, and they're both looking for you."

Oh great. Just what Cassandra wanted.

Before she could say another word, the door opened yet again.

This time, Amity came in.

CHAPTER THIRTY-TWO
Dance Break Down

Cassandra took one look at Amity and turned around and walked into a stall. She closed the door and locked it.

"Cassie, it's not what you think," Amity said.

Silence reigned. Cassandra didn't say a word.

Amity cleared her throat. "Could we be alone for a moment?"

Andrea and Farrah murmured noises of acquiescence, and Cassandra wanted to call out to them not to leave. She did not want to be alone with Amity. She heard the swish of the door, followed by their footsteps exiting the bathroom.

Amity spoke again. "Cassie, will you come out so we can talk? He was just being my counselor, I swear."

Cassandra kept quiet. The fury still coursed through her, accompanied by tendrils of hurt, betrayal, and disappointment. But not surprise. She had expected this, really.

"Really, Cassie. Let's talk. Unlock the door. Please?" Amity waited another moment, then she said, "If you don't come out, I'm going to crawl under that stall and we'll talk in there."

Amity would. Cassandra did not want to be in this little tiny stall, shoulder to shoulder, with her. So she undid the latch and came out.

Amity stood at the double sinks and offered Cassandra a smile. Cassandra did not return it. She moved her eyes away and focused on her reflection. She turned on the water and splashed her face, wishing she didn't look so splotchy.

"We were just talking, Cassie. I promise, that's all it was."

Cassandra didn't want to talk with Amity. She pressed her lips together. Things would be better if Amity would just stay away.

"Cassie," Amity said. "Please. Don't be angry with me."

Cassandra crossed her arms over her chest and faced Amity. She stayed a good three feet away from her, keeping her distance. But she didn't say anything.

Amity sighed. "I really like Elijah."

"Yeah, him and ten other guys," Cassandra bit out.

Amity paused, a hurt look crossing her face. "I never knew you thought that about me."

"Because I was too nice to say anything," Cassandra snapped, aware she was lashing out irrationally but unable to stop herself. "But you weren't. I knew exactly what you thought of me."

"I don't think you have any idea," Amity said. "You were our friend, and you dumped us like an ex-boyfriend. Like you had no more use for us."

Years of hurts and frustrations rolled into Cassandra's throat and boiled over. "I was the butt of every joke. I was the one you turned to when you needed a shoulder to cry on but was quickly forgotten when you needed a friend. I was left out and hurt and everyone's last pick over and over and over again. I was the ignored one, the forgotten one, the invisible one. And if I liked a guy, he was as good as free game, because no guy would ever choose me over you. And you made sure of that."

Amity hadn't moved. She swallowed and blinked, and Cassandra thought she might cry. "Did you even like me, Cassie?"

Oh crapola. Cassandra burst into tears again. She buried her face in her hands. "I loved you! All I wanted was for you to love me too!"

Amity's hand touched her shoulder, but Cassandra jerked away. She took several deep breaths and then lifted her face.

"I'm sorry for what I said. I would never intentionally hurt you," Cassandra said.

Amity nodded. "Elijah will hurt you, Cassie. And he won't care. Just like he didn't with me."

"I know," Cassandra said softly. "But it doesn't seem to change how I feel."

The bathroom door opened again, and Farrah came in. Amity looked like she wanted to say more, then she shook her head. "We'll talk later."

"Amity," Cassandra said as she moved toward the door, "thank you for caring enough to come talk to me."

Amity gave a wistful smile, and then she left.

"How are you?" Farrah asked.

"I suck," Cassandra breathed out. She grabbed another paper towel and wiped her face. "Elijah is a player, and I fell for him."

"They are the worst to fall for," Farrah said. "But also the easiest. They know exactly what to say and how to act."

"I've caused enough drama." Cassandra tossed the paper towel into the trash can. "Let's go out there."

They walked out of the bathroom and turned the corner, bumping into Amity and Elijah as they approached the bathroom. Elijah slipped his arm around Cassandra.

"Come on, let's dance. And talk."

He squeezed her side, and Cassandra hated how much she enjoyed his touch.

He led her onto the dance floor and repeated Amity's story. "She just wanted to talk. She told me how she felt and asked for advice on a few things."

Cassandra kept quiet, listening to him speak. Had they concocted this story together? How much was true? "Can I say something?"

"Sure."

She met his eyes, again marveling at the blue color. "We're not dating. I don't own you and you don't have to tell me what you're doing. But I wish you would have told me you were leaving."

His eyes widened, and Cassandra could just imagine him planning his escape from the dance. So she quickly added, "If you had, I wouldn't have spazzed out when you left. What did you think I would think when I saw you leave with her?"

"You saw us leave?"

Cassandra nodded. "And I watched during every song for you to come back."

Elijah hugged her close. "I'm sorry."

Cassandra couldn't seem to stop talking. She spoke into his shoulder, but she knew he could hear her from the way he held her.

"I don't even know how you feel for me. But I feel good about you. I'm jealous of Amity, and insecure, because I know you two had something going on." He rubbed her back, and she kept going. "I'm stupid for liking you. I'm going to get hurt."

He pulled away. "I'm not going to hurt you."

She knew like she knew the sky was blue that wasn't true. But her heart didn't hurt so bad now, so she just smiled and nodded. "And I'm sorry. You probably think I'm a possessive freak."

He touched her cheek. "You're just fine."

The next song started, and Elijah pulled her back into his arms. They were dancing close, too close, but no chaperones came over and separated them. Cassandra closed her eyes and clung to him, enjoying the feel of his body next to hers, never wanting to let go.

The dance ended and the lights came on. Elijah took a step back.

"Let me get your phone number."

"Me too," Cassandra said. She felt light enough to fly. "I probably won't ever call you, but it will be nice to have."

He laughed. "Same here. We're heading to Braum's after this. You coming?"

"I don't know. It depends on my dad."

"Okay, well, maybe we'll see you."

Elijah left first, with James. Amity and Andrea left shortly thereafter, offering Cassandra a wave before getting in the car.

Mr. Jones didn't show up until ten o'clock, when nearly everyone was already gone.

"We've got to go to Braum's," Cassandra said, hopping into the car.

"You're driving," he said, getting out.

She ground her teeth together and hurried to the other side, not wanting to drive right now. She just wanted to be there. She turned on the radio and pulled the car onto the interstate.

Mr. Jones changed the radio station, putting on an oldies one.

"Hey!" Cassandra exclaimed. "I'm driving, I choose!"

"It's my car. I have the final say."

Cassandra fumed and pressed harder on the gas. He changed the rules whenever he felt like it.

"Slow down, Cassandra!"

She did, but only because they were coming to a red light. She glanced over to Braum's on her right and breathed a sigh of relief when she saw all the cars in the parking lot. They were still there.

She went inside with her dad behind her and smiled when she saw James and Elijah. Elijah was sitting next to Farrah, and Cassandra shoved down the jealous monster biting at her throat.

"Cassie, you made it!" Elijah said. He scooted closer to Farrah, making a tiny spot next to him. "Come sit."

Cassandra squished in beside them. "I'm only here for a moment. Daddy, this is James and Elijah. They're from Tahlequah."

"Hello, gentleman," Mr. Jones said, shaking their hands.

Elijah leaned close to Cassandra's ear and whispered, "You looked really good tonight."

"Not as good as you," she returned, wishing she could turn her face to see him.

"We better get going, Cassie," Mr. Jones said.

She hated to leave, especially since Farrah and Elijah would still be there. But at least Amity and Andrea hadn't come to Braum's. "Okay."

She stood up and gave Elijah one last look, not sure what else to say. He wasn't hers. They weren't dating. But she felt like they were.

"I'll see you soon," he said, smiling.

She smiled back, clinging to that hope, and followed her dad back to the car.

⁂

Riley shook her head.

"Wow. I miss a few dances, and it's like the whole world exploded."

Cassandra laughed.

They stood in the bathroom before school, putting on makeup after their early church class. Cassandra knew Grayson was here; she'd seen him in the hallway before class. But she didn't want to talk to him, didn't want to think about him. Right now she wanted to focus on her budding feelings for Elijah.

"So when do I get to meet Elijah?" Riley asked.

"I don't know. The next dance, I guess."

"Do you think Amity will come?"

"I don't think so. I don't think they'll come again."

Both girls were silent at that, and Cassandra felt a tiny sadness for the closing of that season of her life. Then she smiled. "At least thinking about Elijah gets me through my days without worrying about a certain other person."

"There's always that," Riley agreed.

The day passed uneventfully. She saw Grayson in fourth hour, but she didn't make eye contact, and he didn't say anything to her. In spite of her best efforts, a dull ache throbbed in her heart. They were nothing to each other now.

She pulled out her poetry notebook and scribbled while Mr. Reems lectured.

The Drifters

I've watched you as you drift away.
Knowing we're moving farther apart.
I reach for your hand.
But you don't see me.
I cry out. but you hold it in.
Fighting some internal war.

Your path is far from mine
And I can't bridge the gap.
Now it's too much to bear.
I know I can't stay.
You barely glance up
As I start to move back.
I know you're not strong.
But this time, you're on your own.
Take a deep breath, and I will too.
You made your choice, it's time to go on.
Slowly, painfully, I withdraw my hand.
And without any tears, I look up.
This time, I walk away.
I'm letting you go.
Softly I whisper as you disappear.
I love you. I always will."

Cassandra said hello to Amity in choir, and Amity returned the greeting, but nothing else was said. The drama might have passed, but there were no warm fuzzies between them.

Mrs. Ragland praised Cassandra's poem in English class. "It was from the heart and full of imagery we can all relate to," she said as she handed their poetry back to them.

Cassandra accepted hers and filed it into the spiral binder she kept with her always, the one with her poetry in it.

"Cassie," Nicole said from the back of the classroom when Mrs. Ragland set them to their own devices with a reading assignment. "Come sit by me."

Cassandra picked up her books and scooted back.

"Can I read your poem?" Nicole asked.

"Sure." Cassandra pulled out the binder. "It's this one."

Nicole read through it, then turned the page and read the next one.

Cassandra did her assignment while watching Nicole, who continued reading the other poems.

"These are so sad," Nicole said softly. "Obviously he had a great impact on your life."

Cassandra didn't respond.

"Who are they about?"

Cassandra shook her head. "I can't say."

"Why?"

Cassandra fingered the plastic on the notebook. "It's over now and doesn't matter."

"So why can't you tell me?"

Cassandra hesitated. What would Nicole think of her? "It was a relationship that could never be. He was involved with someone else."

"He had a girlfriend," Nicole said in understanding.

"Yes."

Nicole looked back at the poems, reading another one. "Life is hard, isn't it?"

Cassandra had to look away. She hated the familiar sting of tears in her eyes. "Yes."

CHAPTER THIRTY-THREE
Hard Truths

"Cassie." Cara called out to her when she got on the bus. "I want to talk to you."

Cassandra moved over to Cara's seat, feeling a knot of worry. Certainly Cara had heard about the dance by now. What had Amity and Andrea said?

"Everyone's changed since starting high school, haven't they?" Cara said.

"I suppose so," Cassandra said. "We've all really grown up since last year."

"Doing different things, with different people."

"I miss Janice," Cassandra said. "We were so close. But she has her new friends, and they're all older."

"You changed," Cara said.

Cassandra looked at her, a twist of discomfort in her chest.

"Over the summer," Cara continued. "You matured all of the sudden. I think we weren't a strong enough support system for you. Suddenly it was like you were stronger than all of us, and we were holding you back."

Cassandra wasn't sure how to respond. In some ways, she'd thought the same thing when summer ended. But she hadn't really verbalized it that way. "Is it a bad thing?"

"No. A good thing for you. But sad for us, that we couldn't be there for you. That we couldn't keep being your friends."

She wanted to tell Cara they were still her friends. But being friendly and being friends were different things. She took Cara's hand and squeezed it, certain her angry words to Amity had reached everyone's ears by now.

"But you guys helped me so much when I needed it. I was lonely. And you were my friends. I'll always be grateful for that."

⸙

"So I guess there's a test in math today." Miles stopped by Cassandra's locker before school while she was talking with Riley.

She frowned at him. They weren't in the same class, but they had the same math teacher. "She didn't say anything about a test yesterday."

"Yeah, it was a surprise to me too. But I just walked past the classroom, and she has it written on the chalkboard."

Cassandra's eyes went wide, and she tried not to panic. She was not prepared for a math test today. "When do you have her?"

"First period. I just saw you and thought I'd let you know, since you have her third hour."

"Oh crapola," Cassandra said. "Thanks for the heads up."

She spent Spanish class going over her notes and trying to figure out what equations would be on her geometry test. Math was by far her worst subject, and she could feel herself getting sick with worry.

She walked out of class and headed toward health, and then she heard Miles calling her name.

"Cassie!"

She turned around to see him hurrying toward her.

"Did you do your review sheet?" he asked.

She had completely forgotten there even was one. "Maybe like three problems."

"The teacher collects it for a grade."

Now she knew she was going to panic. The review sheet was due on top of a test? "There's no way I can get it done! Even if I work on it during health class!"

Miles glanced around, then stuck his hand out. "Give it to me."

She pulled it out of her binder and handed it to him, looking at him with worried eyes.

He stuck it in his own binder. "I'll give it back to you after class."

"Miles!" She grabbed his arm. "I have to get it done!"

"I'll do it for you, Cassie. I'll find you after this hour."

He would actually do that for her? Cassandra wanted to grab his face and kiss him. "Your handwriting doesn't look like mine."

"I can have very girly handwriting." He winked and then went the other way with her review sheet.

Cassandra took several deep breaths and tried to calm her panicked heart all through health class. It would be okay, no matter what the outcome. That was what she had to tell herself, over and over and over again.

Just as he promised, Miles found her after second hour.

"Here's your review sheet."

He handed it to her, and she examined all the answers he'd carefully written. She threw her arms around his neck and hugged him. "I owe you one."

"Glad I could help." He stayed to talk to Harper, and Cassandra hurried on to math class.

The teacher did not collect the review sheets, but she did walk around and make sure they were done. Cassandra exhaled in relief that Miles had done that for her. The test itself was brutal, but Cassandra had expected nothing less.

And now for the worst part of the day. Biology.

She stalled, hating that she had to go to this class. She stopped and got a drink at the water fountain, then stepped to the side and knelt to tie her shoe.

A foot appeared in front of her face, pretending to kick her. She looked up, startled, and saw Grayson at the end of the foot.

"Careful," he said, his mouth lifting into an easy smile.

"Grayson," she said, unable to keep the surprise from her voice. "Um, hi?"

"Hi."

He stood there in the hallway and waited while she finished tying her shoe, and then he walked beside her. She was painfully aware of him, though he didn't say a word. When they neared the classroom, he said, "Cassandra, what did you get on your test yesterday?"

Cassandra. The way he said it. She could listen to him say her name over and over and over again. "Oh, I don't remember. It wasn't that great. You?"

"Nearly perfect score."

"Really? How did you do that?"

His lip curled into a half smile. "I memorized the text."

Her heart melted at the allusion to their personal joke. She raised her hand out, so close to grabbing him, and then pulled back. She pushed past him and entered the classroom before him, not saying another word.

Why didn't Elijah call? He would do a lot to take her mind off Grayson. She checked her phone and pulled up his name, about to send him a text. But then she chickened out. If he wanted to talk, he'd contact her. She closed her phone and put it away with a sigh. Pulling out a sheet of paper, she penned another poem.

I Believe

I believe
That everything that needs to be said
Has already been said.
I wish I could say
I no longer need you.
I no longer want you.
But I know it's not true.
And down deep
I think you do too.
Sometimes the look in your eyes
Says you know how much I love you.
I wonder if you do.
Sometimes your look is mocking me.
Laughing and cutting me down
And that hurts.
But worse are the times when it's not
When your eyes say that somewhere. somehow.
You are loving me too.
The scary part is. how quickly you change.
How deeply you wound.
Yet still. whenever you become
Who you used to be.
Instantly. without doubt. I accept you.

Somehow. I still believe in you.

In me

In us.

"You're such a foolish girl, Cassandra Jones," she whispered to herself, reading back over the poem. "When will you let him go?"

When, indeed?

CHAPTER THIRTY-FOUR

No Joke

"Farrah!" Cassandra waved at her friend Sunday morning, but Farrah just looked at her and then went the other way.

Cassandra frowned and said to Riley, "Was that my imagination, or is she avoiding me?"

"It seemed like something's definitely up," Riley said.

Farrah didn't say anything to Cassandra the rest of the day at church, and her paranoia increased Monday morning when Farrah left church class before Cassandra could say hi.

"I should have called her yesterday when I thought something was wrong," Cassandra said to Riley in the bathroom while they put on their makeup before school. "Do you think she's mad at me?"

"Did you guys fight?"

"No! There hasn't been anything that I can think of." Had Cassandra done something she couldn't think of? Had she somehow offended her friend? She wished they still had P.E. together so they could talk it out, but they didn't.

The subject had nearly slipped her mind when Farrah called out to her before she went into her seventh hour class.

"Cassie."

Cassandra turned in the hallway, surprised to see Farrah. "Are you mad at me?" she blurted.

Farrah shook her head. "There's something I have to tell you," she said, avoiding Cassandra's eyes.

A knot formed in her stomach. Judging from the look on Farrah's face, whatever it was couldn't be good.

"Okay," Cassandra said warily. "What's up?"

"I can't tell you now. Meet me after school. I'll give you a ride home and tell you everything."

Cassandra wanted school to end so they could have this talk right away. "What is it, Farrah?"

"I can't—" she exhaled. "Not now."

Cassandra scrutinized her friend. Was that a guilty expression on her face? The anxiety boiled up in her and made her feel nauseous. "I'll find you after class."

Farrah nodded and walked away.

Cassandra could hardly sit through her seventh hour class, one foot tapping up and down on the floor while she wondered what on earth Farrah had to tell her.

The moment school ended, she hurried to her locker and switched out her books, then went to the back door of the school where Farrah kept her car parked and waited.

Farrah showed up a few minutes later and gave Cassandra a weak smile.

"I hope I didn't keep you waiting."

"No, you're fine." Cassandra fought the urge to bite her fingernails. *Just spit it out!* she wanted to say. But she knew she had to wait for Farrah's timing.

The silence between them as they climbed into Farrah's car was thick with expectation. Cassandra put her backpack at her feet and clasped her fingers together to keep her hands still.

Farrah didn't say anything the whole way down the street to the stop light. Only after they sat waiting at the light did she exhale heavily and say, "I went on a double date with Elijah on Saturday."

Whatever Cassandra had been expecting, that wasn't it. Her heart dropped into her toes, and she moved as physically away from Farrah as she could, leaning against the door and staring at her. "You did what?" She had to have heard wrong. Farrah wouldn't do that to her.

"Not me and Elijah," Farrah said quickly. "I went with James, and Elijah was with Amity."

The breath rushed out of Cassandra, and she could find no words. And then they came, and Cassandra turned her indignation into anger. "You went on a double date with them? And you didn't tell me? You didn't call me when you knew who it was to tell me what was happening?"

"I'm sorry. I should have. But Cassandra—it's not just that he went on a date with Amity. It's what he did to Amity."

All of Cassandra's righteous indignation ground to a halt. "What do you mean? He did something to Amity?"

"I don't know exactly, Cassie. We took her home first, and she asked me to walk with her to the door. Then she started crying and said he did things to her. They were alone in the car a few times. She wouldn't tell me what, but it must've been really bad."

Farrah glanced at Cassandra as if to see how she was taking it.

Cassandra didn't know what to think or feel. First she had to deal with Farrah's betrayal, going on a double date with Elijah and not telling her.

And then there was her anger on Amity's behalf.

"What did he do to her?" Cassandra asked again.

Farrah shook her head. "She wouldn't tell me. All I know is it was bad, Cassie, and that could've been you."

The statement struck her heart. How foolish she had been, to think Elijah actually cared for her! How stupid to take all of his flattery and compliments at face value. He knew how to sweet talk a girl, how to get her to like him. That's what he was good at.

She turned her face away from Farrah and looked out the window. "I have to talk to Amity." A part of her couldn't believe Amity would go behind her back like that, accepting to go out with Elijah after the serious conversation they had, but the bigger part of her was not surprised. She'd been expecting it, really. That didn't stop it from hurting.

But more than the hurt, she felt concerned. If Elijah had hurt Amity, she would kill him.

⁂

Cassandra couldn't sleep that night. She was bothered by what Farrah had told her, and Farrah's actions, but worst of all, by what might have happened with Amity. She got back up around midnight, went to her desk, turned on the lamp, and pulled out a notebook. She proceeded to write Amity a note.

Amity:

I'm not sure how to start this note. Farrah told me you went out with Elijah on Saturday. At first, I was really angry. I thought you betrayed me, and I guess you did, but you also took a bullet for me. I don't know exactly what happened. Farrah didn't even know, but I want you to know I don't blame you. And even though we don't talk much and sometimes I'm really angry at you, I still care about you as a friend. And I am angry at Elijah for hurting you and angry at myself for being stupid enough to like him. If you want to talk about what happened, I'm here for you.

Always,

Cassandra

She felt much better having written the note. She climbed back into bed and pulled the covers around her ears, shivering in the early January air permeating the room. Tomorrow she would give the note to Amity and put this whole thing behind her.

She didn't say much to Farrah the next day in church. It wasn't that she was angry at her, exactly, but she did feel like a wall had been built between them, and she wasn't quite ready to tear it down. She didn't tell Riley what happened, saying only that they'd had a disagreement.

She felt the outlines of the note to Amity burning a hole in her pocket. She was anxious for fifth hour to arrive so she could deliver it.

"Cassandra Jones."

She stopped dead in her tracks on the way to first hour. She would know that voice anywhere. She turned around and smiled when she saw Grayson, stepping toward her and shaking his pencil. When he reached her, he tapped the pencil on her forehead.

"You don't even say hi anymore."

"Sure I do." Though she knew it wasn't really true. She spoke to Grayson if he spoke to her, which wasn't often.

He smiled, that characteristic upper twist of the right corner of his mouth that she had permanently engraved in her mind. "No, you don't. It's been, like, forever." He mimicked a girl's voice, even batted his eyelashes and threw up his hands.

Cassandra's breath caught. "Say that again."

He focused on her, more serious, and said, "Say what?"

"That last word you said."

"Forever."

He said it again, the word thick with his northeastern accent, and Cassandra treasured the way the word formed to his lips.

"Thank you." She hurried into her classroom, not waiting to see the pity in his eyes.

Instead she replayed the phrases in her head, putting her two favorite ones together.

"Cassandra Jones. Forever."

The words still playing through her head, she flipped to her poetry notebook and penned her feelings.

It's Better This Way

Hush, my heart, be still.
I know you feel love for him
And he's making you ache.
But you don't know what's best for you.
It's better this way, you'll see.
Shh, my heart, don't cry.
You know it would never work.
It's better this way, they say.
Listen, listen, my heart.
Through the bitter truth.
Others speak wisely.
Just accept it, please.
Cheer up, dear heart, smile.
He may have left you.
But dry those tears.
Someone's waiting, someone real.
Be ready when he comes, my heart.
For he will come, you'll see.
Hush, my heart, be still.
For you know as well as I
It's better this way.

For the next few hours, all Cassandra could think about was choir. When lunch ended, she made a beeline for the choir room, wanting to arrive before Amity. Cassandra did, and then she stood in the doorway casually looking at her phone while holding the note beneath it.

She spotted Amity coming down the hall. When Amity stepped through the doorway, Cassandra moved in front of her.

For a moment Amity looked startled, and then Cassandra thrust the note toward her.

"Here."

That was all she said, and then she hurried to her seat.

Mr. Cullen called them to attention before the bell even rang, lining them up on the risers again. But this time he put Cassandra on the first row, much to her disappointment. She stood there watching him line everyone else up when Amity stepped up and whispered something to him. He nodded, and then Amity looked at Cassandra and beckoned to her.

Really? Mr. Cullen was going to let them talk during class?

She stepped off the risers and followed Amity into the hallway.

Amity moved toward the bathrooms and then stopped, turning to face Cassandra with her arms folded over her chest. She looked stern but vulnerable, and Cassandra wondered how to broach the subject.

"I'm sorry for whatever happened," she said. "You don't have to tell me anything."

Amity shook her head. "You deserve to know. I'm sorry I went behind your back."

"That doesn't matter now. What happened?"

Amity kept her face emotionless, arms still crossed over her chest. "He did things to me in the back of the car. He put his hands in places where I didn't want them to be. And even though I took his hands and moved them away, even though I told him to stop, he still did it." Amity dropped her eyes. "Those are things I've never done with any guy. And I should be the one to decide who touches me and how."

Cassandra's hands clenched into fists, and she closed her eyes, fury lancing through her veins. She took a few deep breaths to keep her emotions under control. "I want to punch him."

"And I never want to see him again."

"He will never come to another dance. I can promise you that."

"Just stay away from him, Cassie. He is the guy our parents warned us about."

Cassandra wanted to hug Amity, but the space between them still felt too large. "Thank you for telling me."

Amity nodded, and both girls walked back to the choir room. Cassandra vowed she would never again trust a guy just because he was smooth-talking and handsome.

"I can't believe he did that," Riley said. She clutched her books to her chest as she and Cassandra made their way down the A-wing before first period.

"I know." Cassandra still wasn't over it. She shuddered, so angry she wanted to hit something.

Two boys bounced through the hallways, laughing and yanking on each other's jackets, knocking into people. Cassandra raised an eyebrow and pulled Riley against a locker before they got run over.

"Isn't that—?" Riley began.

"Yes," Cassandra said. "It's Grayson."

He hadn't noticed her. He was busy trying to get something out of Kevin's hand. The object flew from Kevin's grasp and spun across the floor, coming to a halt at Cassandra's feet.

She looked down at the little square foil packet, and her heart skipped a beat.

"That's Grayson's!" Kevin shouted, skipping over and picking it up. "Where did you get it, the vending machine?"

"No," Grayson said, and he was no longer laughing. His face had gone bright red, and he avoided Cassandra's eyes as he took the packet.

Kevin was still laughing, looping an arm around Grayson's shoulder. "Condom Sense? Been hanging out in Fayetteville?"

Grayson didn't respond. He shoved the packet in his pocket and strolled down the hall without a second look.

"Was that a condom?" Riley said.

"Yes." Cassandra found her chest had tightened to the point she could barely breathe. She wanted to deny it. Grayson and Charlotte . . . She couldn't think. She pushed away from Riley and walked to her class, feeling numb inside.

"What's wrong?" Mia asked, studying her when she sat down. "You look like you saw a ghost."

"Nothing." Cassandra focused on her notebook, then uncapped her pen and began scribbling, angry words of disbelief and hurt, whatever tumbled from her mind.

Ms. Elliot asked her a question, and Cassandra answered without even looking up. She didn't care if she got it right. What was Spanish next to real life?

She'd already written a poem about him this week, and she hated how he affected her enough to make her wax lyrical. But maybe she could purge these negative emotions. She kept writing, ignoring the assignment Ms. Elliot had put on the board.

"What are you doing?" Mia whispered.

"Meditating," Cassandra responded.

Alone

There stood a girl on the edge of the world.
Knowing her place, yet needing one person.
There stood a boy in the midst of the world.
Surrounded by friends, and yet all alone.
Once they stood together, separate but whole.
Then he stepped away, and half of her left.

Blinded, lost, something's gone from his soul.
But he doesn't yet recognize what it is.
In misery he turns to the dark.
Changing his personality, looking for love.
He searches in vain, for he's missing the mark.
Love is not found in rebellion, anger, or sex.
Somehow, ignorantly, he still looks there.
And the girl, far from him, beckons him hopelessly.

Pain she feels, and hurt, and fear.
In tears, sobbing, she prays for him.
Pleading with God, "Please, don't let him be lost!"
For she truly loves him, always has.
If only he'd stop, if he just knew the cost!
She knows it's not likely he'll ever come back.

Yet still, as long as she lives, she can't let go.
If she could give her life for his, she would.
So much he's losing, and he doesn't even know.

He is a fool, acting like someone he's not.
Still she knows not the outcome of their lives.
Only that she wants him to have joy
And she knows that he doesn't, not at all.
She can't forget him, and so she writes.

There stands a girl on the edge of the world.
Knowing her place, yet needing one person.
There stands a boy in the midst of the world.
Surrounded by friends, and yet all alone.

She read over the words, and her heart tightened. They didn't make her feel better.

Cassandra replayed the hallway scene in her head as she walked to health class, unable to keep the tears at bay any longer. Grayson had a condom. There was only one purpose for that. She wiped at the tears and set her face to impassive.

Harper was laughing with her friend Amelia, and her eyes flicked toward Cassandra when she sat down. She said something to Amelia, and then moved to the empty desk in front of Cassandra.

"What's wrong, Cassandra?"

Cassandra shook her head. She had no right to be crying over a boy who wasn't hers and never had been. "I'm fine. Just having an emotional morning."

Harper made a noise of understanding. "I know how that goes." She tapped her pen against her chin thoughtfully, then her blue eyes lit up. "There's a thing at my church this weekend that might make you feel better. Want to spend the night tomorrow? We could go together."

Cassandra looked at Harper and evaluated her seriously for the first time. With her long blond hair, light eyes, and easy smile, Harper was well-liked and easy to get along with. But Cassandra didn't know her that well. "Could I bring a friend?"

"Yeah, sure. You mean, like Riley?"

Cassandra nodded. "She's my best friend." And Cassandra would feel more comfortable having her there.

"Here's my number." Harper wrote it down on a slip of paper. "Call me tonight and we'll work out the details!"

"Thanks," Cassandra said, a little surprised. And it did make her feel slightly better, that someone wanted to hang out with her.

CHAPTER THIRTY-FIVE

Church and Soap

Although it was normal not to speak to each other, fourth hour felt more awkward than usual as both Cassandra and Grayson silently avoided looking at each other. Cassandra trembled to be near him with what she knew now and wished she could have some space. Some time away from him.

Her wish was granted when he didn't come to school the next day. But neither did Charlotte, which meant Cassandra didn't actually feel a whole lot better. At least she had the sleepover at Harper's house to concentrate on.

Riley was coming also, and she rode home with Harper. Cassandra wanted to go with them, but her mom needed her to babysit first. She climbed on the bus and watched the two of them drive away, Harper honking and Riley waving. She felt a flash of jealousy and pushed it down. She'd be with them soon enough.

Except it wasn't soon enough. Mrs. Jones was running late and didn't get home until after six o'clock.

"Mom, we have to go!" Cassandra said, shouldering her purse and her overnight bag. "Harper's activity started at five!"

"I know. Things ran late at work. Let me change my clothes real quick."

"There's no time for that!" Cassandra said, but she couldn't convince her mom to skip it.

It was almost seven by the time Mrs. Jones pulled in front of the chapel in downtown Fayetteville.

"You know where to go?" she asked.

Cassandra already had her phone out. "I'll just text Harper and Riley and find them."

"I don't want to leave you until I know this is the right place."

Cassandra's phone dinged with a message from Riley. "It is!" She waved the phone. "I'll see you soon!"

She ran inside, following the sound of the music to a large auditorium. The lights were dimmed as a band played on the stage, and she scanned the rows of kids, looking for her friends.

"Cassandra!" Harper spotted her first and waved from a bench. Riley sat beside her.

Cassandra waved back and joined them, putting her overnight bag underneath. "Sorry I'm late."

"No worries!" Harper hugged her. "Glad you could come!"

Cassandra glanced around, taking in the massive auditorium and thumping music. Kids littered the room, some from her school and some from others. She didn't know any of the songs, but it didn't take long to catch on. She clapped and danced next to Harper and Riley. Harper's friend Amelia was there, but she kept scowling at Cassandra, so Cassandra didn't talk to her. Even Riley acted a little weird, hanging on Harper and looking put out every time Harper talked to Cassandra.

Miles was there also, and he sat with the girls for a bit, laughing at their goofy antics.

A speaker got up on stage with a microphone, and the music quieted down so he could talk. He spoke about the difficulties facing teens today, and how each person needed to be a light for someone else.

It was the second time Cassandra had heard a sermon about being a light to those around her. Her thoughts immediately went to Grayson. She'd tried to be his light. She wanted so badly to help him, to be something to him. She now knew she couldn't be. He was beyond her influence. Who would be his light? She brushed at tears, furious he still affected her this way.

Harper hooked an arm around her waist. "Don't be sad."

"I'm just thinking of a friend of mine. How he needs someone to be his light."

"We can pray for him," Harper said.

Cassandra nodded. That was all she had left.

❧ ⚘ ❧

When the event ended, Harper drove the girls over to her house to spend the night. Amelia, Harper, Riley, and Cassandra stayed up late talking.

"What did you think?" Harper asked.

"It was fun," Riley said.

"I enjoyed the music," Cassandra said.

Harper elbowed Cassandra. "Time to spill your guts. Who is this guy you keep crying over?"

"Ugh." Riley rolled her eyes. "He won't get out of her life."

"Oh." Cassandra heaved a sigh. "I don't even know how to describe him. We were something. Once. And I can't get over him even though he has so moved on."

"Do you love him?" Harper asked with a knowing look.

Cassandra looked at Riley. She hadn't admitted this to very many people and didn't know how to talk about it now.

"Yes," Riley said.

"Point him out to me in school Monday. I want to know who this guy is."

"We're too young to fall in love," Amelia said. "You probably only think you love him."

Cassandra turned her gaze to Amelia, irritated this girl who knew nothing about her thought she could cast judgment on Cassandra's feelings. But she only shrugged. "I'm sure you're right. It just feels like love."

"That's why you shouldn't date," Amelia continued. "You'll know what real love is someday."

"Leave her alone, Amelia," Harper said. "We can't help what we feel."

"Sure we can," Amelia said, not about to back down.

"We didn't date," Cassandra interrupted. "And I still fell in love with him."

Amelia gave a disbelieving snort. "You can't love someone you never dated."

Cassandra's chest tightened with indignation. She didn't feel like defending herself. So she just buried into her pile of blankets on the floor of Harper's living room. "I'm tired. I'll see you guys tomorrow."

The others whispered a little longer before quieting down and also going to sleep. But Cassandra thought on Amelia's words. How had she fallen so hard for Grayson? She hoped Amelia was right. This wasn't real love. That experience was still in front of her.

⟲~❀~⟳

"Harper!" Mrs. McGraw flipped on the light in the living room, jostling Cassandra from sleep. Mrs. McGraw bent over and shook Harper's shoulder. "You're running late! Everyone will be at the church already!"

Cassandra opened her eyes and blinked. She grabbed her glasses and put them on so she could see the clock under the television. Almost nine. "What time does it start?"

231

"At nine!" Mrs. McGraw said.

Harper sat up, running a hand through her long hair. "Chill, Mom. No one cares if we're late."

"I can be ready quickly," Amelia said.

"Me too." Cassandra pulled herself up. "I just need to brush my teeth and put in my contacts."

The girls split up, making use of the two bathrooms. Cassandra got her left contact lens in with no problem, but the right one irritated her. She hadn't brought the solution with her, only the case filled with enough liquid to get her through the night. She tried to clean the lens with the remaining liquid, but it still hurt when she put it back in. She plucked it from her eye and held it in her hand, then went back to Harper's room.

"Harper?"

Only Amelia sat on the bed. "She's in the bathroom."

"Oh." Cassandra paused. "I need contact solution. Do you know if she has any somewhere?"

"No, she doesn't use contacts." Amelia opened a bag and pulled out a small bottle. "I do, though. You can use mine."

"Thank you!" Cassandra hurried back to the bathroom, dousing her lens in the solution before popping it into her eye.

An intense burning immediately followed, and she blinked rapidly at the shocking pain. The veins on her right eye swelled, leaving the whites riddled with red lines. She tried to grasp the lens to pull it out, but her eye was tearing too much, the large drops making it impossible to get a grip on the lens or her eyelids.

What had she put in her eye? She grabbed the bottle Amelia had given her and read it.

Contact lens cleaner.

It was soap, not solution. With her one good eye, Cassandra stared at it in disbelief. Had Amelia really misunderstood her? Or had she given her the soap on purpose?

Cassandra wasn't going to ask. And she wasn't going to take the lens out again, either. She gritted her teeth and waited for the pain to pass.

Every time she blinked, the whole drive to Fayetteville, her eye stung. Every time her eye stung, it welled with tears, and the tears burned. It took about an hour for the pain to fade, and the whole time Cassandra fumed at Amelia.

CHAPTER THIRTY-SIX

Shock Value

The day at Harper's church activity passed much like the evening had, with lots of singing and skits and sermons. Cassandra laughed and cried and clung to Harper, feeling a connection to the other girl she'd never expected. When the day ended, Riley's mom picked her up from the church in Fayetteville, and Harper drove Cassandra home.

"I had such a great time," Cassandra said, giving Harper a hug at the door when they got to her house. "Thanks for inviting me."

"It was a blast!" Harper said, grinning broadly. "I'll call you. We'll hang out again!"

Cassandra waved goodbye and slipped into the house, her heart lighter than it had been in days. Harper had succeeded in lifting her spirits.

Harper found Riley and Cassandra Monday morning by the lockers.

"Why do you guys get to school so early?" she asked.

"We have an early morning church class," Cassandra said.

"She was just telling me her dream about Grayson," Riley said, giggling.

"You dreamed about Grayson?" Harper lifted an eyebrow. "Do tell!"

"Oh, it was nothing," Cassandra said, her face growing hot. "I dreamed that he got in trouble for skipping school, but instead of going to detention, he was assigned to clean the cafeteria. So we were all eating lunch and throwing our trash on the ground for him to pick up."

"Where is he?" Harper glanced around. "Show him to me."

"He has class across from me." Cassandra led the way down the hallway, and they stopped next to her Spanish classroom. "We'll see him."

But the minutes ticked by with no appearance of him, and finally Harper said, "Well, is he coming? I have to go to class."

Cassandra shrugged, feeling lame. "He's usually here by now."

"Maybe he's cleaning the cafeteria," Riley said, and they laughed.

Cassandra was still laughing when she went to health class. She moved her seat closer to Amelia and Harper, even though she was certain Amelia didn't like her. They relived the weekend, giggling over the funny jokes and skits they'd seen.

Cassandra was in good spirits when she got to fourth hour. She seated herself, hoping Grayson would be absent again. Her days went so much smoother when he wasn't there.

No such luck. Her head lifted almost of its own accord when he came in, as if she could sense his presence. He met her eyes and just as quickly looked away. She swallowed and turned back to reading her text book, telling herself it didn't hurt. She didn't care.

Harper moved her chair next to Cassandra in choir, and Cassandra felt the rush in her soul from their new friendship. They walked to sixth hour together. They were in the hallway talking when Cassandra saw Charlotte walking down the corridor.

She nudged Harper's arm. "That's Grayson's girlfriend," she whispered.

Harper cast a quick glance her direction. "What's so special about her?"

The loyalty warmed Cassandra's heart. "Grayson likes her. That's all that matters."

As if on cue, Grayson came up the stairs behind Charlotte. He called out to her, then slipped his arm around her waist and buried his face in her hair.

Had he seen Cassandra? Had he done it on purpose? Did he not care for her at all anymore?

Anger pumped through her veins, anger at Grayson and anger at herself for not being able to control her feelings. She turned and stormed into her classroom, dropping her books on the desk with a thud.

"Cassandra!" Harper stood in the doorway and beckoned to her.

Blinking rapidly, trying not to cry, Cassandra pushed past the desks and joined Harper.

"What?"

"I'm assuming that was Grayson?"

"Yes." Cassandra sucked in a breath. "I wish he would disappear. I wish he'd move! I can't get over him until he's gone!"

"What happened between you guys?"

"Nothing. We were friends once. That's all." It was too complicated. She'd never be able to make someone understand. "I wish he would drop out of my life."

Harper nodded in understanding. "It might hurt at first, but in the long run it would be for the best. I know that feeling."

Cassandra brushed furiously at the tears in her eyes. "I hate him so much."

Harper squeezed her arm. "It would be so much easier if you did, wouldn't it?" She gave Cassandra a hug and then a loud, noisy kiss on the cheek. "I'll call you later."

Cassandra took a deep breath and returned to class. She sat by Nicole, where she could scribble her poetry in misery and still feel like she had a friend.

⟲⟳∗⟲⟳

Riley called Cassandra that evening. "Harper said you got upset in school. Everything okay?"

"Oh, it was just stupid Grayson. I'm over it." Such a lie, and Cassandra suspected Riley knew it. But she let it slide.

"Want to go to a music concert in St. Louis in a few weeks? My mom said she'd buy tickets for us."

"Really? To see who?" Not that Cassandra cared. She'd watch her dad's favorite band for a chance to travel to St. Louis with Riley.

"I don't know yet. We'll have to see who's playing. Hey, I got my ears pierced again. A second hole. I love it."

"Lucky." Cassandra stepped into the bathroom she shared with Emily and examined her earlobes. "I want a second hole, but my dad won't let me."

"I guess when you're eighteen?"

"I have to wait so long for everything." She couldn't even date yet. "I want a belly ring."

"You do?" Riley sounded surprised. "I didn't think that would be your style."

"Nobody really knows my style," Cassandra said. "Everyone thinks I'm just some quiet, smart girl. Maybe I should shock everyone and dye my hair green and get a belly ring."

"That would shock everyone. You could shave it off like Elise."

Was that what Elise had been going for? Shock value? "I'm tired of meeting everyone's expectations and fitting in their little box."

"So do something different."

Cassandra pulled a needle out of the bathroom drawer. She plugged in her curling iron, an idea occurring to her. "Maybe I will."

"You could just get your hair cut. That would be drastic enough."

"Mm-hm." Cassandra pressed the needle to the hot curling iron, letting the heat sterilize it. "Yep."

"What would you do if you cut your hair?"

"I don't know." Cassandra put the phone on speaker and set it on the counter. She lifted her shirt and pinched an inch of skin from her belly button to her navel. Crapola. That felt thick. How bad would this hurt?

"You would look good with hair my length."

Riley kept her hair shoulder-length or shorter. Cassandra had never seen it longer. "Yep." She took a deep breath and plunged the hot needle into her skin.

Crapola! It hurt worse than she expected. She pulled it back out, hands trembling, tears stinging her eyes. "Oh."

"What is it?"

"Nothing." She didn't want to say until she accomplished the task. "What color would you dye your hair?"

"Blue. Blue would be awesome."

Cassandra tried again with the needle. But this time she didn't try to go as deep. She pushed it through the skin all the way into the belly button. There. She exhaled. She'd succeeded.

Now what? She spun around to the jewelry box on her dresser and fished through it until she found the starter earrings, the ones she'd had when she got her ears pierced. Following the tread of the needle, she forced the thick silver stud into the same spot. Then she gripped the edge of the counter and took several deep breaths, trying to breathe through the pain.

"What do you think?" Riley was asking.

Cassandra had no idea what they were talking about. She examined her newly decorated belly button, a surge of pride rippling through her. "I just pierced my belly button."

"You did what?" Riley screeched.

"Yep. I did it."

"I want to see!"

Cassandra laughed. "I'll show you tomorrow."

She felt a surge of anticipation and excitement at her actions. Cassandra Jones, someone bold, spontaneous, and fun. Right on the brink of sixteen and independence.

Maybe this would be at start of a new her.

EPISODE 5: SWEET SIXTEEN

CHAPTER THIRTY-SEVEN

Belly Ache

Cassandra's favorite part of the next few days was telling people she'd pierced her belly button.

She was known for being a rule follower. A sweet, quiet girl. Someone who didn't do anything impulsive or rebellious.

Maybe she wanted to change that.

The shock value made the pain of poking a hole in her skin in her bathroom all worth it. Mia wanted to see in Spanish class, and Sue and Farrah made Cassandra show them at youth night.

"You shouldn't have done that, Cassie," Farrah said, which only annoyed Cassandra.

Riley loved it.

"Did you show Harper?" she asked when they saw Harper coming toward their locker before school Thursday morning.

"No way!" Cassandra said, shaking her head quickly. "She'd never approve!"

"Well, I think it's so cool."

Cassandra nodded, and then they quickly dropped the subject when Harper reached them.

Cassandra didn't let on that it hurt, especially when she twisted or bent over.

"Cassandra," Mrs. Jones said after school, "it's time to start making plans."

"Making plans?" Cassandra looked over at her mother from where she sat doing homework at the table.

"For your sixteenth birthday party."

Her sixteenth birthday party. It was coming. It was really happening.

She put her pen down and leaned back in her chair, wincing a little when her belly button tugged. "What should I do?"

"Well, it's your sweet sixteen. You can have as many people as you want."

"As many as I want?" Her eyes went wide. "Boys and girls?"

"Yes." Her mother smiled. "You'll be able to date now."

"Can the girls spend the night?"

Mrs. Jones hesitated a moment, then she nodded. "Yes."

"All of them?" Cassandra breathed.

"Yes. All of them."

"Ha!" Cassandra laughed and pulled out a new sheet of paper. "This will rock!"

✦

Cassandra's belly button hurt on Friday morning. She woke up coughing, and her throat ached also. She stepped into the bathroom and turned on the hot water in the shower, then pulled off her pajamas while she waited for it to warm up.

"Ouch," she murmured when the fabric touched her belly. She glanced down at it and frowned. White pus was coming out of the hole with the earring in it.

She cleaned it up the best she could in the shower, then snuck into the laundry room to get the rubbing alcohol and sterilize it. She hoped it wasn't infected. She didn't want to try again.

She drank lots of water while she got ready for church class and ignored the pounding in her head. There was a dance on Saturday, and she couldn't be sick for it.

"Can I see your belly ring again?" Mia asked in Spanish class.

Cassandra didn't want to admit it had been hurting her. She checked it real fast to make sure there was no new pus, then lifted her shirt to show Mia.

"That's so cool. I can't believe you did it yourself," Mia said.

Cassandra smiled, but it was more like a grimace. She didn't feel well.

She waited for Amelia to leave the classroom after health so she could talk to Harper alone, but Amelia didn't seem to want to go. She lingered as long as possible. Finally Cassandra hooked her arm through Harper's and dragged her from the room, leaving Amelia behind.

"What is it?" Harper asked, freeing herself.

"Want to come to a dance tomorrow?"

"A dance?" Harper looked intrigued. "When and where? I like dances."

"At the Jones Center. Tomorrow night. It's put on by my church."

239

"Your church does dances?"

Cassandra nodded. "Yes, and they are so much fun. You should come!"

"Well, maybe. I'll talk to my mom."

Harper called Cassandra that night.

"Hey, my said yes! So what do I wear? How does it go?"

"Great!" Cassandra was anxious to replace her memories of the last dance with a new one. "It's Sunday dress, so just wear something you'd be comfortable wearing to church. And it's at seven o'clock. Do you know where the Jones Center is?"

Harper scoffed. "Of course."

"Then I'll see you tomorrow!"

By the next morning, Cassandra's throat hurt even worse than the day before. She could barely swallow, and it was a struggle to stand up long enough to brush her teeth. She checked on her belly button, and it was red and swollen. She got that sinking feeling in her gut. This didn't look good.

She was going shopping that evening with her mom, so the ring would have to come out anyway. She removed the stud, hoping she'd be able to get it back in.

Mrs. Jones came in an hour later while Cassandra was reading in bed. "You don't look so great. How are you feeling?"

"Terrible." Cassandra shook her head. "But you promised to take me shopping for the dance tonight, so I'll be fine."

"I've never seen you so determined to go shopping."

Cassandra grinned. "We've never gone shopping for my sixteenth birthday before."

The pain in her throat spread to her neck throughout the day, making it difficult to turn her head from side to side. But she had a wonderful time at the mall with her mom, picking out a long black skirt and a fluffy gray and white top to wear to the dance that night. Mrs. Jones also bought some cold medicine to help her feel better. It seemed to work, at least numbing the ache in her body enough that she didn't notice it as much.

Harper wasn't there when Cassandra arrived at the Jones Center promptly at seven p.m. Neither was Riley. She stood around for a moment, feeling awkward and out of her element in the ballroom.

And then Riley arrived, coming up behind Cassandra and scooping her hair in her hands.

"There you are!" Cassandra turned around to face her. "I was worried you weren't coming!"

"Just running late."

"Hey, Cassie. Riley." Zack appeared, waving at them.

Cassandra turned and flashed a big smile. "Hey, you're here!"

"I'm here." His smile matched hers. "I don't miss dances often."

"Me neither." Cassandra put her hand on his arm, feeling bold after having known Zack for so long. Not to mention the exchanged phone calls and the humiliating love notes she'd sent him. "You'll dance with me, right? It's my birthday in two weeks."

Zack put his hand over hers and gave her a squeeze. "Absolutely."

"Cassandra!"

She turned around to see Harper stepping onto the ballroom floor, a fitted blue floral dress wrapped around her waist. Her long blond hair was parted on the side and hung around her shoulders, and she looked gorgeous.

She gave Cassandra an uncertain look. "If this is not fun, I'll kill you."

Cassandra laughed and clapped her hands in delight. "You're going to love it!"

"Attention, attention." The DJ paused the music and spoke into the microphone. "Time for a little dance competition! Grab your partners! Put on your best dance moves and out-dance the couples around you! We'll have judges tapping the shoulders of couples to let them know they're out. If you get tapped, move to the outskirts of the dance floor. The last couple standing wins!"

"What is this?" Harper said, her expression murderous. "I don't even know how to dance!"

"You don't have to! Just don't stop moving!" Cassandra spun around to find a dance partner and spotted James, a friend from Tahlequah. He saw her at the same time and extended his hand. Cassandra took it and let him pull her close.

"Dance, Cassie?" he said.

"I'm all yours."

"I know better than to believe that." James twirled her onto the dance floor and spun her three times before pulling her back into his arms. Other couples danced in a slow circle around them, but James was far more energized. "Hi, guys," he said, letting go of Cassandra to wave to another couple. Then he turned around as if to dance with Cassandra, and instead started dancing with another boy.

"Oh! Sorry. You're not my partner."

"James!" Cassandra couldn't stop laughing.

James pulled her in close, then spun her again, then pulled her in again. Around them the judges kept tapping different shoulders, but not hers or James'. He kissed her cheek, and then he whacked his face.

"Shame on you, James, taking advantage of a nice girl like Cassie!"

She couldn't even speak through the laughter.

James took her hand, tango-style, and marched her across the floor. Then he turned her around and marched her back.

The song ended, and Cassandra looked around.

"And we have winners!" the DJ crowed.

"Us?" Cassandra said, surprised. "We won?"

The other dancers clapped and cheered, and Riley and Harper ran over in giggles.

"What did you win?" Riley asked.

"A free trip for two to Bermuda," Cassandra said.

"With separate rooms," James added.

Cassandra cracked up again, and James turned to Harper.

"I don't know you."

"I'm Cassandra's friend."

"Would you like to dance, Cassandra's friend?"

Harper looked questioningly at Cassandra, who nodded quickly. "Um, sure."

Cassandra clapped as James led Harper onto the dance floor.

She turned around to find someone to dance with and spotted Zack talking to his brother along the wall. Before she could make her way over there, though, Beckham intercepted her.

"Dance, Cassie?"

"Of course." She let him take her hand.

She danced every song after that, and she couldn't help noticing that Harper danced a good number of them with James.

Then the DJ announced the second to last song. Cassandra scanned the room for Zack, not wanting to leave before she'd danced with him.

"Any room on your dance card for me?" Tyler drawled, coming over and taking her hand before she had a chance to respond.

"Oh, yeah. Sure." She spotted Zack then, asking a younger girl to dance. Cassandra maneuvered Tyler a little closer to Zack, then leaned over and whispered, "Zack."

He turned and gave her that killer grin.

"I get you on the next song."

He laughed softly. "Okay."

"Can't even wait till we're done dancing to flirt with Zack?" Tyler said, sounding amused.

Cassandra swiveled back and grinned at him. "Not like I was going to flirt with you."

"No, we don't really do that, do we? Too much like brother and sister."

"Yep." She remembered having a crush on Tyler the previous year, but this year all she felt were platonic feelings of friendship.

The song ended, and Cassandra released Tyler and spun around.

Zack was already there, turning from his partner to Cassandra. "Cassie."

"Zack." She beamed at him.

"How are you these days?" he asked, taking her hand in his and resting his other on her waist.

"Oh, you know, pretty good. Same as always. Except I'll be sixteen in three weeks."

"No way. When I met you, you were just a wee fourteen-year-old."

"I'm all grown up now." She paused, heart racing, and then blurted, "Will you come to my birthday party? You and your brother, of course."

"When is it? If we don't have soccer games, we'll come."

Now she felt stupid for asking. Of course he was too busy. "Friday night in three weeks."

"I'll let you know."

Cassandra kept up a steady stream of conversation, and Zack laughed through most of it.

The song ended, and she let go of his hand reluctantly. "Thanks for the dance, Zack."

"Anytime, Cassie."

She moved away and scanned the dance floor for her friends. Harper and Riley stood by the door, laughing and talking together.

"Cassandra!" Harper gestured her over and looped an arm through hers. "You'll never believe this. James kissed me!"

"What?" Cassandra swiveled around to find James and demand an explanation, but he was nowhere in sight.

"They already left for Tahlequah," Harper said, her eyes dreamy. "Oh, I can't wait to see him again!"

Cassandra nodded, but she fought back a grimace. James better not be playing games with her friend.

CHAPTER THIRTY-EIGHT

Dog Sick

As much fun as the dance had been, by Sunday morning, Cassandra could hardly move her body. Mrs. Jones gave her more medicine, but Cassandra begged to stay home from church and sleep. Mrs. Jones didn't question her and let her rest.

She slept all day and even missed her church class the next morning. She didn't catch the bus, and Mrs. Jones came into her room after seven.

"Are you missing school?"

"No." Cassandra groaned and pulled her pillow over her head. "I can't miss school. There's too much going on."

"Then we need to leave now. Traffic will be horrible at this time."

"Okay." Cassandra forced herself from the comfortable blankets and into the bathroom to get dressed.

She remembered her belly ring when she lifted her shirt. The site remained red and inflamed, and when she tried to get the stud back through the hole, the pain nearly brought her to her knees. She would have to wait a little bit longer.

Mrs. Jones dropped Cassandra off at the high school right before the bell rang. A few people greeted her as she walked into Spanish, but she only gave a half smile and kept her head down. It felt like someone had stuffed her brain and ears with cotton. The world sounded muffled and underwater.

She felt Harper's eyes on her as soon as she walked into health class second hour. Amelia looked at her also, and turned and murmured something to Harper. Harper gave her a scowl and said, "Hush!" Then she smiled at Cassandra as if hoping the exchange hadn't been noticed.

Cassandra had noticed. She just couldn't bring herself to care.

"Are you okay?" Harper asked Cassandra as she sat down. "You have big shadows under your eyes."

"I don't feel well." She gave Harper a wan smile. "How are you?"

Harper blinked and chewed on her lower lip. "I haven't heard from James since Saturday. Don't you think that's weird?"

For a guy to kiss a girl and then fall off the face of the earth? Definitely weird. "No, that's not weird. Guys are different, you know? They don't think about things the same way we do."

"Yeah, I guess." Harper didn't look convinced. "I'll just wait. Maybe he'll call after school today."

"He'll call soon. I'm sure of it." Cassandra made a mental note to call James herself and chew him out.

They walked out of class together. Just as they started up the stairs of the A-wing, Cassandra heard Grayson's familiar voice.

She couldn't help it. Her body turned toward him, leaning his direction.

He stood at the bottom of the stairs talking to Andrea and Melanie. Andrea and Melanie! Of all people! She didn't even know Andrea was still friends with the girl they'd all despised in ninth grade. Melanie wore her tiny cheerleading uniform and giggled at his every word.

A surge of longing and envy flooded through Cassandra's veins like a heady wine. She gripped the banister and stared, for the first time wishing she had stayed close friends with Andrea. He might still talk to her. He might still like her.

"Cassandra?" Harper asked.

She shook her head, frustrated at the burning in her eyes. Her throat ached, though she wasn't sure if it was from being sick or trying not to cry. "Maybe he'd like me if I were a cheerleader."

Harper followed her gaze and gave her a knowing look. "You don't want to be a cheerleader just to get a guy."

"Maybe I do." She pictured herself in the tiny uniform, plastic smile in place, laughing and flirting with Grayson. He would like her again. He would be interested.

A poem flew through her mind before she'd even gotten to third hour. She sat down at the desk, sniffling and aching, and wrote the words out.

I Remember

I remember you.
I remember your face. your gentle smile.
I remember how you talked.
How important I was to you then.

I remember how your hand felt.
Touching my hair. squeezing my shoulder . . .
Making me melt.
Have you really forgotten?
I remember the nicknames you gave me.
The teasing affection in your voice.
Now it seems my name is only a word
Spoken when you have no other choice.
I remember you said you don't care about much.
But I could always talk to you. always. Liar.
I remember your laugh. your physical touch.
Then as it was ending.
I remember saying good-bye in my mind.
Someday. I'll say it to you. or the you you've become.
Then I'll stop living in rewind
And I'll remember to forget you.

Cassandra couldn't move.

She tried to pry her eyes open, but her lids were too heavy. They were glued to her eyeballs, refusing to obey.

Her bed jostled, but she didn't react.

"Cassandra?"

It was her father's voice. "Are you getting up?" he asked. "It's time to leave for class."

"Mmm," was all she could manage.

She felt him rise from her bed, and then all was silent.

Time passed. She drifted in and out of sleep, her head and throat aching. Her body hummed with pain, every muscle and limb complaining.

A cold hand touched her forehead.

"Cassandra?"

Her mother this time. Mrs. Jones ran her hands over Cassandra's face. "You're burning up. I don't want you to go to school today."

Sounded good. Answering took too much energy.

Sometime in the afternoon, her phone rang. Cassandra found the strength to open her eyes and sit up in bed. She felt woozy, groggy from laying down and doing nothing for hours.

It was Harper. "Hello?" Cassandra whispered. Nothing louder would come out.

"You sound terrible. Are you sick?"

"Yes."

"Explains why you weren't in school. I don't feel so hot either. I hope you didn't give it to me," Harper joked.

"Yeah," Cassandra said. It was all she could muster.

Harper sighed. "James never did call me."

That jerk. Cassandra would have to find the strength to call him. "He will."

Harper talked a little bit more, but with Cassandra unable to give adequate responses, the conversation floundered.

"Will you be in school tomorrow?" Harper asked.

"I don't think so," Cassandra said. She couldn't imagine this illness passing in time for her to make it to school.

"Well, feel better. I'll see you soon."

The moment they hung up, Cassandra rallied herself and went to the kitchen. She searched the church directory until she found the phone numbers for the Tahlequah congregation. There was James' family. Moving to the living room and collapsing on the couch, Cassandra called the number.

"Hello?" a woman greeted.

"Is James there?" Cassandra asked.

"No, he's not. He should be home in about an hour. Can I tell him who is calling?"

"Cassandra Jones. I'll try back later." She hung up and dropped the phone on her chest, letting her eyes slide shut.

A moment later, her phone rang, snapping her back to attention. She held it over her face and stared at the Tahlequah area code. Then she answered. "Hello?"

"Cassie? It's James."

Had it already been an hour? "James, why haven't you called Harper?"

"You sound terrible. Are you sick?"

Besides the point. "She keeps asking about you."

"Harper?"

"Yes." Cassandra felt a flash of indignation. "She said you kissed her."

"I did." James sounded reluctant. "I like her."

"So call her and tell her!"

"It's kind of complicated."

"Why?" She waited for him to say he lived too far away, or Harper was too different, or some other lame excuse.

Instead, he said, "I have a girlfriend."

She bit down on her lower lip, annoyed. "James!"

"I know. I shouldn't have kissed her." He sighed. "I thought I'd be breaking up with my girlfriend, but it's not that easy."

Why wasn't it? Why when a guy liked a girl who wasn't his girlfriend could he not just break up with one to go out with the other? "You call her and explain it."

"I will. I'll call her right now."

"You better," Cassandra growled, which hurt her throat more. "I'll talk to you later." She hung up the phone and waited to see what would happen next.

◌◠◠◌❀◠◠◌

The next morning Cassandra woke up a little before lunchtime. She could swallow a bit better and didn't feel as hot, which meant she had to be recovering.

Mrs. Jones brought her a bowl of chicken noodle soup. "I want you to stay home from school one more day."

"That means I'll miss three days," Cassandra said.

"Yes. But you were really sick. You need to be better."

Cassandra sipped the soup, feeling the tenderness in her throat, and decided her mom was right.

Harper called after school.

"James dumped me," she said, fury in her voice.

"I'm so sorry," Cassandra said. "What happened?"

"It turns out he's with another girl. I was just like a side-show or something. Stupid idiot guy."

"Guys are jerks," Cassandra said, falling back on the line everyone used.

"I thought he was different. Because he goes to church and all."

Cassandra laughed. "Church doesn't make people honest."

"Yeah, I guess not. Will you be in school tomorrow?"

"No. One more day. I'll be there Monday, I'm sure."

"Okay." Harper sighed. "Guess I better start looking for another guy."

"You'll find one." Cassandra was certain of that. Harper was too cute

248

and outgoing not to find one soon.

Mrs. Jones came in again after Harper hung up. "Guess who's coming to church with us on Sunday?"

Cassandra couldn't even begin to guess. "Who?"

"Elek."

"Elek?" Cassandra gasped, staring in surprise. She hadn't heard from Elek in at least a year. The boy from Greece had lived with her family for a few weeks when she was in seventh grade, and she had a special place in her heart for him. But a year later he'd been arrested and gone to jail. She hadn't talked to him in person since then. "Is he out of jail?"

Mrs. Jones nodded. "He's out and wanting to change his life. So we'll see him Sunday."

Cassandra instantly felt nervous and anxious. So much had happened. Would he still be the person she remembered?

⌒∿⚬∿⌒

By Sunday, Cassandra was well enough to go to church. She didn't have the energy to stand for long periods of time, so she did her hair and makeup sitting down at her desk in her bedroom. She tried to hide the rings under her eyes, but anyone looking would know she'd been sick. Her hand trembled too much to put her contacts in, so she went without, dumping her glasses in her purse in case she needed them.

As soon as the family pulled into the church parking lot, she spotted Elek. He stood near the chapel doors, thinner and older than the last time she'd seen him. His normally bronzed skin had a yellowish pallor to it, and his thick, curly brown hair was shorter. He stood up straight and smiled when the Joneses got out of the car. His smile seemed a bit timid but otherwise the same.

"Elek!" Mrs. Jones greeted him with a crushing hug. "How good to see you!"

"You too. I'm so happy to see you guys."

Mr. Jones hugged him next, then Cassandra and Emily.

"Thank you," Elek said to Mrs. Jones. "For making me feel welcome. I'm so nervous about being here. After everything."

Mrs. Jones gave his hand a squeeze. "You are like our son. Come sit with us."

Cassandra followed behind as the group moved toward the chapel. She spotted someone sitting in a chair in the foyer, though she couldn't tell who it was without her contacts in. The person waved, so she did also. Only when she got closer did she recognize Zack.

"Zack!" she said. "Hi!"

He laughed. "Hi, Cassie."

She smiled brightly at him, wanting to remind him of her birthday party in two weeks but staying quiet. He knew.

Elek didn't say much during the sermon, but he listened intently. His demeanor was different, and Cassandra was relieved to see jail time hadn't made him a darker person.

Several people came over after the sermon to welcome Elek, and he beamed each time. The Springdale congregation began to clear out, and Cassandra saw Zack take up the position of usher at the doors, welcoming people to the Fayetteville congregation. She moved that way.

Zack looked up when he saw her coming and offered her one of the printed programs.

"No, thanks," Cassandra said. "I don't need another."

"I want one!" Her little sister Annette reached out and snagged a program. She scanned it, frowning. "Mom, why are their programs prettier than ours?"

"More money," Mrs. Jones said, and Zack laughed.

"I'll see you later," Cassandra said, pulling her family along before they could make any more embarrassing comments.

Cassandra, Emily, and Annette walked out of the building with Elek, heading for the car. But Mr. and Mrs. Jones must have stayed in the chapel talking, because the four of them were still just sitting in the car ten minutes later.

"Let's go back in," Annette said.

"I have a better idea." Cassandra reached into her purse and pulled out a spare key to the van, as well as her glasses. She slipped them on her nose. "Let's practice driving."

"You can drive?" Elek looked at her uncertainly.

"No," Emily said.

"I'm learning," Cassandra said, grinning at him. She moved to the driver's seat and started the ignition.

Annette screeched. "I'm putting my seatbelt on!"

Cassandra put the car in Drive and pushed on the gas. The car lurched forward. Elek gripped the handle above the door, and Emily laughed. Cassandra pushed on the gas a little slower this time, and they began a leisurely crawl around the parking lot. She didn't give it a wide enough turn, though, and they bumped over the curb.

"Be careful!" Elek said. "You don't want to hurt anything!"

The car jostled as Cassandra moved them off the curb. "Oh, we're fine," she said. "This is what makes driving fun."

"Maybe I'd rather not drive with a fun driver," Elek said, to which the sisters giggled endlessly.

There was an announcement in first hour on Monday about cheerleading tryouts in April. Something tightened in Cassandra's chest. She had never wanted to be a cheerleader. She had scoffed at all of her friends in junior high for desperately wanting to make the squad, knowing they only wanted it for the social status and the prestige cheerleading would give them.

Not to mention that Cassandra was not coordinated or flexible. She had never done dance or gymnastics or any of those activities that generally helped people be cheerleaders.

And yet she could not get the image out of her head of Grayson standing there in front of the stairs, hanging on every word of Andrea and Melanie and the other girls in their tiny little skirts. She wanted that, and if she were a cheerleader, he would notice her.

She turned around and faced Mia. "Are you trying out for the squad next year?"

Mia nodded. "Of course."

Cassandra hesitated. The only person she had told her ambitions to was Harper, and she wasn't sure she wanted to give her hand away to someone else. But she would need Mia's help if she was going to do this. "I was thinking of trying out."

Mia's eyes went wide in surprise, and she lifted an eyebrow. "You would be so cute on the team."

"Could you help me? I would need someone to practice with, someone who could coach me."

"I'd be happy to help you."

Cassandra nodded and then turned around to face the front. Excitement squirmed in her chest like an anxious worm, but she also felt a little embarrassed, as if she had sold herself out. She didn't really want to be a cheerleader. She thought the sport was vain and silly. All she wanted was Grayson's attention, and she had mocked other girls for trying out for similar reasons. It made her a bit of a hypocrite, but she couldn't worry about that right now.

She had to make cheerleading.

CHAPTER THIRTY-NINE

Bathroom Jam

Cassandra dropped her bag beside her chair in first hour and flipped around to see Mia.

"Is it still okay if I spend the night tomorrow?"

Mia nodded. "Yes. We don't have the tryout music yet, but we can practice one of my old routines."

Cassandra beamed. She hoped practicing with Mia would help her become more flexible, because right now her moves were pathetic. "Great!" She spun back around before the teacher could get on to her for talking during class.

The high school choir kids had been assigned to help the judges at a choir festival at the Jones Center. So instead of going to second hour, Riley and Cassandra rode with Harper to the festival.

"This is going to be so boring," Riley said.

"It's better than sitting in class," Harper said.

"Gotta love that," Cassandra said, not in the least bit sad about missing health. "I don't think Amelia likes me." Cassandra had never told Harper about the soap in her eyes incident, nor had she admitted to seeing Amelia talk about her.

"Oh." Harper twirled her hand, waving off Cassandra's worries. "She's definitely jealous of me spending time with you and Riley. But I don't see what the big deal is, she's still my best friend."

"Of course," Cassandra said, though she had a hard time seeing how they were best friends. Cassandra never saw them hanging out together, and Amelia wasn't a smiley, friendly, pleasant person, at least not to Cassandra.

They pulled up at the art center where the judging would be taking place.

"Mr. Cullen said we could get something to eat before we head back to school for fifth hour," Harper said, locking her car door. "Where do you guys wanna go?"

"We could just go to McDonald's," Riley said.

"Please no," Cassandra said. "Anywhere but McDonald's."

"Don't be such a fast food snob," Riley said, annoyance flashing across her face. "It's not like you eat the meat anyway."

For some reason Riley's comment rankled. Cassandra fell silent, irritated.

The girls got to listen to the other choir sing while they helped the judges. They each took turns passing papers between the judges and the recorder, collecting notepads, and getting them bottles of water.

"Our choir is better than theirs," Riley murmured.

"They're just junior high choirs. What do you expect?" Cassandra hadn't quite let go of her earlier irritation, though it didn't seem as big a deal anymore.

"Yeah, but I'm sure we sounded better in junior high," Riley said.

She was probably right, but Cassandra didn't say so.

Around noon they finished helping with the judging, and the three girls piled inside Harper's car.

"Where to?" Harper asked.

"All the guys are going to McDonald's," Riley said. "That's where we agreed to go."

Cassandra didn't know if that was true or not, but it didn't matter. Harper was already turning her vehicle that direction.

She catcalled when she parked the car and opened the door, grinning widely. "Look at them hot seniors!"

Cassandra and Riley both laughed, and Cassandra's face grew hot when a few of the older boys glanced at them.

They went inside the fast food joint, where Miles and John and several boys who had been helping the judges with the boys' choir stood in line getting burgers and fries. Cassandra ordered a milkshake and fries, since Riley was right, she didn't eat burgers.

She spotted Janice at a table with a few friends from her special choir. Janice waved her over, and Cassandra followed. She missed talking to her. Of all her friends from junior high, Janice was the one she'd wanted to keep.

"How's life treating you, Cassie?" Janice asked.

Cassandra nodded a greeting to Janice's friends, a collection of upperclassman who she didn't know. "It's good," she said. What else was she going to say? She certainly wouldn't delve into the drama that had been her sophomore year so far, not with all the strangers sitting around.

And it kind of felt like Janice was one of those strangers. She watched her friend laugh and joke with the other kids and felt a definite sense of loss.

"Cassandra!"

Cassandra looked over to another table, where Harper and Riley stood, food in hand and beckoning. "Well, my friends are waiting for me. I better go," Cassandra said, relieved she didn't have to stay and try to make conversation.

"It was good to see you, Cassie," Janice said, flashing a smile. "Give me a call sometime, I'd love to hang out."

"Yeah, that would be super fun," Cassandra said, knowing she would never call.

She and her friends finished eating their food and headed back to the car.

"Do you guys wanna come over after school?" Harper asked.

"I would love to, sure," Cassandra said. "That would be fun!"

"Yeah, I think so," Riley said. "I just have to ask my mom first."

"Uh-huh," Harper said, digging through her purse. "Well, just let me know what she says." She looked up, her brow furrowing. "I can't find my keys."

"Oh, no." Cassandra looked back toward the fast-food restaurant. "Do you think you left them in there?"

"Yeah, we'll have to check." Harper looked distracted as the three of them paraded back inside.

They didn't find any keys at the table where they'd sat, and nobody had turned any in.

By this time it was getting close to the time they needed to be back at school, and Cassandra was feeling anxious. She looked back at the car.

"Do you think you locked them inside the car?" Riley asked.

Harper shook her head. "I never do that. I always lock my car with the clicker."

"We were a bit distracted when we got here," Cassandra said. She remembered how Harper had stopped to gawk at the senior boys walking into McDonald's at the same time.

"I guess I better check," Harper said, sighing.

They returned to the car and plastered their faces against the windows.

"I see them!" Riley said.

"No!" Harper said. She tried the door handle, but it remained stubbornly locked. Cassandra and Riley tried the other doors, but no luck.

"Great," Harper said, pulling out her phone. "I'll have to call my mom to bring me the other key."

Cassandra watched the other students pile into their cars and head for the high school.

"Maybe we should catch a ride," Riley said, speaking what Cassandra was thinking.

"I'm not leaving my car here," Harper said testily.

Cassandra had been thinking they would leave Harper there with her car, but she decided not to point that out. She glanced at Riley and Riley shrugged. Cassandra exhaled and crossed her arms over her chest, trying not to look perturbed. She would just have to resign herself to the fact that they would be late.

Fifteen minutes later, Harper's mom pulled into the McDonald's with an extra set of keys. She unlocked the door for them, and the girls took off for the high school, already late.

Harper parked the car behind the stadium, and they hurried across the courtyard, heading toward their daily sixth-hour classes.

A familiar figure with short, light brown hair walked in front of them. Cassandra's eyes glued to the back of his head.

Riley elbowed her. "Look who's there."

"I know," Cassandra said, not tearing her eyes from the figure. Like she wouldn't know it was Grayson.

Harper caught on also. "That's him, isn't it?"

Grayson opened the door to the building in front of him just as another student came barreling out, nearly knocking him over. Thus far he didn't seem to have noticed the girls.

"Watch where you're going, Grayson!" Riley called.

He turned around and gave her a scathing look, one that left Cassandra's skin crawling and grateful he hadn't looked at her that way.

Riley's face turned a mottled shade of purple. She sputtered, but Grayson had already gone into the building.

"What's wrong with him?" Riley said, fury in her voice. "How dare he look at me that way!"

"Totally not cool," Harper agreed.

Cassandra's face burned. She wished she could defend Grayson, but she couldn't. She couldn't even explain his behavior.

She hoped he hadn't seen her, because she would hate to think the look was directed at her.

Riley's mom ended up saying no to Riley going to Harper's house, but Cassandra didn't mind. She kind of liked having Harper to herself.

"I understand how you feel about Grayson," Harper said as they sat on her bed looking through old photo albums. "There was a guy I really liked last year. I thought I'd marry him, but we were too young."

"Is he in here?" Cassandra asked, looking up from the photo album.

"Somewhere." Harper gave a wisp of a smile. "His mom wouldn't let us go out anymore. And then they moved. So." She shrugged. "It's over. But I can't forget him."

"What was his name?"

"Alexander."

Cassandra shared her friend's small smile. "I wish Grayson would move. Then maybe I could let go."

"Maybe." Harper shrugged. "Or maybe you would never let go."

Cassandra hoped that wasn't so. She hoped some day she would get over this.

⟡

The RSVPs continued to roll in for Cassandra's birthday party in one week. She prickled with excitement. She'd be sixteen. Sixteen! And so far over thirty people had said they were coming.

Cassandra went home with Mia on Friday, ready to get down and practice some cheerleading moves. Mia's little sister was home.

"I'm a cheerleader also," Shannon said, leaning over the couch in the living room and watching them. "I cheer at the junior high."

"Yes, we both made cheerleading together," Mia said, rolling her eyes and shoving her hand in her sister's face.

"But I'm a year younger than you," Shannon said, sticking out her tongue. "You look like a cheerleader, Cassandra."

"And I don't?" Mia said, sounding irritated.

Cassandra studied Shannon. She certainly seemed like the cheerleader type. Her short blond hair was stylish and highlighted, her make-up thick, and her clothes form-fitting on her slender body. Mia, on the other hand, rarely wore make-up, though her freckled complexion and red hair complemented her skin tone naturally.

"Of course you do." Shannon moved into the kitchen. "Let's make macaroni and cheese for dinner."

Cassandra went down the hall. "I've got to use the bathroom. It's this way, right?"

"First door on the right," Mia said, following Shannon into the kitchen.

Cassandra let herself into the bathroom and locked the door. She examined her reflection and wondered about what Shannon had said. Did Cassandra seem pretty and outgoing and desirable? That was what she wanted to be.

She used the bathroom and washed her hands, then unlocked the door and turned the knob. Nothing happened.

She frowned at the door and twisted the lock again. Maybe she'd turned it the wrong way.

The door still wouldn't open.

Cassandra stared at it a moment. It wasn't panic time, not yet. She turned the knob and pulled. She pushed. She turned and pushed and pulled again. She rattled the door as gently as she could.

Nothing.

Heat crept up her face. She had no choice. Either she spent the night in the bathroom, or she called for help. She tried the door one more time, then pressed her mouth to the crack and called, "Mia?"

No answer. Sighing, she shook the door harder. "Mia? Shannon? I'm stuck in the bathroom!"

This time she shouted, and a moment later Mia's voice came from the other side.

"Cassandra?"

"Yep. It's me in here."

The knob rattled. "I can't open it. You have to unlock it."

"Pretty sure I did." Cassandra twisted the little button several times, to no avail. "It's still not working."

The door rattled on the other side. "I don't know. It seems to be stuck!" Mia said.

Yes. That much Cassandra had figured out.

She heard Shannon's voice join Mia. "Should we break the door down?"

"With what? Your twenty-pound frame?" The door shook as someone threw their body against it. "Yeah, that's not gonna work."

Cassandra studied the doorknob from inside. "There are a bunch of screws in the knob," she said slowly, not excited about proposing this idea. "If we unscrew them all, we can probably remove the doorknob."

"I know where a screwdriver is," Shannon said, and her footsteps padded away.

"So sorry, Cassandra," Mia said. "We'll get you out of there."

It took ten minutes, but they succeeded in removing the doorknob and freeing Cassandra from the bathroom. Mia hugged her, and they all had a good laugh. They sat down to dinner and then put on a romantic comedy, which seemed perfect after the humorous start to the evening.

By the time Cassandra crawled up on the couch under a pile of blankets, she felt content and happy with how their friendship was developing.

But the one thing they didn't do was practice cheerleading.

CHAPTER FORTY

Ground Rules

Cassandra stayed at Mia's house the next day until lunch. Mia took her outside to the backyard and finally showed her a few cheerleading moves, just the basics. But after twenty minutes, Cassandra had a new respect for cheerleaders.

"This is really hard," she admitted. "I'm feeling really unflexible." She couldn't even touch her toes, let alone do the splits or high leg kicks.

"You're doing great," Mia said graciously. "You'll learn it. You have one month until tryouts. It's plenty of time to become more flexible."

Cassandra nodded. "I'll practice every day."

"So you're going to be fine. Come on. Let me show you a few more things."

⁕

Jason Reeves called Cassandra Sunday night.

"Church class tomorrow morning has been canceled. Can you call people and let them know?"

"Sure. Why is it canceled?"

"The church building is being used for something else. So we can't use it, but we'll be able to on Tuesday."

"Great." Cassandra hung up and then went to tell her parents.

"So I get to sleep in?" Mr. Jones said jokingly.

"Yeah. You'll still take me to school, right?" She held her breath. If he said no, she'd have to catch the bus, which she did not want to do.

"Yes. You have to be ready by seven-fifteen, I don't want to be stuck in school traffic."

"You got it." Cassandra turned and went back to her room, excited by the prospect of an additional hour of sleep.

Mr. Jones came into her room at 6:55 the next morning, just as Cassandra was putting her books in her bag for school.

"I'm almost ready to go," she said. "I just need to grab breakfast and put on some make up."

"I'm not gonna be able to take you. You have to catch the bus."

Cassandra straightened up and stared at him, panic flitting through her veins. "I can't! The bus will be here in two minutes! You told me you would take me!"

"Well, something came up, and I can't. So you need to go now."

"Dad! I don't have time! I'm not ready! You said seven-fifteen!"

He shrugged. "Change of plans. You better get out the door."

She threw her backpack over her shoulder, fighting tears. How could he be so unfair? He knew the plans they'd made.

Cassandra grabbed a banana as she rushed out the door. She didn't really want it. She unpeeled it as she ran to the bus with her younger siblings, taking a few bites before chucking the whole thing into the grass.

The younger kids got off the bus at the elementary school before her, and finally the bus pulled into the high school lot. She got off in a bad mood and went to her locker to swap out books. She'd get what she needed for Spanish and health right now, then come back for . . .

She fished through her backpack again. Where was her health book? Her assignment was in it! She remembered grabbing the book from her desk when she was loading up her backpack. It had been in her hand!

She searched the backpack one last time. No health book. She groaned and slapped her hand to her forehead. She must've put it down when her dad came in and left for school without it! She needed her assignment! She took a steadying breath and reached into the side pocket of her backpack for her phone. She hated to call and ask for help, but she would have to.

Except, her phone was not there.

No way. Not only has she forgotten her health book, but she left her phone behind also? She was fighting back tears by the time she finally accepted that she had no phone. She walked dejectedly to the office.

"Can I use the phone?" she asked the receptionist, trying to sound more confident than she felt.

The woman gestured to a phone on the desk without looking at her, and Cassandra dialed her mom's number.

"Hello?" Mrs. Jones's voice said over the line.

"Mom?" Cassandra tried to sound in control, but the strain of the morning was too much, and suddenly she was crying. "I forgot my health book. I had it on my desk, but when Dad came in and made me leave so quickly, I forgot it. And I need my homework assignment!" She spoke as fast as she could, wiping at her eyes and hoping nobody in the office was paying attention to her.

Mrs. Jones heaved a sigh. "All right, Cassandra. I'll have it to you in half an hour."

Cassandra clutched the phone. "Thank you! Thank you so much!" She swallowed back the tears, her spirits lifting slightly. At least her mom was willing to help her out.

The day smoothed out after Mrs. Jones brought Cassandra her health book. She turned her assignment in and went through her other classes without any disturbances.

She was still mad at her dad, though, so when her parents pulled her into their bedroom for a "counseling session" after dinner, she got all kinds of nervous.

"What's going on?" she asked. "I haven't done anything." Not that she could think of, anyway.

Her dad cleared his throat. "You turn sixteen on Friday."

"Yes." She looked at him fearfully. Was he about to take away her driving privileges?

"You will have more freedom than ever before. We need to set some ground rules."

She let out a breath of relief. Ground rules she could handle. It wasn't like she planned to go off and cause a ruckus. "Okay. Like what?"

"No speeding," Mrs. Jones said.

"No more than two people in your car at a time who are not family members," Mr. Jones said.

The state law said only one, but Cassandra didn't point that out.

"We'll give you money for gas, but if you go through your gas allowance, you have to pay for it."

Money. "I'll get a job. As soon as I can drive, I'll start looking."

Mrs. Jones nodded in approval. "You have a curfew. Ten p.m. on Friday and Saturday, nine every other night."

Cassandra nodded again. She could not imagine what she would be doing that would require staying out late. Maybe this freedom was about to open up a whole new world of activities.

"And about dating." Mr. Jones cleared his throat like he found the subject uncomfortable.

Cassandra arched an eyebrow, enjoying his discomfort.

"Just group dates right now," Mrs. Jones said. "No pairing off, you and one other guy. Double dates are fine."

"Okay." She sure hoped her parents weren't about to launch into a kissing talk.

"We would rather you not kiss any boys," Mr. Jones said.

"Oh, please." Cassandra stood up. "I've already heard all the talks. I already know what's okay to do and what's not, what's appropriate and what isn't. We do not need to talk about this."

"It's important you remember these things, Cassie," her mom said. "When you get involved with a guy, it's too late to make these decisions."

Cassandra waved her off. "I've already made my decisions. I know where my boundaries are."

Her mom looked relieved, but Mr. Jones said, "Things can change."

"If anything ever does happen, Cassie," Mrs. Jones said, looking at her seriously, "something on accident, something serious, something against your will—you can come to us. You can talk to us about anything."

She felt the heat rushing up her face. "Right. I'll remember that."

CHAPTER FORTY-ONE

Starfish Guts

"I hope you didn't forget," Mr. Reems said on Wednesday. "We're dissecting starfish today."

Cassandra paused halfway to her desk. Dissecting starfish? Today? Oh, heck no.

She put her books down and went up to the teacher's desk at the front of the classroom. "Mr. Reems. I can't dissect things."

He looked at her skeptically. "Everyone can dissect, Miss Jones."

"I can't," Cassandra said. "It makes me sick. I got a pass for all our dissections last year in junior high."

"You're not in junior high anymore." He slapped his grade book against the table and pushed away, moving toward the lab in the back. "Pull on your big girl pants, because you're dissecting."

Cassandra stared after him, disbelieving. He was really going to make her do this!

Ashlee watched her as she came back to her desk. "Want to be partners?"

"You don't want me for a partner."

Ashlee glanced over at Andrew and lowered her voice. "I'm not gonna ask one of the boys."

"Fine."

She followed Ashlee into the lab, and they set up at one of the tables. Mr. Reems put a rimmed tray in front of each pair of students and plopped a spongy starfish on top of them. Cassandra stared at the five-limbed, yellowish creature, and her stomach turned over.

"Starfish are interesting creatures," he said, turning around to face the class. "Their body system is very different from ours. They have no brain or blood, which makes them ideal for dissecting. They have eyes, also—one at the end of each arm."

Cassandra peeked at the arms of the starfish in front of them, intrigued in spite of herself.

"Make sure you've got on your gloves, and then flip your starfish over."

Ashlee and Cassandra both pulled on the white plastic gloves. Ashlee gripped one of the legs between her two fingers and flipped the creature over.

"In the center between all the legs, you'll find the starfish's mouth. Unlike us, starfish don't put food in their stomachs; their stomachs exit the body to digest the food."

Cassandra leaned forward with Ashlee, peering at the fish's mouth.

"So, let's get started. Here's what you're going to be looking for."

Cassandra didn't really hear what he said next, because suddenly a scalpel and tweezers landed on the table beside their yellow tray, and her queasiness returned in full force.

"I can't do this," she said, sweat beading along her hairline.

"You take notes, then," Ashlee said. "I'll do the dissecting."

Cassandra tried not to watch. She jotted down what Ashlee said but couldn't help stealing glances at the dead starfish as Ashlee hacked it to pieces.

"What is this?" Ashlee squawked, lifting something stringy and white from within the starfish.

"I certainly don't know!" Cassandra said, though she *was* certain she was going to throw up.

"Those are the starfish's guts," Mr. Reems said, making his rounds over to them. "Impressive digging, Miss Pitts."

Ashlee looked pleased with herself, but Cassandra put her hand to her mouth, dry heaving. She pushed away from the desk and hurried to the trashcan at the back of the room. One hand clutched at her hair while the other clutched at her stomach, and she hoped everyone was too busy with their starfish to notice her.

No such luck. The water turned on at the sink by her shoulder, and she lifted her face to see Grayson filling a plastic cup with water.

"Starfish and snakes, ha? Not your thing?"

Before she could even find the words to respond, he handed her the cup of water.

They weren't speaking. They never said anything to each other. But he remembered the incident with the snake months ago. "Thanks," she murmured, accepting the cup of water.

"You'll be okay."

She would be sick a hundred times over every single day if it meant he would talk to her.

He had already returned to his desk. But he looked up when she walked by, and he gave her a smile.

⚘

Cassandra went home with Harper so they could work on their extra credit project for health.

"I picked the nursing home," Harper said, parking her little red Ford at the old people place. "It's close to the school, and all we have to do is visit with them for an hour."

"That sounds pretty easy," Cassandra agreed.

They got out of the car and walked inside. Cassandra lingered behind Harper at the reception desk and let her do all the talking.

"We're here for our health class," Harper said. "I guess we're just supposed to visit with the residents."

"Sign in here," the receptionist said, and both girls did so.

"Go through these double doors and down the hall. If the doors are open, the residents would like visitors. If they're closed, it's private time."

Harper and Cassandra nodded, but as soon as they walked through the doors, Cassandra's confidence faded.

"What are we supposed to do here?" she asked Harper.

"I don't know. Let's find a door that's open and see what happens."

The hallway smelled funny, like a mix between alcohol and lemons. Somehow the old smell still lingered.

"Here's an open door." Harper grabbed Cassandra's arm and pulled her inside.

A single bed sat in the room. An old lady was nearly swallowed up inside the plush chair beside the bed. Her white hair was short and she stared at the television, humming and clapping her hands as if singing along.

But the television wasn't on.

"Hi," Cassandra said.

The woman didn't react. She just hummed and clapped and even rocked a little bit in her chair.

Cassandra looked at Harper for help, but Harper looked just as lost. So Cassandra turned back to the lady.

"What are you singing?"

When the woman still said nothing, Harper whispered behind her, "You might as well be talking to the wall."

It looked like Harper was right.

"Well, nice to meet you." Cassandra turned around and left the room, and Harper followed. She grabbed Cassandra's arm and leaned forward.

"What was that?"

Cassandra shook her head. "I have no idea." This assignment might not be hard, but it sure wasn't easy.

Eventually they found a few people cognizant enough to realize they had visitors. One lady had a line of hand-drawn cards on her windowsill, and she spent ten minutes showing them off and describing the family members that had given them to her. Another insisted on leading them to the cafeteria, where she sidled up to the piano and played songs.

"You're a very good pianist," Cassandra said diplomatically.

The woman beamed.

Harper checked her watch. "It's been an hour. We can go."

"Right."

The two girls left, clinging to each other and giggling as they returned to Harper's car.

"That was one of the most awkward things I've ever done," Harper said.

"At least we don't have to do it again," Cassandra said, climbing into the car. "And hey, it raises our health grade!"

She and Harper stopped at a fast food place for dinner, and then Harper took Cassandra to her music lessons. They talked about everything from church to boys to clothes to horrible ways to die during the car ride.

"You'll be at my birthday party on Friday, right?" Cassandra asked before she got out of the car.

"Of course, girl! I'm spending the night."

"Fantastic." She gave Harper a quick hug. "Thanks for all. See you tomorrow."

After music, Cassandra went through the list of people she was still waiting for RSVPs from. She paused when she got to Cara's name. When she'd talked to Cara about her party on the bus the day before, Cara had asked her to call. Cassandra hadn't done so yet, but now she did, even though she felt some trepidation. The two girls hadn't really spoken to each other since the previous semester.

"Cassie, hi!" Cara said, her voice chipper and excited.

"Hi." Cassandra settled into her bed, leaning against the pillows and holding the phone close. "How are you?"

"I'm so great!" Cara launched into an excited monologue, talking about her new boyfriend and how fun the semester was going at school.

Cassandra sat and listened in silence, marveling at the change in her friend. Cara was so quiet and shy last year. Now she seemed to have an overflowing amount of conversation. Cassandra laughed several times.

"Sounds like everything is wonderful for you. Are you making it to my party tomorrow night?"

"I'm not sure how long I'll be able to stay, but I'm definitely coming. A few of us are coming. I wish we could stay the night, but there's a lot going on this weekend."

Cassandra's heart soared. The fact that they would come at all meant so much to her. "That's okay. It will be so great to see you guys."

"We're excited! See you tomorrow, girl."

"Tomorrow," Cassandra echoed, smiling as she hung up.

☙❦❧

It was the night before the big day.

Tomorrow Cassandra would be sixteen years old.

The school day had gone incredibly well. While a number of people couldn't make it to her party, it looked like more than fifty people would come, and most of the girls were staying the night. She had friends coming from Tahlequah and Fayetteville and Rogers. It would be the biggest event ever for her.

The only part that made her feel bad was that Grayson didn't know. She'd seen him after school walking with Charlotte. He'd glanced at her once, even given her a quick smile before looking away. Charlotte clung to his hand and also turned her face when he did. If looks could kill, Cassandra would've keeled over right then. She couldn't help wondering if he would come to her party. Would he keep it a secret from Charlotte and come to wish her a happy birthday?

She would never know, because she didn't have the guts to invite him.

She changed into her pajamas and sat on her bed reading her scriptures and listening to music, humming along to the anxious excitement in her heart. Tomorrow. Tomorrow she would be sixteen. Who would be the first guy to ask her out on a date? She wiggled with anticipation.

A knock sounded on her bedroom door, and she paused her music as her parents came in.

"We wanted to wish you good luck tomorrow," her mom said.

"Since you'll be driving by yourself. For the first time." Her dad looked rather anxious about this.

Cassandra gave a bright smile. "Thanks!"

"And we have something for you," Mr. Jones said. He pulled out a long, slender box from his pocket and handed it to her. It jangled as Cassandra accepted it.

Her heart leapt. What could it possibly be? It sounded like car keys. Had her parents changed their minds about the black clunker they'd bought her? Might there be something much nicer waiting in the driveway? She held her breath as she lifted the lid.

A gold necklace with the number "16" and a sparkling blue gem attached like a pendant set nestled in the soft tissue. Cassandra inhaled, trying to hide her disappointment.

"For you to wear tomorrow and remember us," Mrs. Jones said, and her eyes shone. "As our baby girl takes to the road."

"It's beautiful." Cassandra returned the lid, smiling up at them as if all she ever wanted was a necklace. "I'll wear it tomorrow. And I'll drive very carefully."

Her parents both hugged her and left the room, and Cassandra returned to her music. This time a genuine smile spread across her face. And even if it was an old black clunker, she had a car to drive tomorrow.

Tomorrow. She'd be sixteen tomorrow.

CHAPTER FORTY-TWO

The Big Day

Cassandra woke up half an hour before her alarm went off. She lay in bed, a smile plastered to her face as she grinned at the ceiling, excitement flowing through her veins.

Sweet sixteen today.

She got up and dressed carefully, putting on tight jeans and a black shirt with roses embroidered on the left side. Today she did not want to look like a little girl.

Her parents were waiting in the kitchen when she came out. Mrs. Jones stood up and wrapped her in a hug.

"Happy birthday, sweetie."

"Thanks," Cassandra answered, beaming with giddiness.

Her father held out the car keys. "Remember the rules," he said. "Drive carefully. Go slow. Watch for other cars. Be defensive."

"Right. Right, I know." She clutched the keys tightly in her fist, anxious to get past her parents and into the car.

Her mom gave her another hug. "Well, we won't keep you. Be careful and have a wonderful day."

"I will." Cassandra managed to escape her mom's third hug. "See you guys later!"

She turned around and hurried for the front door. She stepped outside into the frigid March morning, and immediately an attack of nerves replaced her excitement. She stood on the porch steps and stared at the black Honda in the driveway.

Show time.

Cassandra's heart pattered in her throat as she adjusted the driver's seat to her leg length. She stuck the key in the ignition and took a deep breath. Then she bowed her head and said a little prayer for safety and wisdom. When she opened her eyes and exhaled, she felt ready. Cassandra turned the key in the car, and it roared to life. A little giggle escaped her lips, then she backed out of the driveway and headed for the pick-up spot.

Mrs. Isabel wasn't there yet, so Cassandra parked her car along the side of the road and waited. Another vehicle pulled up behind her, and a moment later, Riley popped out, running the distance between their two cars and climbing into the passenger seat beside Cassandra.

"Happy birthday!" she said, throwing her arms around Cassandra.

"Thank you!" Cassandra squealed. She put the car back into Drive, and the two of them giggled and chatted like a couple of over-excited squirrels the whole way to church.

They were one of the first vehicles to arrive at the church parking lot. Cassandra had just parked and was getting out of the car when Tyler and Jason arrived.

Jason saluted her as he shut his car door, and Tyler said, "Happy birthday, Cassandra."

"Thanks," she said, beaming.

The whole class wished her a happy birthday when she came in, and she barely heard a word that was said during the hour, she was so excited to get back in her car and drive again. There was something exhilarating about being behind the wheel and being responsible for her own destination. She loved it.

Farrah joined her and Riley after class. "I don't have my car today. Can I get a ride to school?"

"Absolutely!" Cassandra said, glad for the chance to drive someone else around.

"Drop me off at the back of the school," Farrah said as they arrived at the high school. "I have to take care of some things in drama."

"Right here?" Cassandra pulled around the back.

"Not this way!" Farrah said. "It's one way!"

"Oh!" Cassandra said. "How do I turn around?"

"You don't! Park here, just park here."

Farrah's voice took on a snappy edge, and Cassandra pulled the car into an empty spot.

"I'm just gonna get out and go to class," Farrah said. "When you back out, go the other way."

Cassandra looked at her and nodded with wide eyes, feeling like she'd already failed something important.

Farrah got out and moved away from the car, giving Cassandra a stern look as she walked away. Cassandra waved apologetically.

"She's gone," Riley said, peering out the back window. "You can back up now."

Cassandra put the car in reverse and very slowly backed out of her spot before turning the wheel to drive in the correct direction. "That didn't go so well, did it?"

Riley began to giggle. "It's not like you knew! But did you see her face? She was totally freaking out!"

Cassandra began to giggle also. "Oops!"

The girls had plenty of time to find a good parking spot in the gravel pit, so they parked in the sophomore lot and then sat in the car putting on their make up.

"It's like having our own personal bathroom," Cassandra said, outlining her eyes in dark black.

"Without all the stinkiness that usually comes with the bathroom," Riley said.

"True that." Cassandra put away her make up. "I still have to get the school parking sticker for my car." She opened the glove compartment. "Which one of these is the car registration?"

"Maybe that blue one?" Riley pointed at the document in Cassandra's hand. "It looks official."

It did. Cassandra stuck the official document into her binder and climbed out of the car. She waited for Riley to get out before locking it. "Let's hurry. I don't want to get a ticket for parking with no sticker!"

They crossed the street and walked into the office together.

"I need to get a parking sticker for my car," Cassandra said to the receptionist.

"Registration, please," the woman said, glancing up from the computer.

Cassandra put the document down on the desk.

The woman gave it one cursory glance before saying, "That's your title. I need the registration."

"Oh!" Cassandra tried not to panic. "That one's still in my car."

"But you do have it?"

Well, how would Cassandra know? She had thought the title was the registration. Certainly her dad had gotten the required documents. "Yes. It's in the car."

"As long as you have it, that's fine." The woman opened the drawer and pulled out a small blue sticker. "Put this on your windshield, sticky side up, in the upper left corner."

Cassandra nodded as she took the sticker. "Thank you!" She turned and ran from the office, Riley at her side.

"It's official!" Cassandra said, unlocking her car and carefully adhering her parking sticker to the glass. "I'm a legal driver and I can legally park at school!"

The excitement did not end there. All her friends knew it was her birthday, and people greeted her in the hallways, calling out to her as they walked by. Her face felt flushed with happiness by the time she walked into Spanish class.

"Today we're going to play Spanish bingo," Mrs. Elliot said, closing the door behind them. She handed out sheets of paper. "You have to go around the class, asking in Spanish if any of your classmates have experienced the activity in the square. If they have, they sign that square. Once you have a bingo, we're going for blackout bingo. The first person to get all of the squares filled gets an extra ten grade points."

That got the class excited and murmuring. Cassandra accepted her paper and skimmed over the questions. One of them caught her eye.

Turned sixteen this year.

She elbowed Mia and pointed it out to her. "Too bad I can't sign my own," she said, grinning.

"Mrs. Elliot," Mia called out.

The teacher looked at her, and Mia said in halting Spanish, "*Cassandra tiene dieciséis hoy.*"

Mrs. Elliot looked at Cassandra. "Today's your birthday?"

Cassandra nodded, her face flushing.

"Well, happy birthday! Class, I want everyone to have Cassandra sign the birthday square. Today she's sweet sixteen!"

The attention had her body growing hot with embarrassment, but her face warmed with pleasure. She smiled as she signed each square, and her classmates wished her a happy birthday.

So far, so good.

❦

Mr. Reems stood in the classroom doorway as students approached for fourth hour.

"We have a field trip today, so head for the bus lot," he said to each student.

Cassandra turned on her heel before she reached the classroom and headed for the buses. She swiveled her head from side to side, looking for Grayson. But as her class lined up outside, her heart sank. He wasn't here.

She told herself that was a good thing.

Another class was already waiting inside the bus as her class climbed on board, and she spotted Mia toward the back.

"Mia!" She waved, and Mia scooted over in her seat to make room for Cassandra.

"Where is Grayson?" Mia asked, peering around Cassandra.

"He's apparently skipping class today, that poop head," Cassandra said, which only made Mia laugh.

They rode the bus to the Jones Center, where the high school science projects were on display. Cassandra wandered around beside Ashlee and Mia, thoroughly bored but not complaining because at least they were missing school.

After about half an hour, Mia said, "Let's get some lunch."

A number of students had already gathered at the cafeteria, and Andrew and Emmett waved from a table when the girls came in. They stood in line and ordered their food, then sat down.

"Where did everyone go?" Cassandra asked, glancing around for Andrew and Emmett. The cafeteria was nearly empty now.

"What time is it?" Ashlee asked. "Maybe it's time to go."

"I heard yesterday they left four students behind," Mia said.

The three girls looked at each other and then jumped up as one, making a beeline for the exit.

They got outside to see the bus fully loaded and ready to go. The door was still open, and they put on a burst of speed, running for it. Their peers poked their heads out the windows and hooted at them.

They scrambled on and went all the way to the back of the bus before collapsing into an empty seat, panting and laughing.

"That would have been a disaster," Mia said.

"Terrible!" Cassandra agreed. "We could've been left behind!"

"What a way to celebrate your birthday," Ashlee giggled.

The rest of the day passed uneventfully and smoothly. Cassandra saw Grayson after school getting in the car with Charlotte, which meant he had only skipped fourth hour. He didn't see her, and Cassandra was grateful. He couldn't give her what she wanted.

Riley joined her in the parking lot, just as giddy as Cassandra. "Let's go get your party ready!"

"Yes!" She pushed thoughts of Grayson from her mind and concentrated on her upcoming party. Cassandra carefully drove them home, alternating between excitement and nerves. "And then tomorrow, my first real church dance!"

"It's real for the rest of us, too," Riley said.

"Yeah, but you can't date yet. So it's not really real."

Riley frowned at her, and Cassandra backpedaled, trying to cover her superior attitude. "It's still fun to meet potential dates, of course."

"No one's asked you out yet," Riley reminded her.

But that's about to change, Cassandra thought. She didn't say it, though.

"How many people are coming?" Riley asked as they decorated the basement with party favors and streamers.

"I'm not sure. About fifty, maybe. I think fifteen girls are staying the night." Cassandra prepped a movie on the big screen TV and made sure there were plenty of blankets and chairs to sit on.

"That's a lot of people."

"Yeah." It did occur to her that the one she most wanted to be there didn't even know about it.

No, no, out of her mind. She put up the card table in the game room with lots of gaming options. "Let's move all the food to the dojo. My parents will be home soon, and I want this set up first." Her parents would be around to supervise, but they had promised to keep themselves scarce.

They put up the table with the food and set up the radio, with pop music playing.

"Now what?" Riley asked, stepping back to survey their handiwork.

"Now we wait," Cassandra said. It was almost five. One more hour before the party started. The nerves hit her in full force. She clutched Riley's hands. "What if no one comes?" This could be the biggest social disaster ever.

"Silly, everyone's coming!" Riley pulled her hands away. "Just you wait!"

Cassandra didn't have to wait much longer. The doorbell rang only moments later, and she opened it to find a Tahlequah group there. James and Andy and Brooklyn and Owen.

"Hi, guys!" she said. "I'm so glad you could make it!"

"We are a little early," James admitted. "We thought it took two hours to get here, not one."

"You drove all the way here for my birthday even thinking it was a two-hour drive?" Cassandra said, touched. "Come in and have some food!"

They munched on chips and played card games for the next forty-five minutes until the next person, Farrah, arrived. She brought Cassandra a rose and apologized for being cross that morning.

Slowly the other guests showed up, and immediately they began to make themselves comfortable. John, Emmett, and Miles crowded onto the couch in the basement, and Nicole came with her brother Shawn. Cassandra hadn't seen Shawn since the year prior when they went on a date.

"I'm so glad you could come to my party," Cassandra said, leading him over to the table of food. "How's college treating you?" She had heard from Nicole that his initiation into the fraternity had been grueling and time-consuming.

"It's fine. I got a little carried away in the beginning focusing on social groups, but I'm focusing more on classes now."

He still had the most intense blue eyes, and Cassandra wished he were younger. They had a lot of fun on their date together, and she would've enjoyed hanging out with him more.

"I'm sure you'll do great. If you're anything like Nicole, you're brilliant."

He smiled. "I'll tell her you said so."

Cassandra laughed, and then he gave her a hug before saying he had to go.

Elek came by briefly also, giving her a card and telling her to be careful driving. "My brother wanted to come," he said. "But he had to work today."

"It's totally okay," Cassandra said. Nothing could dampen her happy mood. So far she had counted about thirty people floating in and out of her house. "Thanks for coming."

Harper arrived late because she also had to work. She greeted James stiffly and then ignored him the rest of the time, even though James looked pathetically remorseful every time he looked at her. Served him right.

Cara, Andrea, and Maureen came by briefly. Nobody else from Cassandra's old group of friends came, but she didn't let it bother her. It turned out those friendships had only been skin deep.

A few kids from church came, but not Zack or his brothers. That disappointed her, but she didn't linger on it.

The party went on for hours. Most of the girls were staying the night, but a few trickled out with the boys after ten. She hugged her Tahlequah friends goodbye while they left for their hour-drive home.

Just as she closed the front door, a huge crash came from downstairs.

She hurried down to see what was going on and was greeted by laughter. Miles and Emmett and John stood, staring down at the couch, which was now tilted to one side. Miles looked up, a guilty expression on his face.

"I think we broke your couch."

"It looks like it," Cassandra agreed. "I better tell my mom."

Her mom and dad had sequestered themselves in their bedroom. Cassandra knocked on the door and poked her head in.

"Mom? I think some of the boys broke the couch."

"Are they okay?" Mrs. Jones asked, looking alarmed.

"They're fine. Not sure about the couch."

Her mom threw her arms in the air. "If we survive this night with all these hooligans running around and all we get is a broken couch, I will say a prayer of gratitude."

Cassandra grinned at her. "I think we're going to survive it."

CHAPTER FORTY-THREE
Emotional Crash

The last boy did not leave Cassandra's party until after midnight. By then, several girls had already crowded into blankets and sleeping bags in various rooms throughout the house. Cassandra went around making sure no boys were trying to stay under cover, and finally she was able to pull out her own sleeping bag. She crawled into it beside Harper and Riley in the game room, giddy and content with how her sixteenth birthday had gone.

A movement in the darkness woke her. She rolled onto her back and made out the shape of a person hovering close to her, their mouth near hers. Cassandra gasped and started to shriek before a hand clamped over her mouth, and Harper said, "Cassie, Cassie, chill! I didn't do anything!"

It was Harper? Cassandra relaxed. "Harper?"

"I'm off to work and was just gonna kiss your cheek, and right then you rolled over!"

Cassandra digested the situation and started laughing when she realize how close her friend had come to planting one on her mouth.

Harper leaned over and hugged her. "I'll skip the kiss next time. See you at the dance tonight?"

The dance! Cassandra nodded. She had almost forgotten. It would be her first dance as a sixteen-year-old. Excitement stirred in her gut. Would this be the night that most of the boys asked her out on dates? This could be the start of something big.

It was a few hours later before Cassandra woke up completely. The girls began to leave, one by one, until it was just Cassandra and Riley.

"Don't forget you have to take Riley home before the dance," Mrs. Jones said as they picked up the food and trash left over from the party.

Cassandra shot Riley a startled look. "Why? I planned on taking her to Rogers with me."

"Church policy. The youth are not allowed to drive each other."

"That's ridiculous!" Cassandra could tell from Riley's expression that she felt the same way.

Mrs. Jones raised her hand. "It's not something I can change. Just drive her home, and her mom can take her."

Cassandra and Riley grumbled about it as they took the trash upstairs.

"Who are they to get to say who we ride with when we leave our houses?" Cassandra said.

"Right? They could at least let us ride to church together."

But no amount of grumbling could change the rules, so Cassandra finally drove Riley home an hour before the dance. Then she returned home to get ready.

"You know how to get to the chapel, right?" Mrs. Jones asked Cassandra as she put her makeup on.

"Sure, I've been there dozens of times."

"But you've never driven there," Mrs. Jones emphasized. "It's different."

Cassandra shrugged, confident in both her driving and her navigational skills. "I'll be fine." She pulled on a snug white shirt with dark jeans, then curled the edges of her hair. She smiled at her reflection. She looked pretty.

"You should go, honey," Mrs. Jones said. "It's a half hour drive. You don't want Harper to get there before you!"

"I'm trying to be fashionably late!" Cassandra said. Honestly, she hoped to make an entrance.

But her mom was right. She couldn't leave Harper there alone.

She hopped in the car, elated energy rushing through her veins.

Half an hour later, though, as she drove down the interstate toward Rogers, a vague sense of uneasiness settled over her. She studied the signs as she headed north and realized she wasn't sure which exit to take. Why had she never paid attention before? She had thought she would recognize it, but each exit looked the same. She panicked, certain she'd driven too far.

The last four exit signs had all indicated she was in Rogers, so she put her blinker on, taking the next one. She drove down Walnut, the main street in town, searching left and right for a church building. She remembered it being right off the main street. Lots of restaurants, a mall . . . where was it? She turned at a light and ended up in a suburban neighborhood. She blinked rapidly against the burning in her eyes. Why couldn't she find the church?

She'd have to call her mom. Cassandra pulled the car over to the curb, put it in Park, and fished her phone out of her purse.

A rapping on her window startled her, and she looked up with a gasp.

An old man stood there, knocking on her window with his knuckle. She rolled it down just a crack.

"Can I help you?" he asked, his kind eyes crinkling. "You look lost."

She swallowed her pride, hating to admit this. "I'm looking for a church. We have dances there every month, but I don't know where it is."

"What's it look like?"

She described the odd-shaped triangular building with a tall, needle-like spire out front. The man smiled and nodded.

"I know that church. Go right at the signal and straight until you get to Dixieland. Turn left, go through several lights, and you'll see it on your right."

She exhaled, her shoulders wilting in relief. "Oh, thank you!" She put the car back into Drive and made her way to the main street again.

Right . . . Left . . .

Was he sure? She frowned as she continued down Dixieland. The church couldn't be this far away!

Just when she was about to pull over and ask for directions again, she spotted the familiar structure. She'd made it! Her hands shook as she parked the car. Only half an hour late.

Harper and Riley saw her when she came in, and they both ran over and hugged her.

"What took you so long?" Harper demanded. "I was about to freak out without you!"

Cassandra wiped the stress from her face and smiled big at them, not about to admit the truth.

"Wanted to make an entrance. How's the dance going?"

"Great!" Harper said. "I've danced with Tyler twice already!"

Of course. Tyler always liked her friends, even though he'd never shown any interest in Cassandra. She shrugged off the sentiment. It wasn't that she wanted Tyler's interest; she wanted *anyone's* interest. Wasn't there anyone who wanted her?

Brother Moda, one of the chaperones who frequently showed up at dances and church camp, came over to the girls. "Who did you bring to the dance, Riley?"

Harper smiled at Riley, and Riley said, "This is Harper. We're friends from school."

Cassandra stood quietly to the side, waiting for Harper to say, "I'm

Cassandra's friend too." But she didn't, and as the conversation between Brother Moda, Riley, and Harper continued, Cassandra's injured feelings grew. She turned around and stalked off, waiting for them to notice her absence.

They didn't. The dance continued, with Tyler dancing almost exclusively with Harper and Cassandra feeling like a lame wallflower. She spotted Zack once and he waved, but not even Zack asked her to dance. Where was the line of boys eager to ask her out on dates? Riley came over to chat, but Cassandra wasn't feeling talkative. She found the only boy not dancing—he looked about fourteen—and made him dance with her.

By the time the night ended, her bad mood had morphed into full-on self-pity. As the other kids made plans to meet at Braum's for ice cream, Cassandra got in her car and drove away without a backward glance.

Except, of course, she got on the interstate going the wrong way. When the interstate dissolved into the small town of Bella Vista, she realized her mistake. To make matters worse, it had started to rain.

"Crapola!" she said, finding a spot to turn around.

She may as well go to Braum's now, since she had to drive past it on the way home.

The whole gang was there, Tyler wedged next to Harper, who was next to Riley and Farrah and Beckham and Jason. They greeted her with a smile, but Cassandra didn't sit.

"I can't stay," she said, coming up with a lie on the spot. "It's raining. So I have to hurry home."

"Are you mad at me?" Riley asked, and Cassandra's face grew hot.

"No," she denied.

"I'll follow you out," Harper said, sliding from behind the booth.

Cassandra cupped her keys in her hand and stopped inside the first set of doors. The rain came down in torrents now, and a bit of uneasiness brewed in her gut.

"Is there something wrong?" Harper asked.

Cassandra rolled her eyes. "No. I didn't dance as much as I wanted. And I got a little, I don't know. I felt left out when Riley introduced you as her friend and you didn't mention me."

"Really?" Harper looked at her in surprise, and Cassandra felt defensive.

"Yes. I get a little jealous sometimes."

"Ah, babe." Harper gave her a quick hug. "Me too. Who did you want to dance with?"

Cassandra opened her mouth to say something, but as she did, Grayson's face flitted behind her eyes, and then she was back at

Homecoming, waiting for the dance he had promised her. "Grayson," she said, and she burst into tears. "Stupid! I should be over him by now, it's been six months!"

Harper wrapped her arms around her. "No, you shouldn't be. Sometimes we never get over these things." She squeezed Cassandra tight. "Now stop crying or you'll get in a wreck."

Cassandra wiped her eyes and smiled weakly. "Thanks."

She slipped out of the fast food joint and ran for her car, feeling only slightly better. The rain slammed against the windshield so hard the wipers didn't have any affect. And she cried. She drove slowly, blinded by both tears and rain, letting the blackness of the night act as a mask for the hurts she still carried in her heart.

⸙

A dull beeping in Cassandra's ear slowly penetrated her hazy dream state. She blinked into the dark night and then sat up as she realized it was her alarm. She swept her phone up into the palm of her hand and groaned when she saw the time.

"Five forty-seven!"

She was supposed to be at the pick-up spot already to get Riley!

She leapt from the bed, tearing her pajamas off and throwing on clothes as fast as she could. She whipped the toothbrush over her teeth and plopped her contacts into her eyes in record time.

Even so, a glance at the phone showed 5:49. Crapola! Church class started in eleven minutes!

Emily slept on. The lights were off in the house, her parents oblivious to her sleeping blunder. Cassandra grabbed her backpack and the car keys, then flew out of the house. Her heart raced in her chest as she put the car into reverse and backed out of the driveway just a little too fast. 5:50. Ten minutes to go.

She moved the car into Drive and raced out of the circle driveway, gravel kicking up behind her. She took the turn at the end of the road and sped down the hill past Beckham's house.

Suddenly the wheel spun in the opposite direction, slipping out of her hands. The car veered to the right, heading for the ditch.

Cassandra didn't even have time to scream. She grabbed the wheel, holding it tight in both hands, and slammed on the brakes. The car whipped around so hard the trees outside blurred past, and then it slammed to a halt.

Her breath rattled in her throat, and Cassandra panted, staring out the windshield.

She was still on the road. Only now she faced the opposite direction, looking back toward her house.

"You're okay. You're okay," she whispered. Her heart thrummed in her ears.

Very slowly, much slower this time, Cassandra turned the wheel and circled around until she faced the right way. Her hands shook on the wheel as she took her time continuing down the rocky road.

By the time she got to the pick up spot, Riley was long gone. Cassandra continued on to the church and parked her car. She took several deep breaths before going into the building. She'd made it here, even if she was twenty minutes late. Her classmates glanced at her as she came in but didn't say anything, and Cassandra dropped into a table beside Riley.

"Where were you?" Riley hissed. "We waited!"

"I woke up late," Cassandra breathed, pulling out her scriptures and notebook. "Sorry."

By the time class was over, Riley had forgotten about being abandoned. "Let's get breakfast at Braum's!" she said, following Cassandra to the car.

Cassandra looked it over, making sure no damage had been done from her one-eighty spin. She still felt anxious and a little jumpy, but she kept that to herself. "Sure." She willed a smile. "Let's do it."

Riley chattered the whole way there, and Cassandra found herself relaxing a bit. She pulled into a parking spot at the fast-food restaurant but didn't like the angle of her parking job. "Give me a second to re-park," she said, putting the car into reverse. Then she switched back to Drive and turned the wheel hard to the left, heading for a spot on the other side of the lot.

But there wasn't enough room, and instead of turning the car around, she drove it into the door of a blue pick-up parked two spaces over.

"You hit that car!" Riley gasped.

Cassandra panicked. "I barely tapped it. If I can just keep going . . . I'm sure I can clear it." She drove forward, but instead of skimming the side of the car, she gouged into it. The sound of crunching metal and shattering glass followed.

"Cassie!" Riley said.

Cassandra realized she'd made a mistake. She should have backed up as soon as she hit the car. Heat crept along her forehead. She flipped into Reverse and backed away from the truck. She stared at the damaged metal and paint, her heart battering in her neck. This was bad. Very bad.

"What should I do?" she whispered.

She knew what she should do. She should march into the restaurant and find the owner and confess she'd hit his car.

But that wasn't what she wanted to do.

For a moment, all her good intentions of honesty and integrity failed her, and she wanted to run and hide. "Should we just go? Not tell anyone?"

Riley only stared at her, eyes wide.

A man emerged from the store, and she knew it was too late for her half-hearted plan to flee.

"Hey!" he shouted, his face purple. "You just hit my car!"

Cassandra got out of her own vehicle, her hands shaking. "I'm so sorry. I miscalculated my turn." She tried to control her voice, but her eyes burned, and hot tears filled her eyes.

"Do you even know how to drive?" The man pulled out a cell phone.

"I have insurance," Cassandra said, the tears escaping and flowing down her face. "Let me get my card."

"I'm calling the police," he said, not even looking at her.

Riley got out too. She rubbed her arms and stood next to Cassandra. "It'll be okay, Cassie."

"Hello, yes, there's been an accident at Braum's," the man said into his phone. "Some kid hit my car. She obviously doesn't know how to drive. I doubt she even has a license. Looks like a little girl."

Indignation flooded Cassandra's veins. "I do too!" she blurted. "I can get my license for you!"

"Let's wait in the car," Riley said, guiding Cassandra away.

Cassandra sat in the driver's seat and bawled. "I have to call my parents and tell them. They're going to take my license away." How could this happen? Three days of driving, and now she'd wrecked her car!

Another man with a flannel shirt and white hair stepped out of Braum's. He walked over to his vehicle, parked several paces away from Cassandra, and gave it a careful once over, all while glaring her direction.

"I didn't hit your car, idiot!" Cassandra yelled through the window. Of course he didn't hear her, but it made her feel a little better.

A police cruiser pulled into the lot, lights flashing. Cassandra opened the glove compartment and got out her required papers, then climbed out of the car.

"I'm sorry," she sobbed, handing the papers to one of the policemen while the other talked to the truck owner. "I just made my turn wrong."

The man checked over her papers and handed them back. "Hon, it's okay. This isn't as bad as it seems."

"I hit his car," she choked out.

He patted her arm. "No one's hurt. We don't have to issue a citation. It's just a car."

The other policeman stepped over. "Tell me exactly what happened."

Cassandra replayed the events, leaving out her first inclination to flee the scene.

"It's all right," the second cop said. "You just give him your phone number and he'll follow up with you to get this fixed. We've taken a police report. Everyone's okay. You're going to be fine."

Cassandra took a deep breath and nodded. She felt a bit better having spoken with them. She turned to the man, wishing she didn't have to talk to him. "Here's my number."

She watched him write it down, then the policemen told them they could go to school.

"I need to call my parents," Cassandra whispered. She drove very slowly the half a mile to the high school, wishing she could let Riley do it.

"Class starts in ten minutes," Riley said.

Cassandra parked in the back and squeezed her eyes shut.

"You should check your car," Riley said softly. "See the damage."

Her eyes flew open. "Have you?"

Riley nodded.

Crapola. One more thing. Cassandra slammed the door behind her and went around to the passenger side, where she'd hit the car. Her stomach roiled with nausea as she took in the dangling light and crumpled metal. "My damage is worse than his!"

Riley shouldered her backpack and joined her. "I have to get to class. I'll see you in fifth hour."

Cassandra swallowed hard and pulled out her phone. Time to face the music.

CHAPTER FORTY-FOUR

Squad Girls

No one answered when Cassandra called home. The tardy bell was about to ring, and she would have to wait until after first hour to try again.

"Are you all right?" Mia asked when Cassandra slipped in right before the bell rang.

Cassandra faked a smile and nodded. "Fine." She didn't feel like telling everyone at school what had happened.

"Don't forget the cheerleading meeting after school today," Mia said. "It's mandatory. You and your mom have to come."

Great. Cassandra had the feeling her mom wouldn't want to do anything that night.

By the time class ended, she felt numb inside. She needed to reach her parents and get this over with. She ducked under the stairs before second hour and called home again.

"Hello?" Mr. Jones said, answering the phone.

Whatever numbness she thought she'd felt dissipated in an instant, and Cassandra burst into tears. "Daddy?"

"Cassie? What's wrong?" He immediately sounded alert and concerned.

"I—I—I hit a car this morning!" She sobbed the words out.

"You hit a car?"

"Yes!"

"Are you hurt?"

"No. It was in a parking lot."

"Is the other party hurt?"

"No. No one was in the car."

Her dad let out a loud sigh. "Cassie, honey, it's okay."

She blinked. "It is?"

"Well, it's not great. But these things happen. I'm glad no one was hurt."

Her throat tightened. "Aren't you angry?"

"Honey, I'm so sad for you."

Now her eyes welled up again, but for an entirely different reason. She'd thought for sure she'd be grounded for life.

"We'll talk about it more when you get home," Mr. Jones said. "For now, just get through your day. Don't let this affect you too much."

Instantly she felt loads lighter. She wiped her eyes and straightened up, finally believing it would be okay. "Thanks, Daddy."

Throughout the day, her friends asked if she was okay, noticed her bloodshot eyes, but Cassandra didn't say a word. She was too embarrassed.

Her parents were waiting for her the moment she got home after school. She could tell her mom had another headache from the way she sat hunched in her chair, but both of them greeted her in the living room with big hugs.

"Have a seat," Mr. Jones said, gesturing to the couch. Cassandra sat.

"I'm glad you told us when you did. The man whose car you hit called a few hours later, and at least we knew what he was talking about."

"Tell us what happened," Mrs. Jones broke in.

Cassandra sucked in her breath and slowly let it out. "I was trying to move to another parking spot and miscalculated my turn. So I hit his car."

"Who called the police?" Mr. Jones asked.

"He did. When I told him what happened." The tears stung her eyes, unbidden. "He was a jerk."

"He called the police while you stood there bawling your eyes out?" When Cassandra nodded, Mrs. Jones said, "That was really cold. We should drop bombs on his house."

Cassandra laughed, a cross between a snort and a hiccup. "I don't think we're allowed to even say things like that."

"We're not going to punish you," Mr. Jones said. "But you do have to pay for the damage to his car. It's almost two thousand dollars."

Two thousand dollars. Cassandra gulped. Her monthly allowance of twenty dollars would not cover that.

"So I suggest you get out there tomorrow and look for a job," Mr. Jones continued.

Cassandra nodded. "Okay." She waited, and when nothing else was forthcoming, she ventured, "Is that it?"

"That's it," Mr. Jones said.

That wasn't so bad. She'd wanted a job anyway. And she got to keep the car. She turned to her mom.

"There's a cheerleading meeting tonight. We both have to be there."

"Oh, honey." Mrs. Jones closed her eyes. "I'm not feeling well. I can't get there."

"But if I don't go, I can't be in cheerleading," Cassandra said, panic again whispering through her chest.

"Let me call the coach. Maybe you can go with Mia and her mom, and I'll meet her later."

"That's not how these things work," Cassandra said.

"Cassie. It's either that, or you don't go."

Cassandra bit back any further misgivings. "Okay."

In the end, the coach let Cassandra show up with Mia and her mom. Once again Cassandra drove into town. She took a deep breath and pulled open the doors to the cafeteria, the only person without a parent there. Heads turned her way, and she avoided making eye contact with anyone as she scanned for Mia. Spotting her, Cassandra hurried to her table and sat beside her with a quick smile. Then she checked out the other kids in the room.

Cheerleaders and dance squad, almost every one of them. They sat casually with an arm slung over the back of a chair or resting on the table in front of them, wearing cheerleading shirts and ribbons in their hair to give them away as team members already.

The coach was talking, and Cassandra tried to tune into her words.

"Not all of you will make it," she was saying. "Even some of you currently on the squad won't make it. We have incoming freshmen and new people trying out. So don't miss any practices, and bring your A-game to the tryouts."

Cassandra swallowed, her heart plummeting as she stole another glance around the room. These girls were experienced. They knew what they were doing.

This was going to be hard.

❦

Cassandra began to make the rounds after school, stopping at different fast food places and picking up job applications. She tried Subway first.

"We don't do applications in the store anymore," the lady behind the register said. "Everything is online. You just fill it out, and if we have an opening, you'll get a call."

"Oh. Okay," Cassandra said, feeling slightly deflated. She had really hoped to get an answer today about the job.

"It would be great to have some more help around here," the lady said.

Cassandra offered a smile. "I'll go online and fill it out tonight."

She bypassed Wendy's. While she was sure she could get a job working with her mom, she didn't want to. She did stop at Taco Bell, one of her favorite places to eat, but they told her the same thing: go online and fill out an application. Was job-hunting always this impersonal?

She stopped at one last fast food place on her way home, Burger King. She offered a smile to the guy behind the register.

"Can I talk to the manager, please?"

Sure," the kid said, and he walked away.

"Hey, Cassie!" a boy called from the back.

Cassandra craned her neck to see Andrew waving from the food prep counter.

"Hey, Andrew," she said.

"What are you doing here?"

"Hoping to get a job."

The manager came up to the counter from the back, glasses and stubble decorating his face. "Can I help you?" he said, looking bored and uninterested.

"You want to hire her," Andrew shouted. "She's awesome."

Cassandra shot him a grateful smile. Then she faced the manager. "I was hoping to fill out a job application."

He squinted at her. "Well, most everyone applies online these days. But since Andrew put in a good word for you, go head and take this paper one." He fished one out of a drawer and handed it to her. "We'll put you down as a referral and get you bumped to the top of the list."

Cassandra's heart soared. "Thank you!"

She practically skipped back out to her car. Maybe finding a job wouldn't be so hard after all.

Cassandra prepared her application that evening and put it in her backpack. With any luck, she would soon be gainfully employed at Burger King.

It was nine weeks testing again the next day, which meant she'd be able to leave school in between tests. And this time, she would be driving.

But first she had to get through her biology test.

Grayson did not even glance at her when she walked in, which was so normal that she didn't know why she even looked. But she did, and his lack of response squeezed her heart, making it constrict painfully in her chest. How was it that she could be invisible to him after what they had almost been?

She tried to shake off the oncoming gloom and focus on her test. But suddenly all the things she had studied jumbled around in her head, and none of the questions made any sense. Multiple choice would've been nice, but they were short answer, and she fumbled for a long time, making up answers and stringing technobabble words together, half hoping she could fool the teacher into thinking it was correct because it sounded good.

The bell rang to indicate the end of class, and Mr. Reems said, "If you're not done, you may stay and take the time you need. I'll still be here."

Cassandra was not done. She had finished three of the four pages. She risked a quick glance over her shoulder and saw Grayson, still concentrating hard on his own exam.

Suddenly her desire to get out of the classroom, to get away from him, was stronger than any fleeting ambition to get an A on the exam. She stood up, not even bothering to guess the answers for the rest of the questions. She walked to the desk and left her paper there. Then she hurried out of the classroom, head held high even though she'd just sealed her doom.

She met up with her friends in the choir room. Riley, Harper, Betsy, and Miles were all there, and they greeted her with such enthusiasm and excitement that Cassandra managed to put off the negative feelings from biology.

"Are we ready?" Harper asked, jangling her car keys in her hands.

Cassandra pulled her own keys from her purse. "Where are we going?"

"Fayetteville. We have time. They've got some nice restaurants off Joyce Boulevard."

"Sounds like a plan," Cassandra said.

The teenagers split into two groups, with Cassandra taking Riley and Miles in her car. Being one of two people who was able to drive made her feel special.

Harper called Riley while they were driving.

"I had to stop at my house and get something," Harper said. "I'll be about half an hour behind you."

"You got that?" Riley asked Cassandra as she hung up.

Cassandra nodded. "What are we supposed to do for half an hour while we wait for her?"

"There's plenty to do in Fayetteville," Miles said. "Where do you want to go?"

Immediately Cassandra thought of the pet store. It had always been one of her favorite places to go as a kid, and now she could drive herself there anytime she wanted. "The pet store!"

"And I thought you were going to say the bookstore!" Riley said.

Cassandra grinned broadly. "Not this time."

She made the ten-minute drive to Fayetteville without incident, and she very carefully parked her car in the back away from other vehicles. The memory of hitting that other car was still too fresh on her mind.

Her friends lingered in the entrance of the store when they walked in, though Cassandra immediately took off for the den of ferrets. One of her favorite things about this particular store was that most of the animals were in open cages with the tops off. Customers were invited to reach out and touch them and find the animal most suited to their personality. Even the birds flitted about freely on a small tree, their wings clipped so they couldn't fly away.

Cassandra reached into the ferret cage and pulled out one of the wiry animals, rubbing her face into the fur and smelling the musky scent. Ferrets reminded her of cats with their cuddliness, but their long torsos and tiny faces enabled them to maneuver about in smaller places. It was her dream to own one someday. She had asked her mom half a dozen times, but Mrs. Jones always said no.

"Hey, Cassie!"

She turned around when Miles called out to her and nearly screamed when she saw the snake wrapping itself around his hand. He only laughed.

"It won't hurt you!" He took a step toward her.

Cassandra put the ferret back in its home and backed up.

Riley stood behind Miles and stroked the scaly back of the snake. "Oh, Cassandra, it's so nice. You should touch it."

Cassandra shook her head rapidly. "No way!"

Miles held it out toward her, and he and Riley both cracked up when she shrieked and ran the other way.

They were still chuckling when they finally left the pet store twenty minutes later and headed for the car.

"Most snakes won't hurt you," Miles said.

"You're looking at this all logically," Cassandra said. She fastened her seatbelt and turned the car on. "It doesn't work that way in my head. I'm terrified of them."

"You'll never get over it if you don't start touching them," Riley said.

Cassandra didn't answer, but she wasn't concerned. She didn't feel the need to "get over it."

They arrived at Kirby's, a standard American restaurant, or so the sign out front claimed, at almost the same time as Harper. The six of them settled into a table, Riley and Miles sharing their exploits at the pet store with Harper and Betsy. Cassandra's face burned, but she couldn't help giggling along with her friends.

"One boy and five girls, huh?" The waiter came by with menus and winked at Miles. "Looks like it's your lucky day."

Miles' face turned bright pink, and Cassandra was happy to join in the laughter at someone else's expense.

They took their time at lunch and finally headed back to the high school for their last hour of testing. They met up again as soon as class ended with the intent to go to Harper's house. Cassandra was so busy talking with her and Riley that she didn't see Grayson at his locker until he stood up and glanced at them.

She stopped talking abruptly, wondering how she had missed him. He met her eyes and nodded before turning around and continuing down the hallway.

A lump formed in her throat, and she swallowed hard. A nod? Was that all she deserved? What bad luck to run into him!

Harper glanced from Cassandra to Grayson and back. "That wasn't Grayson, was it?"

Cassandra nodded, not taking her eyes from Grayson's retreating back. "Yes. That was him." That aching sadness was back, and she forced a smile. She couldn't let him rule her emotions. "I'm okay, though. I really am."

She would be, anyway.

CHAPTER FORTY-FIVE

Tornado Clean Up

The weather had turned nippy by the time the two girls walked outside to get to their cars, and Harper pulled out her weather app.

"It looks like it's supposed to snow tomorrow."

"It better not!" Cassandra said. "I've got too much going on!" Snow in the middle of March? She was ready for sunshine!

It had started raining by the time they got to Harper's house. The girls crowded into Harper's living room and watched a movie, but Cassandra's thoughts went back to Grayson. How had she managed to lose him? How had everything gone so wrong?

Harper found a second movie after the first ended, but Cassandra stood up.

"I better head home," she said, not in a fun mood anymore.

Harper followed her to the door. "You okay?"

Cassandra rolled her eyes. "Just more of the same."

Harper gave an understanding smile. "Hey, you know that tornado that happened in Arkadelphia this week?"

"Sure," Cassandra said. She'd heard something about it on the news, anyway.

"My church youth group is taking a trip down there during spring break to help clean up. Want to come?"

Harper was inviting her and not Riley? Warmth touched Cassandra's heart. "Yes. I'd love to. I'll ask my mom, but I'm sure it'll be fine."

"Great." Harper gave her a big hug and a loud kiss on the cheek. "See ya later, babe. Drive careful."

"Will do."

Cassandra stopped at Burger King on the way home and asked for the manager, but he wasn't in. She gave her application to another woman, who glanced over it and said they'd call her. Then she stuck it in a drawer.

Cassandra crossed her mental fingers as she walked out, hoping they would call her with a job offer soon.

❦

Cassandra stopped by Harper's house after school on Friday to drop off the permission slip for their trip to Arkadelphia during Spring Break the following week. Then she picked Mia up so they could practice cheerleading.

"Ready to go to my house?" Cassandra asked.

"Let's do something first. Like, go to the mall."

Cassandra grinned. "Can we go to the pet store? I want to show you the ferrets."

Mia looked a little unsure, but she nodded. "Okay."

Cassandra parked in front of the pet store and led her friend inside. Cassandra went straight to the ferret home and lifted one out.

"See? Aren't they the cutest?" Cassandra rubbed her cheek against the prickly fur.

Mia took a step backward. "I don't want to touch it."

Cassandra laughed at her and put it back. "Fine. What animal do you want to see?"

Mia looked around and went over to the bird tree. She put her finger out, and little bird landed on her. "I like birds."

Birds were only slightly more interesting than fish. Cassandra wandered over to the glass cages and peered down at a sleeping lizard.

"Do you want to hold it?"

Cassandra lifted her face and was surprised to see one of the employees standing beside her, a sleepy expression on his young face.

"Well, sure."

The kid opened the top and pulled out the lizard, then handed it to Cassandra. She accepted it and lifted an eyebrow at the scratchy little claws as they wrapped around her hand. The creature had bumpy skin and a fat, squishy tail.

"Oh!" Cassandra exclaimed, delighted. "He's awesome!" She held him toward Mia. "Mia, you have to touch him!"

"No, I don't!" Mia covered her face as if afraid the lizard might jump on her.

Cassandra shoved it toward her. "Come on, Mia. Just pet it."

Mia shrieked and pushed Cassandra's hand away.

Suddenly the lizard jumped from Cassandra's palm. It landed on the linoleum and took off running.

Mia's scream echoed through the pet store, and the kid-employee mumbled something and charged after the lizard. Cassandra stared open-mouthed, fighting back the hysterical laughter bubbling up in her chest.

"It's probably time to go now." She grabbed Mia's arm and hauled her toward the exit.

It took the girls half an hour at Cassandra's house to stop giggling after the pet store excitement and start practicing. Mia led them through a standard routine slowly, correcting Cassandra's arms and straightening her body.

"Okay," Mia said. "Let's go a little faster this time."

Cassandra nodded. She almost kept up with Mia, only messing up at the end.

"Good," Mia said. "Now up to tempo."

Mia chanted out a count and then started the routine, much faster than Cassandra had anticipated. She kept up for a total of eight counts, and then she spent the rest of the routine trying to figure out where Mia was.

This was terrible.

Mia finished and beamed at her. "How did it go?"

"It was all right," Cassandra fumbled.

"Should we try it with the music?"

Cassandra hesitated. Bracing herself, she went for full honesty. "I'm really bad at this, Mia. I think I'm changing my mind. I won't make it. Maybe I shouldn't try out."

"No way!" Mia exclaimed. "You'll do awesome. We just have to keep practicing. It would be so much fun to have you on the squad with me!"

"Okay." Cassandra sighed, sensing the futility of the effort. "Let's do it again."

"Cassandra!"

Cassandra jolted awake at the sound of her name and blinked into the hazy darkness of her bedroom. Was it time to get up? Wasn't school out this week?

The light turned on, and Mr. Jones stood over her bed, his lips pressed down in a frown. "You're supposed to take me to the airport before you go to Harper's!"

Harper's. The Arkadelphia trip. The memory slowly crashed through the fog of Cassandra's brain, and she sat up. "You were supposed to wake me!"

"Well, we have to go now or I'll miss my flight!"

"Okay. Okay." Cassandra scooted out of bed and searched for her duffel bag. At least she'd already packed for the trip.

Her dad returned to the kitchen while she brushed her teeth and dressed. She'd barely plopped her contacts into her eyes before he returned.

"Let's go, let's go!"

She shouldered her bag and followed him out to the car. "Am I driving or you?"

"You drive." He settled himself into the passenger seat and opened his laptop. "I've got work to do."

Cassandra put the car in reverse and backed out of the driveway, then continued down the winding country roads to the regional airport in Cave Springs.

"Here's some money for your trip," Mr. Jones said, pulling a twenty dollar bill from his wallet.

"Just put it in my purse," Cassandra said, concentrating on taking the switch-back curves slowly.

"Where's your purse?"

"It's on—" she cut herself off abruptly. Usually her purse was in his seat, but where had she put it? Her eyes went wide. "Oh no! I forgot my purse!" Which meant she didn't have her license, either! She gripped the steering wheel tighter as panic flooded her.

"It's all right, calm down. Just drive home really slowly, get your license, and continue to Harper's house."

"Okay. Okay." Cassandra nodded and took deep breaths.

She dropped Mr. Jones off with only half an hour before his flight and then turned around and went home again. She drove slower than the speed limit, super anxious about being pulled over. She breathed a sigh of relief when she finally parked at home. She ran inside, grabbed her purse, and left again without saying a word to anyone.

As soon as Cassandra pulled up to Harper's house, Harper flew out the front door.

"There you are!" she said, her long blond hair flowing behind her. "What took so long? We'll be the last ones there!"

"Sorry, sorry," Cassandra said, too embarrassed to admit she'd had to drive home again to get her license.

She drove them both the short distance to Harper's church. Only after she'd hauled her things out of the car and locked it did she feel she could relax. She followed Harper onto the bus and collapsed into the seat beside her.

Miles Hansen and Todd Wilcox sat behind them, and Harper turned around to chat with them. Cassandra leaned her head against the window and let the exhaustion lull her to sleep. She didn't sleep well on the bus, because for some reason Todd thought it very funny that she was trying, and he kept poking her and waking her up.

Hours later, the bus pulled into a church parking lot in Arkadelphia. Cassandra sat up and surveyed the tornado-ravaged town. Insulation erupted from broken houses like cotton from a stuffed animal. Branches and trees criss-crossed the roads, and upturned vehicles dotted yards and parking lots. Shards of glass littered the ground in driveways and in the street.

"It's terrible," Harper said, leaning over Cassandra's shoulder to look.

"Yeah," Cassandra agreed. She was glad for this opportunity to help them.

The bus squealed a sigh as it parked in front of a large brick church, and one of the youth leaders stood up in the front and spoke to them.

"Get your bags from under the bus and take them into the church. There's a room for girls and a room for boys. Then gather in the lobby, and we'll take you to the warehouse for our first assignment."

Cassandra stood and filed off the bus with the other kids. She did not expect the hot, sultry air that smacked her in the face the moment she stepped outside. Back home, five hours north, spring was just getting its feet on the ground. Here it seemed to have dug in its nails and gotten a fever.

Inside the church was only slightly cooler. She put her bag next to Harper's and went back to the lobby.

"I'm going to divide you into groups of five," the youth leader said. "We'll be sorting clothes and food, and I'll assign each group a task."

Easy enough. Cassandra stood next to Harper and got put in her group with Miles, Amelia, and an older girl she didn't know.

The bus drove them back to the warehouse. If anything, it was even hotter inside the building than outside, and it also stank. Piles of cans, boxes, and clothes littered the interior. The youth leader stepped over to the older girl in their group.

"Beth, I'm putting you in charge." She nodded, and he continued. "All these cans of food here? They've been donated, but they're a mess. We need to sort them. Let's get them separated and into piles."

He walked away, and Harper said, "I'm going to see what Todd's doing."

Beth rolled her eyes as Harper left. "So much for being in our group. Everyone pick a food item and start sorting those cans."

"I've got green beans," Miles said.

Cassandra smiled. "I'm tomato sauce."

"This is you, then," Amelia said, tossing a can of tomato sauce at her.

Cassandra caught it easily and started a pile beside her. "What are you, Amelia?"

Amelia glanced through the food. "Sweet potatoes."

Soon cans were being tossed back and forth between them. Cassandra squealed when one got away from her and rolled across the floor and laughed out an apology when she knocked over the pile Miles was building.

In less than an hour, they had finished with their job, and Beth went to the youth leader to get another. She came back and said, "Now we need to sort clothes according to gender and size. The clothes are over here."

The smell in the warehouse grew worse as they moved toward the clothing. Cassandra wrinkled her nose. "This won't be quite so easy."

"Lots of piles," Beth said. "Let's start by separating boy from girl."

Amelia picked up a blue shirt with a streak of mud on it. "And dirty?"

Cassandra also pulled out a pair of pajamas wet enough to cling to her hand. "Did these come out of ruined houses?"

Beth looked disgusted. "Let's just do the best we can."

The next hour passed slowly as they separated moldy clothes from clean, ripped clothing from usable. Cassandra's hands smelled, and she kept them away from her face.

The youth leader finally called a halt. Amelia passed around a disinfectant, and Cassandra applied it liberally.

The group headed to a frozen yogurt place after, and Amelia's brother Chris kept teasing Cassandra. He stole her yogurt and then picked her up when she tried to get it back.

"You are such a flirt!" Cassandra said, laughing and hitting him.

"A what?" He grabbed her in a headlock and ran his knuckles over her head. "I'm a what?"

"Nothing! Nothing! You're not a flirt!"

Everyone was laughing by the time he released her, and Cassandra beamed at him. At least there was a cute guy to talk to on this trip.

The next morning started out much the same. They went to the warehouse and divided into groups and sorted clothing. Cassandra wondered if the donations were items people found in their basement that they no longer wanted. It was all wet and stained.

After lunch, though, they drove into town where a few families from the local congregation had asked for help sifting through debris.

"We should have the girls over here, going through the kitchen things," the youth leader said to another leader. "The boys can do the heavy lifting."

Cassandra took offense to that comment. Just because she was female didn't mean she was weak. She kept her mouth shut, but when the boys were directed outside, she followed along with them.

The youth leader began yelling out instructions to haul away branches and bricks that had fallen into the living room and what remained of the master bedroom of the house, which no longer had a roof. Cassandra knelt down beside Chris and got her hands under a large piece of tree.

"What are you doing?" he asked, giving her a startled look.

"I'm helping." Without waiting for his response, she heaved a portion of the tree into her arms.

It was heavier than she expected. Her forearms immediately began to ache, and only because Chris was watching did she force herself into a standing position.

He laughed, his eyes following her as she carried the piece of tree over to the trailer hauling away debris. "You're much stronger than you look," he said, something like admiration in his tone.

Cassandra couldn't respond; it took all her concentration to place the wood on the trailer. Then she turned back around and gave a breezy smile as if it hadn't been hard at all.

"I do karate."

She wasn't sure where the lie came from. She didn't do karate. She didn't do any physical activity, for that matter. But Chris didn't question her.

"Well, karate girl, you can come help me with this one."

Karate girl. Cassandra liked it. She stepped over to his side and got on the other end of a log much heavier than the one she had carried. Chris did most of the work, but together they cleared away a good chunk of the debris in the bedroom.

"Good job, karate girl," Chris said, holding his hand up for a high five.

The smile did not leave Cassandra's face for the rest of the day.

CHAPTER FORTY-SIX
Crush Material

The bus stopped in Tulsa on the way home from Arkadelphia so the kids could get out and stretch their legs, get food, and play laser tag.

Cassandra and Harper wandered around the Tulsa mall, eating pretzels as they talked.

"I really like Todd," Harper said. She paused as if for effect, then said, "He kissed me on the bus."

That explained why Harper had switched seats with Miles and seated herself next to Todd.

"He did?" Cassandra looked at her in surprise. "Are you dating now?"

"Well, I don't know." Harper sat down on a bench, and Cassandra joined her. "He doesn't seem like the committed type."

"Really? And you let him kiss you?" Cassandra raised an eyebrow.

"It was all in fun." Harper sighed. "I want to be his girlfriend, though."

"Hmm." Cassandra considered the two of them. Todd was thinner than he'd been in elementary school and wore glasses now. He also had a bit of an acne problem. He should consider himself lucky to have a girl like Harper interested in him. "Maybe he'll change his mind."

"Maybe."

They finished up at the mall and joined the group of kids outside the laser tag studio. Chris spotted Cassandra and moved to her side. He bumped her with his bulky shoulder.

"How's Karate Girl?" he asked in a deep voice.

Cassandra hid a smile. "Ready for some laser tag."

"You gonna kick our butts in there?"

Now she laughed. "I'm not really a great shot."

He grinned down at her, at least two heads taller than her. "Then I'm gonna take you down."

"You can try."

They went in and suited up with the electronic vests and glowing lights. Then they were released into a series of dark tunnels and stairs.

Immediately the kids vanished, and Cassandra clung to the wall, whipping her weapon around corners and shooting at anything that moved. She crouched as she walked and shrieked when someone leapt out at her and stunned her.

Her vest made a noise as her attacker walked away, indicating that she had died and couldn't play anymore. She slipped into a corner, waiting for it to reboot so she could shoot again.

She heard someone on the other side of the wall, and the flashing green light on her gun told her she could play again. She spun around the corner and shot the laser dead center into Chris's back. "Got you!"

He gave a yell and whipped around, his elbow colliding with her eye.

"Ugh!" Cassandra cried, reaching a hand up to her face. She knelt and bowed her head.

"Cassandra! I'm so sorry!"

She blinked, her eye numb from the force of the impact. But something didn't seem quite right. She blinked again and looked around, unable to focus on the lights or surroundings with her left eye.

"Did I hurt you?" Chris crouched next to her.

Cassandra reached up and felt around her eye, then gingerly poked at the iris. "My contact lens is gone!"

"I knocked it out?"

"Yes!" She hadn't even known that was possible. "We have to find it!" Each lens cost over seventy dollars, since they were colored and opaque to cover her dark eyes. She dragged her hands along the filthy ground, feeling for something sticky and wet.

Chris ran his hands along the bottom as well. "Can't you just get another at home?"

"They're yearly lenses. And they're colored."

"Let's use the laser light." Chris aimed his gun at the ground and pushed the trigger, lighting up a circle of red on the ground.

Giggling teenagers ran into the hallway, and he spun around, stretching his arms out wide.

"Don't come through here!" he said. "We lost a contact lens!"

They turned around and went the other way, and he resumed flashing his laser on the black floor.

"Here!" Unbelievably, Cassandra found the small disc. She lifted it up, and Chris blinked the laser on it a few more times.

She blew on it. "It's bound to be dirty." She knew she wasn't supposed to do this, but right now was practically an emergency. She plopped the lens into her mouth and cleaned it the best she could with her tongue. Then she held her breath as she pulled it out. Anticipating pain, she stuck it back in her eye.

Sure enough, a searing burn caused her eye to tear up. She blinked rapidly and clenched her fists, and to her relief, the pain receded.

"There." She smiled at Chris.

"Are we good?" He exhaled, his face worried.

Cassandra looked at his weapon, the one he'd fired countless times to help her find her lens. "I'm afraid your score won't be very good."

His worry creased into a grin. "Shooting a contact lens five hundred times should count for something."

〜◈〜

Cassandra called Riley as soon as she was home on Thursday.

"Did you have fun?" Riley asked.

"I had a blast," Cassandra said. "Come over, I'll tell you all about it."

"Come get me."

Cassandra could. She had a car now, and she loved being able to drive herself everywhere. "Be there in fifteen."

She and Riley stayed up late talking about the trip.

"There was this guy Chris," Cassandra said. "He was so nice and flirty. I really liked hanging out with him. I think—" she hesitated. "I think I might be getting over Grayson."

"Well, that's about time," Riley said with an eye roll.

"I know. But it's not like I could make it happen."

"So tell me about Chris."

"Well, he's Amelia's brother. He's got red hair and is tall and muscular. A football player."

"Ha." Riley lifted a shoulder. "Those guys only like cheerleaders."

Cheerleaders. Cassandra's stomach tightened. "Maybe I'll be one next year."

Riley frowned. "But you'll change if you become one."

"I'll have to change. That's part of being a cheerleader. They care about clothes and makeup and hair and stuff." Cassandra considered the matter. "I should probably change my look now."

"I don't want you to change."

Riley had always been a supportive friend, no matter what Cassandra looked like. "Tell you what," Cassandra said, grabbing Riley's hands. "Let's go tanning tomorrow and then get our hair cut."

"You mean you want a trim? You've never cut it short." Riley eyed Cassandra's hair, flowing halfway down her back.

"No." Cassandra shook her head. "I want something different. I'm going to cut it off." A chin-length bob. That was what she'd do.

"Okay, if you want to," Riley said, arching an eyebrow.

Cassandra smiled. She did.

It was time to get ready to be a cheerleader.

EPISODE 6: CHEERLEADING AND OTHER FIASCOS

CHAPTER FORTY-SEVEN

Two Masters

Cassandra Jones woke her best friend Riley, who had spent the night, around ten on Saturday morning.

"Wake up!" she said. "We have to get our hair cuts!"

Riley yawned and tumbled from the bed. "I still don't believe you're going to cut it short."

"New me, here I come." Cassandra brushed her teeth and smiled at herself in the mirror. She was sixteen now, a sophomore in high school, and about to try out for cheerleading. It was time to stop looking like the same little girl from junior high. A few weeks ago she'd tried to pierce her belly button, but it had gotten infected and grown back. She hadn't tried again. A haircut would be more visible, anyway, and would probably make her look older.

They left the house around eleven and went to the tanning salon. Cassandra paid for both of them and crossed her fingers that she'd have a job soon so she wouldn't keep spending her measly allowance.

"Have you done this before?" the girl with bleached blond hair and orange-colored skin asked as she led them down a hallway with multiple rooms.

"No," Cassandra said, casting a nervous glance at Riley.

"So it's easy. You go in the room and set the dial for how long you want to tan. I recommend ten or fifteen minutes for your first time. Once you do that, you have three minutes to get inside the bed. Put on the eye covers and pull the top of the bed over you. Then just sit and wait for the timer to ding. When it does, hop on out."

"Do we take everything off?" Riley asked.

"Unless you want tan lines. We have little stickers, too, if you want to compare your skin to before and after."

Cassandra took a slow breath, trying not to imagine being stuck inside a box shooting hot rays at her. "I'll take this room." She pushed the door open and went inside.

The bed looked like a space-age device, sleek and oval with light bulbs inside the top and bottom. A little pillow waited for her head. Cassandra set the timer for ten minutes, then stripped down to her underwear. The cool air in the room raised goosebumps on her arms, and she covered herself. Then she dove into the bed, pulling the top down and protecting her eyes with the little plastic goggles.

Now she waited. Her heart thrummed anxiously. At least the bed was open on the sides so she didn't feel trapped.

A hum filled the room seconds before all the lights on the bed turned on. Cassandra closed her eyes. A slow heat radiated upward and around her, comfortable and soothing. She let her breathing slow. It wasn't too hot.

Just as she was drifting off to sleep, the humming and lights turned off, casting Cassandra into darkness and cold.

She pushed open the lid of the bed and sat up. That hadn't been so bad. She checked her underwear line and was pleased to see a slight difference. Cassandra dressed quickly and went out to see Riley.

Riley emerged around the same time, but her face was red, and even her arms had a pink hue to them.

"You got sunburned!" Cassandra exclaimed.

"I only did ten minutes," Riley grumbled.

"Same."

"I'm never doing that again. How dumb."

Cassandra didn't respond. She might do it again.

"Hair cuts," she said, hooking her arm through Riley's. "I'm ready for this."

They had appointments at a salon in downtown Springdale. Cassandra drove them to a small white building near the industrial part of town, just before the railroad. She parked the car and walked in, Riley trailing her.

"Are you Cassandra?" the woman asked. She was larger with thick dark hair and a heavy Southern accent.

"Yes."

"Sit here." The woman waited while Cassandra sat, and then she worked her hands through Cassandra's long hair. "What are we doing today? You have some of the longest, healthiest hair I've ever seen."

"Well." Cassandra took a deep breath. "I want to cut it off. Into a bob. No longer than my chin."

The woman's hands stopped their movements. "You want to cut it off?"

"Yes."

"Are you sure?"

Cassandra met her eyes in the mirror. "Positive."

The woman looked at Riley as if for confirmation, and Riley nodded. "Well, okay then. You're so brave."

She shampooed Cassandra's hair and set to work with the scissors. Cassandra's smile slipped a little as she watched the dark strands of hair fall past her shoulders and to the ground. She swallowed hard against a sudden lump in her throat.

It was too late to back out now. Half her hair was gone.

But by the time the woman rounded to Cassandra's other side, her certainty and confidence had returned. The look was good on her, and it was time to stop looking like a little girl.

"What do you think?" the woman asked when she finished blow drying it.

Cassandra spun her head from side to side, looking at the short strands of dark hair. "I love it." She met Riley's eyes in the mirror. "What do you think?"

"It's great," Riley agreed.

Riley got her hair cut next, just a trim, and then the two of them walked out to the car.

"You really like it?" Cassandra asked, opening the mirror visor for another look.

"It's great. I thought you were going to cry for a second there."

"Me too!" Cassandra admitted. Happiness bubbled up inside her. She looked so much older. "But I love it now! Hey!" She swiveled to face Riley. "Let's go surprise Harper at work."

Harper, the newest member in the trio of their friendship, worked at the local grocery store just around the corner.

"Sure," Riley said, grinning.

They found Harper at the check out line, wiping down the conveyor belt. She glanced at them and went back to cleaning. "Hey, ladies. What's up?"

She hadn't noticed! "Not much, just stopping by to say hi," Cassandra said. She leaned on the counter and smiled.

Harper didn't look up. She rearranged a few things on the checkout counter and wiped down the register. "It's been so slow today. Like, no one's coming in. So I've been cleaning all morning." Harper lifted her eyes and finally looked at Cassandra.

Harper's eyes widened. She brought both hands to her mouth and gasped, stumbling backward and colliding with the cash register behind her.

Cassandra and Riley both burst out laughing while Harper pressed a hand to her chest and took several deep breaths.

"Your hair!" Harper exclaimed.

"I cut it," Cassandra summarized.

"I can't believe it! It looks so different! You look amazing! Everyone at school is going to flip."

That was the reaction Cassandra was hoping for.

She couldn't help the tiny part of her that hoped Grayson would notice her.

Harper didn't get off work for a few more hours, so Cassandra and Riley went to the mall and walked around before returning to Cassandra's house. They were in the middle of watching a movie when a number Cassandra didn't recognize showed up on her phone. She stepped into the kitchen to take the call.

"Hello," she said, answering with some trepidation. Occasionally she got telemarketing calls, and she hated dealing with them.

"Hello, Cassandra?"

"Yes." It was someone who knew her, anyway. Her curiosity was piqued.

"Hey, this is Chris."

"Oh, Chris!" Delight fluttered in Cassandra's belly. He remembered her! "What's up?"

"I'm going with a couple of people to the movies in about half an hour. Want to come?"

He was inviting her to the movies! Cassandra immediately started thinking up ways she could go with him. Then she glanced over at Riley, watching the movie without paying any attention to Cassandra. She couldn't ditch her friend for a guy. She couldn't be one of those girls.

"I'd love to, but I have a friend over right now. Can we go another time?"

"Yeah, sure. Have fun with your friend. I'll talk to you later."

Chris hung up, and Cassandra grinned. Just wait until he saw her haircut.

⁓⁕⁓

It took Cassandra nearly half an hour Sunday morning to figure out how to blow dry her hair, but she finally got it. She wasn't used to having to style it. When her hair was long, she showered the night before and just let it dry naturally while she slept.

She bounced on her heels excitedly, anticipating the reaction of her peers when they saw her new look. The person she most wanted to see was Zack.

"Can I stay after church today and say hello to Grandma?" Cassandra asked her mom before they left for church. "I want to show her my hair." She knew her mom would have a hard time saying no to that, seeing how she wanted to foster the relationship between her daughter and her mother. Since her grandma lived in Fayetteville, she went to the same congregation as Zack and his family.

"That's fine, but I don't want you more than half an hour behind us."

Cassandra bobbed her head. "That's no problem."

"Can I stay with you?" Annette asked.

Cassandra looked at her ten-year-old sister. "Sure, that's fine with me."

The first people Cassandra saw at the chapel were Tyler and Jason Graves. Jason glanced at her, opened the church door, and then did a double take. He reached out a hand to shake hers as she arrived.

"Cassie. Your hair looks really good like that."

Tyler held the other door, and he appraised her. "I like your haircut."

Cassandra smiled, pleased with their attention. "Thank you!"

The rest of the day was much the same, with people congratulating her on her new look. Finally the Joneses left, and Cassandra stayed behind to look for grandma/Zack.

She spotted Zack's mom first when she came into the chapel, and they waved at each other. Then she saw Zack come in behind her. He was talking with another boy and didn't notice her.

Cassandra stood against the wall watching him. He finally glanced her way, and she smiled. Zack blinked twice and then smiled back.

And then he walked into the chapel with his friend.

Not even a hi. Not even an indication that he noticed her hair.

Cassandra let out a sigh. That was that. Zack wasn't going to stick around to talk to her.

She found Annette on the other side of the building, and they went to the library where their grandmother worked. She seemed delighted by Cassandra's haircut, and they chatted for a few moments before Cassandra took Annette's hand and led her out to the car.

She was definitely making waves with her new haircut. But she wasn't catching the attention of the people she wanted so far.

There was no shortage of people before school on Monday who complimented Cassandra's hair.

She saw Chris before first hour and called out to him.

"Hey, Chris!" she said.

He glanced around like he heard someone say his name, but if he saw her, he didn't acknowledge her.

Cassandra frowned, not satisfied with his reaction.

"Amelia thinks you have a crush on Chris," Harper said as they walked together after second hour.

Cassandra's face warmed. "I guess I kind of do. Not super strong, though. Just kind of like, I need someone to focus on."

Harper nodded. "I get it. Todd didn't even talk to me at church yesterday. Now I'm wondering who else I can crush on."

"If only it were as easy as that."

Cassandra didn't see Grayson all morning, and she felt a flicker of anxiety before she walked into fourth hour. What would he say when he saw her hair?

Ashlee and Emmett noticed right away.

"OMG," Ashlee said. "I've always thought your hair was so beautiful, I didn't think it was possible for it to look even better short!"

Cassandra smiled at her. Out of the corner of her eye, she saw Grayson walk in. "Thank you," she said, studiously not looking at him. "I knew I wanted to do something different."

"It looks amazing on you," Emmett said. "I've never seen you with anything except super long hair."

Behind her, Grayson settled down at his table, dropping his books with a bang. He turned to Katie, the girl who sat next to him, and said a little too loudly, "I got so drunk over spring break. I went home to New Hampshire, and if they have any laws about underage drinking, nobody enforces it."

So that was his reaction. Or lack thereof. As if she were some stranger, some girl he didn't know.

Even worse, Cassandra was starting to believe that Grayson was someone she didn't know.

⟡

Harper wanted to eat lunch with Tyler, so she grabbed Cassandra's arm and pulled her over to his table instead of going to the secluded bench where they usually ate. Cassandra had always seen him, but they had never eaten together. They were really only friends at church.

But apparently he was the object of Harper's newest crush, because she giggled and flirted with him throughout all of lunch. Tyler seem to enjoy it, flirting right back and even including Cassandra in his teasing. It made Cassandra laugh, but it also made her angry. Why was he always super nice when he liked one of her friends?

"Cassie."

Cassandra turned as they left the cafeteria and saw Cara walking toward her.

"Hi, Cara," Cassandra said, giving her a side hug. "How are you doing?"

"I'm good! Hey, I wanted to see if you could do this modeling thing with me."

Cassandra cocked her head. "Modeling thing?"

Cara nodded. "It's at Dillard's, trying on prom dresses and showing them off on a runway. They asked me to find a friend or two, and you're the first person I thought of."

While flattering, Cassandra hardly considered herself the modeling type. "I think you're better suited for that." Cara had the perfect figure for it.

"Do it with me. Please? It'll be fun."

The fact that Cara actually wanted her there was enough to make Cassandra consider it. "When is it?"

"It's on a Saturday."

Cara told her the date, and Cassandra's heart sank. She had way too much going on that weekend. Friday evening was cheerleading tryouts, and she was also supposed to have a song ready for clinic Saturday morning. She felt like she had completely neglected her music because of cheerleading, and Miss Malcolm was not pleased with that. She needed to take care of her song . . . But she wanted to do this modeling thing with Cara.

"I'll try and make it work."

Cara nodded. "Great! Hope to see you there."

CHAPTER FORTY-EIGHT
Different Mold

Cassandra had to pack for the concert with Riley. They were leaving Friday right after school. Cassandra had to admit she didn't really know much about the band they were going to see, but she didn't care. They were taking a road trip to St. Louis!

But she was desperately short on cash. She needed a job, and quick. It had been over a week since Cassandra had applied at Burger King, and so far nothing. She booted up the computer and pulled up several fast food websites. Subway, Dominos, Little Cesar. She was a smart, motivated young woman. Somebody had to hire her. She filled out six applications before calling it a night.

On Friday, Riley and Cassandra rode with Mrs. Isabel for the five-hour trip to St. Louis. They checked into the hotel before getting ready for the concert that night.

"I don't really know anything about this band," Cassandra said. "I listened to some of their music online, but it seems like pretty heavy stuff. Do they play anything lighter?"

Riley shrugged. "I don't have any of their albums, so I just hear the stuff on the radio. I guess it's pretty hard, but at least it's not heavy metal. More like alternative."

Cassandra didn't care that much. "I'm sure it will be so much fun."

She and Riley wore matching striped tops, except Riley's colors were orange and black with white while Cassandra's were blue and black with white. They brought their phones, cameras, and money to the concert, stuffed into pockets because they didn't want to bring their purses.

A long line had already formed outside the concert hall.

"We don't look like the usual crowd," Cassandra said, eyeing the tattoos and multiple body piercings and unique haircuts on the people in line. Riley looked down at the camera she held in her hands.

"I feel silly with this."

"Me too," Cassandra admitted, glancing at the camera around her wrist. "You have a smart phone. Let's just use your phone."

"Good idea."

The two girls ran back to the van where Mrs. Isabel sat. She planned to wait for them in the car until the concert was over.

"We're leaving our cameras here," Riley said.

She and Cassandra deposited their cameras and ran back to the line, which had nearly doubled in length while they were gone. A few teenagers pulled out cigarettes and leaned against each other while they smoked. At least there was no alcohol allowed on the premises, though Cassandra did not see anyone going around and enforcing that.

The concert attendees got louder and more rambunctious the closer it got to the concert start time. Finally, the doors opened, and an usher in a black suit forced everyone into a single-file line. He checked tickets as they came through, nodding as he let each person pass.

Riley held the tickets, and Cassandra wished she had her own. They were some of the youngest people there, and she couldn't help feeling jittery. What if they had the wrong dates, or this wasn't the correct concert, or they weren't old enough?

But the man looked at hers and Riley's tickets and bobbed his head at them to go on.

Riley squealed as soon as they were inside. She turned around and hugged Cassandra. "We're here! We're really here! Come on, I want to buy a T-shirt."

She took Cassandra's hand and hauled her through the pressing crowd until they found a booth selling shirts. Riley couldn't decide between the black one and the gray one, but Cassandra was getting impatient to go into the arena.

"Shouldn't we find our seats?"

Riley shrugged her off. "It's assigned seating. Our tickets have our seats on them. We can go whenever we want."

And Cassandra wanted to go now. These people made her nervous, and she wanted to sit down and get her bearings.

Riley finally selected the black shirt and paid for it, then pulled it over the shirt she was wearing.

"Relax," she said, hooking her arm through Cassandra's and steering her toward the doors that led to the arena. "We still have twenty minutes until the concert starts."

It was a good thing, too, because they had a heckuva time finding their seats. They finally located them at the opposite end of the arena, almost in the very top row.

"These are lousy seats," Riley complained. "Look how far away the stage is from here."

It was on the opposite side of them. The performers would be nothing but Lego people. But since Cassandra had not paid for the ticket, she didn't feel she had the right to be ungrateful.

The lights dimmed in the arena, and the ones on stage flashed brilliantly. In a moment the crowd was on its feet, screaming, and Cassandra and Riley stood also. Cassandra peered down into the open space between the bleachers in front of the stage, filled with hundreds of bodies standing and rising.

"Are we allowed to go down there?"

"That's the mosh pit," Riley said, peering into it also. "My mom said absolutely not. It could be dangerous."

"Dangerous?"

"Yeah. Apparently people have been trampled from the crowd's excitement before. You know, stepped on."

"I don't see how someone could not notice a person under their feet," Cassandra said.

"I don't know either," Riley answered.

But Cassandra barely heard her, because by now the opening singer had come out, and the screaming and enthusiasm was so loud that Cassandra heard nothing else.

The woman struck her electric guitar loudly, then clicked forward to the microphone on a pair of boots that rose all the way to her thighs, which were exposed by her mini-dress. She gripped the microphone in both hands and shouted into it, "Are y'all ready for this?"

The excitement was contagious. Cassandra had no idea who this woman was or what she would sing, but she cheered and clapped her hands with everyone else.

The woman began to shriek into the microphone, and Cassandra's expectations plummeted. It sounded more like she was screeching, screaming angry, hateful emotions at the crowd. The audience roared its approval at her, echoing the sentiment. Cassandra wrinkled her nose. She could hardly call this music.

Luckily the woman only sang two songs before leaving the stage with a wave. Cassandra pressed forward on her toes, anxious to see the real band come out.

Gavin Shrub, the lead singer, came onto the stage next, flanked by his two band members, each carrying electric guitars. His shoulder-length brown hair was parted down the middle and hung around either side of his face. Video cameras recorded his performance live and projected it to a screen in the middle of the arena.

The lead singer really was dreamy, with smoldering eyes and high cheekbones. Something about him reminded Cassandra of Grayson. He hit a few chords on his guitar, and then he and his back up singers broke into their throaty, hard rock sounds, which included a wide variety of growling and screaming and yelling.

Cassandra had not been a fan of their music when she listened to it on the Internet, but now she was caught up in the infectious adoration of the crowd, and she wished she knew the words so she could sing along. In the mosh pit below, bodies wove above the heads of the people as hands carried them toward the stage and then back again. She could see the danger in it now, though the energy radiating from the crowd made her wish she was there also.

Gavin paused his singing in the middle of the third song, but the music didn't stop. It sounded like every person in the arena except Cassandra knew the songs, and thousands of voices lifting up without accompaniment sent shivers down her spine. She found herself looking at Gavin and his entourage with the same adoration.

"I wish I had my camera now," she said to Riley.

Riley fished her phone out of her back pocket. "I completely forgot. I'll take pictures for both of us."

Cassandra caught on to the lines of the chorus, and she screamed them as loudly as the fans around her. By the end of the concert, she had hardly any voice left, but her spirits were soaring.

She had not intended to spend her money on anything, but as soon as the concert was over, she made her way over to table and bought one of Gavin's CDs. The music and the fervor had embedded itself in her veins like a heady toxin, and she definitely considered herself a fan.

In all the excitement of the concert and going out of town, Cassandra had forgotten to practice for one thing: cheerleading.

To be perfectly honest, she had also forgotten to practice for the music festival, which was the Saturday after tryouts and the same day as the modeling activity with Cara. She brushed that worry aside. Music was easy for her; she would have the chance to memorize the song after she learned the cheerleading routine.

Monday was the first day of the cheerleading clinic. Cassandra and Mia went to the gym with all of the other wannabe cheerleaders. Cassandra waited in the group and looked around at everyone while the cheerleading coach explained that she would be putting them into pairs, one experienced cheerleader with a newbie. Cassandra's stomach knotted. Almost everyone present was currently on the squad, and they looked different than those who weren't. They had their hair in the same ponytail, high up on their head with a ribbon around it, be their hair blond, red, brown, or black. Prepared for a vigorous workout, they were short shorts and tank tops. Cassandra was dressed in a pair of soccer shorts and a T-shirt. Did she look as out of place as she felt?

A girl with light brown hair and lots of freckles stepped up to her. "Cassandra?"

Cassandra forced a smile. "Yes."

The older cheerleader also offered a smile. "I'm Jennifer. I'll be your partner today. We'll work together and learn this routine."

Cassandra nodded. "I've been practicing," she said.

"Great. I'm sure you'll do awesome."

Cassandra kept her doubts to herself. The cheerleading coach stood with a few of the senior cheerleaders in front of the gym and showed them the dance routine. Cassandra was grateful for Mia's instruction beforehand because she knew how to do most of the moves. Putting them together with the music, on the other hand, would be a new challenge.

"Now we'll break it up into sections so you can start learning it," the coach said, as if it would be that simple. She went through the moves again of the first part of the routine.

"Okay, let's try it together," Jennifer said. She pulled on her ponytail and faced Cassandra. "Ready? Go." Immediately, fearlessly, Jennifer launched into the routine, shouting out the words with a big smile on her face as her arms bent and punched and she lunged and kicked.

Oh, crapola.

Cassandra gave it her best shot, which was pathetic.

Jennifer didn't stop there. She did it again. And again. After four rounds, sweat rolled down Cassandra's face and her sides ached, but she was no closer to matching Jennifer's speed or precision.

This was much harder than she'd expected.

A glance around the room showed that most of the cheerleaders had mastered the routine within minutes. Even Mia had it together.

"How did you learn that so fast?" Cassandra asked.

"You get used to it," Jennifer said with a shrug. "It's kind of the same motions all the time. So it's not hard to learn."

The coach blew her whistle and gathered the girls in. "Let's work on the next section!"

That had only been the first section? Cassandra watched with a glazed expression. Her mind flashed back to the three tests she had to take tomorrow in school and the job she still didn't have, not to mention the music she needed to learn for clinic. Cheerleading? This didn't fit in the picture. She wasn't cut out for this.

CHAPTER FORTY-NINE

Bonked

By Wednesday they'd been shown the entire routine, even if Cassandra felt like she was the only person who hadn't mastered it. Several girls had quit, though, so she knew it wasn't just her.

"You're doing great," Jennifer said, patient as ever. She had to be so tired of Cassandra by now. "You'll learn how to pick it up fast."

Cassandra wasn't fooled. She wasn't doing great. She could not remember what move came next when the music started, and she knew two more days wasn't going to change that. She couldn't even remember why she wanted to do this. She felt inadequate and foolish.

Her body ached from the constant practicing, but she went home with Mia after the clinic so they could practice some more.

"If I make cheerleading," Cassandra said, "it will be the most shocking thing I've ever done."

Mia laughed at her. "You're going to make it and we'll be cheerleaders together."

Cassandra wasn't even sure she wanted to anymore. But she didn't tell that to Mia.

There was no school Thursday, so Cassandra stayed the night with Mia. The plan was to practice cheerleading all day before the mock try-outs that evening, but instead the two girls goofed off and watched movies. Then they went to school for the mock try-outs.

Cassandra did terrible. She remembered how Cara had supposedly stopped during her cheerleading tryout in eighth grade and just smiled at the judges. Cassandra didn't have the guts to do that, but by the time the music stopped, she was still eight beats away from being through the routine. She'd really screwed it up somewhere.

She drove home determined to get this right. Even if she didn't make cheerleading, she would fail with dignity.

Mrs. Jones came into her room as Cassandra ran through the routine for about the tenth time.

"You look great," Mrs. Jones said. "I think you're going to make it."

Cassandra shook her head. "No matter how fast I am, I'm not with the music. No matter how high I kick, everyone else kicks higher." She knew she was doing a lot better than a few days ago, and maybe with another month she could get it. But she only had twelve hours.

Mrs. Jones patted her shoulder. "You look exhausted."

"I'm worked to death," Cassandra admitted. "Just one more day."

"And then you've got Festival on Saturday."

Cassandra nodded. As soon as cheerleading was over, she'd focus on her song.

⟲~·⟳~·⟲

Friday.

The day of cheerleading tryouts.

Cassandra's stomach was a mess of nerves. It was all she could think about. She smiled vacantly when her classmates talked to her, her mind going over the routine in every class. Counting. Trying to get her arms and legs working together.

Chris passed her in the hallway before second hour and poked her belly. Cassandra grinned at him.

"Christopher!" she called after him, grinning goofily.

"Cassandra!" he called back.

A happy warmth filled her insides, and she hurried to class.

"You should come over tonight after cheerleading tryouts," Harper said in health. "We can go see a movie or something."

"That sounds like fun," Cassandra said, her stomach twisting again. After cheerleading tryouts. That meant she had to get through them first.

Mr. Reems put on a documentary about nature in biology. Cassandra had seen the movie before, probably in junior high. She remembered the leaping frogs. Right before they began their dance in the rain, Cassandra said, just loud enough for Ashlee and Emmett to hear, "This movie is so corny."

Her friends giggled. She hadn't thought anyone else heard, but then Mr. Reems twisted his large body toward the class and said in a jovial tone, "Who called the movie corny?"

The class tittered.

"Cassandra," Grayson said from behind her.

317

Cassandra froze. Something like molten lava poured over her shoulders, coating her all the way to her feet. Usually she felt invisible to him. But no, he'd heard her, and he'd even said her name. She squeezed her fingers and toes, willing herself not to turn around and look at him. She knew, deep down, that she was trying out for cheerleading for him. So that he would notice her and say her name again. And again and again.

The school day finally ended. Cassandra dumped her books in her locker and made her way down the hall over to Mia, who had just deposited her own things.

"Ready?" Mia asked.

Cassandra nodded, though she felt like puking. "As much as I can be."

The two girls made their way to the auditorium where the tryouts would be. A room adjacent to it had been set up as a holding pen for the girls waiting their turn.

"Hey, girls!" Mia's mom greeted them enthusiastically when they stepped into the waiting room. She gave them both a hug and a frosted cookie on a stick that read, "Good luck!"

"Thank you," Cassandra said, a little overwhelmed by the gesture.

"Hey, you two!" Stacey, captain of the cheerleading squad, came next with a basket under her arm. "I want to wish all of you the best of luck today!" She pulled out long-stemmed roses from the basket and handed one to each of the girls. "We can only have so many people on the squad, but each one of you deserves a place, and I hope you do your very best during the tryouts. We'd love to have you in our family!"

It was a heartwarming sentiment, and Cassandra found herself also wanting to be a part of that unit.

Jennifer arrived a little later, and she gave Cassandra another Good Luck cookie.

"You've worked hard," she said. "I hope you do well."

Now Cassandra felt bad she hadn't brought any gifts for the other girls. It hadn't occurred to her to do so. "You too. Thanks for all your help this week."

One by one, each girl was called into the gym to try out, and each time, Cassandra's resolve weakened. Her legs felt like jelly.

And then it was finally Cassandra's turn. Her heart rattled in her chest as she walked into the auditorium with four other girls. They stood on a line and faced the judges, and trepidation filled her. She gripped the poms in her hands, trembling, nauseas.

"Ready?" the cheerleading coach said. Giving them all a smile, she started the music.

Cassandra lurched, just a second behind the beat, and then her limbs caught up with her and she sprang into motion. She tried to envision what came next while she counted in her head. "One, two, three, four, five, six, seven, eight, one, two, three, four, five, six, seven, eight . . ." She moved and twisted and turned, but her heart sank. She wasn't quite on tempo, and her movements were not as precise and sure as they needed to be.

In a flash it was over, and she straightened up, breathless, staring at the judges.

"Thank you, ladies," the coach said. "We'll post the results on the gym door tonight."

Cassandra dropped the poms into a box as she walked out the door. She already knew the results. There was no point in coming back to check.

⊙↝⚜↝⊙

"It was terrible," she told Harper that evening while they ate ice cream at the kitchen table.

"Don't you want to go check?" Harper licked the spoon before digging out another bite.

"I know I didn't make it." Cassandra shook her head, hot with embarrassment. "It was stupid to try."

"I'm glad," Harper said. "I didn't want you to make it. That's not who you are."

Riley had said something like that a few weeks earlier, and it had bothered Cassandra. Now, though, she agreed. "Yeah." She felt a stab of disappointment in her heart. She was certain if she was one of the cheerleaders, Grayson would notice her again.

She stayed with Harper until it was almost her curfew, then she hurried home before she got in trouble.

Mrs. Jones woke Cassandra up at seven the next morning.

"Cassandra! You have Festival auditions in one hour! Get up!"

Festival. Festival! Cassandra bolted upright, panic lancing through her chest. She had not practiced all week, she'd been so consumed with cheerleading. She turned her music on while she brushed her teeth and dressed, trying to memorize the words and the quick changes to the song. She should have practiced! She should know this!

"Good luck," Mrs. Jones said, trying to give her a hug as Cassandra rushed for the door. Cassandra evaded her.

"Thanks."

The exhaustion of the past week hit her between the eyes as she drove to the art center. Her phone rang, and she saw it was Cara, who would be waiting for her at the modeling event. Cassandra waited until she'd parked at the art center before calling her back.

"I haven't forgotten," she said without preamble. "I have a music audition this morning, but then I'll come over to the mall and do the modeling with you."

"Great, Cassie!" Cara said. "I'm so glad you're going to make it. I'll see you in an hour!"

One hour. Cassandra looked at the clock. She would have to hurry.

Ms. Malcolm gave her a frustrated looked when she walked in. "It's almost your turn."

"It's been a long week."

"Let's warm up quickly before you sing."

They ran through a warm up for a few minutes before Ms. Malcolm thought her voice was ready.

"Let's get in there and sing your piece."

Cassandra's head pounded. She flashed a blurry smile at the judge. Here she was, being judged again. Ms. Malcolm began playing, and Cassandra waited for her opening. She opened her mouth and came in —on the wrong note.

"Stop," the judge said, looking up from her copy of the music. "Let's start again."

Start again. Was that even allowed? Fully awake now, face warm with embarrassment, Cassandra waited while Ms. Malcolm started the intro again. She fixed the correct note in her mind, and this time she came in correctly. But right away, she tripped over the first phrase, getting stuck and stumbling on the rhythm.

"Hang on," the judge said, and Cassandra's face burned. Why couldn't she just let her sing? She'd catch up. "Let's clap that rhythm and try again."

Like a school child, Cassandra clapped out the proper rhythm, and again they started the piece. This time she sang the right note and got the rhythm right, but she felt so nervous and anxious through the rest of the song that she didn't put any feeling or energy into it, desperate to sing the right words and not get stopped. She just wanted to be done.

"Thank you for singing," the judge said, looking up at her when she finished.

The woman didn't even smile. Cassandra nodded and exited the room, followed by Ms. Malcolm.

"Cassie!" her vocal teacher exclaimed. "That was terrible! What happened?"

Cassandra rubbed her eyes, blinking back tears of frustration. "I'm tired. I've had a lot going on."

Ms. Malcolm gave her a disappointed look. "Music should be a bigger priority. You've never gotten less than a Superior rating, but you certainly won't get that today. You won't be able to do the recital."

Cassandra nodded, swallowing woodenly. She'd sacrificed practicing her music for cheerleading, and what good had that done her? At least she still had modeling with Cara.

By the time she parked at the mall in Fayetteville, it had been two hours since she'd spoken to Cara. She wandered over to the large department store on the south end of the building.

Several girls stood on a makeshift stage, turning in long formal dresses. Cara spotted Cassandra and gave a small wave. Cassandra smiled and waited to the side. After a moment, the girls moved off the stage, and Cara stepped down to Cassandra.

"Cassie, I'm so sorry. We're all done."

"You're all done?" Cassandra's mouth fell open.

Cara nodded. "That was it. We just did the last one."

"Oh." Cassandra blinked, feeling stupid. One more thing she'd missed.

"Good to see you, though!" Cara said. "I hope your singing thing went well!"

It hadn't. Nothing had, and Cassandra had no one to blame but herself.

She needed to get her priorities straightened out.

CHAPTER FIFTY

Bread Winner

Cassandra realized when she stepped into Spanish class Monday morning that she didn't even know if Mia had made cheerleading. Surely she had. Cassandra set her books down and swiveled in her seat.

"How are you doing?" she asked. The question would work whether Mia had made it or not, and she would take her cue from Mia.

Mia's eyes welled up with tears, and she gave a shaky smile that broke almost immediately. "I'm doing okay."

No way! Mia hadn't made it! Cassandra's heart lurched, and she immediately felt guilty for not contacting Mia earlier. Cassandra touched Mia's hand, feeling bad for not being a better friend. "I'm so sorry. I can't believe it."

Mia nodded. "Are you okay?"

"Yeah." Cassandra rolled her eyes. "It wasn't really me or my thing. But it was a fun experience."

"Lots of other people didn't make it," Mia said, and she listed off a few of the former cheerleaders who had also been reduced to the status of a commoner.

"It will be okay," Cassandra said. "We'll just focus on other hobbies." Like music.

Cassandra felt restless as she went through the rest of the day. She needed something new in her life. Something exciting.

She wanted a guy.

Cassandra also desperately needed a job. Her parents had paid for the repairs on the car she'd hit but expected her to pay them back. She couldn't even think about fixing her own car until she paid for the other one.

Emily had asked for a ride home from the junior high, so Cassandra picked her up. Swallowing her pride, she stopped at McDonald's and Wendy's, the two places she'd sworn never to work at, as they drove out to Tontitown. The restaurants told her the same thing the other places had told her: fill out an application online.

Emily bought chicken nuggets from Wendy's and French fries from McDonald's and hummed happily to herself as she ate in the passenger side.

"What a waste," Cassandra said. "I'm never going to find a job."

"Not quite a waste," Emily said. "I got nuggets and fries!"

⊙⁓⸱⚘⸱⁓⊙

Days went by with no news on the job front. Cassandra pulled into a small Italian restaurant along the highway leading to her house, feeling a little desperate. "Vicenzo's," the name read on the sign outside. It looked like a flea market from the front, just a long warehouse set on a gravel parking lot. But she stepped inside and was greeted by a small market of authentic Italian foods, including dried artisan pasta, vinegars and oils, and sauces. There was even a refrigerated cheese and meat deli.

Behind the market was an open kitchen. Cassandra stepped up to the window and cleared her throat. "Hello?"

A short, portly man with a balding head and a white apron across his large belly poked his head out. "Be right with you!"

Cassandra waited while he washed his hands and dried them on a towel before coming out of the kitchen and greeting her behind the register with a large, friendly smile on his face.

"How can I help you?"

"I was wondering if you're hiring," Cassandra said. She wrung her hands together and tried to smile. "I'd like to work here."

"Oh." The man opened the drawer under the register and pulled out a generic application. "My sister does the hiring. Just fill this out for me right here, and I'll let her know."

Hope lifted in Cassandra's heart. It was more promising than an online form, at least.

"What sort of position are you looking for?" he asked as she filled it out.

"Whatever you need," Cassandra said, not even sure what her options were.

He looked over her application. "I'll have her give you a call this weekend."

Really? Would she really call? Cassandra felt a mixture of hope and cynicism. He seemed genuine, but nobody else had given her the time of day.

"Thank you. I look forward to hearing from you."

Cassandra waited at the designated pick-up spot early the next morning for Riley to arrive so they could carpool to church class together. She sang along to the radio as a car pulled up behind her. Cassandra hit the unlock button on the door so Riley could hop in just as flashing blue lights came from the vehicle.

Cassandra froze. That wasn't Riley. It was a cop!

The man got out of his car and moved around to Cassandra's window, which she promptly pushed down.

"Yes?" she asked timidly. She'd never spoken to an officer by herself before, and she swallowed hard, anxiety tightening her throat.

He shone his flashlight on her. "I need to see your driver's license, registration, and proof of insurance, please."

What had she done wrong? Cassandra's hands trembled as she opened the glove compartment and removed the required documents. She fished around in her purse for her license and dropped it on the floor of the car as she tried to hand it out the window. Crapola! She scooted her seat back to get it and then looked up at him as he read over her information.

"Did I do something wrong?"

He eyed her. "What are you doing out here at this time? And why are you just parked on the side of the road?"

"Um." Cassandra threaded her fingers together. "I'm waiting for a friend. We carpool to church together every morning. Our class starts at six."

He looked at her like he did not believe her.

Cassandra did not want to sound rude, but she didn't know how to prove it, so she said, "You can call my mom if you want. Or if you wait a little longer, my friend will be here soon."

"I'm just going to check out a few things." He returned to his car with her documents and sat there for a few more minutes.

A moment later, Mrs. Isabel pulled up in her van. She rolled her window down and parked on the opposite side of the road. "Cassie? Is everything okay?"

Cassandra nodded.

Mrs. Isabel looked at the cop car like she wasn't sure.

The cop got out of his car again and went around to talk to Mrs. Isabel. A moment later, Riley hopped out of the passenger side and ran over to Cassandra's car just as the cop came over.

He handed her documents to her through the open window.

"You're good. Stay out of trouble."

That was it. Like she was one who had instigated this communication. But she just nodded and put everything away, then waited for him to drive off from behind her before she finally started down the road.

"That was an interesting way to start your morning," Riley said.

Cassandra snorted and rolled her eyes. "At least I had my license with me this time." She could think of at least three other times when she'd forgotten it and had to drive carefully to avoid the attention of the police.

"You're such a troublemaker," Riley teased. "These church girls. Up at six in the morning to devote their time to God. You have to watch out for them."

Cassandra couldn't help but laugh also at the absurdity.

❧⁓⁕⁓❧

Cassandra's phone rang as she left school Wednesday afternoon. She didn't recognize the number, but it was local, so she answered it.

"Hello?" she said.

"Is this Cassandra Jones?" a female voice asked.

"Yes." Cassandra unlocked her car and tossed her backpack in.

"This is Vicki Pianalto, from Vicenzo's Italian restaurant. Are you still looking for a job?"

Cassandra's heart skipped a beat. "Yes! I mean, yes, I am." Someone was actually calling her!

"Well, we're not hiring right now . . . At least, we weren't. But you came highly recommended from my brother. Would you be all right with a hostess position on Fridays and Saturdays? Those are our busiest days, and we could find work for you."

Only two days a week. Better than nothing. "Absolutely!"

"Great. Come in at four on Saturday. We'll fill out paperwork and get you started."

"Thank you. See you then!" Cassandra hung up the phone and did a happy dance outside her car. She'd just gotten her first job!

The week crawled by. Amity surprise Cassandra by sitting down next to her in choir Friday morning. At least, it was a surprise until Cassandra noticed Melanie was absent.

"Hi, Cassie," Amity said. "Everything good with you?"

"Pretty good." Cassandra had nothing important to share with Amity. Not that there was anything important going on in her life. "How about with you?"

"Good. We all miss you, you know. We talk about you all the time."

Cassandra could imagine the sort of things they said about her. "I miss you guys, too." It was a rote response and not actually true. Cassandra didn't miss at all constantly feeling like she didn't fit in or getting her feelings hurt because her friends were "jokingly" making fun of her.

"We're having a surprise birthday party for Cara tonight," Amity said. "You should stop by for sure. She'd love to see you."

Any other person, and Cassandra wouldn't believe it. But she and Cara still talked and tried to hang out from time to time. "What time? I'll try to sneak over."

"Six o'clock. We're trying to get everyone there by five-forty-five, if you can manage."

"I'll do my best," Cassandra promised.

She didn't have time to get a present for Cara, so she stopped at the store on the way home and got a card. She felt lame sticking a gift card in it, since that was what Cara had given her for her birthday, and it had felt so generic. But at least Cara would understand.

There was a lot to do when she got home. She and Mia were going to the movies at 7:15, and Mrs. Jones had plenty of tasks for Cassandra to do first.

"Crapola," Cassandra said, glancing at the clock on the stove. It was already after six. Oh well. She'd missed the shout of surprise, but she could still stop by and wish Cara a happy birthday.

By the time she got to Cara's house, though, it was almost six-thirty, and Cassandra had started to sweat. She needed to be leaving for Mia's house, not stopping at Cara's for a birthday party. She parked behind the other cars, gripped the birthday card in her hand, and hurried to the front door. She could hear the voices in the living room, laughing and talking loudly, so she didn't knock but just let herself in.

A sea of unfamiliar faces turned to her. Her heart suddenly hammered in her throat nervously. What was she doing? She didn't know these people.

Cara's face lit up. "Cassie! You came too!"

Cara looked delighted, though everyone else just looked surprised.

Cassandra gave a smile as if she'd meant to be here this whole time. She stepped over to Cara and handed her the card. "I can't stay. But happy birthday, Cara. Love you much."

"Thank you." Cara beamed at her. "I wish you could stay longer."

Cassandra nodded in acknowledgment. "I've got to pick a friend up to go to the movies. I'll talk to you later, though."

Cassandra slipped out the door in a hurry, glad she wasn't staying. The only person she really knew was Cara, and when Cara was with all of those other people, Cassandra didn't know her either.

She tried not to panic when she got in the car and saw that it was 6:50. By the time she pulled up to Mia's house, it was seven. She laid on the horn and waited for Mia to emerge, feeling bad for showing up so late. Mia flew out the door and ran to the car.

"So sorry I'm late," Cassandra said by way of greeting.

"That's okay. The beginning of the movie is just previews anyway."

"We are not going to miss it," Cassandra vowed. She pressed her foot to the gas and took off through the suburban street. Mia screeched and grabbed onto the handhold above the door.

Somehow, she got them to the movie theater by 7:11.

"I'm not even telling my mom how fast you drove," Mia said, undoing her seatbelt.

"That's probably a good idea," Cassandra agreed.

Mia paid for her ticket and went in first. After Cassandra paid for her own ticket, she barely had enough money left to buy a pickle. Thank goodness she had a job starting the next day! She went back out to the concession stand.

"One pickle, please," she told the kid working behind the counter.

He tossed his wavy brown hair out of his face as he stepped over to her. "We're all out of pickles," he said with an apologetic smile. "Why don't you get some Twizzlers?"

Cassandra looked at the long, red, twisted candies. For one thing, she didn't like them, but she wasn't going to say that. "I don't have enough money for them." That was true. A pickle was only a dollar-seventy-five, and the rest of the candies were three dollars or more.

"Tell you what. I feel really bad about us not having pickles. So pick anything you want, and I'll cover the difference."

Cassandra cast another look at him. "Really?" She felt like she ought to say no, but she wasn't above accepting someone else's generosity.

He gave her another smile, and Cassandra decided he was cute. Too bad he didn't go to her school.

"It's no biggie for me. I get a discount on all the food."

Well, Cassandra wasn't going to give him a chance to second-guess himself. "I'll take a Caramello bar, then." The thing was giant, not the typical five squares, but more like fifteen. She could just taste the gooey caramel and sweet milk chocolate now.

"Give me your money and I'll take care of the rest."

She handed over her cash, and he pulled out his card and paid for her candy.

"Enjoy your movie," he said, handing it to her.

"Thank you," Cassandra said. She walked away wishing all boys were so nice.

❦

Saturday was Cassandra's first day on the job.

She went in early with her documents to fill out paperwork. They had told her to dress nice and hadn't said much else, so she put on a pair of blue jeans and a frilly top. She parked in front of the warehouse/restaurant and took a deep breath to calm her nerves, then stepped inside.

A large blond woman with puffy hair stood behind the register. "Hi," she said. "How can I help you?"

"Hi." Cassandra put on her biggest smile. "I'm starting work here today. I'm Cassandra?"

"Oh, lovely! I'm Donna. I'll get Vickie."

Vickie looked a lot like her brother, but with long, wavy hair. She looked over Cassandra's documents, had her fill out a hiring sheet, and turned Cassandra back over to Donna.

Donna beamed at her. "Let me show you the time sheet and how to work the register."

She gave Cassandra a quick tour, showing her the room behind the kitchen where she would leave her things.

"Here are the time sheets. You write in the time you arrive and the time you leave. And you get one free meal off the menu during your shift," Donna said. "Just make sure and let the kitchen know at least an hour before we close."

Cassandra scanned the Italian menu. It all looked delicious, from the pesto gnocchi to the margherita pizza. She would enjoy working here.

"And this is the dining room." Donna led her to another room off the kitchen with dim lighting and what looked like giant Christmas tree lights strung from the rafters. A small bar with multiple wine bottles sat in a corner, and a line with articles of clothing draped across it served as decor along the walls.

"Sometimes you'll help the wait staff bus tables," Donna said. "You can't actually wait tables because you're not twenty-one, and we serve alcohol."

"Okay." Cassandra wasn't interested in being a waitress, anyway.

"Over here's the dishwashing room." Donna led Cassandra to a small room off of the dining room, where two teenage boys with aprons and rags hanging from their belt loops stacked the dishes on a large green tray before shoving it into an industrial steel box. "On occasion you might help them out with something, but really, your job is to be the hostess."

The boys eyed her. One was tall and lanky, while the other was shorter and more muscular. Cassandra waved, about to introduce herself, but Donna led her back out to the front before she could.

"The dining room is divided up into sections. When a new party comes in, you'll put them in the correct section so that each waiter or waitress gets a turn. You'll also learn how to ring them up. Sometimes people come in and buy items from the market without eating here. I'll show you how to ring those up also."

Cassandra nodded, trying not to feel overwhelmed. "Okay," she repeated.

"It's really not hard. You'll enjoy it."

Donna was right. Cassandra had learned everything she needed to do before the first hour was up.

And then time slowed down. Cassandra waited behind the register for someone, anyone to come in. No one did. She could hear the wait staff in the kitchen, laughing and joking with the cooks. Donna disappeared into the kitchen also, her loud voice echoing in the market.

Well, this was a bit boring. Cassandra doodled on the paper and wished she had brought a book to read.

The bell above the door jangled, and Cassandra straightened up as an older couple came in.

Her first people! She flashed a bright smile. "Welcome to Vicenzo's. How many?"

"Two, please," the man said with a polite smile.

Cassandra nodded and checked her table map. That would be Willa's section. "This way, please."

She walked down the hallway toward the dining room and found a table with forks rolled in a pretty napkin, just waiting for diners. Cassandra seated them.

"Your server will be Willa tonight, and she'll be right with you," she said with another bright smile.

The boys stuck their heads out of the dishwashing room when she walked by, and she gave them another wave before going into the kitchen.

"Willa, you've got people," she said to the short waitress with long brown hair.

"Oh, thank you!" Willa said, and she floated toward the dining room like a distracted fairy.

The bell out front jangled as more people walked in, and Cassandra headed back to her post. Looked like it would be a busy evening after all.

CHAPTER FIFTY-ONE

Working Girl

Cassandra fell into an easy routine over the next few weeks. Since she only worked Fridays and Saturdays, it wasn't difficult to stay on top of her grades. She liked Friday nights at work the most because Donna wasn't there, and it was slow enough that Cassandra could spend a lot of time chatting with the dishwashers. Oliver was super tall, with dark hair that he wore on the longer side and constantly fell in his face. Cassandra had seen him around school before but never spoken to him. The other boy, Tate, was much quieter, a little on the shy side, with red acne that marred his face. Both were friendly and made her laugh, so unless the bell was jangling or Cassandra was helping bus tables, she was in the dishwashing room talking to the boys.

She still practiced for her upcoming recital, though she had to admit singing didn't seem as important to her as it used to. She remembered she used to write, also, but now the only writing she did was poetry. That seemed to be something else she'd forgotten about.

As for Grayson, she only wished she could forget him.

Cassandra did not have to work until five o'clock on Saturday, so she finished up her schoolwork while planning the evening. She was missing an ice-skating activity with her church group, but her shift at work ended at nine, and she hoped a few people would still be at the skating rink at the Jones Center. It was a combined activity with the Fayetteville congregation, and she wanted to see Zack.

She had barely set her purse down in the back room at the restaurant when the bell started jingling with arriving customers. Cassandra hurried to the front, smile in place. Two groups of four had just walked in.

Oliver, the taller boy with dark hair, stepped out of the dishroom after she seated the diners. "Customers already?"

"Yes." She peered around him into the little room with the dishwasher and two sinks. "Where is Tate?"

Oliver looked disgruntled. "He bailed on me today."

"That can't be fun. Hopefully it doesn't get too busy."

"Let's hope." Oliver turned around, disappearing into his domain. Cassandra return to the front, her hostess face firmly in place.

It did not slow down.

By seven o'clock, she had pulled out a slip of paper and created a waitlist. No one had trained her how to do this, so she estimated the wait time for each party. As she would seat a group of people, she would bus as many tables as she could, delivering the dishes to the dishroom in an attempt to help Oliver. The dirty dishes were piling up, and his lips were pressed together, brows furrowed.

"Oh, thanks for the dishes," he said snarkily.

"I'm trying to help you out," Cassandra said, annoyed by his attitude. "You're busy, but it's not like the dishes can stay in the dining room waiting for you."

"Sorry," he said, instantly contrite. "I'm really stressed right now."

Dirty dishes lined both counters, and even from the hallway she could see baked-on cheese in the lasagna boats in the sink. Cassandra nodded, her annoyance vaporizing in sympathy. "I wish I could stay and help, but I have a line wrapping itself around the store out there."

He waved her off. "Go. Just go."

Cassandra did, though she felt guilty leaving Oliver to the piles of dirty dishes.

The night flew by. Cassandra barely had the chance to breathe between seating people and ringing people up and clearing tables.

Marco, the owner, came out of the back when the restaurant closed. "Your shift is over," he said, watching her cash out the register. "You're free to go."

Cassandra hesitated. She knew Oliver was still back there trying to catch up with the night, and she felt bad leaving him. But if she didn't go now, she would miss everybody at the ice-skating party. She took her time card from Marco and gave him a smile.

"Thanks. I'll see you guys tomorrow."

"Great job today. You're catching on fast."

Cassandra nodded and hurried out to her car. The Jones Center was twenty minutes away, if she hurried.

She spotted her group of friends standing outside the Jones Center when she arrived around nine-thirty, laughing and chatting with each other. Cassandra slammed her car door and hurried to join them on the sidewalk.

"Hi, guys," she said, scanning who remained. Tyler, Zack, Jason, Riley, and a handful of other people.

"Cassandra!" Riley gave her a hug.

"You're a little late," Tyler said. "We're all done ice-skating."

Cassandra's face warmed. "Yeah, I know. I had to work." She turned around to see Zack talking to his brother while he tightened the laces on his shoes. She stepped over to him.

"Hey, Zack."

He looked up and flashed her that smile she was so familiar with. "Hey, Cassie." He put a hand on her shoulder, and she felt the warmth of it through her shirt. "Sorry I couldn't make it to your birthday party."

"Oh, it's okay. I know how busy you are." She tangled her key ring on her finger. "But hey, I'm sixteen now. You can ask me on a date."

Zack laughed, a light, easy sound. "You're right."

And that was all he said. No excitement, no agreement, no date. Cassandra suddenly felt foolish for even bringing it up.

"Cassie?"

Cassandra turned toward Riley's voice with relief.

"Can you give me a ride home?"

Cassandra nodded. "Sure."

Riley piled into her car, and the girls stopped at McDonald's on the way to Riley's house.

"I really enjoy work," Cassandra said. "It's nice to be making some money, even if more than half of it goes to my parents to pay for that car I hit."

"Ugh," Riley said, adding an eye roll as she ate her fries.

"Yeah," Cassandra said in agreement.

"And how's the guy situation?" Riley asked. "We don't really talk about Grayson much anymore."

"I've moved on," Cassandra said, even though she only wished it were true. "I kind of like Amelia's older brother, Chris." That was only a little true also. Cassandra desperately wanted to have a crush on him. "What about you?"

"No luck for me. I'm still waiting for my first kiss."

Cassandra gave her wistful smile. She might have passed that milestone, but it didn't mean she wasn't hoping for another.

⟡

Monday morning dawned cooler than the past few mornings had been. April never could seem to decide whether it wanted to be winter or spring. Cassandra sat at the pick-up spot before church class, waiting for Riley. It was cold out, but she didn't have a lot of gas, so she ran the heater for a little bit and then turned the car off to wait.

Just as she was ready to turn the car back on and get the heat going again, Riley's mom pulled up behind her.

"Hi," Cassandra greeted and turned the key in the ignition as Riley closed the passenger door. The car made a chugging sound, but then nothing happened. "That's weird." She frowned at it.

"What's happening?" Riley leaned over to peer at the gauges.

"Well, I don't know, but that seems rather odd." Cassandra tried again to turn her car on, but the same thing happened. Hot fingers of panic crept up her neck. Had she broken her car?

She tried a third time, pressing down on the gas this time as she turned the key. Even from here, she could smell the gasoline, but the car would not turn on.

Someone tapped her window, and she turned her face to see Riley's mom. Cassandra had enough power to roll the window down, at least. She gave a sheepish grin.

"The car won't start."

Mrs. Isabel poked her head inside the car and examined the dashboard. "I think you're out of gas."

Wouldn't that be awesome? Cassandra also stared at the gauges and wished she could refute the logic.

"Do your parents have a gas can?"

Cassandra nodded. Her dad always kept one so he could start the tractors.

"Let's move your car off the road, and I'll take you up to your house to get a gas can."

"Oh, okay," Cassandra said lamely. What an idiot.

She and Riley got out of the car, and Mrs. Isabel said, "Put your car in neutral so we can push it to the side."

Cassandra leaned her head in and grabbed the transmission stick, putting the car in neutral. She pulled her head out and turned around to see Riley behind the car, pushing. The car gained momentum, moving rapidly forward.

"Cassie!" Mrs. Isabel yelled. "You've got to get inside the car and steer!"

Crapola! The car was nosing headfirst into the ditch! Cassandra had to run to keep up with it. She grabbed the door handle and yanked it open, then jumped inside and slammed her foot on the break, stopping the car's downward motion. Her heart pounded in her chest so hard she thought she'd puke, and she breathed a sigh of relief.

"Put on your emergency brake," Mrs. Isabel said, eyeing the car suspiciously. "And then hop in the car with me and Riley. We'll get the gas."

Cassandra put on the brake and joined Riley in her mom's van. She didn't say much as they drove to her house, where she knew she'd be in trouble.

But she spotted the gas can when they pulled into the circle drive, all the lights still off inside the house. She hopped out and grabbed it from where it sat in the tractor seat. Her parents didn't even need to know about this little mishap.

Mrs. Isabel drove her back to the pick-up spot. Cassandra tipped the gas into the car tank, then got inside and turned the ignition.

The car gurgled and churned but didn't respond. Why wasn't this working?

Mrs. Isabel stepped up to the window. "Still nothing?"

Cassandra shook her head. "I don't know why."

"There must be something else wrong with it."

Figured. Stupid piece of crap.

"I'll take you home," Mrs. Isabel went on. "I think you and Riley are skipping church class this morning."

"Looks like it," Cassandra grumbled.

Mrs. Isabel dropped Cassandra off at her house, where the rest of the family was awake and prepping for school.

"What are you doing here?" Mr. Jones asked, looking at her.

"The car won't start," Cassandra said with a sigh. "Mrs. Isabel brought me home. It's still parked at the pick-up spot."

Mr. Jones grunted and turned back to the younger children. "Well, I guess you can ride the bus to school with everyone else."

No way. "I'll wait till we can get my car."

That turned out to not be for a while. Mr. Jones had to leave for work, but Cassandra's mom said she would take her to the car after she got dressed. An hour later, they were finally driving back to the pick-up spot.

"Cassandra, your car is in the ditch!" Mrs. Jones said as they pulled up behind it.

"No, it's not." Though she had to admit it looked like it was. "We stopped it before it got there."

Mrs. Jones did not look convinced. "I hope you don't have any issues getting it out."

Cassandra just hoped it would start.

"Did you push on the gas when you tried to start it?"

"Just once—I think." She couldn't be sure anymore. "I tried everything."

"Most likely the carburetor got flooded," Mrs. Jones said. "It's had enough time to sit now that it should start."

Cassandra nodded, though she didn't really know what her mom meant. She got in her car, said a quick, silent prayer, and held her breath while she turned the key.

The car purred to life, and Cassandra wilted in relief. "It works," she breathed.

She gave her mom a thumbs up sign, and Mrs. Jones pulled up beside the car.

"Go ahead and drive to a gas station. I'm gonna follow you to make sure you don't run out of gas before you get there."

"Okay," Cassandra said meekly. She felt like a little girl again, but she was grateful for her mom's help.

She made it to the gas station without any problems, and after filling up her tank, she continued to school, vowing to never let the tank get below a quarter empty again.

CHAPTER FIFTY-TWO
Vulnerable

Cassandra had her recital on Monday night. Miss Malcolm had been kind enough to schedule it on a weeknight because of Cassandra's work schedule, which made her feel guilty enough that she spent a lot of time on the song.

It was the same one she'd done for Festival a few weekends earlier, but for the recital she sang the song without a hitch. School and work weighed on her before and after her turn to sing, however, and she felt so exhausted she wasn't sure if she even remembered to smile.

Miss Malcolm stopped her before she left after the recital. "Cassandra, that was the best you've ever sung that song. When you practice, it really shows."

Cassandra gave her a wan smile. She knew it was meant to be a compliment, but it just made her feel like she was failing in so many ways. "Thank you."

She meant to practice. She really did. But life was getting in the way.

❧

Cassandra woke up Tuesday morning and remembered just in time that she had a field trip to the Fayetteville aquatic center all day. The aquatic center had a lake and marshes and lots of tall weeds. She dressed in jeans and a T-shirt and tried to find her athletic shoes. Where were they? She sifted through the clothing on the floor and even checked the dirty clothes basket. No shoes.

All of the noise she was making woke Emily, startling her in the bed before she sat up.

"Why is the light on? What time is it?"

"Sorry," Cassandra said. She had to turn the light on to search under the beds. "You haven't seen my shoes, have you?"

Emily got a strange look on her face. "What shoes?"

"My Adidas shoes. With the thick soles. They're black." No way was she wearing her white tennis shoes to parade around Lake Fayetteville at the aquatic center.

"Oh. I borrowed them yesterday."

Emily said it so casually that for a moment, the words didn't register. And then Cassandra straightened. "You what?" She fought back her fury at having her things taken without permission. "Never mind. Where are they now?"

"I left them in my locker."

"In your locker? At school?" Cassandra's mouth fell open, and this time she didn't try to hide her anger. "Emily, those were my shoes! You didn't have any right to take them!"

"Sorry." Emily lay back on the bed, not sounding at all sorry, and Cassandra was not done with this conversation.

"What am I supposed to do?" Cassandra shrieked. "I don't have time to go to your school and find your locker and get my shoes!"

"Well, I don't know."

The bedroom door opened, and Mr. Jones stepped into the room. "Girls. What's going on?"

Cassandra whirled around, blinking back tears of frustration. "I have a field trip to the Fayetteville aquatic center today, and Emily took my shoes and left them in her locker!"

"Wear a different pair."

Cassandra wanted to stomp her feet. "I don't have a different pair, and aren't you going to get her in trouble for taking my shoes?"

"They're just shoes," Emily grumbled.

"Except now I don't have any to wear!" Cassandra shouted.

"All right, enough." Mr. Jones held his hands up. "Here's what we'll do. Get ready for class. When you're done with church, come by the soccer store, and you can pick a pair of shoes before school."

Cassandra took a deep breath and let it out slowly. That wasn't ideal, but it would work. "Okay. I'll do that."

By the time church class was over, Cassandra had pretty much gotten over Emily taking her shoes. She was getting a new pair out of the deal, after all.

The soccer store was still closed, but her father was there. He greeted her with a smile. "I've got a selection of shoes here you can choose from."

"Wait." Cassandra frowned at him. "You're not going to let me pick whatever shoe I want?"

"Well, no, some of the shoes are very expensive."

"I know that. But some of the shoes I don't like."

"Hopefully you can find something you like from what I've selected."

She looked down at the ones he'd picked and groaned. She didn't have many choices, and she was running out of time. None of these were shoes she would buy if it were up to her. She picked a pair of black shoes with three purple stripes. They were cute, except for the tongue that wanted to crawl halfway up her shin.

"Why is this tongue so long?"

"Soccer players like it. It can go under the shinguard and provide extra protection while keeping their shoe in place. Or it can fold back over the laces and provide a spot for kicking the ball."

Cassandra suspected her dad had made that information up right then and there, but she didn't say anything. Instead she doubled the tongue over on itself and tucked it under the laces.

"This will work," she said was a heavy sigh. It would have been much better to have her own shoes.

She was in first hour just long enough for the teacher to take roll before the announcements came on and excused the fourth hour biology classes to the bus lot for the field trip.

Cassandra left her Spanish class and joined up with other students behind the performing arts center where the buses waited. She scanned the line of kids nearest her and spotted Oliver. He bobbed his head at her.

"Cassandra," he said.

Cassandra smiled, a ripple of pleasure spilling through her at the sight of his familiar face. "Oliver. I didn't know you had biology fourth hour."

"Yup. So I'll be on this joy ride of a field trip with you."

Cassandra laughed. Oliver had such a dry sense of humor, but he always made her laugh. She followed him onto the bus and spotted Grayson already in a seat. She averted her eyes and sat with Oliver.

The drive to Fayetteville would only take about twenty minutes, but Cassandra was prepared. She pulled out her math assignment and began working on it. It was due today, but since she wasn't in class, she just had to get it to her teacher before the day was over.

"You're not really doing homework, are you?" Oliver said, elbowing her. "Are you? Are you? Are you?"

Her pencil dropped from her hand and rolled across the floor of the bus. "Oliver!" she exclaimed, but laughter bubbled up in her chest. She bent over and grabbed the pencil.

"Hey, Cassandra."

She gripped her pencil tighter, knowing that voice anywhere. Slowly she lifted her head to see Grayson leaning out of his seat across the aisle.

Looking at her. Why was he looking at her?

"What are you doing?" he asked.

"I'm just working on my homework," she said, inexplicably frazzled.

He smirked, a corner of his lip pushing upward. "Why would you do that? We don't have to go to school today."

There was a teasing note to his voice, something jovial and friendly. But Cassandra could not bring herself to match it. "This is still due by the end of the day. Some of us care about things like that." She settled back into the seat and dropped her head, letting her hair fall as a shield around her face.

"Burn," Oliver said beside her. "I take it you guys aren't friends."

Cassandra's face grew hot. "We've had some interesting interactions," she murmured. Her temples throbbed just from the few words they had exchanged, and Cassandra rubbed the bridge of her nose. It was really too bad they were in the same class.

Oliver proved a welcome distraction. Nicole was in his biology class, and the three of them spent most of the day together at the aquatic center. At one point they had to walk through patches of muddy grass, and Cassandra stepped gingerly, not ready to dirty her brand new shoes.

"Want a piggyback ride?" Oliver asked.

Cassandra looked at him in surprise. That seemed a rather friendly gesture. "Sure," she said, warming to the idea. She gave Oliver a closer study. He was tall and lanky, with dark brown hair just a little too long to be stylish. He knelt, and she crossed her arms around his neck.

"What do you weigh, like fifteen pounds?" he joked as he carried her over to the building where they would be writing up reports.

"A little bit more than that," Cassandra said, laughing again.

She and Oliver settled at a separate table with Nicole. Cassandra couldn't help looking for Grayson and spotted him with two other girls. He was talking loudly, complaining about his job and his mom and talking about how he got an apartment in Fayetteville so he could be alone with Charlotte. His speech was peppered with swear words, and Cassandra's ears burned just from listening to him.

Who was this guy? He was nothing like the Grayson she had met at the beginning of the year.

"Hey." Oliver threw a wad of gum wrapper at her. "You helping us or not?"

Cassandra focused on them. "Totally helping."

"How's Claire doing, Oliver?" Nicole asked.

Cassandra looked at Nicole and then at Oliver. "Who is Claire?"

"She's my girlfriend." Oliver smiled rather sheepishly. "Things are going well."

Cassandra settled back in her seat, feeling a sharp pang of disappointment. Oliver had a girlfriend. Just when she thought he was flirting with her and maybe the beginning of something was starting to develop.

Nope. No boys for Cassandra. They were all taken.

⁂

"I can't believe this school year is almost over," Harper said on Friday.

Cassandra walked sandwiched between Harper and Riley into the auditorium for the last assembly of the year. "I know."

"It's not over yet," Riley said, making a face. "We still have two more weeks."

"Yes, but it's like, the final countdown," Harper said.

The girls quieted down as Mr. Cullen walked onstage with his elite choir, Unity. Their song moved Cassandra to tears as they sang about crossways and goodbyes. She tried not to be jealous when she saw Janice up there. Cassandra would always feel like it should be her singing with them.

"It must be so hard for the leaving seniors," Harper said, her eyes also glossy.

Cassandra nodded, though she was thinking of Grayson. Their paths had crossed early in the year, but they'd moved to different places now. "Are you guys trying out for Unity?"

"Of course!" Harper said.

"Not me," Riley said.

"I am." Cassandra sighed. She'd had such confidence last year when she tried out. Now it felt more like a dream than a possibility. "I'll try out. But I don't really think I'll make it." She hadn't had good luck lately. Everything wrong seemed to be happening.

"I just want to make the advanced choir," Riley said. "I'm not worried about Unity."

Harper scoffed at her. "Of course we'll make the advanced choir. We're singers."

Cassandra nodded. Tryouts had been that morning, but like Harper, Cassandra wasn't worried about it. The advanced choir was a given.

Unity, on the other hand, was not.

Cassandra and Riley went tanning after school, where Riley burned again.

"I'm done with this," she announced. "You can tan by yourself."

Cassandra couldn't stop giggling as she looked over at her friend. "I'm so sorry. How did you get so red?"

"We did twenty minutes this time, that's how," Riley growled. "Now we're going to Farrah's party and I'll look like a lobster."

Cassandra bit back her mirth.

Farrah had set up lanterns and tents in her front yard. Cassandra was surprised at all the people there, many who she didn't know. She had expected it to only be people from church.

"Hey, Cassandra," a deep male voice said.

She turned around to see Chris. He poked her side and smiled at her.

"Chris!" she said, delighted. "Is Amelia here?" She really wanted to know if Harper had come, but Harper hadn't mentioned it.

Chris shook his head. "She doesn't know Farrah. How do you know her?"

"I've known Farrah for ages."

"Cassie!" Farrah popped out of a tent, then ran over to hug her. "I thought I heard your voice. I sure miss seeing you in school."

"I miss seeing you too," Chris said, sticking his lip out in a pout as he looked at Cassandra. "Where've you been?"

"Just around." Cassandra studied Chris, trying to figure out her feelings for him. She liked the attention, for sure. Flirting was fun. But did she like Chris?

Did she even care? She just wanted someone to hold her and kiss her. Never mind feelings.

Chris left around midnight, and though he stayed close to Cassandra all evening, he didn't try to kiss her or hold her.

"I should probably get home," Riley said.

"Me too," Cassandra said, though she wanted to stay. She felt such an aching loneliness in her heart. All she wanted was to find someone to make it go away.

"I'm glad you guys came," Farrah said, coming over and hugging them both. She gave Cassandra a knowing look. "Is there something going on between you and Chris?"

"If there is, I don't know about it," Cassandra said with a sigh.

"Do you want there to be?"

"She'd take something with just about anyone at this point, I think," Riley said.

Cassandra could not deny it.

CHAPTER FIFTY-THREE

For Your Consideration

"Congratulations, Cassandra," Mia said, smiling at Cassandra as she sat down in Spanish class Monday morning. Cassandra turned around to face her, cocking her head. "Congratulations on what?" She couldn't think of anything amazing she'd done.

"On making the advanced choir."

Cassandra blinked. She hadn't thought about that all weekend. It wasn't something she'd worried about. "Thanks. You made it, right?"

"Yes." Mia lowered her voice. "But be prepared. A lot of people didn't make it. They got bumped to fifth-hour choir."

"What?" Cassandra couldn't believe it. "Like who?"

"A lot of our friends."

Ms. Elliot began class then, shooting evil glances at Cassandra and Mia, and they fell silent. Nervous energy rippled through Cassandra's fingers. Did she know anyone who hadn't made it?

As soon as she stepped into health class, she knew she did. Harper's eyes were red from crying, and Cassandra's heart sank as she dropped into the seat beside her.

"Harper? What's wrong?" She was almost afraid to ask.

"I didn't make the advanced choir." Harper gripped the blue pen in her hand so tightly Cassandra worried it might break. "Neither did Riley."

Cassandra pressed a hand to her mouth. "No way."

Harper shook her head. "I'm a singer. I'm known for singing at church. How could Mr. Cullen not put me in it?"

Cassandra didn't even know what to say. She had taken it for granted that she and her friends would be in choir together. "What will I do without you and Riley?" She wasn't even sure she wanted to be in choir if they weren't.

"I might drop out. I'm not a second-rate singer."

"Please don't," Cassandra begged. She understood Harper's feelings, though. If she'd made fifth-hour choir, she'd feel so insulted and angry she would probably drop out also. "We'll still be in choir concerts together."

Harper wiped her eyes. "Maybe. I don't know."

Cassandra searched for Riley all morning but didn't see her in the locker hall. She finally found her on her way to fourth hour. "Riley!" she called, wondering why it had taken this long to find her friend.

Riley saw her and hesitated, slowing her walk. "Hi," she said flatly.

Cassandra stepped into place beside her as they headed toward the science wing. "I'm so sorry," she said.

"You made it," Riley said, proving she had the same topic on her mind. "It's not like you're a better singer than us."

Cassandra nodded. "Of course not. I know." She grabbed Riley's arm. "You should try out for Unity. If you make it, you'll be in the advanced choir for sure."

Riley looked unsure. "But why would Mr. Cullen choose me for Unity if he didn't even put me in the advanced choir?"

"He's not the only judge. Just go in there and wow him. I'll help you find a good song."

Riley considered it, then nodded. "Okay. I'll try it."

They parted at Cassandra's biology class, and she hurried in to sit down. She had two more questions to answer on her homework. She pulled it out and got to work.

She sensed when Grayson walked in but didn't look up. He settled in behind her, then said, "Hey, Cassandra."

What could he possibly want? She spared a quick glance over her shoulder before focusing on her book. "What?"

"Can I borrow a pen?"

He must not have his homework done either, and there wasn't anyone else to ask, since they were the first two in the classroom. She removed a pen from her backpack and barely kept herself from chucking it at him. "Just be sure to give it back."

He accepted it, his eyes lingering on her face for a moment. "Okay."

Why could she not pull away from his gaze? Didn't he know the effect he had on her?

His lip quirked upward as if he did know, and he said, "Even though you never say hi to me."

She blinked and then forced herself to turn around and face forward.

She was some kind of joke to him, someone he could mess with because he knew what she felt for him. The thought made her angry, and she didn't even look at him when he gave her pen back after class.

"Bye, Cassandra," he said on the way out.

"Bye." She went the opposite direction, taking the long way to her locker and hating how she melted at the sound of his voice.

She and Riley stopped by the music store and selected a song for Unity tryouts before going to the Jones Center for ice-skating with the other kids from church. Cassandra hadn't been ice-skating since she went to Tulsa the year before with Cara and her other friends.

"Hi, Cassie," Tyler said, sitting down next to her to tie his skates.

"Hi," she said. She waved to Farrah and spotted Beckham talking to Jason.

A boy she didn't know stood at the counter getting skates. He turned slightly, revealing a shiny gold stud in his ear. His blond hair fell to his shoulders, and when he shifted his gaze, it landed on Cassandra.

"Who is that?" she asked.

Tyler looked also. "I don't know. He's not with us."

A girl walked up to the boy then, smiling, and the two of them moved off together.

"He's with someone," Cassandra said, turning back to her skates in disappointment.

"He doesn't seem like your type," Tyler said.

"How would you know my type?" Cassandra glared at him.

He shrugged and walked off.

"Riley." Cassandra stood and wobbled over to her friend on her skates. "Did you see that guy?"

"Which guy?"

Cassandra pointed him out on the rink. "Him."

At that moment, he glanced over his shoulder and caught her eye again. Her face warmed, and then he skated past.

"Do we know him?" Cassandra asked.

"No, but he's cute. Too bad he's got a girlfriend."

Cassandra grunted. "Story of my life." If she wanted a guy, looked like she'd have to steal him from someone.

She followed Riley onto the ice and fell five times in the first ten minutes. Jason and Tyler kept laughing at her, but then she found her equilibrium and even figured out how to skate backward.

The boy kept looking at her. One time when she met his gaze, he smiled at her.

"Did you—" Cassandra began.

"Yes," Riley said. "I saw."

Cassandra tried not to stare at him across the rink, but she was too aware of him now.

"I need a drink," Riley said after half an hour.

"Same." Cassandra followed her to the water fountain. She waited in line, then bent over to take a sip of water.

"Excuse me."

She turned around and gave a start when she saw the cute boy standing there.

"Hi." He smiled, and he gave a toss of his head, sending the blond hair flying out of his face. "I'm Lee. I noticed you on the rink. Do you mind if I get your name and number? We could hang out sometime."

Cassandra didn't dare look around to check if Riley was seeing this. "Um, sure. You're not here with a girl?"

"Oh, no. She's just a friend. She's the one who told me to come talk to you."

"I'm Cassandra." She smiled at him. "What school do you go to?"

"The U of A. You?"

The U of A. What school was that? It took Cassandra a full second to realize he meant the University of Arkansas. He was in college. College! She cursed her bad luck. "I go to Springdale High."

"High school." He smirked. "I remember those days. Here, let me get your number and I'll call you."

"Sure." Cassandra gave him the info, the whole time wondering what she'd do if he called. Her parents would have a cow.

Then she shrugged it off. *If* he called, she'd worry about it then.

***

Lee didn't call Cassandra that night, which was probably a good thing.

"I need to borrow your car," Mr. Jones said, coming into her room. "I can get you to your church class tomorrow, but then you'll have to get a ride to school."

"Sure." That wouldn't be a problem. "Just remember I've got Unity tryouts after school, and someone will have to come get me."

"I'll tell your mom."

Riley ended up not going to the church class since Cassandra couldn't take her. Cassandra flagged Farrah down after class.

"Can you give me a ride?" she asked.

"Sure." Farrah gave an impish smile. "I'm heading to Chris and Amelia's house. You'll have to come along."

"Really?" Cassandra felt a flash of jealousy. "Why are you going there?"

"I just have to pick up a school assignment."

They had barely gotten to Chris's house when Farrah got a phone call from her mom. Chris came out of the house as Farrah stepped out of the car. She moved to the side and spoke in angry, hushed tones. Cassandra got out as well and exchanged a look with Chris.

Farrah hung up and walked back to the car.

"Cassie, I'm so sorry, I have to go home and get something," Farrah said, her face flushed.

"Is everything all right?" Cassandra asked.

Farrah rolled her eyes. "Just my stupid mom. I have to take you to school now, though."

"I can take her," Chris said.

"What about Amelia?" Cassandra asked. "Will she be okay with that?" She didn't fancy the thought of riding with him and his sister.

"She has her own car. We don't ride together."

That made sense.

"Thanks, Chris." Farrah gave Cassandra a quick hug. "We'll talk later."

"Want some breakfast?" Chris wandered into the kitchen and pulled down a box of cereal.

"That sounds great, actually. Thanks."

"So why do you go to church so early?" Chris poured himself a bowl and one for her as well, then sat down across from her.

"Well." Cassandra paused. "It's a chance to really study the scriptures. It's especially important for me now as a teenager to figure out what I believe and how I want the word of God to shape my life."

He smirked around a mouthful of cereal. "Did someone tell you to say that?"

"No." Her face warmed at the insinuation that she was nothing but a sheep.

"Don't you hate it?"

"Sometimes I hate waking up early, yes," she admitted. "But I like what I'm learning."

"I think church is boring," Chris said. Then he paused and added, "Sometimes it's okay."

Cassandra laughed at that and ate her cereal.

"I have to pick up a friend," Chris said, clearing her bowl when she finished. "So we should go now."

"Okay."

She followed Chris out to his car. He put her in the front seat next to him and then teased her because her backpack was half ripped up.

"It only has to survive a few more days," Cassandra said.

Chris stuck his hand in it. "I could steal all your pencils right now."

"Oo, I'm so nervous."

He grinned at her and pulled up to his friend's house. He laid on the horn, and a moment later a boy Cassandra didn't know came out.

"Hey," he said, giving her a strange look. "There's someone in my spot." He stopped at the passenger side door.

Did he really expect her to move? Cassandra stared back at him, but Chris said, "Cassandra, hop in the back."

Seriously? She gave Chris an incredulous look, but he didn't notice. Huffy, Cassandra climbed between the two seats and buckled into the back.

The boy got in the passenger seat and slammed the door. "Holy —, wait until you hear what happened at the — drive-thru last night."

The profanity didn't end there. Cassandra grew more and more irritated with this boy who swore like a sailor. Even worse was when Chris laughed about it.

"I swear, she wasn't wearing anything under that skirt, and when it flew up—" The guy glanced back at Cassandra as if just remembering her. "You babysitting today?"

"Oh, she's my sister's friend."

"Sisters are good for their friends." The dude laughed, and Cassandra rankled at the veiled insult.

They paused at a four-way stop near the school, and Cassandra undid her seatbelt. "I'll walk from here."

"I'm almost to the school," Chris said, his eyes seeking her out in the rearview mirror.

"This is close enough." She let herself out and slammed the door hard behind her, fuming.

At least she knew where she stood with Chris.

CHAPTER FIFTY-FOUR

Taking a Stand

"Finals are next week," Mr. Reems said in fourth hour as he handed papers out to the students. "So let's grade your practice exams from yesterday and see how you did."

"Those were just for practice?" Ashlee said. "I studied hard!"

"Then you'll be even more prepared for next week."

Cassandra accepted the paper he handed her and saw Emmett's name across the top. She leaned over Ashlee. "Emmett, I got your paper."

"Give me an A, Cassie."

"What's this?" Grayson said. "I got Cassandra's paper. That's it, an F right now."

She turned around, trying to conceal her surprise. "You got my paper?"

"That's your name, right?" His eyes teased her as he held up the test.

"Yes."

"Hmm." He bent over it, marking answers with his pen. "Wrong. Wrong. Wrong. Did you even study, Cassandra?"

"Make sure you put your name on the exam also," Mr. Reems said. "That way I know who graded each one."

Cassandra watched as Grayson wrote his name across the top of her paper, and she knew that was one test she would never throw away.

"Good job," he said, meeting her eyes and giving her a smile when he finished. "You only missed one. You're ready for the final."

She held his gaze, captivated by his mouth. How could he be so kind one moment and act like a completely different person another moment? Why did she still have to fight off the insane desire to plant her lips on his?

She shook it off and accepted her test back. "Thanks."

Unity tryouts were all anyone talked about in fifth hour. It seemed everyone was trying out. Cassandra became more and more nervous as the class time passed.

When school was out, she holed herself up with Riley and Harper in an empty classroom, where they sang their songs to each other over and over. Each time, the feeling of deja vu grew stronger, and Cassandra's heart sank. Who was she fooling? Mr. Cullen knew who he wanted in Unity. It didn't matter how well she did. He would pick the students he wanted. The futility of it left her feeling desperate.

Still, Cassandra sang her heart out on her turn, and she even got the rhythm right on the sight reading. She did better than the previous year.

But she knew she hadn't made it.

Riley went next, and she came out with a light shrug. "I don't know why I tried. Singing solos isn't for me."

They both stood near the choir room and listened to Harper sing through the door.

"You did great," Cassandra said, hugging her when she came out.

Harper burst into tears. "I messed up. I know I did."

"It's okay." Cassandra rubbed her back. "It doesn't really matter, anyway. But we have to be able to say we tried."

Cassandra took Riley home after the tryouts. Her phone rang as she pulled into the driveway at her own house, and she paused to answer it.

"Hello?"

"Hi, is this Cassandra?" a male voice asked.

"Yes," she said, curiosity flooding her. "Who is this?"

"This is Lee. We met at the ice-skating rink?"

"Oh, Lee!" She couldn't believe he was actually calling. "Hey! What's up?"

He laughed, a pleasant sound even though his voice was a little high-pitched. "Not much. I just wanted to talk to you, get to know you more."

Cassandra let herself out of the car and chatted with him as she wandered into the house.

"Who are you talking to?" her mom asked.

"It's Lee," Cassandra said, then she disappeared into her room.

Since Lee was in college, Cassandra knew he was older than her. But he was only nineteen, and the more she talked to him, the more it seemed they had a lot in common.

"So maybe we could go out sometime," Lee said.

Her first date! "I'd love that," she said, excited.

"Great. Think about what you'd like to do, and I'll call you later."

Cassandra hummed as she walked into the kitchen and cut an apple for a snack.

"Who's Lee?" Mrs. Jones asked.

Cassandra straddled a barstool. "Just this kid I met at the skating rink last week. He asked for my number, so I gave it to him."

"And you like him?" Mrs. Jones said.

Cassandra shrugged. "I don't know him. I'm just so happy someone is finally interested in me!" She took her apple slices and went back to her room, anxious for Lee to call again.

⌒⌒⋇⌒⌒

Cassandra didn't make Unity. Neither did Harper or Riley.

It hurt, but not as bad as it had the year before. She no longer believed she was an amazing singer. She was average. Just good enough to be in school choir.

What was her talent, then? She'd written a book a few years ago but completely lost interest in it. She'd never even sent it back to the publisher. Now she enjoyed writing poetry, but was that her best ability?

"How are you feeling about Unity?" she asked Riley when she saw her at her locker before school on Friday.

Riley shrugged and changed out her books. "It was a shot in the dark, you know? Like I didn't really think I'd make it."

"Yeah. Sometimes it's easier not to hope." She glanced over Riley's shoulder and saw Chris coming down the hall. He smiled at her, but Cassandra deliberately turned away from him. "I'll miss not being in choir with you. It's not fair. You'll be with Harper."

"You could always say you want to be in fifth hour choir with us, you know," Riley said, brightening.

Someone tapped Cassandra's shoulder, saving her from having to answer. She pivoted and saw Chris standing there.

"Hey, I'm sorry about yesterday," he said, all humor gone from his face. "Josh sometimes thinks he's funnier than he is."

Well, since he'd brought it up . . . "This wasn't really about Josh," she said. "No one told you to make me move to the back. And no one told you to laugh at his lame jokes. No wonder he thinks he's funny." Not to mention the way he'd put her down. "You supported his stupid behavior."

"I know," Chis said. "I'm really sorry."

Cassandra waved him off. "Just be yourself, Chris. I like who you are."

He nodded and gave her shoulder a squeeze. "I'll make it up to you next time."

She wasn't sure there'd be a next time. Chris was clearly one person when he was with her and someone else around his friends. The thought saddened her.

⁂

"Cassandra."

Mr. Jones stopped Cassandra as she headed out the door for work Friday evening.

"Yes?" she asked, pausing with her sweater hung over her arm.

"What's this your mom tells me about some college kid wanting to take you out on a date?"

"Oh, it's just Lee. We met at a church activity." She didn't mention that he wasn't part of the youth group.

"I don't care where you met. You're not going on a date with someone who's in college."

"He's only three years older than me," Cassandra said. "It's not like we're getting married. Besides, he wants to meet you guys. I figured we would do a group outing." It was the first Cassandra had thought of it, but if it meant she'd get that first date, she'd hang out with her family.

Mr. Jones tilted his head and seemed to be considering that. "I will not allow you to date someone at a different stage in life than you are."

Cassandra rolled her eyes. "There's always something I'm doing wrong, isn't there?"

Mr. Jones' expression hardened. "We'll talk about this later."

"I have no doubt," Cassandra said dryly. She let herself out the door, glad to go to work and escape her dad's omnipresence.

At least there was nobody working with Cassandra behind the register. She liked it best when she had it to herself. She filled out her time card and said hello to everyone in the kitchen before going to the dishwashing room. Tate and Oliver were there, and they greeted her, though Oliver seemed to be in a bad mood. Which matched how Cassandra felt.

"What's wrong with him?" she asked Tate when Oliver took the clean dishes back to the kitchen.

"Oh, he's been fighting with his girlfriend."

"Claire?" Cassandra still hadn't met her, but she remembered talking about her with Nicole at the aquatic center.

"Yeah."

Something in his tone had Cassandra tilting her head. "You don't like her?" She narrowed her eyes at Tate, who had a distasteful expression on his face.

He shrugged. "They've only been going out for a little while, but she seems pretty possessive of his time. So I don't know what to make of her. Isn't your girlfriend supposed to make you happy?"

He asked Cassandra like he thought maybe she knew a thing or two about dating. Which she did not, but she hated to reveal her inexperience. "For sure. Why date someone if they don't make you happy? You're better off being single."

Tate nodded. "And that's why I'm single."

"Right?" Cassandra smiled like it was also a choice she had made rather than something forced upon her that she would gladly change every second of every day.

Oliver came back in, and Cassandra left for the front desk. She put on her best smile and seated customers, then helped bus tables just so that she could take the dirty dishes back to Tate and Oliver. Talking to them was the highlight of every night.

"Are you okay?" she asked Oliver when Tate left to get more rags.

"Yeah, I'm fine," Oliver said. "I'm just PMSing like a girl."

Cassandra laughed. She'd never heard a guy admit to something like that. "Well, that's something I can relate to."

"You?" he scoffed. "I bet you've never been in a bad mood in your life. You always come in here all smiles and good nature." He gave her a twisted smile and bumped her chin with his fist. "It's hard to stay in a bad mood around you."

His praise warmed her heart, and Cassandra wished she could make him feel better. "I'm sure you and Claire will work things out."

His face darkened again. "I'm sure."

❦

Lee called Cassandra on Saturday.

"It's Memorial Day weekend," he said. "I was thinking of going to Devil's Den on Monday. Do you think you and your family would like to come along?"

Devil's Den was a state park with hiking trails, swimming holes, and caves. Her family had been on many occasions. Cassandra had kind of dreaded bringing this up to her parents again. But she knew if she wanted to accomplish anything at all, she would have to get their permission and approval.

"That sounds like a lot of fun. I'll ask my parents."

She and Lee continued to talk on the phone for another half an hour, and he made her laugh a lot. Cassandra felt light and joyful when she hung up. Not because she had a crush on him, but because someone found her interesting. Somebody wanted to spend time with her, and that was encouraging. Maybe her future love life wasn't hopeless after all.

She was in a much better mood when she went into work, and Oliver kept laughing at her goofiness.

"What's your middle name, Cassandra?" he asked. "Happy?"

Cassandra just laughed at him. "No."

He followed her back out to the register. "Seriously. What's your middle name?"

"What's yours?" she returned.

"I've got two middle names. Louis and Daniel."

"Oo, that's much cooler than mine." Still, she didn't reveal her middle name: Maya. Nobody ever asked it.

"Come on, give it up."

"Nope." She smiled to herself and began reorganizing the handmade pastas in the market.

"Fine. I'll just call you Spanky."

"Spanky!" Cassandra whirled around, but Oliver had already run back to the dishwashing room, laughing.

⟨━━━◈━━━⟩

Cassandra's family met Lee at the mall on Saturday, and he followed them out to Devil's Den. Nervousness wracked Cassandra the closer they got, and her siblings teased her endlessly. Her dad stayed quiet, and she knew he didn't like Lee's presence even though he'd agreed to let him come.

Mr. Jones parked in the lot in front of the trail leading to the caves. They got out of the vehicles and met out front.

"We're in luck," Mr. Jones said. "The caves were closed because of the bat sickness. They're open today."

"That's great." Lee smiled at her. He'd removed his earring, which was probably good. Cassandra didn't think her parents would approve. "I love caving."

Cassandra returned his smile.

Mr. Jones led the group down the path through the woods until they reached the Icebox cave, so named because no matter the time of year, the cave remained a frigid forty degrees.

"This is scary," Annette whimpered, stopping in the entrance.

"Oh, no it's not," Cassandra said, rolling her eyes before pushing past her little sister. She grabbed one of the ledges and pulled herself up onto a shelf, then climbed along the ridges.

Lee gave a whistle. "You're really good at this. Kind of fearless."

"I love climbing," Cassandra said, a bit breathlessly. She helped Annette up and shimmied between two vertical slabs of rock.

"You're an acrobat," Lee said, following behind.

They emerged from the cave at the opposite end almost twenty minutes later and completely caked in mud.

"That was awesome," Lee said, and Cassandra beamed.

They changed out of their muddy clothes in the bathrooms and then drove down to the stream to swim while Mrs. Jones set out lunch. Lee tried to teach Cassandra how to skip rocks, standing behind her and holding her arm steady to guide her. But even with his help, she couldn't do it.

"I'm just no good at it," she said, dropping the rock and moving over to the picnic tables.

Lee dropped down beside her. "I can show you another time. You'll get it." He tapped her knuckled with his finger and grinned at her, leaning his head on his fist. "I like you. This is a lot of fun."

She nodded, keeping her smile firmly in place, but the thought of spending more time with Lee didn't excite her.

She knew then she didn't want to date him. She didn't want him as her boyfriend.

Maybe the reason she didn't have any dates was because she liked the idea of a boyfriend more than actually having one.

CHAPTER FIFTY-FIVE

Burning Heart

Three days left of school.

Cassandra was more aware than usual of her classmates, of her teachers, of the end of the school year. She flew through her Spanish final, encouraged by how well she knew the material.

Biology was another matter. She listened to Grayson joking with Katie at his table before the exam started, and then she had to concentrate. In spite of all the studying she'd done, the test was hard.

Still, she finished before Grayson. When she handed in her final, Grayson still sat at his desk, eyes narrowed as he concentrated. Cassandra waited a moment longer, willing him to look up, to notice her. To smile at her.

He didn't, and Cassandra hated how it made her heart ache.

This has to end. Cassandra refused to go through the rest of her high school career pining after him, longing for him to speak to her. At least next year they wouldn't have any classes together. He would be a senior . . . and after that he'd be gone.

Words formed in Cassandra's head, and by the time she got home, they had coalesced into a poem. She jotted them down, going through the cycle of hope and expectation and hurt and rejection and finally acceptance.

The End

I guess that was it
The last time I'll see you.
Somehow. I thought it would be different.

I imagined something else.
I hoped we'd talk a bit.
Maybe I'd finally speak my mind.
At least I wanted you to smile.
I wanted to receive that smile.
One last time. That special smile.
But it didn't happen.
As I got up and left.
I glanced back at you, but you didn't notice.
And so I walked out of the room.
Forever out of your life.
Without even a last look.
I walked away with a sense of longing.
Not believing that was it. That was all.
Still hoping. Still wanting.
Needing to end this.
But that was my last chance.
And stupid me. I let it pass.
Now it's time to close this last note to you
Because I realize that was it.
It was the end.

And suddenly, in a flash of understanding, she knew she had to give this to him. It was time to say goodbye.

Cassandra held her folded note with the poem close to her chest as she walked into the school building Friday morning. She had to find Grayson and deliver it to him before she lost her nerve.

She spotted him at his locker and knew it was too late. She'd lost her nerve. Cassandra continued onto her locker without glancing back.

But the note burned a hole in her binder. She'd always regret it if she didn't give it to him.

She turned around from her locker and spotted Mia walking by. "Mia!" she called, gesturing her over.

Mia switched directions and maneuvered past the other students to Cassandra. "Hey, what's up?"

Cassandra thrust the note out at her. "Can you give this to Grayson?"

Mia furrowed her brow. "What?"

Cassandra shook the folded paper. "Just give this to Grayson."

"Okay." Mia took it with a perplexed expression on her face, which did not inspire Cassandra with confidence.

"Thanks." Cassandra couldn't watch. She turned and fled the hallway as quickly as she could.

Most of the day went easily, as if the teachers were as ready for the school year to end as the students were. Cassandra's thoughts kept going back to Mia and the note to Grayson. Her foot tapped up and down in nervous energy, and she gripped her pencil harder as she worked on her math final. What would Grayson think when he read it? Would he talk to her? Did she want him to? What would she say?

She didn't even call Mia after school but went straight to work, eager to distract herself.

"Cassandra, I'm so glad you're here," Vickie said when Cassandra stepped in the door. "Oliver called in sick and Tate needs help with the dishes. I'll have you work back there today."

"Oh—okay," Cassandra said, caught off guard. She glanced down at her silk shirt and khakis. She definitely hadn't planned for dirty dishes.

"This sucks," Tate said as they set about scrubbing lasagna boats. "I'm about sick of this job."

"Oliver's sick?" Cassandra asked, grabbing a rag and drying the pans.

"Just lazy." Tate rolled his eyes. "He didn't feel like coming in today."

"Really?"

After several hours of doing dishes, she understood why. This wasn't nearly as much fun as being the hostess.

"I'm so mad at Oliver for bailing on me," Tate growled as they ran another tray of dishes through the washer. "He knows how much I hate this job."

Cassandra checked her phone. The restaurant had closed almost an hour ago, and they still had at least one more tray of dishes to wash and put away. "I don't blame you." If Oliver didn't show up tomorrow, she'd be mad at him, also. She definitely didn't want to be a dishwasher again.

In spite of her best efforts to keep Grayson from her thoughts, he kept popping back in.

What about the note? What had his reaction been?

Cassandra gave in after lunch on Saturday and called Mia. "Well? What did he say when you gave him the note?"

"I didn't have the chance to give it to him," Mia said. "It's still in my binder."

"What?" All the tension and anxiety rushed out of her, leaving Cassandra feeling deflated and disappointed. This whole time she'd been imagining Grayson's reaction, thinking about his thoughts, and Mia hadn't even given it to him?

"I will Monday," Mia said, unconcerned. "That's the last day of school."

"Yeah. Okay." Cassandra reminded herself she couldn't be ungrateful. Mia was doing what she herself didn't have the guts to do. "Thanks, Mia."

Still, the news put her in a bad mood, and she didn't feel so chipper as she got ready for work. She was almost hesitant to go in. What if Oliver didn't show again? She did not want to do dishes.

Just in case, she wore skinny jeans and a tight T-shirt, clothes that would be appropriate for hostessing or dishwashing.

She breathed a sigh of relief when she walked into the back and saw both Tate and Oliver.

"Spanky!" Oliver said, his face lighting up when he saw her. He stepped up to hug her, but Cassandra took a step back.

"I had to do your job," she said darkly. "All because you didn't feel like coming in."

"You did the dishwashing for me? I'm touched." He grinned, but when she didn't back down, his face became more contrite. "I didn't have a ride. No one could come get me, so I couldn't come."

"You don't drive?" Cassandra gave him a surprised look.

"No. My dad dropped me off today, but I'm gambling on finding a ride home after work."

That changed things a bit, and Cassandra relented her anger toward him. "At least you're here today."

"Yeah, Marco told me to bring my guitar, that I could play a song for everyone after we close." Oliver smiled, looking particularly happy.

"I can't wait to hear it," Cassandra said. Then she went back to the front desk, where she could do her hostessing duties in peace.

But now the anticipation of Grayson receiving the note was in front of her again, and she couldn't keep the nervous tremor out of her hands. If only Mia had already delivered the poem!

Things got busy right away, and then they hit a lull around eight. Cassandra helped bus the tables and went back to the front, wiping down the register area and the deli.

Oliver popped out of the hallway. "Hey, you okay? You don't seem like your usual chipper self."

Cassandra turned around, mouth open to tell him she was fine, and instead she burst into tears.

Oliver took a step back, his eyes going wide. "Whoa. What is it?"

She wiped her eyes, feeling foolish and glad no patrons were coming in. "It's just a stupid guy."

Oliver came closer, joining her behind the register. "I didn't know you were having guy troubles."

"All year," she confessed, and then the story tumbled out. "We had a thing last fall. Just a small thing. Then it ended, for him, at least, but I can't get over him. So I wrote him a note telling him goodbye, and I'm just waiting on my friend to deliver it on Monday."

Oliver's hand fell on her shoulder, then moved to her back and rubbed the spot between her shoulder blades. "Wow. That's intense. Are you okay?"

"Yes." She gave him a smile, appreciating his concern. "I'm fine, really."

Oliver hugged her, his long arms sweeping her up and pulling her against his lanky body. "I hope so. I don't like seeing you not smiling."

She let him hold her for a second before pulling away, drying her eyes. "You better get back there before someone comes in and sees you."

"Cheer up, Spanky," he said, and she couldn't help smiling as he disappeared down the hall.

Just when she thought it would be an easy night and they'd be out right on time, a party of fifteen came in. Cassandra and Willa, one of the waitresses, scrambled to pull enough tables together to seat them. Cassandra helped fill their drink orders, then settled back to see what else would be needed.

A few other people trickled in, but when the restaurant closed at ten, everyone had left except the large party. Every waiter finished their tallying and headed out except Willa. The kitchen closed and the staff left, but Cassandra had to stay to ring up the customers.

She wandered back to the dish room around ten-thirty. "Are they ever going to leave?" she hissed at Oliver and Tate.

"I was going to play my guitar for everyone," Oliver said, clearly irate. "And now almost everyone is gone."

Cassandra felt a pang of sympathy for him. She remembered how excited he had been. "I'm still here."

Oliver grunted.

Clearly that wasn't good enough.

Tate stuck his head into the dining room, then pulled himself back. "They're getting up!"

"Finally," Cassandra breathed. She returned to the cash register, smile in place.

The last person was rung up by ten-forty-five, and the moment they walked out the door, Marco locked the restaurant. He turned around to face Cassandra.

"I know it's late. Can you help Willa bus the tables? Then you can go."

All she wanted was to leave, but how could she when they needed her? "Sure."

"Cassandra." Oliver stopped her when she walked past. "You're going to stay to hear me play, right?" His expression was neutral, but there was pleading in his dark brown eyes.

"Of course." That hadn't been her plan, but she didn't want to let him down.

He hesitated, then he said, "And could you give me a ride home?"

"Yep." She held back a sigh and went to clear the dishes. She'd be here until the very end, then.

Marco was ready to leave by the time Cassandra brought the last dishes to the dish room.

"Just leave them there, boys," he said to Oliver and Tate. "We can get them in the morning."

The few remaining staff clocked out and grabbed their bags.

"Wait!" Oliver said, his face a mixture of hopeful and crestfallen. "I brought my guitar. I was going to play for everyone."

"Right," Marco said, and his warring emotions played out across his face. Compassion won out, and he shrugged. "Go for it, kid."

Cassandra settled onto the bar stool behind the register and waited while Oliver plugged in his electric guitar. He strummed out a few chords, grinned at them all, and then played a hard rock song she'd never heard of.

"Great job," Marco said when he finished, and Cassandra clapped along with Tate and Willa. "Now let's head out."

"Long night," Cassandra said with a sigh as she led Oliver to her car.

"Yeah," he agreed. "Thanks for the ride home. It's close by. Just go straight through the intersection. It's the first driveway on your right."

Cassandra drove onto the country road, winding past a ditch and a field before spotting a gravel road. She turned onto it and took it all the way to the small mobile home at the end of the drive.

"This it?"

"Yeah. Want to come in for a sec?"

It was almost eleven. But Oliver had a lonely, vulnerable look on his face. "Just for a sec." Cassandra turned off the car and followed him up the steps into his house.

All was dark in the kitchen and small living room. Oliver took his guitar to his bedroom while she stayed in the kitchen, then he returned to her.

"My parents are sleeping," he whispered. "Can you stay for a bit? I want to talk to you."

He wanted to talk to her? Cassandra nodded, flattered to be considered worthy of confidence.

Oliver led the way onto the porch steps. He tried the porch light and grunted. "Out."

"No worries." Cassandra took the few steps to her car and reached inside, turning on the headlights. "We've got light."

"Awesome." Oliver sat down.

Cassandra returned to his side and settled down next to him. "You doing all right?"

He shrugged. "I'm just, I don't know. Life isn't exactly going the way I want it to."

"What's going on?"

He shook his head. "Just me, probably. Being stupid."

Cassandra waited for more, and when he didn't say anything, she prompted, "Does this have to do with Claire?"

"Nah, she's fine. But I miss my ex-girlfriend."

"Who was that?"

"Ciera Lamb."

"Oh, I know her. She went to my elementary school. Did you date long?"

"Long enough." Oliver sighed. "Some things I can't forget."

"Why aren't you still together?" Cassandra asked softly.

"I'm too screwed up for her."

His phone rang before he could finish the sentiment, and he fished it out of his pocket. "Hang on. It's Claire." His voice changed, becoming more perky as he answered. "Hi. No, I just got home from work. It was a long night. I'm super tired. Yeah, maybe we can get together tomorrow. I'm heading to bed now. Everyone's asleep. Sorry, Claire, I don't feel like talking right now. I'll call you tomorrow."

He hung up and sighed. "I'm probably too screwed up for Claire, too. I've messed with too many things, trying to find my place in life. Life sucks."

"Oliver." Cassandra put a hand on his arm. "You are not too screwed up. Everything I've seen of you proves you're a compassionate, caring guy."

"You don't really know me. I've done it all. I slept with Ciera. I've tried drugs, I even thought I had HIV once."

Cassandra blinked, as surprised by his revelation as that he thought he could tell her. "That doesn't make you screwed up. That makes you human."

He rested his elbows on his knees and leaned his head on his hands. "You're the nicest person I've ever met. If all humans were like you, this world wouldn't be so screwed."

His praise brought a warmth to her face. Something bubbled up in her chest, something pleasant and flirty, and she bumped his shoulder with hers. "I'm pretty normal." She looked out at her car and frowned. "Do the car lights seem dimmer than before?"

Oliver's eyes wandered toward her car, and his lip twisted upward. "Yes."

Oh crapola, that couldn't be good. Cassandra stood up and went to the car, then leaned inside and turned the key. The engine sputtered but did not roar to life.

"Oh, no." She climbed inside, turned off the lights, and tried again. This time it didn't even turn over, just clicked at her.

Oliver joined her, a sheepish expression on his face. "The battery is dead. I'm so sorry."

Cassandra looked at her phone. It was a little after midnight! "What am I going to do?"

"I know. Let's move it close to my dad's car, and I can jump-start it. Stay inside and put it into neutral, and I'll push."

Cassandra did as she was told, and Oliver got behind the vehicle. The car wiggled a bit, but that was it. He came back over, panting.

"I'm so sorry. I couldn't do it."

She wasn't surprised, but panic rose in her chest. She had no choice now. She had to call her parents.

They were going to kill her.

CHAPTER FIFTY-SIX

Goodbyes

Her parents didn't kill her, which in Cassandra's mind was nothing short of a miracle.

Mr. Jones picked her up and left the car at Oliver's house. Cassandra expected a lecture when she got home, but instead Mrs. Jones asked what happened and listened without censure while Cassandra explained the situation.

The next morning after church, Mr. Jones took her by Oliver's house to get the car. Oliver was asleep, and even though Cassandra woke him, he was out again by the time Mr. Jones jump-started the car and they were ready to leave.

"We'll have to leave it at the shop overnight," her dad said as she got inside. "Follow me there."

"Overnight?" Cassandra groaned. "Tomorrow's the last day of school and I won't have a car!"

"Next time don't leave your lights on," Mr. Jones said.

She wouldn't. Cassandra would never make that mistake again.

❦

Mrs. Jones let Cassandra use the van on Monday for the last day of school. She picked up Riley at the drop off spot, and the two of them shrieked.

"Last day of school!" Riley said.

"Almost juniors!" Cassandra crowed. She could hardly believe it!

"Still no car?" Riley asked.

Cassandra had told her all about the incident with Oliver the night before. She shook her head. "I get to pick it up tonight."

"And how are things with Lee?" Riley gave her a mischievous smile.

"Lee." He called almost every night, and sometimes his possessiveness and infatuation reminded her of her ex-boyfriend, Josh. "I'm really not into him."

"But he's in college!" Riley sighed.

None of Cassandra's friends could understand why she didn't feel something for him. But she couldn't seem to force it. Should she be able to? "There's just nothing there."

Not like how she'd felt the night before sitting beside Oliver. But she banished those thoughts instantly.

"Oh, well." Riley shrugged. "We'll just have to go ice-skating again and pick up some other guys later."

"Right." Cassandra laughed at the idea.

Cassandra only had choir and English class left, and choir let out half an hour early. She, Harper, and Riley drove to Applebee's in Fayetteville, along with about seven other kids. Cassandra ate till it hurt, and she laughed until she thought she'd throw up.

She saw Oliver after English. His face lit up, and he gave a sheepish grin. "Hey!" He held his arms out, and Cassandra stepped into them for a crushing hug. That same comfortable feeling rose in her chest again, and she hated to step away from him.

"You made it to school!" he said, still grinning at her. He tucked her chin with his knuckle. "I didn't even notice you come get your car."

"I couldn't wake you," Cassandra said, her heart rate increasing at the way he touched her. "I tried, but you were out."

"Sorry about that. I would have liked to see you."

"I'll see you a lot this summer. We work together!"

"And now I know who to bum a ride off of." His hand trailed down her arm, and he squeezed her wrist.

A little shiver sputtered through Cassandra's stomach. She shoved it down. Oliver was her friend. That was all he could be.

Betsy and Riley ran up to Cassandra and bounced around her like a couple of excited children. "Take us to Diary Queen in your mom's van? Please? Please please please?"

Cassandra laughed at their antics. "Okay. Let's go." She jangled the keys and looked at Oliver. "Want to come?"

"Yes. But I can't. Claire's mom's picking us up and taking us out."

"You're missing out," Cassandra teased. "My ride's better."

Oliver shoved his hands in his jeans pockets. "Next time."

She waved and let her friends pull her out the door.

Her phone rang just as she started up the van.

Mia.

Cassandra's heart skipped a beat, and she tried to keep cool. She hadn't seen her friend all day and had tried not to think about her. Now she picked up the phone and pressed it to her ear.

"Hello?"

"I gave him the note."

"You did?" Cassandra let out a deep breath. "What did he say?"

"Nothing. His girlfriend was with him, so I just said, 'this is from Cassandra' and handed it to him."

The words spun around in Cassandra's mind, and her mouth fell open as she pictured the scene. "Wait, what? Charlotte was there?"

"Yeah, the tall redhead?"

Oh no. No no no no. This was not good. Cassandra pressed her forehead to her hand. Why hadn't Mia held onto the note until Charlotte wasn't around? "And then what?" Cassandra asked, trying to keep the tremble from her voice.

"When I looked back, his girlfriend had the note in her hands and was opening it. He was watching."

Crapola.

This could not have gone any worse.

"Thanks, Mia," Cassandra said through stilted breath. "I appreciate it." She hung up the phone and leaned her head against the steering wheel.

That wasn't what she had wanted. The poem was for Grayson and Grayson only. He alone knew her heart.

But he'd let Charlotte take it.

He'd let her read it.

It was done. They were through. She lifted her head, blinking her eyes and clearing her thoughts. Whatever else, it was over. She could move on now.

"Cassie?" Riley said. "Are we going to drive?"

"Yes." Cassandra pasted on a smile and reversed the vehicle. "Let's get some ice cream."

elee

Coming spring of 2021!
Season 7
Springdale Bulldogs Year 2: Age 16

The Extraordinarily Ordinary Life of

Cassandra Jones

Springdale Bulldogs Year 2: Age 16

Tamara Hart Heiner

Yes, now you have to wait until spring of 2021 for the next book in the series!

But don't worry, I won't leave you hanging. There are a few things you can do to occupy your time until the next book comes out!

1—Find me on social media! Join my Cassandra Jones fan club on Facebook. Here we can theorize together on what's going to happen, talk about past events, dive into character feelings, and even give me ideas for upcoming books! Find it on Facebook at "All About Cassandra Jones." And follow me on Instagram @tamaraheiner, where I post all kinds of sneak peeks, do fun giveaways, and enjoy interacting with you! Say hello and I'll say hi back!

2—Dive into the Perilous series, another binge-worthy, high school drama I wrote with plenty of action, suspense, and romance!

3—Preorder Episode 1 of Springdale Bulldogs Year 2: Age 16 right now so you don't miss a thing when it comes out!

4—Go backward in time! Get a free copy of Walker Wildcats Year 1: Age 10 when you sign up for my Reader's Group and see Cassandra where the journey began! Text TREADER to 33777

Happy reading!!

Enjoy this book? You can make a huge difference!

If you enjoyed this book, I'd be honored if you'd leave an

honest review on whatever book haunt you frequent.

Reviews are indie authors' bread and butter, and we

couldn't do it without readers like you!

About the Author

Tamara Hart Heiner is a mom, wife, baker, editor, and author. She currently lives in Arkansas with her husband, four children, a cat, a rabbit, a dog, and a fish. She would love to add a macaw and a sugar glider to the family. She's the author of several young adult suspense series (*Perilous, Goddess of Fate, Kellam High*) the *Cassandra Jones* saga, and a nonfiction book about the Joplin Tornado, *Tornado Warning.*

Connect with Tamara online!
Twitter: https://twitter.com/tamaraheiner
Facebook: https://www.facebook.com/author.tamara.heiner
blog: http://www.tamarahartheiner/blogspot.com
website: http://www.tamarahartheiner.com
Thank you for reading!